D0118773

ALSO BY NIVEN BUSCH

Continent's Edge
California Street
Duel in the Sun
The San Franciscans
The Takeover
The Gentleman from California
The Actor
The Hate Merchant
The Furies
They Dream of Home (a.k.a. Till the End of Time)
Day of the Conquerors
The Carrington Incident
No Place for a Hero
Twenty-one Americans

THE TITAN GAME

Niven Busch

THE TITAN GAME

RANDOM HOUSE  NEW YORK

Copyright © 1989 by Niven Busch

All rights reserved under International and Pan-American
Copyright Conventions. Published in the United States
by Random House, Inc., New York, and simultaneously in Canada
by Random House of Canada Limited, Toronto.

Grateful acknowledgment is made to Ludlow Music, Inc.,
for permission or reprint four lines from the lyrics
to "Amazing Grace," collected, adapted and arranged by
John A. Lomax and Alan Lomax. TRO—copyright 1934
(renewed) Ludlow Music, Inc., New York, N.Y. Used by
permission.

Library of Congress Cataloging-in-Publication Data

Busch, Niven.
The titan game : a novel / by Niven Busch.
p. cm.
ISBN 0-394-57537-7
I. Title.
PS3503.U746T58   1989
813'.52—dc19   88-43223

Manufactured in the United States of America

24689753

FIRST EDITION

To Sue
Only and always the greatest

Irrational streams of blood
are staining earth.

W. B. YEATS

ACKNOWLEDGMENTS

I could not have written this book without the generous help of many people who took time from their own careers to instruct me in matters about which I knew nothing, and set me straight on those about which I knew little. First among these, since I appealed to them most often, have been Don Kennedy, famed adviser to the DOD and to many procurement companies, and John Joss, himself a novelist as well as a journalist contributing articles on electronics and avionics to many specialist magazines. Thank you, friends. And particular thanks to Lou MacTamany of FMC, artificer of the real-world, still-secret robots that will one day supplant my fictional SEDAVS.

The list of those who answered my Mayday calls, literary as well as technical, is long and distinguished, and I bestow on each my blessing and my lasting gratitude: Dr. Alvin Bucalew; Roger Boravoy; Ron Burman; Henry Carlisle; Col. Ed Christof; Stan Delaplane; Paul Erdman; Tully Friedman; Gen. Sir John Hackett, Ret.; Frederick Hill (the world's most creative agent); Gen. Dutch Huyser, Ret.; Ivan Hudson; Gen. Stanley R. Larsen, Ret.; Michael Malone; the Hon. William Perry; H. Ross Perot; John Renshaw; Dwight Taylor; David Thomson (with a key ideal); Jerry Sanders; Vladimir Sakharov; Francis Seidler; Paul Shanley; Martin Cruz Smith; Diana Smith; Col. Charles Steiner; Clyde Taylor; David Wilson; William J. Zellerbach; and the Command and Public Affairs Staff at Aberdeen Proving Grounds, Maryland, and the National Training Center, Fort Irwin, California.

Special thanks also to my incomparable editor, Samuel S. Vaughan at Random House, and his able associate Mark Riebling.

THE TITAN GAME

Weapons are ugly things at best and this one was as ugly as they come: a low-slung iron iguana with a slant steel face, a cannon on top, and treads instead of feet. It could scuttle forward and backward at amazing speeds and even swim, if necessary, in a gurgling, wallowing fashion. On its body it had steel and ceramic scales and in its belly a microelectronic box containing its brain. With this brain it could detect and intercept an enemy or avoid him, direct its cannon to destroy him, and control the engine which, if he became cantankerous, would enable it to flee. It needed help from no man.

Better still, it was cheap. This, above all else, recommended it for production in a world which had long been draining itself and impoverishing its peoples making expensive weapons. Never before in history had there been such a glut of weapons of all kinds: weapons lurking with eyes agleam in the black holes of outer space; weapons that could pop out of the void and kill at ten times the speed of sound; weapons as small as pinheads and as big as cathedrals; weapons that could burrow underground or hide in the genitals of icebergs; weapons that could be slung on dogs, elephants, mules, goats, dolphins, or even children; weapons with fins, with tails, with lungs; weapons by the million and the hundred million stashed in warehouses, depots, forts, catacombs, arsenals, revetments, attics, cellars, suitcases, satellites, and silos; weapons made of sulfurous gases; weapons of light, of air, of new metals, of magnetic pulses. There was, it seemed, no lack of any sort of weapon at all. It is odd then, if one stopped to think, that this weapon was ever fielded or that once it was, it could produce, aside from its military applications, such widespread effects.

Its birth was mysterious. That too is characteristic of weapons—no one person or pairing of persons is responsible for their advent. The notion for a new weapon may blow in from any direction. The Department of the Army, U.S. Material Development and Readiness Command (DARCOM), specifically encourages this practice. To do so, it has issued a pamphlet entitled *Guide for Unsolicited Proposals* (DARCOM Publication 70-8) *"as a means by which unique and meritorious proposals can be made available. . . ."*

One must always, in light of the policy, keep in mind that the birth of a weapon does not take place in a manger, but in the glare of world attention. Only the seminal procedures prior to the birth are complex and secret. Seeds in the wind.

There was, for instance, the report of a young officer assigned to what was known in 1983 as balls-to-the-walls training unit at Ilopango, San Salvador. The recruits this officer was supposed to train were between sixteen and eighteen years old and most of them were shorter than the M-16 rifles and the M-79 grenade launchers he was teaching them to use. Their GI helmets were too big for their heads and their shoes too loose for their feet. The recruits were brave and quick to learn, but their scruffy, rock-and-mesquite training camp was situated in a horizon dominated by Guazapa Volcano, a major guerrilla base.

The young officer felt badly about what he knew was soon to happen to his recruits. He tried to think of ways to protect them.

If only they'd had a paratroop battalion nearby, or a decent air force. Or some armor! From armor the officer's thoughts veered to an engine that would not only help but perhaps *substitute* for his doomed little guys, actually take their place. He wrote out his ideas and sent them to his father, a retired brigadier general knowledgeable about such matters, holding a position as lobbyist for a defense supplier.

That was one seed. Then there was the research analyst at the Rand Institute who sent through a paper at this time relating to *Goliath,* the drone tank the German High Command had tested on the eastern front late in World War II—one of those queer genius-type ideas, like the early fighter jets that Hitler's desperate staffers dredged up and never, fortunately, put into full production.

So it went. The Old Boy Officer Network is always on the *qui vive* to get the best material for its branch and by now, what with one thing and another, there were rumbles in the huge bowels of the Pentagon and its Specified and Unified Commands.

DARCOM knew the score. It knew a terrible fuss was being raised about protecting personnel in combat, and it knew and recognized that the best way to improve armor combat-crew survivability was not to put the crew inside the armor in the first place. DARCOM knew the navy was considered to be way ahead of the army in robotics and it knew had to rip that myth to shreds and the sooner the better.

DARCOM knew too that the Swedes had some mystic crap of their own and that the French, always ready to steal the fillings out of your teeth, were working on components for autonomous, mobile combat robots. DARCOM knew about control algorithms for multiple cooperative robots working on a task. It knew about 3-D stereo vision sensors, also about image processing, mobile platforms and power sources, and about automated computer mission planning and scheduling. DAR-COM began to set up informal talks in the Pentagon for the representatives of great electronic companies, jawbone sessions as they were then called, leading to a *Request for a Quotation,* or, in other words, some concrete guidelines, the step that comes before the *Request for a Proposal,* the real nub of the matter.

A bidding session followed and the bid, the best though not quite the lowest (since DARCOM weighs seriously other factors besides price), went to Advanced Electronic Technologies (ADECT) of Santa Clara, California, a well-known firm headed by the wizard entrepreneur J. C. Streck.

The new weapon also had a name by now. It was called Self-Deploying Attack Vehicle (SEDAV). A respected steel maker bid for the cannon and body plates and a maker of turbo-diesel engines for the motor but ADECT, with its diversified capabilities, prevailed in obtaining the whole package principally because, in addition to the other elements, it surpassed all competitors in its version of the new weapon's "intelligence."

Money was now distributed, and a prototype drone built and triumphantly tested. The project whizzed forward wonderfully when an accident occurred, or if not exactly an accident, then at least a setback of a type rare in the disciplined structure of weapons making. As time went on, other events not easily explained but somehow connected with the weapon or its use or its procurement surfaced it seemed almost as if the weapon itself, rather than any human agency, was at the root of the trouble—yes, as if this thing, this object, from some powers lodged within its iron soul, had produced a force that dragged a whole array of human lives along its course like the tail of some insane and unpredictable comet: ministers and heads of state, spies, soldiers and renegades, arbitrageurs, thieves, plotters and priests, women of high repute and low, and of course a lot of just plain people. Few had the slightest understanding of what was happening to them but one and all experienced certain changes caused by their abrasive rush through time and space with the result that none of them were ever quite the same again. . . .

It had been Jason Streck, by some terrible chance, who discovered what had happened to his father. It was late at night. This in itself was odd since father and son, though in each other's office all day at the plant, with countless details to discuss and, frequently, decisions to be made which were best made jointly, were seldom together after business hours. A certain coldness had settled into their relationship, not a real break, but something less than what they'd once had. Both had regretted this change; both knew and recognized the incident from which it stemmed but neither had known how to repair the damage.

That night, Jason had wanted to be with his father; he wondered in retrospect whether some kind of ESP had made him decide to drive in and call at the cottage where he'd seen the lights from the road.

Jason had been out on a date. Generally he waited until weekends, but on this night he'd felt in no mood to stay at home, so he'd hit the bars. It was a way to go, pretty much the only way available for him now after an early, failed marriage for which he was still paying alimony, and the termination, by mutual consent, of a long-term live-in.

Jason's prowls through the singles' bars had become a highly stylized procedure: first the physical prepping, the shampoo, the lotion, the useful Gucci briefcase containing razor, comb, and toothbrush, also condoms or some other contraceptive in case she wasn't on the Pill. Not a bad idea to toss in a few technical papers (making sure they weren't stamped with the company logo) so in case she peeked inside, as she would if given a chance, she could see you were a worker, a serious person—you had paused in the scruffy bistro where the two of you had met while coming from or on your way to a business appointment. Final rule: her place, never yours. Then you could split whenever you liked; also because in most situations you would not be using your right name.

So it went. You looked around. You bought a few drinks. You drew a number, holding yourself ready for surprises. For, oh, what hang-ups could come to light, what sometimes bizarre demands lurked beneath the profiles of the chic Valley femininity, blessed in some instances with Ph.D.s in computer science or electronic engineering, the most brilliant and irresistible and sometimes the freakiest. Ah, those surprises—the wild little blonde from Bendix who would seize the skin of her lovely belly in a firm grip and pull it up (the first time with the remark, "Would you like to see your free door prize?") until the tip and then more of her rather extraordinary clitoris appeared, a wet pink prong inciting a whole new order of games. He would not soon forget her . . . or the athletic Jordanian MBA who became aroused by nude swimming and would make love in the pool and only in the pool (and in the deep end at that), her elbows propped in a corner of the skim gutter with Jason clamped on to her with an ardor intensified by his desperate need to keep from drowning as she opened her submarine thighs to receive him.

And then, of course, the exceptions, the wondrous ones with some magical, honest way of touching you or rousing you, who effortlessly made you feel, from the moment their sweet breasts sprang out of the nylon bra, that they would induct you into . . . Camelot! A deathless relationship . . . only to have some curious distortion set in as time went by, certain verbal expressions or the husky sexy laugh heard too often— too familiar the deliberate way she rolls down her pantyhose to wash between her legs. You miss an appointment, or you are busy for the weekend, or she fails to be on time. Somehow you are both on the prowl again and it's all over.

On that night there had been no sex. He had seen this particular girl before and had admired but never dated her. She had been a medium-sized brown-haired girl with a rather cool, uncensoring way of taking stock of you and what was going on around you and of crinkling up her small deep-set eyes when she laughed. Jason, who'd skipped dinner, had been eating alone and this girl had come over and sat and talked and a warmth had sprung up, a feeling that could lead to a better-arranged evening. Then he had taken her home, on Sand Hill Road, and after leaving he had seen the lights on his own family's large fenced estate.

He'd realized at once that they weren't in the main house but in a complex known in the Streck family as the cottage. There were several rooms in this—two bedrooms, a living room and den, and a small kitchen, the latter always kept well provided with food and drink. It had been built sometime after the main house and at first had been used mostly by Art and Norma, also assorted cousins and in-laws, when they came to visit. But after a while, J.C., wanting a place in which he could work away from the plant, had remodeled it into an office complex, paneling one bedroom for the use of staff, putting a computer in the other, and extending the living room into a glassed-in porch. He'd also ordered various electronic traps and alarms to ward off unauthorized entry and installed a chain-link, electrified fence, the same height as the great steel fence surrounding the outer grounds.

Inside this second fence, the first thing anybody saw as they approached the cottage was a robot tank, J. Caulfield's pet. It was there now, a compact, camouflaged little monster. It squatted peacefully in a corner of the area which Odille had sardonically christened *The Romper Room,* an acre field where J. Caulfield Streck, for his own amusement and the enlightenment of certain selected weekend guests, programmed it to smash up a sandbagged "fort," leap ditches, swim across a tiny lake, and whack away with its cannon—using subcalibrated rounds, so much more dramatic than laser simulations—at targets painted to resemble Soviet tanks or ground troops which sprang up unexpectedly.

It was a weird sort of pet but, in itself, a piece of history: the first model to come off the ADECT production line. It was designated in the company inventory as TY6o, followed by a long string of numbers, meaningless except to the supplier and its ultimate recipient, the army.

Tonight the tank was alive. Buried in the armor, behind and to one side of the heavy foreplate, a tiny light glowed green, showing that systems were GO. All tanks are blind in front and "see" at night by thermal detection devices, their purpose being to remain invisible, not to headlight their presence to an enemy.

Coming closer, Jason had a queer sensation. His pulse had altered and his skin chilled. He remembered this afterward and tried to account for it, so strange was the sensation. It seemed as if the robot had developed a field of force so strong that it was disarraying the electromagnetics of his own body. This feeling made him stop for several seconds.

The live armored thing crouching there in the dark seemed aware of him. Its sensors had detected his "signature" and it stirred as a living creature might at the approach of a stranger. When Jason got closer he reached out and touched the metal shell, then the cannon. Both were hot enough to make him jerk his hand away. He wondered, as he put it later, whether someone had been "fooling around with it" or whether his father had implemented the machine into the cottage surveillance arrangements, the most formidable part of which were still to be confronted: the attack dogs.

There were three: large gray-brown German shepherds. They had no names. This anonymity was deliberate, a reminder that they were not to be treated as pets, regardless of how one wished to treat the resident robot. They were killers, domesticated animals artfully and cruelly reconditioned into primal savagery. They were known as Dog One, Dog Two, and Dog Three. They were astute as well as aggressive, presumably able to distinguish friends from foes, but . . .

Jason had never been quite sure about this. He was always very careful with the dogs.

He unlocked the gate leading to the cottage and walked in with determined unconcern, then stopped and turned back, curious about Dog One, the largest. It was standing on hind legs at the edge of the fence, its forepaws pushed against the chain link and its head tilted to one side. Dog One was always the most active of the dogs but Jason could not remember it ever standing up that way. There was certainly an oddness about it, its great body stretched up and its square black muzzle held at that strange angle, motionless.

Neither of the dogs on the ground moved as Jason approached. Then he saw why they weren't able to: Dog Two had no head. Its brains, along with a considerable amount of blood, were splattered on the grass. In the beams of the strobe lights, covering portions of the yard from the eaves of the cottage, Jason could see that Dog Three, the young one, had been almost ripped to pieces by bullets, the concussions of the hits knocking out chunks of hide and muscle, embedding bone and fur in the soft lawn. The blood made irregular dark patches, like vagrant shadows, on the grass.

Surely Dog One signaled some gruesome fantasy, standing there dead in that athletic, welcoming position he had never assumed while alive. He had bled hardly at all, but he had defecated in his death throes. The smell of his feces was rank in the air. Jason touched him, exploring, as he had touched the tank, but the light contact was enough to send the body crashing to the ground.

Dog One had been killed by a single shot between the eyes. His mouth came open as he fell and his great pink tongue lolled out. He had teeth like those of the steppe wolves of Eastern Europe, his forebears. Somehow those teeth were familiar to Jason. He had seen them before, but not in Dog One. A flash arose in his mind of himself as a boy of six or seven, standing with his mother in front of a case in a museum. That had been a wonderful time, a day when they had all made a trip to San Francisco to see the sights.

"That's a wolf," his mother had said.

Jason spun around. He crouched beside the huge dead dog, staring at the cottage. The inside lights, like the robot's were on—was the dog killer there, waiting for him?

Keeping low to the ground, Jason turned back along the fence to where his tan Mercedes was parked. He opened the glove compartment and took out the Smith & Wesson .357 Magnum that the security people had given him to keep there. This was the first time that he'd had the big revolver in his hand since the day it was supplied. It was fully loaded. Jason pushed the safety latch into its OFF position. The gun was heavy and he was conscious of its weight and of his lack of training with it. Could he carry it and still use his walking stick? Better not. He could walk without the stick. He would lurch, but to hell with it. He needed one free hand. Hunched over, gun held awkwardly in front of him, he crossed the lighted gap between the car and the back door; he kicked the door. It opened and he was inside the kitchen. His mouth was dry and his lips pulled back senselessly from his teeth like the big dead dog's.

The small kitchen smelled of coffee, gas stove pilots, and some kind of cleaning stuff. He stood against the wall, groping for a light switch; he failed in this but was conscious of light under the swinging door leading to the living room. Lurching, with one foot dragging and the stupid large cold Magnum in his right hand, he had opened the door and got his first look at what had happened beyond.

TWO

Corporate structure provides a simple unwritten manual for disaster. Just as a housewife calls the "disposal man," the "stove man," or the "roof man" when something goes wrong, in a great company there is always a designated person, the expert in the particular type of destruction, inefficiency, or horror you have in hand. So you call him. You set the machinery in motion. From then on you have nothing to worry about. You can turn your attention to something else and so keep busy with corporate affairs the way you are supposed to do.

On discovering his father's body, Jason made two calls.

The first roused Abe Kohn, vice-president, security, from sleep. The second did the same for Ken Garay, vice-president, legal. Both men lived in the Valley. They would come soon. Meanwhile, the incident in the cottage, which would eventually cause such wide repercussions, was still sealed off in space and time, company controlled, a status highly appropriate at this time even though obviously it could not be long maintained.

Turning from the telephone, Jason examined the dead man. His father had died as meanly and miserably as the dogs, his body pierced by bullets, his papers spilled onto the floor, everything fouled by blood.

Sitting that way, dead, in the big white chair, his father seemed pitiful, shrunken, and inconsequential. Jason looked for something to put over him, finally locating a striped pool towel, a weird kind of shroud with its broad gay colors, but big enough to cover his father from head to foot.

This done, Jason sat down to wait for Garay and Kohn. He sat on the floor, his back against the wall; he knew it was important not to disturb anything. Up to this point he had behaved in a clear-headed, almost robotic manner but suddenly a sad fearful anger swept over him and he began to swear.

"Fuck it!" he moaned. "Why did it have to happen this way?"

There was crime in the Valley, there had always been crime, but not crimes of blood.

There was thievery, schlockery, adultery, fraud, and general sleaziness—not killing. There was no need for it. Killing was for city ghettos. Here billions of dollars washed daily through the quiet streets. If you wanted some you just dipped in. The currency was chips and the great factories oozed chips like glucose from an IV bottle. A junkie security guard on a loading platform could get you some, the price would not be high, he had his habit to sustain; aggrieved or debt-ridden executives had ways of circumventing electronic searches, there were even simple souls who salted good chips into the rejects that their firms paid scrappers to haul away.

Then, of course, there were the spies.

Spies were a way of life in the Valley. They had their regular payrolls. They would arrange conveyance of your stuff to France (now a frequent conduit to the Eastern Bloc). Or Austria, Vietnam, the Philippines, as the case might be, way stations to the USSR. Every year students from these sympathetic lands registered for study at the great U.S. science universities and soon knew enough to take home souvenirs, the latest electronic breakthroughs.

There were laws, of course, against the export of defense materials but none to restrain trade publications which blithely printed and circulated technology which the Defense Department might later classify as secret, once its application to warfare had been established.

That was not burglary.

Real, street-level burglary was frowned on, but when it happened to a company it was considered an in-house affair and rarely prosecuted. Courtroom trials were bad public relations, they could reduce confidence in a product! Only in brief, grisly glimpses—a mysterious free-

way accident or the needle-racked, garroted body of somebody scheduled to appear as a federal witness, giving its testimony instead inside
a culvert in the Santa Cruz mountains—surfaced the logos of the
European-style terrorist groups which would use "wet means" to get
what they wanted.

These.

And one also had to assume the KGB, always in the wings if not
actually onstage when the dialogue related to new combat techniques,
a classification into which SEDAV fit all too readily.

Jason looked at the awful little bundle under the bright towel on the
big chair and swore again, bleakly and miserably.

Espionage, like terrorism, is a buzzword, easily bandied about. However, if a person searching for a hypothesis ruled out these words then
he had to fall back on demonology, which is neither a hypothesis nor
an explanation but a fact. There is demonology in all weapons, as anyone
familiar with them knows, particularly the people engaged in making
them, and nobody knew it better than Jason Streck, the only son and
principal inheritor of the technology empire of his slain father, J. Caulfield Streck.

Jason had grown up in the climate of the martial spirit at the heart,
as it were, of the family business. He knew the great plant better than
anyone except possibly his father, the latter as the years passed assuming
more and more the character of an offstage presence, remote and withdrawn, his power passed down the lines of policy rather than personal
contact. Jason was highly visible. There were days when he seemed to
be everywhere at once, his shock of red hair flaming under the neon light
banks of the great production buildings, his muscular, oddly tilted body
speeding with a sidling gait along the trim walkways and through the
corridors inside, to some of which a special ID or knowledge of an
electronic code were required for entry. To offset the tilt and abet the
stride he carried a stick, an unusual accoutrement for a strong and
attractive man in his mid-thirties, but there you were—he carried it and
thought nothing about it.

Early on in his career at ADECT he had suffered a certain unique and
awful type of damage that had left his feet impaired. The older employees knew the story and would, reluctantly, pass it along, though it was
not considered good form to discuss it. Nor did it seem, measured

against the force of the young man's vital presence, to have much significance.

It had happened a long time ago.

If the hurt in question had changed his attitude about his work he had been careful not to let this appear. He had made or helped to make a lot of battle machines so their secret properties were by no means new to him. He was also very much a child of his times: his contact with deadly appliances went far back. He had been seven years old in 1957, the year when people climbed on their rooftops and stood gaping in the fields and in the streets while *Sputnik,* the first man-made object in space, winked past in the winter skies. That was also the last year the United States tested a nuclear device in the atmosphere and Jason Streck had seen that too.

The memory, for no particular reason, came back to him as he sat with the rest of the Streck family members in the forward pews reserved for them with strands of white ribbon in St. Athanasias Church, Cupertino, California, while the Right Reverend Emmet Dalton Phelan delivered the eulogy at the requiem mass honoring the passing of J. Caulfield Streck. Amid the smells of churchly wood and spicy memorial incense he had thought of traveling with his father to see the bomb go off. He had almost not gone. His mother had opposed the outing. She rarely argued with anyone, least of all Jason's father, but she had argued against this furiously.

"How can you expose a child to that?"

"There's no danger in it, Mother," said J. Caulfield mildly.

"Of course there's danger. They say if you look at the explosion you go blind."

"I won't let him look at it."

"Then why are you taking him?"

"So it will be real to him."

"That's a hideous idea. Why don't you let him be a child?"

"He's a child in the nuclear world. He might as well know about it."

His father won the argument.

They had driven all day on splendid roads with little traffic and got up in the dark on a cold morning in Las Vegas. His father made coffee and pancakes. Then a green army truck with a bunch of men in it picked them up and they drove for hours into the desert. There was a road at first, then hardly any road and it was bumpy. The men in the truck passed a bottle around. The sun was just coming up in the blue rim of the desert as they piled out of the truck and went into a long green outhouse. Jason had been embarrassed having to go in front of so many strangers and his father understood this and stood next to him until he was through and they were able to get out of the rank outhouse into the desert air, warmer now and full of the harsh exciting smell of sage.

The sky had turned a clear hard blue and in the distance there were mountains with black grooves in them, topped with sharp straggly peaks.

The men marched in a column, saying little. Overhead circled several large planes—camera planes, his father said. After walking several hundred yards they met some soldiers who were handing out sunglasses. There were a lot of wooden tables lined up with benches placed on one side so that everyone sitting there would be looking out in a single direction.

The bomb was on a steel frame in the middle of a dish-shaped scoop, way out in the sage.

"You are ten miles from ground zero," said a voice on a loudspeaker. It looked a lot closer than that.

"Can I have some more coffee, Dad?" Jason asked in a low voice.

"I don't see why not," said J. Caulfield Streck, and poured him some in a tin cup. Jason drank it eagerly, though he disliked the taste of it. He was not allowed to drink it at home. There were platters of buns and doughnuts on the table and he ate one of each and started to feel better.

Someone on the loudspeaker talked about the bomb. Jason understood not one word of this except the part when the lecturer said, "Serious injury could occur if you attempt to look at the blast with the naked eye. Please put on your glasses when the countdown begins."

Jason put on his glasses which immediately fell down around his neck. To keep them up he had to hold the rims in his hands, resting his elbows on the table. The glasses were not simply tinted but black. Looking through them he couldn't see a thing.

He was starting to feel badly again. Nobody was talking anymore. All the scientists and the soldiers who had been standing around went into a concrete building dug into the side of a knoll and left the businessmen and reporters sitting at the bare tables in front of the bomb. There were no other kids. Jason wondered if he would go blind as his mother had said he might. He wanted to go to the bathroom again.

"Now counting down," said the loudspeaker. "Minus ten, nine
. . . five . . . three, two, one . . . ZERO."

An enormous white light suffused sky and earth, so bright that Jason
could see the bones of the fingers he had cupped around the glasses to
keep them from slipping down.

The ground shook and buckled, making the benches slip around;
seconds later came a blast of hot air and a terrible noise. Jason could
no longer see his fingerbones. Slowly he eased a tiny crack to peek
through.

The men around him were all taking off their glasses so he did too
and sat shivering, watching the enormous thick white wide-topped
mushroom-bottomed cloud of boiling stuff rise up into the desert sky.

"Daddy," he said when they were driving home, "when will the last
day come?"

"What day is that, son?" his father asked.

"The day when they blow everybody up."

"Don't worry, it will never come," said J. Caulfield Streck.

"Then what are they practicing for?"

"Don't worry about stuff like that. Those fellows you met today know
what they're doing. They have everything under control."

But Jason could not put the thought about the last day out of his
mind. He had bad dreams in which the roiling, bulging, inside-out
burning and fiery swelling clouds that followed the airblast and the
explosion were seeping into his room through the windows, the door,
the ceiling. He could not keep them out or hide from them and the
glasses kept slipping off his face and the awful burning stuff was getting
into his bed and around him and would have got into him had he not
saved himself by waking up, usually with a howl. He told no one at home
about these dreams and at school he told nobody about anything, knowing that if he even talked about the trip or the dream they would not
believe him but put him down as some kind of weirdo.

By the time he was in eighth grade the nature of his father's work was
changing. The plant was doing something called Defense. That was how
it was mentioned at home, Defense with a capital letter or some kind
of quotation marks. It had nothing to do with bombs. Nothing whatever. Jason had assured himself of that. Quite a number of the kids at
Santa Clara County Day had parents who were into Defense and these
kids knew about the products being made and talked about them freely
and sometimes proudly. Satellites. Rockets. Missiles. Detection systems.
They knew how they worked and would describe them to you.

These kids were all gearheads. They were into electronics up to their asses and so was Jason. He and Chris Larner or one of his other buddies were into telephone black boxing and Chris was almost arrested for crunching the code into the mainframe data bank at the Smithsonian.

Jason and Chris would go to the computer flea markets and come back with all kinds of treasures which they would try to repair or just pile up to gloat over and compare collections. Chris's mother worked at a plant that made PCs, his father was an SP railroad brakeman. When anyone brought up Jason's father Jason said he was an electronics engineer. He loved and admired his father but that was as far as he wanted to go with the subject of the kind of work he did since Defense had come into the picture.

Although more people than St. Athanasias could hold had been present at the mass, many of them forced to stand outside, only family, and not all the family at that, had gone on to the interment that followed at Maryknoll Cemetery. Jason's sister, Norma, and her husband, Arthur Hulett, Kenan Professor of History at the University of California, Irvine, had hurried straight from the church to the house at Woodside and so were at hand to greet the guests soon streaming in for the gathering that would follow mass.

By the time Jason and the widow Odille (J.C.'s third and final wife) reached the scene, the party was in full swing. Barbecue spits were turning in the patio and on the terraces and the reek of burning charcoal and scorched meat billowed out into the great wooded lawn; lines of men and women clutching plates moved slowly past the buffet tables while, inside and out, waiters in red jackets passed trays of cocktails, champagne, caviar, sausages, and strips of lox rolled into nuggets and filled with cream cheese. Conversations which had started at the halting gait and subdued pitch that had seemed appropriate for the sad occasion gained speed and decibels until the voices merged into a roar indistinguishable from that of a fashionable cocktail party anywhere in the world.

The black limousine rented from the funeral director dropped off Odille at the front door but Jason, who until then had been escorting her, had the driver take him around to the north side of the house. Here a service staircase led to the upper floors, one he seldom used—it was steep and hard for him to climb; he went up now, though, stick and all, rapidly and quietly, to the room that had been his when he had been a student at Stanford and his father had first built this house, moving the family from the little old shingled place at the corner of Hope and Mercy streets in Mountain View where they had all lived so long.

The room had none of his things in it now. He'd moved out completely after graduation, the year he'd gotten his first job and his first apartment. Still, in the depths of his mind, it was *his* room—and it supplied a viewing advantage: from its position in a wing extending over the patio, he could look down at the activities there and even, through a large picture window, at those in the living room. People were still piling in and Odille and the Huletts were busy greeting them.

He would go down soon, but not yet. Now he wanted a few minutes of quiet. There was also something else, some business to be taken care of. The people who had flown out from Washington would be leaving early. So, of course, would the Sacramento people, the governor and his staff, also probably Moses Ricardi, the attorney general, plus assorted local assemblymen and a few others. But it was not the Sacramento people who concerned him. It was the Washington ones. Secretary of Defense Walden Wynans had sent Undersecretary Samuel Truscott to represent the department and present his apologies for not attending in person. Well, that was natural enough, but Jason secretly wished Wynans could have been on hand to see the people assembled here today. He would have known that high-technology leaders and others of importance had thought enough of J. Caulfield Streck to interrupt their busy lives to pay him honor. Also, had he been there, then perhaps he, Secretary of Defense of the United States instead of the Rt. Rev. Emmet Phelan, vicar-general of the archdiocese of northern California, could have read from the pulpit some of the wonderful messages that had been received, including the one from the President:

> . . . heartfelt regret at the passing of one of our Nation's most able and patriotic citizens—

There had been in the congregation at St. Athanasias another governmental figure almost as high-ranking as the secretary, or even, as some might see it, even higher. This person also could have read the messages or even delivered the eulogy. He could have been asked and Jason had thought of asking him but he had not done so. To put emphasis upon the family connection might cause this person embarrassment—something which was to be avoided at all costs and would more than offset the impact to be gained by his being the one to get up there in the pulpit and say a few kind words.

Jason pushed a button on the house intercom and when his call was answered, he spoke through it to Kim Wah, the Strecks' Korean houseman.

"Kim," said Jason, "can you hear me all right?"

The babble coming up from below made this seem unlikely but Kim's reply was that he could hear fine.

"Okay," said Jason, "I want you to go and find Senator John Lighty. Don't interrupt him while he's talking. Just stand near him until he starts to move. Then go up to him and give him this message. Tell him I'm here, upstairs, and I'd like to speak to him, if that's convenient. Will you do that, just as I've said?"

"Yes, sah," said Kim Wah. "Not when he's talking. Just when he move. I onnerstan."

"Thank you," said Jason.

"I tell him, Mr. Jason. You wan' I bring some highball up, some sanawich maybe?"

"No thanks, Kim. Just the message. That's all."

"Okay, Mr. Jason, sah. I hear what you say."

Up to now it had seemed real that there was a death, but not that it was his father's; he had thought that the latter, when it happened, would be so different. He had imagined it would be like when his Grandmother Weyland had died. She had been released from the hospital so that she could die in the house at Mountain View where she had lived so long. The family had known that she was going to die and she had known it. She had felt it was her right, and though it was not in her character to seek attention, she accepted her central role this one time without objection.

One day she had rung the little bell beside her bed and asked for Father Ciccio. The hour had come.

Father Ciccio's church was only a few blocks away. It was a parish left over from the period before the onslaught of technology. In those bygone days, the whole Valley had been one huge prune and apricot orchard, a tossing sea of green in summer, an artfully pruned and patterned design of gray and black boughs in winter. The orchardists had been Italians and Portuguese and they had built the churches and maintained them in the old, careful ways, just as they did the orchards.

Father Ciccio had come over as fast as he could. He, like his parishioner, had a bell and he rang it as he came, the silvery fragile sound hurrying ahead of him to advise the dying person that comfort was on the way. Soon Father Ciccio could be seen, bearing under the humeral veil, in its leather pyx, the Blessed Sacrament. The children were put out of the room while Grandmother Weyland confessed her little old sins and received absolution. Then they had been let in again. They had watched in awe as the tiny old lady, clutching her rosary beads blessed by the pope, closed her eyes and went away.

That was how one died in the Streck family—not shot down alone at night in a guarded place, presumed safe.

The noise below had smoothed into a deep, steady mix, opulent and full. Jason Streck found it lulling rather than disturbing. Waiting for the senator, he took off the dark jacket with the white carnation pinned to its lapel. He laid this on a chair, then loosened his collar and the knot of his black silk tie; a breathing spell, even one as short as this might be, was welcome after the crisis and confusion of the last few days.

In less than a minute there was a light knock on the door, followed by another of the same kind, and without waiting for a response, Senator John Lighty entered, followed by Kim Wah. Contrary to instructions, Kim bore a tray containing drinks and sandwiches. Kim knew what he had to do.

The senator's greeting was hearty. He neither felt nor showed any sense that protocol had been breached when a servant had informed him that he, senior senator from California, now completing his third term and more than an even bet to go in for a fourth, was wanted upstairs at the request of a young man who as yet held no post of importance, either in business or in politics.

A few days earlier, such a summons would have been absurd. Now that was all changed. An act of violence had turned the pecking order topsy-turvy. The young man, though his new standing was not yet confirmed, had become a person of consequence.

The senator had been happy to oblige. Up here in this room alone with Jason Streck, he was where he always preferred to be—at the hub of affairs.

Senator John Lighty was in his early sixties and had a head like a turtle's—bald on top—with a thick neck and a small hooked nose squeezing down on a mouth that could bite through steel. Like a turtle also, he had folds of skin instead of eyebrows and, beneath those folds, the merriest blue eyes in the world. A longtime friend of Jason's father, he had been the de facto godfather of SEDAV. There had been an evening a few years back when, as Senate majority leader, he'd had one hour in which to get a budget resolution passed or the government would go out of business. The point of resistance had been defense and at the nub of the defense bill had been the new weapon.

Feelings ran high. Any way you looked at it, the vote would be close—the focus of clashing forces in the most critical midelection year since Vietnam. Foremost in opposition had been the senator from Illinois, who threatened to filibuster. The senator from Delaware had argued with him. There in the cloakroom they fell to shouting, then pushing at each other. The senator from Hawaii tried to intercede and the senator from Oklahoma, although nearer eighty than seventy, took a swipe at the senator from Hawaii; meanwhile the clock was ticking and inside the great gold and white chamber the other members, indifferent to all this, had started cleaning out their cramped Colonial era desks.

That was when John Lighty had made his move. He had led Illinois into the hall and talked to him. Then he'd gone back into the cloakroom and spoken with Delaware. He located Oklahoma's glasses, which had fallen to the floor. With each distinguished solon, in one form or another, he employed his magic formula, consisting of the question, "What can I do to make it easier for you?"

He had stopped the filibuster. With six minutes and less than that number of votes to spare, he pushed through a consensus, the appropriation had passed, and SEDAV got its funding.

No doubt of it, such moments were a strain, but Lighty could handle them. He got along famously with the President. There were evenings, barred to even the closest insiders, when Lucy Pearl, the first lady, baked certain country dishes herself and the two fierce old men regaled themselves with these, swilling Appalachian rifle whiskey while they laid out the course of the nation.

Even now, Lighty had food on his mind. Jason was glad Kim had ignored his orders about snacks and booze. The two men ate and drank, the old one and the young—a new power team. They wasted no time on the conjecture being passed around downstairs—had J.C.'s killing been an espionage contract? And if so, what would be the government's response? These were matters for the intelligence community to solve.

Jason's problems were more personal. They concerned the outcome of the struggle for control now sure to take place in the executive suites at ADECT. The senator listened to his exposition, interrupting with a few questions; he saved the most pointed for last, and before launching it, reached for the Bushmill's and poured himself one more dab.

"So there's trouble in the wind?"

Jason nodded. "Quite a history attached to it. You'll recognize the key man when I mention him."

"Would his initials be C.A.G.?"

"That's the one."

Charles Adolph Gitlin, an imposing man in his mid-sixties, was vice-chairman of ADECT.

The senator chomped into a chicken sandwich. When he could speak again, he said, "A hard-workin' feller."

For Lighty, "hard-workin' feller" was a formula almost as useful as "What can I do . . . ?" It fitted almost anyone except notorious sluggards and, while innocent of criticism, could be shaded with whatever overtones one chose.

"He's that, all right. He got his ADECT stock by bringing in some venture capital. He sold most of it too soon, but he's tough, and if push came to shove he might raise quite a fuss. I'm not ready for that."

"So you'd like me to reason with him. Is that how the wind is blowing?"

"I appreciate the offer, John, but no, I have a way to handle him. I just want to clear it with you. Is he important to the party?"

"I get along with Charles."

"That's what I thought."

"Put it this way, son. He's a bagman, a fund raiser. He can walk into my office and be welcome. That's the extent of it. We don't discuss his private affairs and he asks few favors."

"I want him off the board, John."

"That's your option, boy."

"Thank you, Senator."

"No thanks due. He's passed the hat before and he'll pass it again, whether he's on your board or not."

"Would you say he has a price tag on him?"

"Most do."

"Now you've answered my second question. This may be the most expensive thing I've done, but I'm going to buy him out before the cost goes out of sight."

"Ah," said the senator, "the troubles of the rich. Praise the good Lord that a political animal is exempted. And would you think now the folk below might be looking for us?"

For those who attended the funeral reception for J. Caulfield Streck, the moment easiest to remember was the appearance of his son, Jason, on the great stairway starting down, with Senator John Lighty beside him. They made an interesting pair: the senator, so famous that he was like an ambulating cartoon, and his young, muscular companion. Jason's good-humored face, with its rough, ruddy features, was bent solicitously toward the great man as if John Lighty was the one who must be watched over and cared for, although it was not he, but Jason, who was using the stick.

THREE

A stick cannot be hurried, particularly on a stairway. It must be poked ahead each time and braced a certain way, with a certain rhythm, before a foot comes down beside it. Thus they descended, the young man and the old one, stick, foot, stick—and they had not come far before all eyes were on them. Jason did not find this objectionable. If he was in for difficulties with the ADECT board, as he had intimated to the senator, this was as good a way as any to caucus, and better than most.

"Where have you been, you rascal?"

The voice was Odille's. She was still in her place in the family receiving line near the front door, with Norma Streck Hulett, his sister, her husband Arthur, plus various in-laws, cousins, and remaindermen of the far-flung duchy of Streck.

"The senator and I had a few matters to discuss."

"Could I guess about whom?"

"I doubt it."

"You underestimate me. Turn slowly and look over your left shoulder."

Jason did as instructed—and immediately regretted it; his eyes, in that unplanned second, met full on the glare of ADECT Vice-Chairman

Charles Gitlin. Gitlin's sloping shoulders and long thin neck were out-lined against the patio window, the sun pouring its beams into his great mop of snowy hair, the hair of a king, of an emperor! The shock of colliding glances had the force of a freeway pileup, with Gitlin the least damaged. He turned his heel and stalked off toward the buffet.

"Well?" said Odille.

"You've always been too sharp for your own good," Jason observed.

"I didn't have to be sharp. I've been talking to him for the past ten minutes and he was probing me—me!—to see how I planned to vote my shares."

"I was wondering about that too."

"Darling, are you serious?"

"About ten percent serious," Jason said. "The other ninety percent trusts you completely."

"Now I know you're joking. But if you have evil thoughts tonight you must get rid of them. We're family, darling. We stand shoulder to shoulder, don't we?"

"All the way," said Jason, with a smile.

All the way? Make that maybe ninety-eight percent.

On the whole he liked her and always got on well with her, a blessed replacement as a stepmother for her predecessor, who had been a high-tech executive with a brilliant mind, a quick temper, and a secret drink-ing habit. Odille's style was different; she had perfected it, as she had perfected herself, in the process of living. Her clothes and jewels were the best. They had come with her—J.C. had bought her little. She was rich in her own right, and a shrewd investor in the stock market. Her hips were too wide, her eyes too tilted, her mouth too full for her tapering face, but possibly because of her defects—the fact that nothing about her quite matched up—she projected an air of low-keyed but heart-stopping sexuality. Jason was sure that Gitlin, the current subject of their concern, had been making passes at her long before his father died—and equally positive that he had met with no success. Odille was now, more than ever, a great inheritor. By the terms of the will, which had contained few surprises, she'd gotten enough ADECT stock to make her a formidable influence in future company affairs.

Jason watched her as she moved on to welcome a shy, cranky venture capitalist—shabbiest of the several billionaires present in her house today. It was she who had organized the reception, ordered the food, hired catering waiters, turned down Norma Hulett's plea for a quiet "just for family" interment, with the words, "Caulfield wouldn't have wanted it that way."

Norma had been furious.

"A European-style gala, after a *murder*? It's in the worst of taste. She has no feelings. I can't believe she ever loved Dad."

Jason had stayed out of the argument; had he gotten into it, he would have sided with his sister. Yet he could not accept the idea that Odille felt no grief. He had stood beside her at the graveside, seen her tears, felt her flinch when the clod of earth, tossed by the Right Reverend Phelan, landed with a small cellary thud on the lid of the bronze casket.

No doubt about it, J. Caulfield Streck had been her kind of man. Certainly they had been close. With the perceptions of a woman of experience, she had made allowance for his addiction to power, his queer strident tenderness, his ruthless ambition and good nature.

Jason circulated through the rooms; he would have liked a few words at least with everyone present; this, in view of the numbers, was impossible, but the mix had now separated into specific groups, small hegemonies, which made it easier. The ADECT staffers, for instance. The upper echelons required no special attention, since he would be seeing them daily at the plant. The lower ones who crashed out of goodwill or because of the desire to be inside the boss's house this one time and tell about it—they could be ignored. Not so the neighborhood folk, the old family friends from the Mountain View days and even earlier; these had clotted in their own corner and he greeted them individually and warmly: Mrs. Greiner, his chemistry teacher, nearly ninety now but spry; Cloris Hyman, a widow of Abe, family banker at the Wells Fargo; Eichelberg, the fire chief; and Karl Gros, the gardener whose burly son, standing with him, still took care of the grounds at Hope and Mercy for the people who had bought it so long ago.

". . . my Emmy, she is gone too, t'ree years yet."

"I'm sorry to hear that, Karl. We all loved Emma."

"You go sometimes the old place by?"

"Oh, yes. Sure do—once in a while. . . ."

Well, he had—once in a while. Not for years now. But, for Karl, he would make this pilgrimage, at least declaratively. Salt of the earth, these old people, inhabitants of a world which had been swept away without their knowing what was happening.

And then, at the opposite end of the scale, the denizens of the new, lunar landscape—heads of semiconductor companies, the great innovators, the entrepreneurs. There was even one very deaf, very frail and strange man who was said to have invented . . . *the transistor*! Was that possible? How old was he? But that didn't matter in an industry so young that its pioneers were still in their seventies.

This group too had its turf, the most clearly defined of any, its members an odd mix. Some were sleek with the patina of business leaders anywhere, others gross or reclusive or tilting toward flamboyance but all, without exception, very private people, imperious, intractable and sealed off. J. Caulfield Streck would have been pleased, Jason thought, that they were on hand to pay their respects. He wondered whether, under similar circumstances, his father would have gone to their houses . . . or to a church where a mass had been said for the repose of their souls.

He turned away. Norma was coming toward him.

"The governor is leaving. Don't you think you should see him to his car?"

"Of course."

A wind had come up. The tall trees thrashed on the lawn; around the cottage the bushes, recently pushed and pulled about by cops in search of shell casings, shed their leaves; chauffeured limousines inched toward the front door, parking boys in white jackets ran to fetch other vehicles, the catering people left in a large green van.

Undersecretary Truscott, invited to stay on, declined. He and Jason could meet in the morning. The senator accepted. He had reservations on the redeye to Washington. There were other matters to see to before he left. A busy man!

Odille ordered a light early supper for the Huletts, the Garays, and a few of the top ADECT executives, which Kim Wah served in the breakfast room. The white wine had run out so they drank champagne; when the family group was alone at last, they moved to the library, where they read the last condolences from the great of the nation, delivered during the reception.

As the fall night closed in, the wind grew stronger. It came from the south, a Santa Ana, as the hot dry blows are called that sometimes savage California. They uncoil off the great deserts, the Mojave and the high scorched mesas of Arizona and Nevada, the borderlands, breathing through the gorges of the Tehachapis, the only mountain range in the state which runs perversely east and west instead of north and south. Winds of ill omen. In them pushes the rage of the Indian gods, the stink of cactus carrion and the bones of dry-gulched wagon trains, their wheel hubs and tattered ribs still found sometimes, buried in the moving dunes with black obsidian arrowheads nearby. Such winds ruffle tempers and burn nerves but at least they scour off the smog that dims the Valley's perpetual bald-headed sky.

A wild and weird night, fit for the passing of a great chief. Branches skittered onto the roof, also a shutter was loose somewhere; it banged with a dull boom, then subsided, then boomed again, forbidding sleep. Jason pulled on some clothes and went out to fix what he could. He was turning back when lightning lit the garden and he saw Odille.

She stood stiff as a piece of statuary, naked, her arms folded across her breasts, facing a shrine with a big gold Christus in it, one that she and J.C. had bought from Sotheby's. She'd never gone near it before, as far as he could remember, but there she was, wet and chilled, her long hair streaming down her shoulders: was she having some kind of fit?

Pointing his flashlight beam at the ground, not to startle her, he drew close; she didn't turn. He took off his sweater to put it around her shoulders. She shook it off, then struck at him. Another lightning flash laid a yellow ring the size of the sky around them with the gentle, termite-eaten face of the Christus tilting down at them from the middle of it. Jason dropped his stick and the light; he put his arms around her to lift her or drag her along but his weak leg gave way with the effort and they both crashed to the ground.

She was up first. With a wrench of her body she pulled free and ran inside the house.

He found her in the pantry, drying herself with dish towels, as composed as if they'd been out for an evening stroll. Her breasts were ample, the nipples large and erect. Jason tried to keep his eyes off them and the flat belly with the dark swab of hair below.

"I want brandy," she said. "The decanter's in the dining room."

It was an order. He trotted off to obey. When he came back she had glasses out.

"Would you get me a coat, dear? A warm one. From the hall closet."

He came back with an ankle-length mink and helped her into it. She'd finished her brandy and was pouring another. He knocked back his own.

"Would it be rude to inquire what in hell you were doing out there?" Jason asked.

"I would have thought . . . that would be obvious."

"Not quite . . . that is, not to me."

She sipped.

"I was saying good-bye to him."

"I thought we did that in church."

"This was my personal good-bye. I feel the better for it."

"I hope you feel as well tomorrow. It was cold out there."

"I'm quite warm-blooded. But you were sweet to care—and come after me."

It did not seem the time to tell her he'd gone to mend a shutter.

"Good night, dear."

"Good night, Odille."

She turned to go, then as if correcting an oversight came back and kissed him. Her mouth, still cold, yielded nothing. As if this too required correction she kissed him a second time, the lips parting deeply and softly, offering the tip of her tongue. With this she was indeed on her way, leaving Jason to the brandy. That night he slept without dreaming. He wakened to find the storm over and a sheen of early light, pale and harsh, over the wrack it had left behind.

FOUR

The wind had died overnight. As usual, the morning sky was gray, but light broke though in shafts, glazing paint and chrome as the lines of cars crawled on the freeways, the morning shift in Silicon Valley on its way to work.

Gradually the oozing river of steel puddled into parking lots and became still. The workers formed new lines, which disappeared into factories built of tilt-up concrete slabs, so much alike in styling and so artfully designed that they appeared to be parts of some gigantic secret campus—interconnected, flowing on and on as far as the eye could see, silent, harmonious and macabre.

The hushed buildings did not look like factories at all. It would have been hard for a stranger coming on to the scene to realize that inside them, around the clock, thousands of people would be busy making weapons, the oldest form of manufacturing known to man.

The ADECT plant was one of the most imposing. It was known as Sunnyvale Three and consisted not of one building but a whole clump. It was located almost at ground zero, the epicenter of the Valley's industries, an area containing some 500 plants within a five-mile radius, many of them world famous.

Jason had never liked the name "Silicon Valley." It was a metaphor, not a place. It had none of the characteristics or properties of a real place. A place had a terrain, an identity on maps; it had sewers, sidewalks, schools, postmen, taxes, cops, garbagemen, judges, and courts. Insofar as Silicon Valley possessed such components it usurped them from the six major towns and four minor ones that encompassed its perimeters, namely Sunnyvale, Santa Clara, Mountain View, Palo Alto, San Jose, Cupertino, Redwood City, Menlo Park, Los Gatos, and Saratoga. These were all real places, not some publicist's fantasies, as he well knew, having grown up in one of them; it sometimes seemed odd to him that, in spite of his travels to distant parts of the world, sometimes with good luck and sometimes without it, he had settled down within spitting distance of his birthplace, all changed now, of course.

He turned off Monroe Street into the ADECT parking lot. From here he could see, to his right, the back of the Intel plant on Bowers; to the left, only a little further off, rose the windowless ten-story box of the NSA center, the Valley's most mystic installation, where satellite surveillance data was decrypted and passed on to its appropriate recipients; not far away was Watkins Johnson, Lockheed Missile and Space, Hewlett-Packard, Varian, Ampex, FMC, Ford Aerospace . . . and on and on, their celebrated logos, crafted in brushed steel or polished stone, displayed out front on well-watered swards of grass.

Jason's father had bought the land cheap. The prune and apricot orchards were already disappearing but the Valley was rich with the potting soil of venture capital; gifted engineers and physicists who had assumed they would be working for salaries all their lives had suddenly found that they could get start-up money for their own ideas. They were swarming in, eager for a piece of the action.

J. Caulfield Streck's infant company did well. He was pleased with the turn it took in the late fifties. A graduate of West Point and a former infantry captain, he was military-minded; down the line he saw glory in serving his country's defense needs, plus the prospect of personal enrichment. He was not, like certain members of his board, disappointed with the early contracts he had negotiated with the Department of Defense, nor impatient with the long qualification process, the endless paperwork, the slow pay involved in dealing with this customer. It would all come right in the end. He was proven correct, but his policies, perhaps too heavily affirmed, created a split in the decision-making levels of ADECT which endured until his death and was the principal problem now facing Jason on this, his first day at work since the funeral.

He parked his car at the far end of the lot. The slot had no name on it; reserved parking would have run counter to ADECT's egalitarian ethic. Had someone else parked there, however, a security guard at the gate would have told the offender to move it. Egalitarianism was not ADECT's first priority, although Caulfield had seen it at other semiconductor firms and adapted it, to a limited degree, for his own use.

Egalitarianism in on-the-job dress, for instance—that was sound. It did away with a certain kind of snobbery and wasteful expense; as a side effect, it created a kind of company uniform. Vice-presidents and senior engineers and famous physicists wore it along with fuzzy-cheeked whiz kids just out of Stanford and Harvard and MIT. It consisted of a plaid L. L. Bean-type woodsman's shirt, tan chinos, and moccasin loafers for men and slightly more decorative shirts or shirtwaists, either jeans or medium-length cotton or wool skirts with sneakers or Hush Puppies for women. Jason had on his own version of the uniform now, with a shell parka added to keep off the early morning chill. His solid-state, test-pilot's watch, an early ADECT product, stood at ten minutes to eight as he joined the file of people moving through the great, guarded gate, past the tall pole and half-masted flag.

The file moved on, electronically swept for dangerous objects and observed by an armed security person seated behind a bulletproof window. Inside they were issued ID badges and happy morning smiles from several attractive young women. Jason enjoyed the process. Egalitarianism was jolly if you looked at it the right way. Some of those near him had attended the funeral mass and some also the reception, and several of these as well as others reached out to shake hands and express sympathy for his loss. When it came time for him, like the rest, to get his ID badge, the girl who gave it out was teary-eyed.

"Jason, I'm sick inside. We all are."

"Thank you, Bobbi," Jason said.

"It will never be the same around here."

"I know," said Jason. "God bless you."

She handed him his badge and he clipped it onto his shirt.

With another card he opened an unmarked steel door and entered the executive reception foyer, where egalitarianism ended and command began.

The foyer was huge. It was furnished in a kind of contemporary art deco that blended well with the high gleaming walls, tile floor, and towering ficus. By nine o'clock it would be staffed and functioning, but at the moment it was empty, except for one security guard.

Stick propelled, Jason crossed straight to an escalator which, dormant until his approach, now chunked into life and took him to the second floor, which ADECT people called The Tower. Here a single office covered all the available space, which until his death had been occupied by J. Caulfield Streck. No one knew better than Jason that the title and hence, one would assume, the quarters of the president and chief executive officer of a public company having several hundred thousand stockbrokers could not be passed on as a family legacy even if the president had so desired. Still, if he wanted that office and that job, the best idea was not to mess around with formalities but to get in there and stake out a claim. Jason had asked Abe Kohn to provide his secretary, Mrs. Purviance, with a key. He was puzzled now to find Mrs. Purviance sitting in the small foyer at the head of the escalator, surrounded by stuff brought over from Jason's former office in another building. The door to J. Caulfield's office was still closed and in front of it, at parade rest, stood a large pale man with a shoebrush mustache.

Mrs. Purviance rushed over to Jason. She was very much upset.

"That idiot won't let me in."

"You have the key?"

"Of course. Abe gave it to me yesterday."

Jason looked at Shoebrush Mustache. He knew most of the plant security by sight. He was sure he had not seen this one before, if such indeed he was. Key in hand, he crossed the foyer.

"Kindly stand aside."

Shoebrush rocked back and forth on his large cop's feet.

"This office is sealed, sir."

"Are you employed here?"

"I am today, sir."

"Let me see your ID."

The man hesitated, then produced a one-day special-duty pass. This type of ID at ADECT required a signature at vice-presidential level. It had such a signature.

Abe Kohn stepped off the escalator.

"We got a problem?" he asked quietly.

"Our friend here says we can't get in the office. I'm afraid he's mistaken."

"He sure as hell is," said Kohn. He addressed Shoebrush.

"Don't I know you from somewhere?"

"I don't think so, Mr. Kohn."

"You're a Pinkerton."

"That's right. And my orders," said the man, "are to keep this office sealed."

"—on a one-day basis."

"That's right, sir."

"Your day just terminated."

"Try me!" said the Pinkerton.

He swung a karate chop at Kohn who ducked it, then kicked the Pinkerton in the groin, slamming him against the door he had so stoutly defended; with one hand between his legs and the other in his collar he dropped him on the escalator, the man sliding and scrambling on the metal-gridded steps, flailing as he tried to get upright again. Kohn spoke on the intercom to the guard in the lower lobby, then turned to Jason.

"They'll take care of him down there. You might want this."

He handed Jason the special-duty pass which the Pinkerton had dropped. "Can we do anything further to help you move in?"

"No, that's fine, Abe," said Jason. "And thanks."

Kohn waved off a salute and headed below, where sounds of a struggle were audible. Jason unlocked the office door and walked in. He sat down at the desk—the biggest desk at ADECT—and examined the contested pass: the signature it bore was Charles Adolph Gitlin.

He beckoned to Mrs. Purviance, presently engaged in moving the files from the foyer.

"Edna, will you please call Mr. Gitlin's office? Tell him I'd appreciate a meeting with him. Try to make it after lunch, one-thirty or two if that's agreeable to him. Or whatever time he wants. And let Ken Garay know about it. I'd like him with me."

Mrs. Purviance made a note.

FIVE

At least he'd cleared the day's first hurdle and this pleased him; he leaned back in his chair, looking around the room—a unique, a beautiful room, filled as it was with historic memorabilia which his father had collected from the four quarters of the nation: Revolutionary War flintlocks and sabers; muskets, bayonets, cannonballs, grenades; a Rough Rider's hat; a chunk of armor from the battleship *Maine,* so treacherously sunk in Havana Harbor; bandages and surgical instruments from seven wars on beds of velvet in glass cases; a piece of the flag that had flown over Fort Sumter; a wheel from the caisson that had carried John F. Kennedy's coffin to Arlington.

A patriot's office—and J. C. Streck had certainly been that. Also a wise and tender father, a prudent businessman, and a mean son of a bitch. It had been hard to tell which of these personalities, at any given moment, you were dealing with. Most of the time Jason had felt he understood his father; he was not so sure that his father had always understood him. There had been love between them, but there had also been that changeableness, that high-pressure feverishness in J.C. these recent years, leading to the break Jason had wanted to fix the night he'd found J.C. dead.

If you went back far enough you could say that the roots of the trouble had been another act of terrorism, one in which Jason himself had been the victim. He had been kidnapped and held for ransom by agents of the MPSI, the Moroccan Party for Social Independence, which had toppled the monarchy. The coup had taken everyone by surprise, including, apparently, the CIA, whose chief of station in Casablanca had been Jason's good friend and tennis pal. In fact, the last game of tennis he had ever played, or ever would, had been with that fellow on an embassy court. The ambassador had left the day the old regime went down, borrowing the ADECT Learjet for his getaway. He bailed out so fast he nearly forgot his attaché case, which a junior officer handed up to him from the boarding ladder. The steward slammed the door—and that was the last they saw of His Excellency.

The Lear was supposed to come back the next day and bring Jason home, but by that time he was in custody.

He had been in Casablanca for a company survey. ADECT had been considering a fabrication plant there. The fab plant in Almeria, Spain, had run into union troubles; Morocco seemed a logical alternative. The climate was fine and the labor was cheap. Jason had even picked out a site; he was working on final details of the lease—always, in Third World countries, it had proven better to lease than to purchase—when he was awakened one sunny summer morning by a loudspeaker truck blasting away in English, French, and Arabic in the street in front of the Hilton:

> People of Morocco! Rejoice, give thanks to Allah, the Compassionate! For today you are free! By one momentous act of revolution your chains have been broken and the bondage of centuries cast aside. From this moment on you take your place among great nations of the world, the Moroccan Arab Republic!

He dressed and went down to breakfast. Less than half of the usual dining room staff had come to work. A tank flanked the statue of General Lyautey in the Place Napoleon III. Soldiers wearing queer green brassards never seen before in public mingled with the crowds listening to the sound trucks.

Jason had trouble getting a cab. He drove to the office of the Bank of Switzerland, ADECT's African agents. The shutters were still up and the doors locked.

At last the irresistible destiny long denied us has been realized. The corruption and filth that has afflicted us is at an end. We embrace a new era!

The papers had no news as yet, but gradually a structure of fact emerged. During the predawn hours a force of cadets from the Ahermoumou Military Academy in the middle Atlas mountains had helicoptered into the city. They had seized the post office, the customs house, the television station, and the docks. At the same time assault squads, recruited from the regular army, surrounded the king's summer palace, killing the guards there. The king, warned in time, had fled.

United under Allah, we seek no vengeance, demanding only recognition of our rights. From now on we stand shoulder to shoulder against all enemies of the Arab world and the new Republic. . . .

There was excitement but also confidence and quiet power in the voice issuing from the loudspeakers. It was the deep voice of a certain Muhammed Guelta, the young general who had organized the junta and proclaimed himself the republic's first president. By nightfall bundles of posters displaying his photograph had been hustled through the city and pasted up on every scrap of vacant public wall.

Jason tried to get through to California, but Guelta had forbidden transatlantic calls. The young Streck ate a good dinner in a harbor restaurant, then walked back to his hotel and went to bed; he was arrested early next morning by an aging sergeant wearing a Hawaiian print shirt and period French field breeches, accompanied by two grinning young soldiers.

The sergeant was respectful. He waited while, at his suggestion, Jason packed a small suitcase—which was then stolen. The detail marched him out through the Hilton service quarters to a Land-Rover where another Republican soldier stood guard, armed with a Kalashnikov rifle so new it was still gobbed with its packing-case grease. Jason was not particularly worried, even when he found himself lodged in La Fosse, the filthy and ancient French prison near the Casbah.

Every year one heard of U.S. executives kidnapped in various parts of the world. The purpose of the kidnappings was ransom and, after due negotiations, the ransoms were paid and the executives released. Abe Kohn had written a report on the situation, urging caution. In a three-year space 170 businessmen had been held hostage in Argentina alone. Coca-Cola, Ford, Kodak, Babic Cement, Lanvin, and Noble Tobacco had all paid ransoms. Exxon had paid $14.2 million for Vice-President Victor Samuelson's release. The record was $60 million paid for Juan and Jorge Born, brothers and directors of Bunge & Born, grain exporters.

Jason's own case might be settled in that way. Or possibly by pressure exerted through the State Department: J. C. Streck had powerful friends in government. Before elections, he contributed generously to the campaigns of both leading candidates. True, he had frequently expressed scorn for people who trucked with terrorists. But hold on—was General Guelta a terrorist or a legitimate head of state? There was a difference! And in any event, J. C. Streck was not the man to sit blowing on his fingers while his son lay imprisoned in a foreign land. He would do something.

Thus, amid the stench and chills of a jail built for no one's pleasure, Jason chewed the cud of sweet and bitter fancy. Three days went by, the last of these memorable for his first meeting with General Guelta and the end of his own efforts to evaluate his situation objectively.

The general had ordered the old palace turned into a school. He made his headquarters a great mansion in the old French quarter. He was a well-knit, slender man wearing U.S.-made jogging shoes and a spotless white uniform without decorations or insignia of rank. His face, too heavy in the jaw, became animated when he spoke. He uttered each word slowly, grandly, as if sending it straight into the lexicon of history. He motioned to a chair in front of his desk and poured a cup of coffee for his hostage from a silver pot—obviously a trophy *de la guerre.*

"We have been in communication with your company in California. I must tell you that the results, so far, have not been productive. I sincerely hope that you will help us make them more so."

He put down his cup opposite Jason's untasted one. With his most captivating smile, he added, "What we need now, my young friend, is a bit of money. Do you follow me?"

"I follow you, General," Jason said, "but I afraid I can't help. You have been communicating, you say. I, on the other hand, haven't communicated with anyone."

"And you haven't been happy."

"I haven't been a goddamn bit happy, General Guelta."

"I understand, my dear sir," said the general in a tone of true concern. "La Fosse is not a spa. It needs modernization. Yet you have a bucket in your cell. There is a tap there so you can wash. You get three meals a day. During exercise period you can converse with other prisoners. By giving a single order I could change all this. I hope I never have to give that order."

He took another sip of coffee.

"Your detention, Mr. Streck, was not an act of mindless harassment. I detest such tactics. You must see my position. The first days of a new regime are critical. We need funds to get through our labor pains."

"Nobody likes dealing with kidnappers."

"You were not kidnapped," said Guelta with no change of tone. "You are under arrest. You were seized by an extremist sector of our party. It was at first believed you were a Jew. This would have placed you in double jeopardy. By converting your disappearance into an arrest, I saved your life. What we ask in return is thirty million dollars, certainly not a formidable sum in view of the issues. One telephone call from you might get it. And also give proof that you are still alive and well. Don't you think your father would like to know that?"

The general set aside his empty cup. He nudged a telephone toward Jason.

"Let's make that call and get through with this nonsense."

That moment, the instant when Guelta set him free to make the ransom call, brought him close to yielding. At the time he had not the slightest notion of what was ahead.

Like many people who have been tortured, he did not know later how he had lived through it; while pain was inflicted on him, he had severed his connection with the real world and entered one known only to the damned . . . but at this point he just stared at the telephone. His will had turned to water. He longed to be put through and hear, within seconds, the voice that would save him. But with no will left he lacked also the will to surrender. He found that he was pulling back the hand which had twitched forward as if to pick up the receiver.

"General," he said, "if I am under arrest, there must be charges. Will I be permitted to know what they are?"

"You will be permitted," said Guelta absently.

Guards conducted him back to a cell, but not the one he had left. This one was filthy. It was approximately two and a half meters wide, three meters long. There was a blanket but no bed and no bucket. When he wanted to relieve himself he had to bang on the door for the guard to come and take him down the hall. He was not allowed to go into the exercise yard and received no word from outside except, as Guelta had promised, a copy of the "charges." These were in Arabic, to which was attached a typed English translation. The document was not presented as a set of accusations but as a list of illegal acts he had performed to which he was now supposed to confess.

ONE: He had conspired to set up a U.S. military base on Moroccan soil. (The plant was supposed to be *military?*)

TWO: He had contracted to bring in foreign spies to staff this base. (The exact number of these "spies" was listed, along with their countries of origin. The number roughly corresponded to the applications received from Mauritanian, Spanish, and Senegalese men and women who had applied for and received work permits after ADECT's advertisement for plant employees had run in the newspapers.)

THREE: He had failed to pay the tax due to the government for leasing the base. (There had been no such tax under the monarchy. It was also hard to figure how, if the "base" was illegal, it could be taxed.)

A subparagraph, stating that he had "lied about his ethnic and religious background" had been struck out; he assumed this referred to his captors' original assumption that he was a Jew. If he had pleaded guilty to that, it might have been enough, from the way the general had touched on it, to make other charges redundant. But how did you plead guilty or innocent to being a Jew? He would happily plead guilty to something perhaps lesser: that he had come to Morocco to make money? To turn out goods for profit? Even war goods, if they insisted on that.

He wouldn't sign the preposterous confession. And ADECT wouldn't pay for his release. He was being sacrificed to the company policy of "no negotiation," a hero role which related to reality only in the fact that he was the president's son.

The method employed at La Fosse for interrogations was an arrangement called The Switchboard. This applied electric current to the genitals. A doctor stood by during Switchboard interviews. He used a stethoscope to check the subject's heartbeats. Several patients had defied the system by dying during the applications. This was to be avoided, particularly with respect to candidates for ransom. A dead candidate was poor ransom material.

Guelta was taking no chances with Jason. He spared him The Switchboard. Guards escorted him to a basement area where an ancient generator drowned out the noises made by confession candidates. They laid him on a gurney, then bound his ankles to a rifle which two of them raised to shoulder level while a third whacked the soles of his feet with a bamboo rod. After several minutes of this they took him off the gurney and made him stamp on the floor, which caused his feet to swell. Then they beat him again. That night he was delirious. The Switchboard doctor examined him and gave him a week's respite from *la falanga,* as the foot treatment was called. After the third beating he signed the "confession." Muhammed Guelta released copies to the European wire services and the Middle Eastern desk of the U.S. State Department. In his eyes it tended to confirm the republic's status as a legitimate regime rather than a cabal of feckless brigands. More to the point, ADECT— while denying all accusations—paid the ransom.

Jason was freed, his case now a cause célèbre. He spent three weeks in the former Royal (now People's) Hospital in Rabat, while his feet healed somewhat. Then he was given new clothes and conveyed by Air France to Orly Airport where a company plane picked him up for the last leg of the trip home.

The girls in public relations had made a big cloth sign that said Welcome Home, Jason! in white, blue, and red. This they hung out front, from the third floor of ADECT's main administration building, and when security flashed word that he was on the way in, everybody in the building and most of those in other buildings crowded into the forecourt and the lobby as his limo swept up and stopped. People were cheering and clapping and some of the girls and the men were crying; inside, as he passed along, using an aluminum walker, there was hugging and kissing and the kind of interfacing that is rare at any semiconductor plant except at the annual Christmas party and by no means always then and in the middle of it all, step by step down the staircase leading from the executive suite, came J. Caulfield Streck.

While not a large man he was not small either, unless you considered five feet six, with lifts, as small, but no man alive surpassed him in sheer force of being. On he came, holding his beaky, glazey-skinned face at a sort of classic angle not unlike the fierce proud angle of the head of the spread eagle, so wonderfully replicated in the tile of the floor on which welcomers were standing. He walked straight up to Jason and embraced him, then shook hands with him, and then embraced him again, and with his arm around his son, he made a short speech. He gave thanks to God for restoring his son to him and thanks to all present who had taken time off from their work today to honor him, finishing with the words: ". . . all our vital operations here at ADECT will be more effective now that Jason is here to move them forward. . . ."

With this, welcomers began drifting off. Having caught mention of the word *operations* when the boss was speaking, they knew enough to take a hint. And with Caulfield holding Jason by the elbow in a fatherly helpful way, they made it to the escalator and thus up to the office with its grand historic souvenirs and all, and Caulfield Streck walked over to the desk. He still seemed emotionally moved, but not as pleasantly as a few moments earlier.

"Son, dear son," he said, "what went wrong out there?" And then, as Jason looked at him stupidly, unable to follow this odd turn in their dialogue, his father fell silent, staring at the son with whom he had just been reunited, apparently unable to complete the speech he had begun.

"But what, Dad . . . what is it?"

The elder Streck recovered his composure. Once more his small, slanty head assumed its familiar, eaglelike tilt.

"I suppose," he brought out slowly, "I . . . can see this is hard for you to understand. But there were factors—my dear Jason, when you signed that piece of paper . . . that confession or whatever they called it . . . that was a mistake, my dear boy—"

"Holy Christ," Jason groaned, "what do you mean, mistake?"

"I mean," said J.C., "it blew our position. Not that I care. Not that I truly care at all, not at this point in time . . . but my boy, my boy . . . *why did you let me down?*"

SIX

hat was the parting of the ways, right then. Right then a relationship pulled apart and was never quite put back together. Jason walked out (and at that point he'd understood why no one had been on the tarmac to meet the long lost son!). The car that had brought him from the airport was still in place outside the administration building and he'd gotten into it and driven back to his condo in the Valley. Apparently Odille—surely it could not have been his father—had foreseen he'd go there, for the apartment was ready, cleaned and aired, the kitchen stocked, the beds made, the utilities functioning, and a housekeeper on the premises to serve him. That night he ate a dinner of packaged food, heated in a microwave, then went to bed and slept with a minimum of his usual bad dreams.

He didn't speak to J. Caulfield Streck again for more than a year, nor did he return to work during that time. His feet were healing, but he slept badly, avoided old friends, made dates grudgingly, then broke them without explanation.

There had been changes in his inner life more damaging than any outside event. Though coming to a climax after Morocco, it had started way back when Jason was still in school and the company had begun to move out of the private sector into products of quite a different kind.

There was always a need for different kinds of machines. What a machine was to be used for was not a maker's concern. His concern was to make it well and swiftly and fitted for what it had to do. Yet the machines changed their makers. They changed J. C. Streck. Jason had lost touch with his father, a heavy toll to pay for the covenant of "business as usual." Part of the toll was not sleeping. Once before he'd had trouble with this—the period when he'd had those dreams about the bomb. Now there were times when he couldn't sleep at all, and when he did he struggled with a new set of nightmares.

Trying to account for his insomnia, he forced himself to talk about Morocco to a psychiatrist, sometimes raging, sometimes with sad, cynical self-abasement while the doctor, a blond, quick-witted woman not much older than he, took copious notes and asked gentle, probing questions.

"Why didn't you make the call when Guelta offered you the telephone?"

"I don't know. Perhaps I should have."

Dr. Clara Straska chewed the end of her gold Cross pen.

"I think you acted wisely. You didn't want a personal rejection on top of what had already happened."

"It might not have been rejection."

"I think it would have been," said Straska with unusual decisiveness. She closed her small, school-type copybook.

They had reached the end of the fifty-minute hour of their ninth session, scheduled for twice a week. She said that they were through.

". . . the last thing you need is a prolonged, formal psychoanalysis. You are, if you'll let me use the cliché, a natural survivor. Morocco will leave its effect on you for the rest of your life, but you survived it superbly—just as, after a while, you'll be able to deal with the trauma of your father's cruelty, which was much worse. He treated you abominably. Just accept the fact. Which leads me to my one mandate—your total, immediate separation from J. C. Streck . . . and perhaps someday from weapons making also. I would suggest you give some thought to that."

Jason spent the rest of the year traveling. He beheld many wonders, lived in some splendid hotels, read a few books, made love to a certain number of women, and acquired a sensational tan. He still liked to have a light near him when he slept, but many people, after all, sleep with a light on, even those who have never been imprisoned in a foreign land.

The idleness, which had seemed so luxurious at first, by degrees became boring. Home again, he let it be known that he wanted to go back to work; the response was flattering but none of the offers he considered seemed quite right. Oh, he could understand why he was bid for. Most Valley firms would love to have old man Streck's son on their roster. Fine! Jason was by no means reluctant to use this leverage. What he needed, however, was a way of measuring, by his new standards, what was right and what was wrong with the situations offered. Once he had focused, it became clear: the firms that wanted him were weapons makers, but he was tired of making weapons.

Dr. Straska had put her finger on it there.

That was the whole packet. It was no longer an open-ended argument. He knew both sides of it. He'd grown up with the side his father had been selling when he'd told him those fellows with the bomb had everything under control.

For a while he'd bought that side or done his best to. The world boiled with contention: wars, coups, conspiracies, rebellions, conquests, suppressions, riots, slaughterhouse solutions. Weapons came to hand for such occasions: Kalashnikovs, Schmeissers, Stens, Italian Berettas of ill fame or the lethal, hard-to-get Czech sawed-off 7.9s; whatever you wanted was readily for sale by the bootleg traders flitting through the customs barriers of every nation, eager for orders. The money plunked down each year in such transactions would have paid the deficit of the most hopelessly bankrupt nation on record with enough left over for a tip. Look for trouble and the weapons would be there. But did they start the trouble? Not on your life. Francisco Franco or Genghis Khan or Muhammed Guelta would have made their runs with the resulting bloody heads and bodies in the streets and tortures and imprisonments even if the only available tools had been sticks and stones and knives and hatchets. That was the plain truth of the matter, so to rack your brains and addle them over the right and logic of it was a waste of time.

That was one side. There was some sense in it; if you were on that side of the argument you had a lot going.

For his own position Jason did not have an argument. He just had a gut instinct that suggested he seek alternate employment. He would not negotiate with this feeling. He would simply pamper it as some people pampered an allergy which made it inadvisable for them to eat a particular kind of food.

He was a production engineer and in due time he would produce something: electronic dolls that would teach a child how to spell or car warning systems that would anesthetize the thief or magic dog collars that would totally protect an animal from rabies or flea bites.

He would let other people make weapons. He would just be more comfortable that way.

Such was his resolve. He had never changed it. It was surprising, most of all to him, that by Christmas he was back at work at ADECT.

He had no way of accounting for this except that, when you got down to it, ADECT was the only game in town.

Now in his father's office for the first time since the accident at the cottage, Jason sat at his desk and touched the key that brought the monitor to life—a lovely sight. He almost laughed aloud; half the meritocracy of ADECT wanted to see him or touch base with him, including several vice-presidents and what seemed a platoon of senior engineers waiting for a word or a conference, looking for a signal of authority that would smooth out a shortcut or affirm a decision already half made.

He fingered Garay's code and the thin boyish face and steel-rimmed glasses of the vice-president, legal affairs, appeared.

"Don't let me forget that meeting with Gitlin."

"Not if that's the way you want to play it," said Garay.

"I do," said Jason.

Plans for the Gitlin confrontation had been raked over numerous times between the two: it was hardly the airy chat that Jason seemed to be proposing. The only strategy left open had been whether go to the meeting alone or with legal backup.

Jason broke off. Mrs. Purviance's voice was on the intercom—"Abe Kohn here to see you"—this announcement still hanging in the air when Kohn himself strode in, looking even more dour than usual. Jason would have expected him to be livelier after his success with the Pinkerton.

"What did you do with that guy?"

"Took away his badge, gun, and shoes. Then I had the boys drive him up on Mount Hamilton. They set him down where he'll have a long walk back to base. But I've got other news for you. Could I steal five minutes?"

"You could, but later would be better."

Kohn's heavy shoulders twitched. He turned as if to go, then hesitated. "This is an *immediate,* as we used to call it. Wasn't that your dad's name for what couldn't wait?"

"Okay, but it better be good."

Jason moved from the desk to a contour chair, listening somewhat impatiently as Kohn discussed the investigation still continuing at the cottage.

". . . we've been over every inch of that area not once but fifty times. We've found some shell casings. We've found some dead dogs—and you found a dead man. But we haven't found one fingerprint or one hair follicle or other trace or signal that would prove anyone had been there that night except J. C. Streck. There was nothing disturbed, nothing taken from the files. Can you account for that? Because I can't. Once we knew what they came to get, we'd have somewhere to start."

"Okay," said Jason. *"What was there originally?* Why don't we start with that?"

"The videos, Jason, that's for sure. He stacked them in a cabinet. He ran them, I guess, when he was alone. The videos were what he liked. Those and the chips."

"What videos, for Christ's sake?"

"The Aberdeen, Maryland, ones. The Yuma Proving Ground ones. The Fort Richardson, Alaska, ones, where we all froze our balls off. SEDAV was never out of his mind, night or day. He was always thinking of ways to make it better."

Jason blinked, hardly believing—yet it figured. "Home movies!" They'd hardly been that, but they made good viewing; he too, like the rest of the ADECT command echelon, had marveled at the crunching, unforgettable tapes of SEDAV prototypes going through their paces at various test sites: leaping trenches, sloshing through foaming rivers, running countless treadmill miles through fields of simulated battlefield radiation that would have reduced most electronically operated devices to inertia and helplessness.

SEDAV had proved up. The superhardened, silicon-on-sapphire chips that were its brain had functioned under all conditions—as the tapes bore witness. DARCOM had made videos. DARPA and TECOM and ADECT itself had all made them. They were coded Confidential— the lowest security category.

"Well," he said grudgingly, "so he ran videos. If they got lifted, it's too bad, but no great harm done except to prove we have a hell of a weapon. But you mentioned chips. You mean he took chips home with him?"

"We're not sure."

"You're supposed to be sure, Abe. This is your turf."

"Are you saying I was supposed to have my guards check the boss's briefcase or go through his pockets?"

"You're supposed to protect this company's product."

"We do protect it. There's a chip check at the end of every workday in every goddamn fab plant around the world. But if you think I could have made J. C. Streck turn his pockets inside out for me, you're jerking off, Jason, if you'll pardon the expression. What happens after somebody leaves here is none of my business. Your father wasn't killed here. He was killed at home, Jason, and that's your turf, not mine. Give me a break!"

Jason failed to reply, distracted by the image of an ADECT chip in a Soviet laboratory and what might happen to it there.

"Okay, Abe," Jason finally said. "Check out everybody who *might* have had chips. It won't be a true count, but at least we'll have something to go on. Will you do that and get back to me?"

"I will, Jason," said Kohn.

But the security man stayed planted. A glint of mockery flicked through his nail-colored eyes. "I gather you don't have much faith in the SDC."

The SDC (Self-Destruct Component), programmed into last-generation military chips, was a tiny fuse triggered to wipe out the lacy web of performance patterns if the lid was removed—a device to prevent reverse engineering. Currently in use in marine detection buoys, always vulnerable to theft on the high seas, the protective device was also fast becoming standard for many industrial applications, the banditry among Valley competitors, not to mention the Japanese, far outreaching anything the Soviets, for all their ruthlessness, had been able to accomplish.

Lead time was the critical factor and ADECT had exploited it. In the weapons field, lead time created a crisis psychology like war itself. More than half of the breakthroughs of the past decade had come out of ADECT's division for circuit design; ADECT culture called for any methods necessary to keep the leading edge.

"I never said I don't have faith. I just don't want to need that much, that's all."

"I know how you feel, boss. I'll run the count you want and we'll see where we stand."

"Thanks. But don't call me boss. I'm not—anyway, not yet."

"Yes, you are," Kohn said, getting to his feet at last. With an abrupt, self-conscious gesture, he stuck out his beefy hand. The two shook, and Kohn left.

Jason buzzed Mrs. Purviance for his next appointment.

Through the next several hours, in his borrowed mantle, he tried, as demand arose, to borrow also his father's magic—reviewing data, assessing schedules, rolling forecasts, taking risks. Twice he called Washington, "ramping up" (in Valley argot) for his interview with Undersecretary Truscott, now postponed until eleven. It was a busy morning and a pleasant one, but behind it lingered the echo of Kohn's statement about the SDC—an odd statement for a man so far separated from the rhetoric of technology. He visualized what would happen if in fact the SDC could be bypassed or, worse, if it failed to function! He'd seen the deadly effectiveness of reverse engineering. He could not imagine the SEDAV system laid bare for photo topology, magnifying the logic and memory systems that power all computers until they were blown up to a scale of 500 to 1. The digitized pictures would be broken into maplike squares, then taped together until they composed a nine-by-six-foot reproduction of the mask originally "scribed" onto the chip—the system that would steer the tank and sight and target its fire.

"They can reverse engineer anything ever made!"

Who said that? Not Kohn—even if in some oblique way he had implied it. The words, as he focused on them, had a foreign tone to them . . . the heavily accented speech of Imry Kraskov, ADECT's Soviet-in-Residence.

SEVEN

Dr. Imry Sergeyevitch Kraskov had been *the* defector of the early eighties. A professor of computer science at the Moscow Academy of Applied Sciences, his papers had brought him international renown but his government had never let him attend the western conferences where his researches were honored and discussed. Finally, in Poland for a lecture, he had pulled out, crossing the Gulf of Danzig, then the open waters of the Baltic in a stolen motor launch. A storm had blown him up on the coast of Sweden where he had applied at once, through the embassy, for asylum in the United States. These maneuvers, plus the fact that, in the launch with him, he'd had a lovely Polish lady (with whom he later set up housekeeping) had jazzed the media but failed to bedazzle the American intelligence establishment, which regarded him with intense suspicion. At Langley, the CIA's professionals put him through months of hostile and sometimes brutal interrogation before crediting, with notable lack of enthusiasm, his *bona fides*.

A time of confusion and trauma followed for the good doctor. No high-tech firm was willing to hire him. He read the technical and defense magazines *Electronic Week* and *International Defense,* and even an extremely esoteric bureau report entitled *Heads of State;* he combed the *San Jose Mercury News* classified section and answered ads offering opportunities:

PROGRAM DIRECTOR, EW SYSTEMS
Top level position with major firm providing prime technical in next generation EW systems. Should have broad multi-discipline experience in large digital programs with emphasis on problem solving in millimeter wave and EO areas, etc. etc.

Large and forlorn, he camped on folding chairs in bright little waiting rooms, his soft gray eyes patient behind their thick lenses, his shirt very clean, his feet in their scuffed loafers tucked back out of sight. Sometimes the pleasant secretary behind the little window would encourage him to come back the following week, but by that time he would be in an identical chamber in some other plant.

OUTSTANDING SALARY AND BENEFITS
in growing defense-systems organization specializing in electro-optics. Hands-on knowledge of systems integration required, etc. etc.

He never quite understood that the classifieds were often cruel frauds, designed to get in résumés, then interview the better-qualified candidates to see what was happening where they last (or still) worked. Sometimes a few might be hired so they could be vacuumed for trade secrets, then tossed out.

As for giving a job to a defector, U.S. citizenship was an unstated but basic qualification for all defense employment.

J. Caulfield Streck broke the rule. Always a bargain hunter, he saw value in this tough, aging man; though his security had been cleared at the lowest level permitting his employment at ADECT, a place was made for him under Derek Shawn, vice-president, research. There were weekends when he appeared, like a new piece of memorabilia, at the boss's weekend parties. J. C. Streck seemed quite taken with him, even to the point of feeling that his gifts were being wasted in the lowly tasks assigned to him. Derek Shawn readily agreed—perhaps too readily, being by no means reluctant to rid his department of an overqualified and somewhat unsettling employee. Accordingly, Streck put through an order promoting Kraskov to a better paid and more responsible position in planning and development. The new job called for a higher security clearance, a detail which in view of the CEO's endorsement could have been routine but this time turned out not to be: the Defense Investigative Service, which presides over such matters, returned the application stamped "denied" in red marker.

Streck was annoyed. There was a story at the time that he had demanded an explanation and that a rep from the DIS had come over and discussed the matter with him privately. Should this have happened it would have been most unusual; Jason rather doubted it. Abe Kohn swore it was true. Abe was relentless in his distate for Imry. By his standards Imry was not the sort of person who should be allowed to work at ADECT in any capacity.

Denial of the upgraded clearance was never lifted and in due time this human souvenir of the cold war slipped back once more into the anonymity enveloping lower personnel. Imry accepted his lot with good grace. He slogged along and, after the required residence span, applied for and obtained citizenship; he kept to himself, eating his lunch alone in the bustling company cafeteria, where the carefully spelled-out egalitarianism did not stretch to include Russians. Jason felt this was a poor show. He sometimes took his own tray over to Kraskov's table and they had some good talks; it had amounted to little more than that. But then one day Kraskov issued him an invitation. He did this with a beaming face but with a shyness that took Jason by surprise.

"On Saturday . . . the fact is, I should be most happy if you could spare the time. Not long, of course. It is at my house, in the afternoon.

"What, a party, Imry?"

"In a way, yes. You might say so . . . a party, to be sure, but also a wedding. Myself and my friend, the lady with whom I live. Entering the solemn bonds and so forth. We should both be greatly honored if you . . ."

"Congratulations, Imry. Just let me know what time. I'll be there."

Jason wondered if the media would pick this up: Kraskov and the Polish lady who had been in the escape launch with him, for surely it was she! It was, he found . . . but when the day arrived, no journalists were on hand. The great defector was no longer news.

. . .

The Kraskov house, a modest bungalow in south San Jose, had been crammed with flowers, candles, food, and serious men in dark heavy suits from the Valley's small Polish community. Jason waltzed pleasurably with the bride, a black-haired beauty of great charm. When he left—far later than he had planned—Imry walked him to his car, thanking him repeatedly for coming, then stood at the top of the lane—visible in the rearview mirror—waving until he was lost to view.

Thus the cafeteria chats had been converted into a friendship; Imry would drop into Jason's office for a game of dominoes after work or the two would go over to the Decathlon Club together for a swim in the pool. Regardless of what the DIS thought of him, Jason liked and trusted the Russian—and his remark about the SDC bothered him: what had prompted it?

He cut short his talk with Undersecretary Truscott so as to break for lunch by noon, Kraskov's regular eating time; he was glad to see that, as usual, no one else was with him. Before the meal had progressed far, he brought up the topic of reverse engineering.

". . . I remember your saying that the Soviets are proficient in that field. . . ."

"The Japanese are better."

"Granted. But so far the Japanese haven't made much headway with self-destruct components in the new chips. We have a lead on them there, wouldn't you say?"

"I haven't been informed on the latest state of the art," said the defector stiffly. And then added, as if out of corporate loyalty, ". . . but I understand our SDC is very fine."

"We believe it's foolproof."

Kraskov concentrated on his food. He seemed not to have heard the remark.

Jason kept at him.

"In your experience, Imry, are such devices easy to subvert?"

"Of course."

"I'm surprised."

Kraskov changed his tone.

"I'm speaking only in general terms. There are many different systems. I have only examined two kinds—the most common, a pyrochemical sealed into the chip in the last fabrication stages under an inert gas blanket like argon, and the second . . . but if I go on I shall be boring you."

"Not at all!"

"The second is an electronic wipe that makes the EPROM unreadable."

The first system, not the second, was what ADECT had been programming.

"And you could bypass either or both of these?"

"I believe so. As I said . . ."

"I'm tempted to let you try."

The Russian smiled.

"I'm afraid I'm not cleared for that sort of enterprise."

"We might be able to fix that."

"Then I should be interested."

"When could you start?"

Kraskov shrugged.

"Whenever I'm relieved of current duties—which, if I may say so, any college freshman could perform as well as I."

"Would you need any special equipment?"

Kraskov looked hard at Jason to see if he were serious.

"Nothing that doesn't exist here. Or that I couldn't make on the job."

"By yourself, or with staff?"

"One or two junior engineers, if I could steal them from you."

"We've had enough stealing by Russians."

"As an American, which I am now, I would have to agree with you."

And with this the defector's bony, peasant face broke into a capacious grin. With his snub nose and peaked, bushy eyebrows, he looked like a character out of Gogol. Jason smiled with him, but his reflection was serious as he surveyed a new idea.

Weapons systems indexed as top secret were sometimes so readily exposed that by the time the Senate Armed Services Committee approved their funding they had already been described in various technical journals and magazines. These publications were bought in bulk on the day of issue by the Soviet Consulate in San Francisco, then airshipped by diplomatic pouch to the USSR where they were translated overnight and available the next day, in Russian, throughout the Soviet Union.

ADECT chips had been better protected. It was vital to keep them that way.

Could gains be made by giving Kraskov a go at reverse engineering? If he cracked it, then ADECT could set to work on a better SDC. If he failed, they could proceed with some confidence that the system was invasionproof.

It seemed like a good idea, but there was no time to take it further now. Jason caught sight of Ken Garay in the cafeteria doorway with his arm up, beckoning.

It was time for their appointment with Charles Gitlin.

EIGHT

Walking as fast as Jason's stick permitted, the two men crossed the lower office floor. They entered a glass-lined corridor passing through one of ADECT's many fabrication buildings, like the rest a busy place. Technicians were at work, to the left and right, visible through the glass. They wore hoods, masks, gloves, and hospital-type robes. They concerned themselves with racks containing sapphire-on-silicon chips. Some set the racks into tubs of acid. Others removed racks from the tubs and put them to bake in microwave ovens arranged in tiers like office filing cabinets. It was exacting work and the people who did it were incredibly clean. Before putting on their curious clothes, they were required to shower and shampoo—but without soap. In the Valley world, soap was a threat and scent an abomination. One flake of dandruff or a single sliver of the most exquisite and feminine pubic hair in this rarefied atmosphere would be as destructive as a nuclear bomb. So would be a single ray of daylight. The light in the baking lab was yellow. In substance, it was like tule fog—the yellow not a color at all but only an absence of it. The lunar figures moving in the nonlight went at their tasks in dreamlike deliberation and savage concentration. Not one of them looked up to see Jason's tall figure tilting by on his thick, spiny stick.

A short flight of steps, a turn or two, and they were in another shed and then another, each dedicated to some phase of imprinting mazes of miniaturized circuitry. Jason, when "paying his dues" (his father's term for his apprenticeship), had worked briefly and uncomfortably in this building a number of years earlier, learning to engineer the three elements which went into all computer systems: the microprocessor (the decision maker), the EPROM (the data bank on which the microprocessor based its choices), and the feedout, meaning the specific trade or military application made possible by the interfacing of the first two blocks. All three elements were housed in a flat ceramic rectangle the size of a fingernail with electrical leads sprouting from it like the golden legs of some ill-made artificial beetle.

Such an insect was the ADECT 3762, the chip that powered SEDAV. Though hardened against the attack of rays or pulses that could impair its thinking, it still retained the tiny round window in its superhardened shell which had been ADECT's major market breakthrough.

"The software," J.C. had bragged, "is inside the machine."

By shooting ultraviolet rays through the aperture, an ADECT customer could program the chip for his particular product, whether a video game, a pocket calculator, or a grocery check-out system. Similarly, once its EPROM was charged with data and its televideo sensors feeding back on-site observations, the robotank could accommodate different terrains and still carry out its battlefield missions.

The two men emerged on to a patio. The midday sun filtered through the smog, hot and gray and veiled; the place was full of women eating sandwiches and drinking coffee and bottled sodas. The food and drink came from coin-operated dispensers, one of the few unregulated amenities provided at ADECT; company policy had never included the carnival props some firms resorted to in order to keep employees satisfied: racketball courts, raffle tickets to Tahiti, hot tubs, beer busts, free orthodontia, or bonuses for recruiting new talent. So far the women had not complained. They were the bottom group, the fab girls. They stuffed boards. They dipped wafers. They stared through microscopes at integrated circuits whose function they didn't understand but whose flaws they were trained to detect. The days were long. A sandwich and a Coke in the sun helped you get through. Amphetamines and a whole spectrum of other drugs helped you get through. In early times, before dispensers, before the cafeteria, the Hell's Angels came around with a food van from which you could buy anything you wanted. Nobody cared as long as you didn't talk, weren't late, didn't make mistakes, or go to bed with the men in your department, not much of a deprivation since, at this level, women outnumbered men at a ratio of eight to one.

Jason had always strictly observed the unwritten law against company dating. What could be worse than having a chick at your elbow to whom you were accountable? The pits! The girls he had dated from other IC companies made him familiar with their problems. They were young, sexy, single, many of them very pretty. Some of the single ones had been left with children to bring up without a man; kids who had to get bedded down with a sitter before Mom could hit the bars along the Camino Real. In the morning, get them up, get breakfast, get them off to school, get dressed, gal, get with it, the hair, the eyes, the nails, the fucking starter that needed a new motor, the bundle for the laundromat, the traffic, get that weekly paycheck, hope that the boom would last, the job would last, that the new guy who came along wouldn't try to live off you. . . .

High technology is a very macho industry. Jason knew all about that. Nobody knew the reason. It was just the way the business was structured. There were few women vice-presidents; the exceptional ones, who by superior looks, ability, and aggressiveness had reached high responsibility, were generally to be found in PR or personnel rather than the better-paying jobs in product design, development, or distribution.

The girls in the patio had all kinds of hair and skin coloring, all kinds of racial mixes in them, but they had one thing in common: they were young, all young; they had their legs up on the redwood chairs, the benches, they had their blouses open to let the weak autumn sun soak into them for these few minutes, for whatever it was worth. Some of them stopped talking as Garay and Jason went by, he with his stick, his odd way of walking, his flame of red hair. The fab girls followed him with their eyes until he was out of sight in the next building.

Although company dating was disapproved, marriages of two people within the company were acceptable and sometimes lavishly celebrated. At one such, reported by the *San Jose Mercury News* and the Associated Press,

> Bride and groom stood before a computer terminal. Rev. Rom typed in RUN WED. And the rites of marriage lit the screen of the world's first marrying computer.

"Hello, my name is Rev. Apple (PRESS SPACE BAR TO CONTINUE)," read the Apple II screen.

"Groom, what's your name?"

". . . in the Valley a computer wedding is a very appropriate means of self-expression," said Reinhard Jaenisch, designer of the program, who likes to be called the Rev. Rom.

Charles Gitlin had moved out of the main administration building after his break with J. C. Streck. They had split over company policy but there was also another reason. Gitlin had got himself an honorary degree from Stanford.

He got it for founding ADECT and he hadn't founded ADECT. He had just come up with the venture capital. J. C. Streck had founded ADECT. How Gitlin had campaigned for that honorary degree was never known except to the extent that his father-in-law had been a member of the Stanford Board of Trustees. You could take it from there.

In some parts of the world, the theft of an honorary degree might have been no great matter. Not so in Silicon Valley. There an honorary degree was a many-splendored thing. From the moment Charles Gitlin absconded with his, he and J. C. Streck stopped speaking. They communicated, when compelled, by means of memos, strange anachronisms in an almost paperless world.

Charles Gitlin had an office in a department where offices had no doors and the walls came up only shoulder high, a habitat of change. The partitions were supplied by Westinghouse. They were painted in bright primary colors. They could easily be regrouped to form new combinations, large or small, but always bright, always cheery in spite of the absence of windows. The air flowing between and over them was neither new nor fresh but it flowed constantly and freely; so did information. The ceilingless and doorless offices stripped away the trappings of power. Such boxes might make the people in them seem themselves like chips attached to a floor-sized board, but this made no difference. They were at the heart of urgency. No one could shut himself off. No underling could keep his knowledge from those above and no manager could insulate himself from contact with those below. In this bright doorless labyrinth there was change and there was flexibility and "that," as J. C. Streck had often said, "is what this industry is all about."

Charles Gitlin embraced his humble office like a hair shirt. It was not, to be sure, quite as humble as might at first appear; Gitlin had put six cubicles together to compose his own monstrous box and he had all kinds of secret perks and little comforts tucked away inside, including a chef to prepare his meals. But being down there curled up among the slaves certainly tended to show that he was the kind of man who bloody well deserved an honorary degree!

In the corridor, Garay nudged Jason.

"Don't mention the lockout. Let him bring it up. I want to see how he'll explain it."

"He won't try. I know this cat. He'll play it cool."

"Putting a Pinkerton outside your door, that wasn't cool."

"It wasn't dumb either. If he could have kept me out that would have been half the ball game, right there. Probably some fucking attorney told him to do that."

"Could be. But if so you can look for some attorneys in there with him right now, plus his moneymen, lackeys, and gunbearers. This isn't the type of deal you wrap up single-handed. Be prepared."

"I am," said Jason. "So let's get on with it."

The vice-chairman came forward to greet his callers with both hands outstretched, one for each; he drew them away from the door into a conference corner of a type seldom found in a semiconductor company, an area of large leather chairs with matching couch and a cocktail table made from a huge polished redwood burl.

"You've had lunch, I suppose? Too bad—I'd have been so glad to have you with me. I've a little galley here, you know—I call it that—it's too small for a kitchen—and a sort of mess boy, he gets out snacks for me. Not that the chow downstairs is bad. Fine, if that's your taste. But I'm afraid I'm spoiled. . . ."

Gitlin could pull rank on you and make it sound like flattery. With his resonant voice, his royal crown of gleaming whitewashed hair, and heavy, prominent features, he embodied the old-fashioned concept of a company president—not that he, thought Jason, would ever be one. He folded his veined, blotchy hands across his stomach—hands that gave him away, testifying to his age and uncertain health.

"Let me correct a misunderstanding, if it indeed exists," he said. "That nonsense this morning—the security chap and all—My dear fellow! What could be more natural? You'd want your father's office! Why not? But it never occurred to me! My one thought was protection! Those priceless historic artifacts and all. Things vanish, even here at ADECT. But by all means stay where you are, at least until the board makes further dispositions. . . ."

Garay shot across a look that said, "Ignore that last crack," but Jason didn't need the warning. His manner was impeccable.

"I appreciate your concern, sir, . . . but from now on everything will be properly looked after—up there."

"Splendid, I'm delighted," said Gitlin, "and now bear with me one step further. Since we're entering a new kind of association, you and I, you must meet some people on whom I greatly depend." He clapped his hands like a magician recoupling a body he has just sawed in half and from opposite sides of the room two people advanced, one tall and puckish, bent by arthritis, the other a Chinese lady with an open, friendly face and a pince-nez.

"Sir Simon Locke-Trevor of Rothschilds, London, and my attorney, Mrs. Thong . . . Mr. Jason Streck, and Mr. . . . ."

"Garay," Ken supplied. Gitlin, he was sure, knew his name well enough: if pretending not to was a crude effort at a put-down, more such could be in the offing.

Chairs were pulled up, drinks offered—and declined. Sir Simon produced a briar pipe, rubbed it against his nose, finally lit it with a wooden match. Gitlin leaned his kingly head aslant, his eyes on Jason.

"May we say the ball is in your court, Jason?"

Jason was happy to take the shot. He felt in control.

"Mr. Gitlin . . . I know that in the past you and my father had certain differences. I should like to make it clear that as far as I'm concerned all that is gone and forgotten. I hope you feel the same way."

"Well said," declared Lawyer Thong.

Gitlin cleared his throat.

"No man alive had more respect for J. C. Streck than I! A tremendous force! Let us invoke his spirit as we carry on!"

Ken Garay said mildly, "Most of the differences Jason has referred to centered on the SEDAV program. Perhaps at this point we might . . ."

"Please!"

Gitlin held up an admonitory finger.

"May I clear the air? I'm a frank person. I don't hold back. This is how I look at what's ahead."

Evidently drawing confidence from Jason's mild preamble, he launched into a rambling policy evaluation to be implemented presumably after his own elevation upward.

". . . Sure we went after the SEDAV contract tooth and nail and we got it—a permanent monument to J. C. Streck and his vision: the nuclear freeze that put the burden of defense back on conventional weapons. We're out in front, but let's not sit on our hands. There are some new notions blowing around and by gosh, my young friend, I think we should have a finger in the wind. . . ."

Jason put in softly, "Would it be silly to imagine a time when there would be no weapons at all? I mean on the scale we're discussing?"

Gitlin stared at his questioner, then felt that he was being kidded—always a trap for the humorless. He smiled indulgently.

"Ah, wouldn't that be blissful? The millennium! And when it comes we'll be first in line to file under Chapter Eleven."

"Still clinging to the leading edge, as it were," said Sir Simon amid his pipe smoke.

Mrs. Thong laughed—a quick dim yelp—then bowed her head in contrition. Garay looked at Jason with surprise. Their joint strategy for the meeting had been to bypass, at least at the outset, Jason's view of the armorer's trade—and here he was, flinging it on the table as an opening gambit. The lawyer hoped Jason knew what he was doing . . . but obviously he was not to be stopped.

"I know how firmly we're committed to the robotank program—I can assure you that I'll give it my best shot. But I won't say I like it. I want to move toward the private sector and I hope we can retake our old position there. I'm convinced that we won't lose by it."

Charles Gitlin looked fixedly at the ceiling, then covertly at Thong and Sir Simon as if to say, "These are the babblings of an idiot." To Jason, with the gentleness with which one might accommodate the mentally impaired, "May we, with your permission, keep this strictly *entre nous*?"

"Whatever suits you, sir. But speaking of the board."

"Yes?" snapped Gitlin. He ran his hands through his extraordinary hair as if, like Samson, to draw strength from it.

". . . Ken here has called a special meeting for next week, with the election of new officers first on the agenda. I wondered if I could persuade you to put my name in nomination."

"You're not happy where you are?"

"I'm seeking an appointment to succeed my father as CEO."

"You have never been mentioned for this post, as far as I can remember."

"Possibly not, though I would doubt that."

"In that case . . . are you under the impression that control can be passed along to you like . . . some sort of family trinket?"

"No, sir. That's why I need your support."

The statement was perfectly true. For in spite of his age, arrogance, and affectations, Charles Gitlin was a man with interests that stretched far beyond the narrow world of high technology. He sat on the board of a famous insurance company, an airline corporation, and a midwestern bank: the father-in-law who had gotten him the honorary degree was chairman of a mutual fund which had invested heavily in ADECT stock and, unlike Gitlin himself, held on to it. Jason knew how bitterly Gitlin must have regretted selling when he did, taking a quick profit that reduced his status at ADECT. That, as Senator Lighty confirmed to Jason, was his weakness—the quick buck. When Jason said, ". . . I need your support," the unspoken corollary was ". . . and I'm ready to pay for it."

They had come to the essence of the matter, but there was a prescribed ritual, like a temple dance, to be gone through before numbers were mentioned. Gitlin was clearly not prepared to commence dancing.

"I can say with confidence that I have always been the board's first choice for CEO. Putting your name up would be presenting my own resignation. Do you think that's what I'm about to do?"

"Certainly not, sir," said Jason. "I never entertained the slightest notion of your resignation from the board. Only of your standing down as candidate for chief executive officer."

Gitlin's normally pale face had turned brick red; a spasm shook his body.

"I'm not standing down from anything," he screeched unexpectedly. "You've got some nerve, handing me ultimatums. By God! . . ." He paused, his breath pumping in noisy wheezes, "I'm too old and too rich to put up with this shit. . . ."

He no longer looked old, he looked strong and alert as if the call to battle had restored a lost vigor. With lowered head, in silence, he glared at Jason with cobra eyes.

"The stats," Garay whispered to Jason.

Jason nodded.

"I think you should look at the whole picture, Charlie. With one decisive gesture you would be helping ADECT through a tough transition period at no cost to yourself—and great personal gain."

Gitlin drew his hands over his face.

"What are we talking about here, a corporate decision? Because I'd never accept that, and I don't have to," he rang out, expanding his caved-in chest and sucking in a great breath of air as if to illustrate his meaning.

The man was a hell of an actor.

"My decision and my money," said Jason. "We could almost leave the figure up to you. And that would be aside from continuance of your regular perks for five years, Charlie, or whatever time seems appropriate—plane, cars, hotels, the works. Plus a special appointment as adviser to the board, with salary."

Gitlin uttered a queer, strangled sound—more acting?—then coughed as if to hide it. He pushed back his chair and strode into a corner of the room, standing there for several seconds with his back to the others. Then he turned on his heel and strode off into another part of his complicated warren. Said Sir Simon, "I daresay he's gone to lie down. He has to when he gets that way."

"I'm sorry if I upset him," said Jason.

"He was a bit edgy. Not uncommon at all. But don't underrate him. A magnificent brain."

"Splendid, sir, I admire that. If I may make one request, will you ask him to get back to us as soon as possible?"

But Sir Simon's pixie face, enveloped in pipe smoke, was no longer visible, nor did any answer issue from him.

Jason and Garay headed back the way they'd come, through the maze of topless and doorless cubicles with their bright basic colors and their population of human chips.

Back in the office, Garay said, "I was afraid you'd blow it when he started yelling, but you hung in there. How do you feel?"

"Tired," said Jason. "I just found out—there's nothing heavier than spending a bunch of money, especially when you don't have some of it."

"How much? You know him better than I do."

"Eight or ten mil in severance alone would be gettin' him cheap."

"Be worth it if he goes quietly."

". . . and hides in the bushes, waiting for another chance to stick it to me. That's the chance I have to take. I'll settle for it."

"At least you reassured him about SEDAV."

"If the company could afford it I'd close out that contract. Default and walk away from it."

"Just as well you didn't tell him *that.*"

Jason applied himself to the new coffee Mrs. Purviance had just brought in. He peered into his cup as if into a fortune-teller's tea leaves. "Ken, I hate the fucking robotank. It's messed up my life. And it . . ."

He pushed his cup away. His hands were shaking. Rising, stick in hand, he strode back and forth in front of the big desk.

"Take it easy, pal," said Garay.

Certainly, J. C. Streck's brilliant son had gone through a bad week: one must expect some aftereffects. ". . . This wasn't my idea, not at first. Abe Kohn was in here earlier. He started the gears meshing. He's been over the layout at the cottage a dozen times, he's worked with the FBI and all the other so-called experts and none of them, not one, found evidence that anyone had been there that night except my father. Wouldn't you say that was odd? Abe thinks so. He let me draw my own conclusions but . . . it's bothered the hell out of him."

"Couldn't a terrorist hide his traces?"

"No, I don't think so. Not with the kind of scrutiny we've been laying on this case. Something weird went on there."

Jason raised his maimed foot in its heavy corrective shoe and smashed it against the desk.

"It was the first thing I saw when I parked my car. The thing's control light was on. Do you think I'm lying to you? And I felt something in my body, something I can't describe."

"But Christ, man. . . ."

"Ken! The gun. *I touched it and the barrel was hot. It had been firing.*"

The two stared at each other across the desk. Then Garay said, "Well, he had a target range there too, didn't he? That wouldn't necessarily mean there was some glitch in the machine."

"No, not *necessarily.* A lot of things happen not necessarily. The kind of guy he was, and the way he prepared me to grow up and live. The atom bomb test in fifty-seven, he took me to see that. So I'd be ready! So I'd realize the kind of world I was facing! Not *necessarily.* Not at all. But just because he *knew,* he had great perception! Then—then we began making the robotank and all that changed. He changed too. He became a different guy. *And then it killed him!* Was that *necessarily?*"

"No," said Garay steadily. "And it might never have happened that way, regardless of your hunch. I think you're fantasizing. Killing—that would be a hell of a tough thing to prove. Isn't there a human factor here we haven't mentioned?"

"What do you mean?"

"In one word—Kraskov."

"Oh, come on, Ken."

"I'm serious. This may be far out, but it should be checked. Sure you like Imry, that's your privilege. He never charmed me to that extent."

"I'm not tracking you."

"Well, ask Abe, since we started with him. He felt the same way. Those times when J.C. had Kraskov at the cottage, letting folks see what a defector looked like. I'm sure the guests enjoyed it, but did it make sense? There were top-secret data and materials around, perhaps more than we've realized. What was to keep Imry-boy from poking into those? Or actually tampering with them? He's smart. He's a top-flight engineer. And he's devious."

"I know, I know," said Jason wearily. "He is indeed and worst of all he's Russian; if he turns on a light switch he can burn out a circuit. I wish this was as simple as it sounds. I'd settle for it in two seconds."

He stood tilted on his blackthorn in the center of the huge, handsome office, his voice tense and his eyes blazing.

"Ken, there's a blank area here, and it scares the shit out of me. Maybe we're a bunch of stupid electronic-minded Frankensteins—we've built some kind of monster that we don't understand and can't control."

NINE

Case Officer Criddle, like many officers with his particular responsibilities in U.S. embassies around the world, was expert in the idiosyncrasies of his fellow staffers; he knew their preferences and their hang-ups, their tense little orbits of openness or meanness, their ambitions and their fuse-points. Nothing, for instance, bothered Pete Owens, the legal attaché, as much as deciding how to rate an intelligence dispatch. He wanted everything low-key, the lowest possible—"then you won't look like an idiot when it bounces back at you. . . ."

Suggest an *Immediate* rating (urgent) and he'd argue with you: how good was the source? Was there a bona fide urgency? So forth and so on.

As for *Flash* (top urgency), forget it. Just suggest a *Flash* and he went bananas. Well, too bad, because in this instance, Criddle felt the situation justified a *Flash,* whether Owens's ass was on the line or not.

"We have to get moving," he said gently.

Owens said nothing. He sat across the table pulling at his lower lip, his sallow, actorish face bland and melancholy. Then he turned and rose as the ambassador came in, the rumble of city traffic suddenly audible from the open windows beyond, receding as the door closed behind him.

"Gentlemen—"

His Excellency sat in with the four gathered here only when momentous issues were at stake and then only, as now, at Spanos House, his official residence, rather than the big bleak new embassy, still plagued by outrageous bugging.

"How long have we been dealing with this agent?"

Owens shot Criddle a heavy look—it was the same question he himself had been asking. Like "legal attachés" in all U.S. embassies around the world, Owens was the FBI rep in residence, his service the one to initiate the stateside activity that would stem from the dispatch. As chief of station, however, McIntyre set himself to answer. The credentials of agents were *his* domain.

"Only a short time here—but more than a year in Silicon Valley. He's been very dependable, very valuable."

"Silicon Valley—yes. Would there be some link, then, between this threat and the Streck thing? But I don't suppose there's been time to sort it out. . . ."

"They'll be doing that in Washington, sir—on a crash basis. I suppose it must be considered a possibility."

"What kind of threat are we talking about, if threat is the loaded word? But again perhaps it's too early to . . ."

"Exactly, sir. But you may rest assured, the appropriate steps will be taken. . . ."

Criddle was hand-lettering *FLASH* on the printout for the crypto crew. Hall, the CIA man, made a note; Owens was pulling on his lip again. From many years' experience in overseas posts he had a deep-seated suspicion of material from double agents. If they were Russians, they were all deceitful; how could you tell which side of their mouths they were talking from at any given minute? That was his instinct and he wasn't about to modify it except on the firmest of grounds. He looked over his shoulder at the wall clock, an exquisitely reconstituted *objet* from Czarist days; 1430 hours, a time when His Excellency, who had served at the Court of St. James, liked to have tea, which was brought up to his private quarters. The discussion would soon end. The message would go out as he, Criddle, had designated it.

In Washington, by Pentagon time, it was 0900 hours and Walden Wynans, secretary of defense, was running late, having been held up for some ten minutes while having breakfast. The call had come in on his secure line, to which only the White House and top intelligence staffers had access—some idiot briefing him about a signal from Moscow just decrypted at Langley: the gist of it ominous—early detecting of a KGB plot being launched to discredit or destroy him. The caller described measures which the Secret Service now proposed to implement for the secretary's protection.

Wynans had listened impatiently. He felt very safe. He knew that he was watched over night and day by concerned and well-trained people. Added vigilance on their part might turn out to be more of a nuisance than a benefit.

A large man, handsome and athletic, he leaped out of his limousine at the river entrance to the great five-sided building and from this point, after a short walk, ascended in a high-speed elevator that bore him without stops to his suite at the hub of the clubby E ring of elite offices, which he entered through a side door.

He never went in the front. To do so would have put him instantly at the mercy of anyone in the waiting room. But even beyond, in the inner sanctum, under the portrait of the late James Forrestal, the first secretary of all (who had sadly and mysteriously leaped to a nightmare doom from a hospital window), he found himself ambushed; Sam Truscott, recently returned from California, was ready to pounce, his ploy a thick computer printout. Greetings were minimal as Sam rose to place the docket on the secretary's desk.

"I think you'll find this interesting."

"What in hell is it?"

"FBI wrap-up on the Streck thing. Rinker was on the horn just now. He wants to come over but he sent this first, so you'd be briefed. Once you give me a fix on it I can handle Rinker, if that's what you want."

S. Cochran Rinker III, director of the Federal Bureau of Investigation, was no favorite of Walden Wynans, as nobody knew better than Truscott, but when Rinker spoke the secretary paid heed as did most others in government, regardless of their placement.

"Give me the bottom line."

"There's no espionage angle. The robot killed Streck."

"Fly that past me again."

Truscott poked the printout with an exploratory finger. "The wonderful little engine that's supposed to revolutionize war. It pumped two slugs in him and made him dead."

"But how did a robot tank get . . ."

"That's where he kept it, a landmark SEDAV—the first model to come off the production line. Serial number TY6o. Just a nice little combat vehicle that he garaged on his own property as if it were a puppy. Only that night it got unleashed and did something a lot worse than poo-poo on the rug."

The secretary slipped on the half-shell spectacles that were such a help when close work was required. He finished the page with the marked paragraph, then scanned several more.

"Wouldn't you say," he said at length, "that the bureau took its time arriving at this concept?"

"I would," said Truscott, "beside which, though they arrived at it, they didn't initiate it. The ADECT security people came up with it. It's all in the report."

It was all there, indeed. First, testimony as to J. C. Streck's fascination with the robot, his pride in it, and his penchant for putting it through its paces. Second, a projection of how he had come by his death. This consisted of computer graphics presenting the event in the sort of mock-up sometimes used in court trials to give an idea of the manner in which a crime has been committed . . . although, to be sure, the term *crime* in its context as a violation of law or an offense against morality could hardly be attributed to a machine, even one artfully endowed with a certain degree of cognitive power (certainly nobody had yet found a way to stick it with a conscience!).

The pictures showed Streck standing in the yard in front of his cottage with the tank trundling away from him, then turning to face him, the cannon revolving on its turretless top. But instead of aiming at the target, fixed that night as usual on its ricochet board at the end of the pool, the deadly muzzle swung around until it was pointing straight at Streck, firing its charges (projected in the graphics by a series of red dashes). The first round struck him high on the right shoulder. Streck staggered, fell, half rose, started to crawl toward the cottage door. The SEDAV fired again, the bullet this time hitting him between the shoulder blades, the impact kicking him down a second time but also propelling him toward the rear or kitchen door of the cottage which he got through, leaving a trail of blood. He passed through the kitchen on hands and knees, made it as far as the large chair in the living room where, as he reached for the telephone, he collapsed and died.

Wynans raised his head. He pulled a page from the docket and waved it at Truscott.

"Here's where it falls apart—right when the shooting starts. SEDAV carries a 30-mm cannon. That first hit at close range would have blown Streck away in bite-size pieces and taken out the cottage at the same time."

"It would, boss," said Truscott diffidently, cautious about reminding his superior, old and close friend though he might be, of a technical detail he should have remembered, "but for testing those thirty em ems anyplace except on an official target range we've been subcalibrating them with a diminished inner barrel. The rounds used in Streck's set conformed to the Skoda ammo for the Walther PPK9, an automatic handgun . . . okay, okay. I know what you're going to tell me," he declared with confidence, well aware that the secretary had been about to tell him no such thing, "the Walther is used officially in several international spy services, but that's pure coincidence. Or so Rinker seems to feel."

Wynans leaned back in his chair. He took off his glasses and laid them on the desk.

"S. Cochran Rinker, Third, is a horse's ass, Sam, and don't you ever forget it."

"I never do, sir," said Truscott.

He could tell from the signs that the secretary, having studied the material, was now ready to enunciate the department's position.

"Sam," said the secretary, "a while back you used a curious phrase. You said this tank 'got unleashed.' That kind of language has no application to modern warfare. A robot weapon won't get unleashed. It has no leash. It's not an animal. It's an engine. This engine has been tested and countertested. It's been approved and it's in full production. It should be protected against any shitty talk that would reduce confidence in its effectiveness. Do you agree?"

"Absolutely, Mr. Secretary," said Truscott.

"Okay, then," said Wynans in a milder tone.

He picked up the FBI report once more and shuffled its pages back together, then laid it aside.

"You handle Rinker. Tell him we don't give a flying frig for his report. It's well intentioned but it has obviously been prepared by individuals unfitted for the task they undertook. We're not in the crime detection business. We're supplying the armed services with automated machines that are combat-ready and will function so under all circumstances. That's where our responsibility begins and that's where it ends."

"I agree," said Truscott.

"Fine, then," said the secretary, brightening. "Make him aware that release of this material would be counterproductive and misleading . . ."

"And a threat to national security?" suggested Truscott blandly. "I believe that's SOP."

"Precisely. We'll put together our own report—the true solution. Also try to find out how far this crap of Rinker's has circulated. What would be your guess?"

"Well," said Truscott guardedly, "certainly Langley. And maybe . . . maybe even the Situation Room . . ."

The presidential bunker! That would be the printout's ultimate destination. Or, if the great Pudknocker cared to come up for air that day, then the Oval Office. And once in either place, once the presidential ranges were chewing on its contents, God only knew what you might be in for . . . and today of all days when he, the secretary, had made other plans!

TEN

President Claude C. Gantt was peremptory in dealing with his cabinet ministers. They were supposed to carry beepers with them at all times so that the President, beaming a signal from the White House, could summon them to his bidding in nanoseconds.

Walden Wynans had not *refused* to carry a beeper. He simply *did not* carry a beeper. It was not the kind of thing he did, not his style, any more than it would have been his style to wear, for instance, a tie woven with the stripes of some British regiment in which, not being British, he had never served, or the colors of some club to which he did not belong.

The White House had never applied pressure about the beeper. There were ways of closing the gap between the office of the president and the secretary of defense but pressure was not one of them. Nor could any amount of pressure have reduced the social gulf that separated the two men or altered the fact that Wynans had been born at the highest rung of a tiny but by no means vanishing elite while Claude C. Gantt had originated deep in the peckerwood gulches of a hillbilly proletariat.

This was a Wednesday and the October weather mild and clear; on such Wednesdays the secretary liked to drive out to the Middleburg Circus and Steeplechase Club, a spin-off of the famous old Middleburg

Hunt, and play polo. Also today he had a date to pick up his daughter, Ilena, at her school and drive her with him to watch the game. She liked polo and he enjoyed having her along.

Ilena had been watching for him. She ran out as soon as the driver, Linton, touched the horn, but she was agitated. She'd been kept in. She didn't say why. It could have been grades, but as a rule her grades were good. Behavior, then. It must have been behavior. She could be uppity, as nobody knew better than her father. At the moment she was in a hurry and quite breathless. She had another girl with her, a slender dark-haired busty girl with long lovely legs and more eyeliner than was generally approved at Miss Clampett's.

"Daddy, you remember Jacqueline? She's been to all my parties . . . Jacqueline de Saban—Daddy. Can you give her a ride, Daddy? She really needs a ride."

"Of course," said the secretary.

The secretary smiled at his daughter's friend. A smile seemed all that was required, but Jacqueline de Saban shot out her small paw at once, the wrist curved in a particular way as if, like some European women, but usually older ones, she expected him to kiss it. He was content with shaking it.

"Thanks, Daddy," said Ilena. "Her father's in the game but he went on ahead. That's why she needs a ride. I'll see you later, Daddy. I'm sorry I got kept in."

"I'm sorry too, sweets," said the secretary. "Bye, now."

"Bye, Daddy," said Ilena. And with a twirl of her tall, trim body, she was gone.

Mademoiselle de Saban, meanwhile, had popped into the car. Walden Wynans took a seat beside her and the trip to Middleburg began—the vehicle of conveyance not departmental wheels but the secretary's personal Bentley town car.

The secretary, if the truth was known, felt less than overjoyed at having this child with him for the next forty-five minutes. It would have been different if Ilena had come. He could have put them both up front with Linton. They could have sat there together and chattered to their heart's content, leaving him to his own devices—a TV news program, perhaps. Then some calls on the car telephone. Should he wish to scramble calls from the car, he could do so and generally did; he remembered a night at the White House when they had all laughed uproariously at satellite interceptions (with overlapping translations) of Soviet ministers chatting with each other on their car telephones; he did not wish to provide the same type of amusement in Moscow. He could have telephoned in the girl's presence, but it was not departmental procedure to conduct business with a third party listening while you both rolled along the Virginia-Washington Parkway, particularly if that party was the daughter of a foreign diplomat.

But the news. He could certainly still have the news.

"Do you mind if I turn on the television, Jacqueline? There's a program that I'd like to listen to."

"Oh, no, sir," said Mademoiselle de Saban demurely. "I should enjoy it." She spoke without a trace of French accent, unusual for one of her derivation; few of the frogs the secretary had known ever seemed to lose it.

"They don't let us have it except for about two minutes in the evening," she went on rather unnecessarily. "I detest that. So stuffy. Don't you think?"

This she brought out with complete composure, sitting with her rather phenomenal legs crossed, squarely in the middle of the back seat of the Bentley instead of over on her side, where she belonged. She had that degree of confidence—or presumption—which only considerable charm can make acceptable. And charm she had. Closer examination established that without question. She was a beauty. A real one. And young. Fearfully, devastatingly young, though perhaps somewhat older than the Clampett average. The secretary laughed.

"I do, but never let Miss Clampett hear of it. She'd put both of us in detention. Like poor Ilena."

A thought about this Mademoiselle de Saban flickered through the secretary's mind. He rapidly, firmly, pushed it aside—only a tiny residue of it remaining, out of sight. He put it to himself that she was not the ordinary finishing school product. Or he hoped not, though he had been suspicious from time to time about Ilena. Half of them, he'd heard, were on the Pill.

Today for the first time in almost a week the newscaster hardly touched on the Streck affair. Lacking new developments, public interest had evidently slacked off, certain proof that at least up to date the FBI wrap-up had not reached the media. The announcer's reference to "alleged KGB participation" would hardly set the airwaves afire.

He listened a moment or two longer, then turned off the set; he leaned back, pillowed in the car's deep upholstery, watching the fall countryside roll by: the dogwood and maple burning yellow and red, the water oaks still green but turning brown, the elms dropping their leaves. It was easy to imagine the lovely blend of boughs and color as a painting—a Monet, for instance, a painter of whose work he and Barbara owned an excellent example. The car's smooth motion was soothing; the secretary's breathing changed. A sigh, then a light snore came from him. He was drifting off, and well content to do so, except . . . except that in his delicious, half-waking, half-sleeping state he was conscious that something had changed. At first he wondered if Mlle. de Saban had moved closer. Then, forcing himself to a greater degree of awareness, he knew damned well she had. She had also shifted her arm. That was it! She had stretched her arm along the soft cream-colored upholstery of the seat.

With an effort, the secretary raised his heavy eyelids. He noticed that the . . . paw, as he thought of it . . . the little paw she had presented to him in such an absurd way in front of the school was now lying in another, even more ridiculous position with the fingers curved once more but differently and the pointed and tinted nails actually . . . by Jesus . . . touching the secretary's leg!

The secretary's eyelids now rolled up all the way. His great stallion eyes, veined with tiny skeins of good living, opened to their fullest extent. Without moving his head, he looked at the hand, then at the girl. His mouth made a new shape, not a shape of reproof but not one of connivance either. It required a great effort on the secretary's part to produce this shape and he knew it was just right. It expressed complete understanding of—what was going on. It was also a clear statement of what was *not* going to go on!

Mlle. de Saban got the pitch. From her theatrically designed eyes she shot back a look of her own, a look full of fire! She withdrew her hand and the secretary settled back into his own corner of the big car and composed himself again.

Ho, he reflected, so much for that.

It would have been pleasant to doze off, cool down his brain in preparation for the coming game, only . . . now it was hard to think about polo because . . . his thoughts had veered off on another direction. Now he had identified the memory that had brushed his consciousness, as with a feverish wing tip, when Ilena had introduced this nymphet outside the school:

"She's come to all my parties . . ."

Precisely! Yes, it had been just so, at one of those delightful afternoon affairs in the spring, the young people there together with a few of his own and Barbara's friends, a mix of all ages, to which affair Mademoiselle de Saban had been a recent addition—a luxury import, as it were.

He'd been inside the Georgetown house, having a quiet drink, looking out onto the terrace in the dusk as the older guests were leaving and he'd noticed her out there with a boy.

He had not been able to see either of them completely, one of the terrace pillars partially intercepting his view. The girl had her back to him. She'd had on a backless cotton dress, the curve of her arm and part of the naked and fleshy but very pretty back visible through the window. He could hardly see the boy at all but he could see the tenseness of his body, his head turned away as he leaned back against the pillar, one of the other pillars supporting the half-roof of the terrace. They were not kissing. From their attitudes, they undoubtedly had been but now they were not because they, or one of them, was doing something else. The lower portion of both bodies had been hidden from him by a planter box but what was going on was apparent.

So what. You might well say so what. When had it been? This spring or the spring before? Ilena had just had her sixteenth birthday. They probably did more than what that girl was doing, most of them, a hell of a lot more, probably everything in fact. They were *all* precocious! Was that so extraordinary? Not too different from himself at that age or Barbara either. Just the dimensions of it different, what was accept-able and what was not and how much discretion you cared to observe. There'd been plenty of fucking then and everything else. Young stuff! And this French kid—she was *young stuff* personified. There had been that feeling in the air. She'd made the first move. All he'd had to do was take her up on it and bring on . . . Hiroshima!

Linton was turning the Bentley into the club drive. The alteration in speed and the different texture of the road conveyed this to the secretary. Otherwise he might not have noticed it because, in spite of the upheaval in his blood, he had dipped back into sleep again, wiped out, probably only for a minute or two, but . . . holy cow! . . . long enough to start an erection. And there on the club steps stood the Marquis Jean-Loupe Marie Gerard de Saban watching for his daughter's arrival. Probably he'd telephoned the school to find out what time she'd left; with a daughter like that, one did well to check, one did damn well to check! There he was, elegant in white moleskins and Hermès boots boned to a high shine, ready to play, smiling a welcome.

Out of courtesy, Wynans would have to be first out of the car. Some-what hunched over, he reached in to help the girl to alight, then turned to shake hands with de Saban.

The marquis thanked him elaborately for transporting his daughter.

"I'm afraid I've put you to a great amount of trouble."

"Not at all, sir," said Wynans. "We had a fine trip, most enjoyable. Though I'm afraid I slept most of the way."

Not a bad touch, that last.

"We are grateful indeed. I am sure Jacqueline feels as I do. Don't you, Jacqueline?"

"Certainly, Papa. Mistair Wynon has been most kind."

With her father, the secretary observed, the child affected the accent she had been sent to Miss Clampett's to lose—aside from whatever other reasons.

They separated in the hall, the de Sabans heading for the dining room, the secretary to the locker room upstairs where he got suited up to play.

The Wednesday games were informal round robins, players entering the lineups or leaving as they felt inclined, even changing sides when that was appropriate to keep handicaps balanced. But today the climate on the field was different somehow. Play had gone on only a few minutes when the umpire called Penalty Four against Red—a free shot from 25 yards out, with one defender.

De Saban, who had committed the offense, was the man in the goal. Wynans sent the willow ball in a lovely arc high over the Frenchman's head to make the score.

De Saban's foul had been dangerous and stupid. He had defied the rules of the game, bumping the secretary across the boards at a dangerous angle, although Wynans had been riding on the line of the ball. In a clutch situation, with everyone going all out, that kind of thing could happen—but it was unusual and unnecessary in the relaxed style of a Wednesday afternoon. He had almost come unseated. And then, by God, as he struggled to stay aboard and straighten out his mount, he'd seen de Saban looking back at him—and *laughing*!

Heaven deliver me, he thought, from a suspicious father. Jealous husbands had been bad enough . . .

Very well. If that was how the frog wanted it, then that was how he'd get it. Wynans had never had much use for him or for the rest of the Gallic corporate establishment which had fled France helter-skelter when the Mitterand gang came in—a case of the sinking ship deserting the rats.

One had to grant, however, that aside from trying to unhorse you in an otherwise friendly game, the marquis had a lot of style; he was on every Washington hostess's A list. He'd arrived in the United States without his wife, without his horses, grooms, or trainers—without everything, indeed, except his daughter and his money. By European standards he was a formidable player, carrying a five-goal handicap. Wynans was now a four, but he'd once been a seven and could put out at that level again at least for a chukka or two. He'd grown up with polo, playing on bicycles at Meadowbrook and at the Phippses' field in Palm Beach before he'd been big enough to sit a horse and hold a full-length mallet. There hadn't been much in his life except polo until he was well over thirty, polo and the good life and certain women.

His family had accepted that. One didn't look for too much from Waldy. They were mystified and not entirely approving when he opted for a career in public life. He had tried numerous times, always vainly, to explain this conversion to his brothers, both older than he and even richer—both large, comfortable men with cautious, complacent opinions about most affairs of life and complete cynicism about politics. Brother Cleve was chairman of the Murray Hill Trust of Manhattan, the Wynanses' bank. Brother Roger presided as senior partner of the law firm which represented Murray Hill and most other family activities: Wynans Development (a venture capital arm); Wynans Foundation (a nonprofit organization which also served as a major tax shelter); Trinity International (oil, dairies, airlines, high tech, etc.). Cleve worked with Americana. He liked restoring rotting Colonial era paintings and pots and even villages to pristine condition. Both he and Roger felt that the government could be conducted as if it were a partially owned subsidiary of their businesses. They did not see that to be engaged in public affairs required skills, even though quite different ones from those involved in acquiring money, collecting stuff, or even practicing a sport. A collection only had a certain mass just as a game had a score but someone else would soon put together an equal or larger mass just as a score, well, a score would soon be forgotten unless it were a record and even then it would someday be surpassed. Political power was another thing entirely. Having it, you stepped on to the stage of history; above all it gave a surge and excitement to life that only the rarest moments in a sport, the moments when one broke through some hidden barrier, went into a high beyond one's ordinary limits, could ever equal. Only an idiot would sit in a counting house directing employees to make more loot when he already had enough.

Walden Wynans now set service above all else—all except those basic values such as love of wife, family, and country, which, of course, came first in the lexicon of any decent citizen. Just the same, he would never give up polo. Never! He would not give it up nor would he conceal his scorn for men who ignored sportsmanship by bringing a personal antagonism—not to mention a completely ill-founded one—onto the field.

Everyone was flying now, charged with a feeling unusual for this sort of polo, the result of the rivalry, perceptible to all, between the two top players. A purist in field etiquette would have been disgusted at the absence of teamwork; once a rider got on the ball he tended to stay with it rather than risk losing the attack by passing. Halfway through the last period, de Saban, on a rawboned black that looked more like a steeplechaser than a polo horse, drove a tremendous neck shot up to the college boy playing Number One for Red. The kid's try for goal was short, but his pony, turning, scored on behalf of his rider, kicking the ball through and setting off a bedlam of horn blowing from the cars along the sidelines.

A throw-in, then a melee followed, no one, least of all the umpire, clearly seeing what then happened in the churn of whirling, trampling hooves, foam-flecked rumps, red and white jerseys and whacking mallets.

Wynans could have told him. He had betrayed his own standard of fair play, sticking a foot under de Saban's stirrup as the frog leaned over the black's croup, then giving the foot a hoist that tumbled its rider out of the saddle. By the rules, play continued even with one man dismounted, since no injury had occurred. De Saban was still chasing the black horse, afoot, when the game ended. . . .

Once more back in the Bentley, driving toward the Capitol, the secretary kept this scene before him—the big black out in midfield, reins trailing, with the Frenchman waddling behind.

He saw the shape I was in when I got out of the car. Well, too bad. He or somebody should have taught the girl to behave.

For his own conduct, he had nothing but approval. He had performed impeccably, with perfect propriety—but—he shivered at the thought. *Young stuff!* God! The dangers of it . . . woe and destruction! He'd seen it happen to the few who tried because . . . you did something stupid. Or someone tipped off the parents. Or the kid got guilty feelings and spilled it. Always, without fail. Then you were done for.

Well, he'd kept his wits about him. Let de Saban suspect anything he liked. Nothing had happened. Nothing ever would. But as Linton, having been so instructed, headed for the Pentagon, the secretary marveled again at the curve of that little paw on the seat, the fingertips touching him. . . .

He shook his head as if warding off a blow. Then he leaned forward to turn on the four o'clock newscast.

Ten minutes later, in his office, on the clean surface of the great walnut desk once the gift of a grateful nation to John J. "Black Jack" Pershing, general of the army in World War I, Secretary Wynans found a message from the White House communications room:

"President Gantt would like to see you at 2200 hours."

No agenda was mentioned. There was no need for one. The secretary's nerves pulled a little tighter but he felt that he was ready. Just to make sure he ordered his office tape to play back what he'd said earlier to Truscott on this subject. There could be no impugning of SEDAV, no crap about its having killed anyone: his position on that was ironclad. The integrity of the Department of Defense and the profile of future combat strategy rested on it. There would be no turning back!

ELEVEN

For months now there had been only two functioning approaches to the White House. The West Gate was blocked. Foot traffic entered by day from the walkway and parking area on East Executive Avenue on the far side of the Executive Mansion, next to the treasury building. Tourist passes were no longer issued. Federal cars with special license tabs came and went under tight inspection; outside the grounds, on all approaches, reinforced concrete barriers compelled a zigzag entry. There would be no head-on bombing runs. Huey gunships also patrolled around the clock to keep the incumbent safe from attack by air; the Secret Service had insisted on this after some kook tried to destroy the White House and the Capitol by means of a homemade atom bomb sent aloft in a balloon!

The threat presented by such lunatics was only too real as was the increasing sophistication of international terrorists. President Gantt took due and proper recognition of such dangers. If it seemed appropriate to conduct the nation's business in a bunker two thousand feet underground he would do so no matter how absurd this might appear in a postnuclear age with the arms race, unabated, focusing on conventional weapons such as this new and wondrous robot, SEDAV.

Wynan's vehicle passed through three electronic checkpoints on its way to the visitors' garage, built directly over the bunker and designed to hold a maximum of twenty cars. It was barred to all except cabinet-level officials, top White House staffers, and a few others of comparable rank who might be summoned here from time to time. Entry was obtained through a computerized voice-recognition system, each individual registering into the voice box his private code designation, changed daily. A marine here held the small microphone through the lowered car window so that Wynans could speak into it.

"Straight Arrow," he said.

"Thank you, Mr. Secretary," replied the computer.

The car ran down the ramp into the garage and the driver cut the engine. Wynans got out. He walked a few feet along a red-carpeted corridor to an elevator carrying him to the presidential anteroom two thousand feet below. Whoosh! A crazy run: you didn't realize you were falling at the speed of a bank safe dropped from a high building until your liver and lights came up, soft as silk, with a sigh that could turn into a fart, and did so now, before settling back where they belonged.

An attendant took the secretary's hat. This he placed on a tubular steel rack which already had another chapeau on it, an old-fashioned black Borsalino which looked somewhat familiar.

"Kindly be seated, Mr. Secretary," said the young lady attendant. "The President will be with you in a few minutes."

She had about her the professional good cheer encountered in the better grade of dental nurses. "Don't worry," her warm voice seemed to assure him. "The man will shoot some stuff into your gums and you won't feel a thing."

Not true, of course: once you were facing that yellow-eyed Pud-knocker in his lair you were between a rock and a hard place. The issue usually didn't rest on what you could tell him but on what you might be hiding. Make one mistake and the President would reel off the very facts and figures which, because of your negligence or general untrustworthiness, you'd never heeded or—worse!—forgotten. Forgetting—that was not advised. It was as bad as contradicting yourself—a deadly peril. Any lapse from an opinion once expressed was proof of unreliability and a suggestion of . . . treachery. Woe! At such times the Pud-knocker's fearful eyes would cloud over. A film would appear in them resembling that to be seen in the eyes of a fish when it is no longer very fresh. Then look out!

Wynans's large, muscular body was ill-suited to the miserable chair now required to support it. He shifted this way and that, trying not to stare at the Borsalino but forced then to observe, as he had a thousand times before, the rest of the decor down here, the spindly cactus plants in their helmet-liner pots and the gas-chamber-reject green of the rugs, walls, and ceiling.

He never felt well in this subterranean burrow—he felt ill. His skin itched and his bones ached. Then there was the congestion in his nose. He carried tissues in his pocket against this failing. The trouble was the air, the way the weird air conditioning machines affected your breathing—could one imagine a President of the United States building such a hole to crawl into when he could be conducting his affairs like any proper chief executive, in the superb, historic chambers aboveground?

Oh, the air was clean, all right. That was probably what was wrong with it. Gantt had ordered a special conditioning system. He'd had complicated and supposedly tamperproof fans and chemical filters created just in case some ingenious terrorist tried to kill him by injecting poison gas into the White House pipes. In his vigilance to ward off assassination Gantt thought of such schemes as that—he was brilliant at it; if he himself had been a terrorist he would have eliminated himself in no time at all. Yet he also had a reckless side. Every year—usually during the congressional recess—he would go back, as if for some renewal of the spirit, to the spiny hills of his origin. Shaking off the Secret Service by some devious, boondock strategy, he would disappear, sometimes afoot, sometimes on horseback, camping out alone and showing up unexpectedly, like some tattered migrant, in a country town to gab with the people and listen to their complaints about his conduct of the nation.

Wynans's head tilted forward. It dangled on his neck like a sinker on a fish line. A wave of sleepiness had wiped him out. Wishing he had drunk less wine at dinner, he gulped down deep drafts of the claustral air but . . . there was no relief to be found here. The whole place was so cramped, it was like being in a submarine, some vicious, newfangled little craft plunging through chartless seas on a desperate mission. Forced to uncouple his legs at last, he bumped a side table on which stood a carafe that opened with a key. All carafes and liquid containers of any sort in the night offices were kept locked; if you wanted a drink, you asked for the key and someone gave it to you, as in doctors' offices they handed you, on request, the key to the john . . . and come to think of it he had need of just such a facility right now! Didn't this bloody dungeon include a latrine? It must, of course, it must . . . but before he could make the appropriate inquiry a door opened noiselessly behind him and Senator John Lighty appeared from inside, bless him! Obviously the black hat could have belonged to no one else. Taking a few steps forward, his mad, merry eyes twinkling like rescue beacons, he jammed his mouth an inch from Wynans's ear and said laconically, "Hang tight! I'm with you all the way."

And with this he clapped the Borsalino on his head and vanished into the elevator.

"The President is free, Mr. Secretary," said the office lady. "He would like to see you now."

The inner door was made of heavy metal but it had been surfaced to look like mahogany with a bright brass handle in the middle of it. Wynans turned the handle and went in, lifting his knees higher than necessary as he always did when entering this room. He stood awkwardly and stiffly, blinking in the dim light, waiting for an invitation to sit down.

The room was long, low, and wide, and splotched with pools of shadow. Wynans had been in it many times before but he had never been able to remember anything about it except that it was—so dim and gloomy. Key lights at odd angles created a confusing pattern and to make it worse, the trouble with the secretary's breathing was intensified and he had to blow his nose again.

What—allergic to the President of the United States?

I'm afraid so, sir.

Take the bugger out and put twelve slugs in him.

Right away, sir.

A harsh, milky glare fell from a recessed spot onto a huge desk where nobody was sitting.

"Over here!" said a quiet voice.

A deep voice. Basso. Presidential. It made everything different.

You couldn't see him well. He was over on a couch to one side of the room. He'd pulled some kind of linsey-woolsey blanket around him, the kind of woolen stuff they make in the back country. With that to enlarge him, he looked like a monster instead of the gaunt person he really was. He looked weird. Huge.

He held some papers and the light fell on his hands—big, gnarled hands like a workman's.

Presidential hands.

"Kindly be seated," he said in that deep, gentle voice. He leaned forward and his crooked nose and bright squirrelly eyes were caught in the light for a second before he settled back again.

The Pudknocker from the moonshine stills and the red clay cuts.

"H'it won't take me but a wink to look this over. H'it's somethin' you handed me a piece back."

Standing on a podium, before a world audience of satellite-linked listeners, wearing on his chest a computer speech synthesizer programmed with phonemes, the basic sounds that make up the language, as well as with rules of pronunciation and stress, he could bring out his words like a Harvard professor.

Odd then, indeed, that he seemed more impressive, the dignity of his language more evident, when he let the country speech take over.

He finished the thick batch of papers quickly, then laid them aside; he threw off the shawl and stalked over to the desk, long and lanky and bony. He walked like the Tin Man in *The Wizard of Oz*. He sat down behind the desk and studied a note . . . and as the posture of authority laid its measure on his tongue, his speech shed its dialect twang.

"Why are we dealing with Advanced Electronic Technologies on this tank? I thought TRW had that contract."

"They did, sir, at the start. But there was a vulnerability factor in the C_3 system when exposed to heavy radiation . . . such as a tactical nuclear explosion . . ."

The secretary's nerves tensed as he attacked his own memory, trying to dredge up details.

The President cued him.

"A Hewlett-Packard subcontract, wasn't that what it was?"

"Yes, Mr. President. But when we duplicated battlefield conditions at the test site . . ."

". . . you blew every piece of electric gear in Yuma, Arizona, including the street lights."

"Yes, Mr. President."

Not easy, this kind of thing—dealing with a chief executive who could run his eye over a sheet of military specs and retain trajectory velocities, spall spread, impact per square centimeter, or whatever else was there. But with regard to the robot and its supplier, Wynans was truly well-informed; he felt prepared for any question—and handled with ease the next series, though thrown at him at racetrack speed.

"This still a sole service contract?"

"Yes, sir."

"Should have a backup!"

"Not as long as ADECT keeps the leading edge, sir."

"Who'll run the store with the old man underground?"

"I believe the board favors his son, Mr. President: Jason Streck, a longtime company executive."

"I want a rundown on him."

"You shall have it in the morning, sir."

Though actually quite without facts and figures to back up his notion that the younger man would make a satisfactory supplier, his recital gave the impression of a secretary of defense so vigilant that he had every detail of his vast domain at his fingertips.

Oh, it was fine, glorious, to be sitting at ease with the most powerful man in the world, the only person in that world of whom, for some idiotic reason he, Walden Wynans, was afraid—wonderful to have his respectful attention, to meet all his onslaughts with instant aplomb. How absurd, how distant seemed his malaise of a few minutes ago, stuffed into that hideous anteroom with the potted plant and the ghastly green rug . . . surely he would never feel that way again!

Gantt continued scribbling notes, though everything was taped. But he did it . . . he scribbled . . . and sometimes his massive hand would come up out of the shadows and he would dip into a bowl of mints— some throwback to the Reagan era jelly beans. He would put the little candies in his mouth and gnash on them with his boondock fangs. And now—now in the flow of his easy talk, in this mood of heady exhilaration, Wynans too reached into the bowl! He too took one of the mints, then several. He too sucked them; he too rolled them around with his tongue—the grapes of Olympus.

Gantt leaned back. He knotted his ropelike fingers behind his head, aimed his nose like a mortarpiece at the low, key-lighted ceiling.

". . . figure you saw Rinker's report on that . . . industrial accident . . ."

Industrial accident! Ah, bless the man—what an incredible solution! The only way out! He might have known that Gantt's backwoods savvy would come up with something like that.

"I had an opportunity to make a quick evaluation, Mr. President. I'd say deep-six it."

"You're on target. I've so ordered."

"We can't allow anything that would diminish faith in the robot."

"I agree again. But those investigators came close, they came pretty doggone close to the nub of it. You may have noted—they never call it an accident."

"I observed that."

"And they don't call it a crime."

"No, sir."

"They were sniffing around. They got a whiff of something."

"I'm afraid I don't quite understand, Mr. President . . ."

Out of the secret coils of power within his strange spirit, the Pudknocker shot Wynans a look like a thunderbolt.

"Mr. Secretary, did you ever stop to think how many wars in history were started just by weapons? They kin do that, invoke their own use and purposes. They could do it when they were just dumb inanimate objects and now we've put brains in them, Mr. Secretary. Robots! They bear watching, Mr. Secretary. Cram them full of new ideas, they liable to take off on you."

TWELVE

The late-night or early-morning "workshops" in the presidential bunker were scheduled two or three times a month. They consisted of lectures usually accompanied by movies along with computerized maps and graphics which enabled experts to brief key members of the cabinet and the departments on new policies and strategies: this was the swat team, the land's highest opinion-making group, delegated to bypass, convert, or crush any resistance, legislative or industrial, that might confront the President's intentions.

Tonight General Lucius Shotwell, chairman of the Joint Chiefs of Staff, was recommending a shift in relations with Morocco. Since coming to power, General Guelta had made democracy a hold-your-breath exercise.

Civil liberties were still a luxury which Guelta said Morocco could not yet afford but in a fit of annoyance he had kicked out the Soviet "advisers" whose support had put a halt to *perestroika*.

A trade seemed in the wind.

Would he send troops into Angola? Well, he just might, providing that the United States supplied weaponry to replace the Soviet hardware, already obsolescent.

Lights in the bunker dimmed. An oil painting of John Quincy Adams rolled into the ceiling and a projection screen rose from the floor.

Gantt was bored. These hours of relative quiet were precious to him; he should have let General Shotwell harangue the National Security Council instead of coming down here with his military chatter and his light-struck desert films.

The President longed to be alone again, back in the quietude where he could think and plan. Earlier on, he had been warm and full of vigor but now his legs and the tips of his fingers felt numb.

When the briefing ended and he could claim once more the peace of his study he wondered if a chill was coming in; he took a couple of pills, then stalked across the thick blue carpet to a leather couch against the wall and lay down there, wrapping around him again the woolen blanket that some woman in Breathitt County, Kentucky, had sent him as an inauguration gift.

Women were always making such things in the high country. His grandmother had made cornshuck dolls. She had made walking canes out of hickory wood and varnished them and sold them. To save money in smoothing the canes, she used a piece of sharp glass instead of sandpaper.

The President pulled the blanket up over the mail-order pants that covered his dry shanks. Soon the pills would work and he would feel better. Waiting for the warmth to come, he closed his eyes: he had always known how to refresh himself with short snoozes. He had even, on occasion, nodded off while sitting at his desk in the great hall of the U.S. Senate. Some of his colleagues had ridiculed him for this. They'd called him the senator from Nappalachia. He didn't care. He had always done what he'd had to do. Napping or not, he had represented his constituents fearlessly and well.

He had come far—far! Some newspaper man had nicknamed him "the last of the log cabin presidents"; a silly epithet and wrong, of course! He'd never had logs around him or thatch over him, though he knew some in the nearby creases such as Lost Creek, Grassy Branch, Toulose, Pippa Passes, Stanville, Caney Creek, and Van Lear who did and had. Logs would have been an improvement for Granpappy Lavrety, his mother's pappy. Old Lavrety had lived in a tar paper shack, but the Gantts (of Hessian descent) kept a general store in Pine Top and lived over the store in four big airy rooms. Later they had moved to a hilltop prefab home with a cinder block wall around it as fine as any mine owner's!

Politics had always been a basic part of mountain life. Men and women in the creases took sides fiercely and argued passionately and endlessly about public issues. In politics, they felt, lay their only hope for betterment.

Claude Gantt hoisted himself on the sofa. The pills were working—he could feel his veins enlarging and the blood flowing better. Yes, he had come a far piece from when he had ridden the high country, crease to crease and house to house, getting the vote out. You had to get it out and hold a true count with careful watching at the polling places or you'd never beat the system which for years had been yoked to the county slate.

The slate was rigged. The district boss would fix the price the candidate had to pay to get his name on the slate, set up so there was a slot on it for every county office: judge, jailer, sheriff, tax collector, and so forth. Minor offices went cheap, higher ones for as much as five thousand dollars, though the man could make that much and more back in a few months if he knew what to do. The going price to a voter for his vote was five dollars, although if the slate seemed in trouble it could go as high as six or seven.

A candidate's abilities were not taken into much account.

Claude C. Gantt had been getting out the vote for three years. He was bucking for his law degree when the party held a caucus and the chairman informed him that he was in line for recognition, and what office would he like to be put down for? Gantt had said and truly meant it: "If I could be undersheriff of Breathitt County, that would satisfy my life's ambition!"

"You got it, Claude," the chairman said. And he wrote in his name.

Life's ambition! Lord God Almighty, he thought, pulling in long, slow breaths, tasting again that ancient triumph, what an ambition *that* had been! A good thing he'd got more than he'd asked for, even if by no means more than his deserts. Undersheriff, sheriff, state district attorney, in that order—the many suits fearlessly and successfully fought, forcing the installation of mine safety equipment, implementing reforestation, environmental protection. Then senator! And now—ha!

The presidency, for such as he, was supposed to have been a joke, a freak! Fine, let them laugh. Let the cartoonists have a field day. Let them sneer at his barricades, his guards, his pills, his air-conditioned bunker. *He was President!* He knew what bullets and bombs could do; it took only one, and he wasn't fixing to be blown away like John F. Kennedy or his brother or that poor bastard contractor out in California. He was

President and he .wanted some steel and concrete around him before they took *him* out to Arlington. He had only one skin and it looked better without holes in it.

He reached for his glass of fruit juice. It was empty but he felt too peaceful to get up and go for more. He still had a journey to go; he knew what he had to do to get the job done and the kind of people who could help him do it. That fellow Wynans and others like him—he'd put a burr under his ass about the SEDAVs.

The President chuckled at the memory, his great bony shoulders heaving. Oh, it was so easy to put Wynans on just by caricaturing the hillbilly act ever so little. He was so straight, so solidly, gold-platedly *elite*! And yet . . . and yet even while, as President, he was in the midst of such raillery he knew that he was putting himself on too, yielding to something deep in his own nature—for he was by troth the very redneck bastard in whose cap and bells he enjoyed capering. He was, *he was* that Pudknocker with hill-country superstition in his bones. He had studied, he had learned about electronics—basic mystery and universal tool and genie of modern life and, more to the point, modern war—but when you came down to it, wasn't all this science just an updated version of sorcery? Had we not fused the Magus into the transistor?

Walden Wynans could be kidded, all right, but he had a place of respect in government. No one could buy him. Even the ones who'd had their money a long time weren't always like that but he could handle that kind too. There were ways. He'd thrown away the rule book long ago. You didn't play by the rules when the rest of the world was playing kick-you-in-the-balls, the only game that everybody understood. He hadn't been elected to play by the rules. He had been elected to represent the people, all the people: the city ones, the corporate ones, the cheaters and the honest ones, the lost and displaced ones and Those Others, the peckerwood ones out there, the ones he'd been chosen from . . . *"the longest enduring society* [as he had declared in his inaugural acceptance speech) *of free men governing themselves, the marvel and mystery of twenty centuries . . ."*

The people, all the people: the ones he had sworn to protect and defend! If you were going to be President you had to know where they were and what they wanted, the ones out there in the great stretch of the land between its oceans, all of them. You represented the cities and the towns, the huge combinations, unions, churches, corporations, con-sortiums, conglomerates, leagues, clubs, societies, all that—but when the chips were down, it wasn't the groups or the knowing ones, but

Those Others who got the money on the line, Those Others who sent their sons to fight the wars, who did the praying and the voting and the begetting of America, the ones out on the flats and the creases, with the RFD boxes and the farm-owned telephone lines stapled onto trees since there were more trees than fence posts along roads made of clay as often as of hardtop, sometimes not much bigger than ropes, it seemed, winding across the wild, jagged land.

What they wanted above all else was peace—and somehow out of this desire had been born the giant dichotomy of the defense establishment with its incredible and ever-growing arsenal of hardware designed to maintain peace but developing at the same time a mystic and fearful field of force whose whimsies could neither be predicted nor controlled. The robot tank seemed at first a modest step in the reduction of this madness, but if even this engine could turn against its makers, what did you do about it?

A light flashed near his head. That would be Lucy Pearl, his wife. She didn't like the bunker, called it a rabbit hutch; if he wanted to consort with her he had to come upstairs. She'd fixed up the Lincoln bedroom and she slept up there, but early every morning, if he didn't come up, she'd call to say good night and tonight was no different. They spoke briefly and tenderly; she would pray for him tonight. The President was tired. In the gloom and warmth and the deep subterranean silence of the bunker he could hear Weaver, the black man who looked after him, moving quietly about, setting things to rights; presently he felt a light additional blanket dropped over him and he knew that all the lights except one tiny bulb no bigger than a possum's eye, in a nook by his Pullman couch, had been turned out; still sleep did not come at once and in its stead advanced an army of robots. Their antennae twitching, their cannon elevated, they slithered sullenly into a battle without purpose in a war that would never end.

THIRTEEN

The uncertain weather of September cleared into an October of Indian summer—soft golden days with breezes just strong enough to lift the smog. On one such, coming to work at his usual time, Jason found Abe Kohn waiting for him in the big office—an infallible signal that some hassle had developed or was about to at Sunnyvale Three.

"I see," said Kohn without preliminaries, "that we've upgraded brother Kraskov."

"Not really, Abe, by no means. What gives you that idea?"

"Man has new job, with staff yet? And he's screening the junior engineers to see who he wants with him."

"I told him he could have some help. And the job is only temporary . . ."

Jason stood his blackthorn against the wall and sat down, picking up the coffee Mrs. Purviance had just planted on his desk.

". . . as a matter of fact, a remark of yours was what got me started on this. You told me I had no confidence in the SDC, and you were right, so . . ."

"You're opening up the whole ball of wax."

"Nothing that extensive. Just a reappraisal. Why?"

"No reason, except that Imry is the last man I'd let loose with a special program."

"You and I differ on that, Abe. And without pulling rank on you unduly," Jason went on without humor, "I'm running these programs, for better or worse."

"You run the programs, boss, but the Defense Intelligence Service runs the security rating system. Even J. C. couldn't bypass that. He applied for an upgrade for Kraskov and got kicked in the ass, if you'll recall. Something that rarely happened to J. C. Streck. He didn't care for it."

Jason finished his coffee and set down the cup.

"Abe," he said genially, "the DIS is free to kick my ass at any time. It has been kicked before. This isn't a permanent assignment. Kraskov may wrap it up and be all through before the DIS knows anything about it."

"I wouldn't bet the ranch on that. May I ask a question?"

"Shoot."

"Why did you pick Imry?"

"He's overqualified for what he's doing, and this is a place where he can give us quick action. It was my idea, not his."

"And he jumped at it."

"He neither jumped at it nor turned it down. I suppose he was happy at having a challenge, even if it can't last long."

"Not long might still be too long. I don't think he can be cleared. But if you insist on using him we ought to try."

"Your recommendation received and noted. Thank you very much, Abe. Is there anything else on your mind?"

Abe Kohn allowed that there wasn't. He left with an appearance of good humor which obviously cost him an effort. Jason understood his feeling. Abe went by the book but in his specialty you went by the book if you were any good at all and Abe was the best; through twenty years or more with the company he had also become a friend insofar as ties of friendship were defined in the corridors of stress and the tilt-up conference rooms of the high-tech corporate world. He, Jason, had been short with this friend. He'd cut him down at the shoe tops.

So what else was new? Abe had always disliked and distrusted Imry: a Russian. A snake. An outlaw. So Abe suspected him. Abe was an expert in suspicion. He suspected everybody.

Jason's instinct was different. He knew that Imry was a gifted person and he felt deep in his heart that Kraskov was an honest and trustworthy person. He had confidence in the accuracy of his instinct.

Jason picked up his cudgel. He walked up and down the deep-pile carpet of his office, ignoring the bleak memorabilia of wars past and present in their neat glass cases. He needed no session with Dr. Straska to advise him that his own nerves were stretched tight. The six weeks since his father's death had not been easy; he'd had to give himself on-the-job training he hadn't known he'd need, tap into the brains of those around him for guidance and reassurance. He felt he was coming through all right, but in addition to the fearful pace of the rapidly expanding market he'd been drained and troubled by a secret problem: his preoccupation with a certain rogue engine and its continued presence somewhere in the coils and crannies of the great busy plant.

There is no computer language for love or hate. There is only a yes or a no, a one or a zero. And yet Jason hated, and the hate was eating him up.

He *hated* the machine he'd made—not the profile of a robotic combat vehicle, SEDAV—but a particular example, the specific individual robot which had killed J. C. Streck. Serial number: TY60, followed by a string of additional digits, adding up to a ghastly threat loose in the world—not only in the Valley's spooky foundry of kill machines, but also the great vulnerable hemispheres beyond. It was about time to do something about that, and riding the adrenaline flow started by his interview with Kohn he sent for Tom Heyn, vice-president, ordnance, and told him he wanted SEDAV TY60 trashed.

It was a freakish order, sure enough.

Heyn didn't feel at first that he was hearing right or that his young boss's dipstick, on this bleak morning, quite reached the oil.

He whipped a notebook out of a pocket in which, in earlier times, an engineer would have carried a slide rule.

"The shell, you want that scrapped?"

"Yes."

"The treads and engine?"

"Absolutely."

"The control box . . ."

"Tom," said Jason, "I want the entire vehicle trashed—all of it. I want it torched. Then I want the junk hauled off the plant area. Am I making myself clear?"

"Whatever you say, sir," said Heyn. Tucking the notebook away, he left the office with a mien defensive and reproachful, dismayed as much by the new CEO's irritability as by the illogical and unprecedented order.

Some people couldn't take the heat there at the top . . .

A few minutes later, however, he called back on the plant intercom.

"That TY6o, Jason? I'm afraid it's not available."

Jason felt his annoyance rise again.

"What do you mean, Tom?"

"The army has it, sir. They took delivery at 0500 yesterday."

Jason blinked. This he hadn't foreseen. He asked Heyn for the out-shipment invoice number. Getting it, he punched in the code for Colonel Nolan Jared, the officer in charge of ADECT's permanently stationed army section.

As at all major defense plants, a staff of specially qualified army engineers—here some fifty of them in their own building, with their separate support staffs—inspected and reported on each step in the manufacturing of every SEDAV on the ADECT production line. When the units were tested and ready for shipment Jared accepted them as the army's representative and signed the invoices which ADECT's accountants would later use to substantiate their billings.

A West Pointer, Jared had graduated near the top of his class, then gone on to take an advanced degree at MIT. He and Jason were on relatively good terms, though without much personal warmth on either side.

"I have a problem, Nolan," Jason said as the colonel's thin, spectacled face appeared on his screen.

Said Jared, "Then I will rub my magic lamp and it will go away."

"Well, you'd better rub extra hard because this is a tough one. Once we've delivered a product to you, is there any way we can get it back?"

"We're talking about a SEDAV?"

"Nothing else."

Jared's eyes, behind their steel frame spectacles, were sombre.

"Hmmm. I don't think we've had that one before. When was this vehicle delivered?"

"Heyn says yesterday at 0500. Couldn't it still be here at the plant?"

"I don't know. I'll check, if you have the serial number."

Jason gave it to him.

Jared was back on the screen in less than five minutes.

"My lamp isn't working very well."

"I was afraid of that."

"The vehicle in question was on last night's out-shipment for Aberdeen Proving Grounds."

The Maryland location is the army's largest armor arsenal and demonstration site. Not only prototypes, as in years past, but—in conformity to an updated DOD requirement—all production-line models of every new weapon are tested there.

"How long does that take?"

"A week. Give or take a couple of days."

"Why not recall the whole shipment?"

"I'd need a goddamn good reason."

"A manufacturing flaw."

"Not after my people have inspected and passed it."

"Even your people can make mistakes."

"Not when *my* ass is on the line," said Nolan. "If we did, what would be recalled would be me."

"Then let's look at something simple. Suppose one, just one vehicle in this shipment gets lost en route. Wouldn't that be possible?"

"The army doesn't lose weapons. Combat vehicles in particular it doesn't lose."

"The hell it doesn't. How do you explain those videos of Communist crews riding around in the stuff we used in Nam?"

"Jason," said Colonel Jared, "those weapons are obsolete. I want to help, but do you mind if I ask, off the record, what this is all about?"

Jason hesitated. Jared's question was natural enough, but in terms of plant/army protocol it was also out of line. In any relationship as complicated as the interfacing of the intelligence establishment and any branch of the Department of Defense there are queer overlapping areas, unforeseen crosscurrents, gabbers and snoopers on lifelong prowls, shredders that don't quite shred, and so forth, no service or branch of any service or department ever being quite free, no matter what due diligence is taken, from invasion by others. The DIA stonewalls the CIA, the CIA has its moles in the FBI, and the FBI flutters the files of the Bureau of Narcotics and Dangerous Drugs. So on—an endless chain. And in each and every one of these covens the IRS pokes sticky fingers, not exempting Air Force Intelligence or the Council on Foreign Relations. Aside from this web there is the spy work of the great companies on each other and the rich lodes of electronic and personal data to be parlayed from subornation of their rivals' security forces or disgruntled office staffers.

Almost anyone can deal himself in.

"We intend to paint this unit red and use it as a logo piece out by the flagpole. Anything more convincing than that you'll just have to invent, Nolan."

The colonel was not amused.

"Forget I asked, Jason. I'll try to think of some way to oblige you, but I'm not too hopeful."

"Thanks anyway," said Jason. And with this he phased Jared off his screen. So for the time being the matter was dropped.

It was to be resumed.

FOURTEEN

Regardless of whatever intramural face-offs rippled the course of Jason's first weeks in office, there was no question as to the leaping prosperity at ADECT. It had started while J.C. was still very much alive and continued its surge with equal velocity into the adjustment period following his bewildering demise: a steady, then a spectacular increase in Pentagon purchases, foreign contracts signed or pending, all this requiring and receiving crash production schedules, round-the-clock work shifts for personnel . . . and at the hub of it all, the generating force, that crazy little bug, the robot attack vehicle.

Even the general public now was interested, investment houses putting out brochures, arbitrageurs cocking their sights. *The Commercial Weekly* (as required by federal law) churned out the figures and the Dow Jones reflected them in an ascending spiral which continued into the new year.

Up and up. Every day the new quotation zipped across Jason's PC screen on the same line as the date and weather forecast. He was getting richer. That was nice to know but not enough to ward off a certain discomfort when Ken Garay passed along to him *The Wall Street*

Journal's "Insider Trading" column, several lines of which were circled in red:

> *Sold:* by Mrs. Odille Streck, a member of the board: 1,879,000 shares of Advanced Electronic Technologies owned directly and 3,844,334 shares owned indirectly through J. C. Streck Trust Estate at a rounded price of $42.50 a share.

So his esteemed stepmother was cashing in. Well, he supposed such was her right—but two big parcels! A lot of shares. She might at least have called to say she was doing it. He remembered the funeral reception when she'd proclaimed with such touching conviction, "We stand shoulder to shoulder, don't we?"

Since the bad night when he had seen the cottage lights from afar and driven up the wide pale drive to find nothing good at the end of it, Jason had been back at the home place many times, not as one who belonged there but who came by invitation, without right of entry unless prior arrangements had been made. The invitations were welcome, always delightful, whether for a Sunday brunch on the terrace or a black-tie dinner given in honor of some friend of the lady in residence.

Odille had a wide acquaintance with the great of the world, an attribute that had always impressed J. C. Streck as it had the former husbands and lovers whose wealth and position had helped to bring it about. Her entertainments had been modest, as befitted a new widow. Nevertheless, without ostentation, she'd had in her house, among others, a former prime minister of Italy, a French film star, and an Irish poet who, having stayed the night, seduced the upstairs maid and stole a piece of silver plate.

Silicon Valley celebrities, when included in the receptions, were not briefed on whom they were to meet. It was they, they themselves, the hermit scientists, the mad armorers, whom she displayed as a guide in a waxworks museum might call attention to the exhibits entrusted to his care. The visitors loved the show and Odille was pleased. By creating what she called "combinations," she set up the climate in which she could move most freely and in which alone she felt truly at ease.

Sometimes she delegated cohost duties to Jason. At cocktail time he saw to it that glasses were kept filled and canapes circulated; at formal seatings he presided at the foot of the table and later helped to escort the departing guests to their vehicles. He was not unaware that such exercises implied a relationship which the Europeans took for granted but which disturbed the local gentry, particularly certain ladies not lacking in corporate ties.

"Are you aware," said a letter to a member of ADECT's board,

> that your Chief Executive Officer is shacked up with his father's widow? He may be having a grand old time but to me what he's advertising is the moral desolation and operational irresponsibility of the people who put him where he is in the boardroom if not in the bedroom. Sign me
>
> Disgusted in Santa Clara

"I think we'll shred this," said the board member. "May I take care of it for you?"

"I'd be much obliged. And thank you for your courtesy," said Jason.

The absurdity of it all was that he was not Odille's lover. A legacy she might be, of a sort—but not a forbidden fuck one might lay, like a secondhand wreath, on a parent's grave. He was satisfied with their relationship the way it was. Her odd behavior in the stock market was what he wanted to check out.

The Dow shuddered only slightly under the big sales; after a few nervous days optimism reasserted its contagious magic. Procurement was a hot investment field, and money managers and counselors from coast to coast linked arms and three-martini lunches to keep it that way. In ADECT's executive suites Ken Garay still expressed worry; Jason was less disturbed. Odille still held a lot of the family voting stock; the main thing now was to keep her from hemorrhaging any more of it. Probably a few words with her would set everything straight.

Jason took this errand on himself. Failing to reach her by phone, he left word that he would like to drop in for a chat on his way home from work. He was none too pleased to find, when he arrived, a Rolls-Royce Corniche parked in the turnaround, the driver still at his post, reading a newspaper by the glow of the dash. A rental car. If it had been a local Rolls Kim would have known the man and invited him in to sit in comfort in the pantry and perhaps knock back some of Odille's booze.

So—the lady had a visitor. Or visitors!

He regretted coming, but it seemed stupid to back off now. He followed Kim into the living room where a fire was burning and four people sitting by it drinking, all in evening dress like some scene from a Noël Coward revival. Odille, ever her cordial self, sprang up to greet him as if indeed she had expected him all along—though he felt somehow that she'd never gotten his message or, if she had, then forgot it.

"My dear, charming stepson," she called him, presenting him to the others, a gaunt dark sallow woman with blond hair piled up in ringlets and stuck full of jewels and a man in a green dinner jacket.

". . . Count and Countess von Leventaller. Jason is the coexecutor of my late husband's estate."

Ha. Coexecutor—that was the loaded word. This dear charming person to be dealt with and got rid of, God bless us, as fast as possible— he in his chinos, his checked shirt, the pens in the shirt pocket, the stubble on his face, the sport coat of excellent cut and fit but bad, all bad in the face of the present company, obviously about to go out to some dinner party.

The immense, green von Leventaller, from his chair beside the blazing logs, hoisted himself up in sections, slowly, but with an inexpressible dignity; he took Jason's hand without looking at him and then, with the sections reversing their action, sat down again.

"Can you excuse us for five minutes, Hulga darling? And Eric? Because I must spend the tiniest moment alone with Jason."

"No, no," said Jason, "I'm sorry. Some other time. I apologize. Please don't let me interrupt . . ."

Everyone ignored this. Odille pressed a glass of champagne into his hand; her arm through his, she led him out of the living room into the library.

"Darling, I'm so glad you came. You have no idea how bored I am, and later it will be worse. We're dining with the Hambrechts. Do you know them? But sit down, sit down. Whatever brought you in here at this hour?"

"I telephoned."

"I know. But I thought you'd be here earlier."

"I meant to be. Anyway . . ."

"Oh, I know. It's about the stock. God, I am so sick of hearing about the stock. You'd think I'd murdered someone. Everyone's been calling, asking the most ridiculous questions. I should think why I sold it would be obvious. I needed some money, quite a lot of it. Isn't that why people sell things? Good heavens . . . Did I really do something bad?"

"Not all that bad. But if you needed money all you had to do was say so. The company would have made you a loan."

"Really?" She seemed genuinely surprised. "I never thought of that. But if I had—" she went on blandly, "I don't know, dear—the explanations. Board approval and all. I might not want the entire world poking into my affairs. Even you, darling. I have—" her voice trailed off, "certain responsibilities, private ones—"

"I understand."

"All right then? You've stopped hating me?"

"I love you more than ever."

"That's what I wanted to hear."

Obviously this was no time for cross-examination about the "responsibilities," unheard of until now.

"—but I have a request: your word that if you decide to sell any more shares you'll offer them to ADECT first."

"Why not? Of course I will. And for your information I'm not selling any more. I'm all through with that."

"Great. Then we have a deal."

"A deal. And my solemn promise."

"The kiss of the spider lady," commented Ken Garay when Jason told him how she'd sealed their compact.

"Maybe. I do have the feeling she's up to something. Does the name Eric A.C. von Leventaller ring any bells with you?"

"Leventaller-Atlas Electronik, Hamburg. Spin-off of Atlas Société Anonyme, Belgique. Submarine detection systems, etc. That one?"

"Right. Doesn't Atlas own some of our stock?"

"About two percent, last time I looked. But why Leventaller?"

"He's some kind of count. A social item. Which might explain why he and the countess were sitting with Odille when I dropped in. Or it might not."

"*Or it might not.* In case the count has acquisition on his mind. The only element that doesn't fit is that your stepmother has been unloading shares, not buying more. If you were thinking of her as a possible participant . . ."

"Which I am. Unloading the way she has, she's brought the price down while at the same time covering for anyone else interested in taking us over. Provided you can think of such a person . . ."

"You know damn well I can."

"The guy with the golden parachute. We don't have to name names."

"We don't."

"Enough said then. Takeover is the name of the game. We may be making all this up, our own version of a prime time soap, but I don't think we are. In any event precautions are in order. You're the legal beagle. So for openers, what do we do?"

"We lay on a shark repeller."

"Run that past me again."

"A professional takeover fighter, a lawyer who makes a business of defending corporations facing this kind of threat. He won't come cheap but he'll be worth the cost ten times over. Unless you plan on losing your company."

"I'm not going to lose it, Ken. I'm not gung ho for making weapons, but the company is something I intend to keep. No matter what. Are you tracking me?"

"All the way."

"So how do we get this shark killer?"

"As of this moment I can't tell you, boss," said Garay, "but give me a few hours and I'll have some ideas for you.

Takeover fighters were available for hire.

A former Sullivan and Cromwell partner, celebrated for his corporate victories, submitted a résumé but was turned down due to conflict of interest—he was a member of the board at FMC, an ADECT competitor.

Garay flew to Los Angeles to talk to another candidate. This one had represented the raider in Schlumberger's takeover of Fairchild (a win) and the defense when Bell went after Dalmo Victor (a loss), but on review the counselor's age (he was well past seventy) had ruled him out.

Gustave Kasten of Washington, D.C., had no such handicaps. He was a wit, a political power broker, and a diner out. His black Brioni suits, bowlegs, bow ties, and sad, pouched Mafia eyes inspired immediate confidence as did his war cry: "I've never lost a company that I've defended."

He accompanied this with a triple mandate photocopied on a single piece of his personal notepaper:

No director has ever been held liable for rejection of a takeover offer.

No director has a duty to accept or negotiate a takeover offer.

No director should undertake to meet personally with a raider.

He forthwith demanded and was provided with a staff which consisted of (a) a proxy solicitation team, (b) a public relations firm, and (c) an investment banking consortium to "familiarize company personnel and directors with guidelines for stock buy-back strategies."

With all this in place, a new buoyancy pervaded the ADECT boardroom, a spirit only slightly dampened when Charles Gitlin, the offstage presence everyone had been so careful not to name (though Kasten had sniffed him out at once and been awaiting him impatiently), called in from Florida, asking for an appointment with Jason.

Silicon Valley had not seen or heard of the great Gitlin since he had zoomed off in his golden parachute to parts unknown. *The Wall Street Journal* had carried nothing about him. Only the indestructible columnist Liz, who tracked the untrackable, ran an item reporting him in Palm Beach ". . . in a vintage Addison Mizner mansion within a stone's throw of the Everglades Club—and I can think of certain folk who would love to throw the stones . . ."

"That's vintage bullshit," said Charles modestly when Jason braced him with the item. "You know my tastes—I could never stand a mansion. I'm a meat and potatoes guy all the way."

And with this he patted, without remorse, the belly that now padded out his once cadaverous form.

"Well, I'm glad you're getting some, wherever you're billeted," said Jason.

In spite of the added adiposity the former vice-chairman looked well, his deep tan contrasting splendidly with his mop of silver hair.

"Oh, it's Palm Beach all right," he said. "But condo-land—a pool, a hot tub, and my own ticker. I had to knock down a wall to make room for it but it's the greatest—like a wife, only it never talks back to me. I spend half my time with it."

"We watch the action too, Charles," said Jason. "Every day we post a graph of ADECT Class A Common. There's been a lot of movement."

"A solid stock," said Gitlin heartily. "At the top of my list. I buy a little, don't sell much. I know this company inside and out, my boy. Your father and I went through the years together, you know?"

Jason nodded. Feeling that the charade of genial banter had finished its run, he said with little warmth, "What's on your mind, Charlie?"

"Control," said Gitlin with equal bleakness. "I'm your biggest shareholder, gentlemen. Did you know that?"

Well, no. They didn't.

It was an interesting piece of information. It gave the ADECT defense team something to mull over: Jason, in the big chair that had been his father's; Ken Garay and a law clerk flanking him on the right. Guarding the left flank hunched the famous takeover repellant, Gustave Kasten, in his usual black suit, fantastic shirt, and alligator loafers with the floppy tassels.

Gitlin also had a lawyer with him, a slender fellow with blond thinning hair and large round horn-rims; at a cue from his boss he cleared his throat and read, in a pleasant Harvard Law School baritone, from a typed memorandum to the effect that Gitlin-Atlas-Leventaller, hereinafter known as GITLIN, owned together more than five percent of Advanced Electronic Technologies, hereinafter known as ADECT, and had now, as required by law, filed with the office of the Securities and Exchange Commission their intention to obtain control of the company by means of a tender offer to shareholders at a rounded price of fifty-eight dollars for the remaining shares outstanding until a total of fifty-one percent or more had been acquired.

"We wish to make clear," he finished, "that our proposal is not to be construed as an adversary move but rather as a logical realignment designed for the ultimate profit and betterment of both ADECT and GITLIN. As an affirmation of the spirit in which the offer is submitted we respectfully call attention to the fact that while GITLIN could legally begin purchasing tendered shares two weeks after presenting this offer we shall stipulate thirty days as a more appropriate period for friendly and full consideration and discussion leading to an amicable and prompt transfer of ownership."

A silence lasting for a beat of ten or more engulfed the five men who sat clumped around Jason's desk at the east end of the great room, a gray light from the windows articulating them like figures in a steel engraving.

Two round spots the size of dimes had appeared on Jason's cheekbones but if these could be taken as a symptom of tension his voice did not reflect it.

"I'll address my remarks to you personally, Charlie, on the basis of the longtime association you've referred to. That association ended when we bought you out. It cost a bundle, most of it my own money, but I never found any way to spend it better. I wanted to run the company my way and that's how I'll keep on running it. I never could abide your policies, Charlie, particularly weapons making. Someday ADECT will not make any weapons at all. That's a major commitment for me, and I want you to remember it. Let me emphasize this too: with all respect to Leventaller-Atlas and whoever else is in with you, I'm goddamn sure you don't have the funds or the muscle to challenge us. This company is not for sale. That's all I have to say, and since we have no other business on hand I'll declare this meeting closed."

As ADECT settled down to its own reflections after the raiders' departure, Kasten put one of Jason's statements to question.

"You were right when you said they didn't have stock enough for what they want to do. That's how it looks now but things could change if they have an as-yet-unrevealed ally on the board. Somebody who would vote with them when the chips are down. At one time you mentioned in confidence that your stepmother might . . ."

"She's in it up to her ass," said Jason gloomily. "She might even be screwing Gitlin. I wouldn't rule it out. She can wear corruption like a social grace."

Garay nodded vigorously. In private he still had his own sobriquet for her—"the spider lady."

"She still holds a big chunk of family voting shares."

"All right then," said Kasten quietly, "let's consider that if they're coming to us as burglars they've got tools for the job. That's not where they're vulnerable. There's a different clue—the thirty-day concession before starting to buy shares. Does that mean anything to you?"

"Kasten," said Jason, "you're here on a million-dollar retainer. Don't make us play guessing games."

"This is no guess. A hostile raider dealing from strength doesn't give thirty-day concessions; he'd gladly cut purchase time down to ten days, five days, one day if he could. They're giving us thirty because they genuinely need a nonhostile climate—time to convince your shareholders how bad your management has been and how good theirs will be. Gentlemen, new federal law requires SEC approval for defense-related takeovers and the SEC doesn't like hostile takeovers. Hostile takeovers where a foreign corporation is involved it dislikes even more. There's a good chance that in our case, if we resist, the SEC will withhold approval, but to make sure, I'd advise using your muscle in Washington. You have friends in high places. One or two calls might be enough—like from a senator, for example—"

Said Jason, "The senator you're thinking of, Kasten, plays his cards close to his chin. He's a friend, yes, and I'll go to him if I have to, but I'm thinking of an individual with more at stake—*Walden Wynans.*"

He looked confidently around the table, but Kasten was not reacting. He seemed hardly indeed to be listening, his face half turned away, his fingers doodling with a pencil.

"You don't like that idea?"

"I'm just not all that positive—"

"You mean if the secretary of defense wanted something, the SEC would refuse him?"

The lawyer sighed.

"I have great respect for Secretary Wynans . . ."

"Well?"

". . . at the moment there are, well, rumors. Maybe just gossip, there's always gossip in D.C. But—I talk to my office every day and the latest story is that the secretary is in trouble of some kind. I don't know the details but from what I hear he may be on the way out if he isn't out already. . . ."

FIFTEEN

A month or less before the take-over crisis at ADECT a series of events, several of which would affect its outcome, began on the opposite side of the earth. Let us look first at Saudi Arabia where the young king of that country, Hisham al-Rahman al Saud, rose on a blue-cold February morning at five o'clock, an hour earlier than usual. He waited until sunrise to face Mecca and pray, after which he had his tea, then did some aerobic exercises, western style, and dressed.

Today he was driving to see a demonstration of the interesting robot weapon which might prove such a breakthrough in desert warfare.

Already, in the vast forecourt of the palace, the motorcade was assembling, two hundred cars, or approximately three hundred less than he took along on his annual pilgrimage to the Holy City, but enough for a quick sortie such as this.

The Cadillacs of the security people led off, followed by the king's Wanderlodge, a four-wheel-drive motor home built on a huge General Motors truck chassis, powered by a rear drive turbo diesel and containing a bedroom, a throne room, a sauna, gymnasium, and a horn programmed to play many popular tunes including "Amazing Grace," the king's favorite.

It was playing that now as the cortege wheeled out of the palace gate into the wide shadowy streets of Riyadh.

When King Hisham al-Rahman al-Saud traveled he liked to do it on the ground, preferably in the desert, his true home. Educated at Andover Preparatory School, Massachusetts, and Queen's College, Oxford, he was the most powerful and only absolute monarch in the world and by all odds the world's richest man. No law, custom, or public outcry separated his private purse from his nation's near-trillion-dollar-a-year income based on oil reserves conservatively estimated to last 256 years at full production—full production being a level reached only once in the last fifty years at which time it lowered the royal family's income drastically by producing a horrendous glut.

> *Amazing Grace! How sweet the sounds*
> *That saved a wretch like me*

Hisham's geopolitical power suffered only a single impairment—his total dependence on the U.S. defense industry. From that commitment neither he nor his supplier could ever pull back, he because of the warlike neighbors on his borders, the United States because any retreat would despoil its honor in the Middle East, demoralize its allies, and provide the Soviets with a market opening which President Claude C. Gantt, like all his predecessors except Jimmy Carter, had been vigilant to foreclose.

> *I once was lost but now am found*
> *Was blind but now I see*

Clear of the city, King Hisham sat down at an IBM desktop computer and began the daily stint of paperwork which he attended to personally and could not escape whether at home or abroad. At forty-one he looked less than his true age, a tall, strong, lean man with the great beaky nose of the Aziz royal family and the weak grape-shaped family eyes, mild and moist behind pebble lenses. His eyes belied his nature, which contained nothing that was mild; he took after his grandfather, Abd al-Aziz Ibn-Sa'ud, the Lion of the Desert, who had consolidated a handful of warring nomad tribes, isolated in nearly a million square miles of sand, into a world power of the first rank.

In King Hisham's palace hung a magnificent mural of Ibn Sa'ud, dismounted from his black war-horse, in front of his camel cavalry, flinging handfuls of sand in the direction of his enemy, the gesture with which the Prophet Muhammad had charged into battle fourteen centuries earlier.

Ibn Sa'ud had slaughtered the Ikhwan riflemen, annexed the Hejaz, cooled the Nejd, and wiped out the Hashimite raiders. He had dealt warily with European exploiters but welcomed American prospectors and written the first oil contracts by which Saudi Arabia received fifty percent of the profits of all drilling. Of his fifty-three legitimate sons Hisham's father, Abd al-Rahman al-Aziz, had been his favorite, and Hisham treasured a photograph of himself as a small boy, standing beside Ibn Saud outside a desert tent. In that photo his head had been level with the Lion's knees. Ten years later he had grown to Ibn's full height of six feet five inches.

The motorcade turned north, the Wanderlodge pulling the long struggling line into an inverted C formation: the limousines of the wives and the royal ministers, the officers' staff cars, the tent trucks, the commissary trucks, the spare parts and radio trucks, and the buses containing the servants, the servants' servants, and the grooms who would tend the thoroughbreds brought along in air-conditioned horse-pullmans so that when the expedition made camp that night the king could ride out in the desert as he liked to do before his evening prayers.

The king had been brought up in the Wahhabi ethic. He abstained from alcohol and tobacco and strictly observed the puritanical limitation of marriage to four wives at a time. His one point of departure was resistance to the Wahhabi notion that sexual congress should be conducted in the dark with entry from behind and climax to follow as soon as possible within the capacities of the male. When a wife professed that she considered face-to-face or oral sex risqué Hisham conducted his lovemaking with respect to her scruples but these wives he did not take along on trips; for him such excursions were a time of relaxation, of escape from palace protocol and renewal of his spirit in the great free spaces.

That night the motor caravan made camp at a small oasis some twenty miles from the old fort and modern air force base at Tebuk, and in the morning not long after dawn an acrobatic team of combat planes flew out from the base to execute various breathtaking patterns in his honor, an earsplitting tribute that he could have done without.

He prayed as usual, then breakfasted sparsely and climbed into a jeep for the short drive out to the test site.

. . .

The SEDAVs had been painted the bleached bone noncolor of the Saudi desert—fifty of them, sent over specifically for this show. You saw them first, if you saw them at all, as arrowy little plumes of sand converging out of the southeast into the attack proscenium, but you heard them well before that: the queer high howling of the supercharged gas turbines that could push along at eighty miles an hour.

The king applauded their entry as did the cabinet ministers seated with him behind the bulletproof glass window of the observation trailer: billionaires and princes, one and all, uncles or cousins or brothers or half brothers, all over six feet tall, all with the Aziz beaky noses and weak eyes and all arrayed like Hisham in checkered headdresses and long white cotton robes. Power was in the blood, for Ibn Sa'ud, as the saying went, had forged his nation with a sword of steel and installed its rulers with a sword of flesh.

In the row behind, the governor of the Saudi Arabian Monetary Agency passed a plate of rice cakes to the Riyadh representative of the friendly Chase Manhattan, the bank which served as investment adviser when large enterprises were afoot. Present also were the ADECT reps, three senior engineers, the SEDAV program manager, the Defense Department people; also the military attaché from the embassy, a handsome, squarely built man with a chest full of medals and clumps of gray hair sprouting from his nose and ears.

Colonel Nolan Jared, as the officer best equipped to answer the king's questions should he have any, stood in for the U.S. Army.

Creee-hee howled the SEDAVs . . .

They were in the trees now—palm trees, big ones, trucked over from the north coast and dug in here where no tree had ever been before. The howling little iron machines ripped them to splinters, toppled them over, spun them off in tangled stacks: wonderful to see! This done, they charged into their next obstacle, a river in a land that has no rivers, a pipeline having made it flow a week earlier after backhoes and bulldozers had dug its bed.

The SEDAVs muddled through. They made it. Swimming was not their forte but, by God, they could handle it, they swam like certain bony breeds of dogs which, by desperate paddling, manage to keep a few inches of nose in air to breathe by.

Amazing, though—how what looked to be solid truncated beetle-nosed pieces of steel could survive imminent drowning under fire pouring down from enemy emplacements, then scramble up the steep bank opposite, none the worse for their daredevil feat.

Now they had to take the gun positions.

Here the odds were hardly fair.

The artillery of the "defenders" (there were actually no human defenders in the redoubts) consisted of laser beams, registering hits and misses on an electronic signal system while the robots were shooting live ammo. Nothing phony, though, about the redoubts; they were no old-style mud huts but reinforced concrete pillboxes, the latest state of the art.

Too bad. Here the robots' turretless, self-loading, automatically sighting weapons were delivering... *rockets*... with hairline accuracy. First sand, then concrete, then bent and burned steel girders flew skyward and the robots raced up the hill to consolidate their victory.

Once more, applause from the king's trailer. Coffee and tea and sweet cakes went around again. Hisham made notes while Jared supplied a briefing on the next part of the exercise: the air raid phase.

Sand was flying again as the robots on the conquered hill dug themselves in, thus becoming aircraft batteries.

"Selective firing will begin at ranges determined as optimum by the autonomous sensors of the individual SEDAVs. . . ."

The colonel's voice droned on, and keeping pace with him, as if part of a slide lecture, planes from Tebuk Air Force Base appeared in the sky dragging white wobbly contrails behind them like angels' graffiti. These were F-15s, once the workhorses of the Saudi Air Defense but now obsolete, put back in service for menial jobs such as this today, which was towing targets. They came in high, the drone target planes behind them small and dark but highly visible until *whapwhap whapoo* went the robotic spunky cannons upon which the drones condensed into fierce little pinpoints of fire, then black smoke, then nothing.

Good. Very good indeed, but this time the very important group in the trailer with the big window and the glass roof kept their binoculars in action and failed to applaud as they had done during the previous drill because the second wave of F-15s was coming over and this time something was not right but horribly horribly wrong, in fact . . . obscene . . . because *whap* and another *whapwhap,* and if you could believe your eyes certain SEDAVs—it was impossible to tell which or how many, although certainly not all—had not bothered with the targets or were missing them with hideous ineptitude since you could clearly perceive that what they were hitting was the poor old bullfight horses, the F-15s, more smears of burning fuselage up there in the cerulean dome and then the sodden black death packages twisting down with the pilots inside them, those young proud Muslim loverboys serving their king with such élan and costing all that money to train, now dead out there somewhere and not only dead but . . . cremated . . .

There were also special cases, different cases, these the worst of all, these certain situations when a plane, not squarely hit, did not ignite, just suddenly disintegrated but the pilot had time to eject and his parachute opened but some berserk gun picked him off midway in his descent and the chute dutifully came on down with the shattered corpus delicti or whatever was left of it swinging gently, frivolously in its cords.

In the trailer the prince-ministers were on their feet now, shouting and gesticulating; not so King Hisham who remained seated, still staring out at the sands of destruction, the large moist eyes behind the thick glasses sheathed in a glaze of arctic ice, his desert warrior face wearing the look that came upon it only at the worst of times "such as," one of the cousinly ministers commented later, "the day his horse lost the Grand National."

The princes knew that in this mood he was best left alone. They made way for him, then fell in behind him as he strode out in the blazing air and signaled for the car that would take him back to the Wanderlodge.

In Washington, D.C., at approximately the same moment, although, due to the difference in time zones, it was ten hours later, Walden Wynans touched the button that stopped the closed-circuit telecast. He pushed himself out of his seat and left the room as fast as he could, followed by Sam Truscott and the bewildered witnesses from DARCOM and DARPA and the White House advisor in the crumpled gray flannel suit.

Every day in the Pentagon and sometimes many times a day the secretary strode past these same walls festooned with portraits of prior secretaries of defense in great gold frames. He had little curiosity about them, these great vanished chiefs. They had come and they had gone and some of them hadn't gone soon enough but there were only a handful who had left a signature behind them. James Forrestal was now remembered less for his organizing abilities than for his suicide; Charlie Wilson's leap into space, nearly as disastrous for his career, had been his statement that what was good for General Motors was good for the United States. Whiz kid McNamara from Ford Motors couldn't sell the Edsel but did a hell of a job peddling to L. B. Johnson a war that seemed hideously expensive until Caspar Weinberger proved that peace could cost more than conflict.

None of them, not one, Wynans knew, had credentials like his own. He had SEDAV, the magic weapon, a better and brighter accoutrement than any of his predecessors could lay claim to. It was his administrative handiwork, also a kind of job insurance.

Or had been, until this business at Tebuk . . .

He had been little disturbed that the robot's sole corporate supply source had recently been the target of a murder and a spy scam. There were always thefts, leaks, sabotage, stock manipulations, sellouts—such matters were the grist of arms purveyance. Even the slight shade of dissatisfaction in the Great Pudknocker's manner when discussing ADECT vis-à-vis TRW, for instance, had been inquisitive rather than significant.

This was different—unprecedented.

In the conference that followed in Wynans's suite in the elite E circle, the secretary knew that for the first time in his expansive career he faced a true crisis: a loose cannon. No telling what it might lead to. He was even reacting physically, his nerves jangling and his heart bumping in a preposterous, unruly way. He tried to take his pulse at the wrist, under the table, but desisted when he saw that the troll from the White House was watching him.

Enough of this! To reestablish control he expanded his lungs with deep drafts of high-level Pentagon air and performed his private version of biofeedback which consisted of contracting and relaxing his muscles at regular intervals, the powerful deltoids, the polo-hardened trapezii, but still, no doubt of it . . . he was upset. Had he been less so he might not have put down so peremptorily the gearhead from DARPA who suggested that the malfunction could have been the work of a single robot somehow programmed to perform differently from the others.

"—we went into the rogue or mad-dog concept at the time of that incident at ADECT. There was nothing in it."

But DARPA persisted.

"With all respect, sir, I don't think we ever eliminated the autodidactic potential of electronic brains. Recent experiments, as one keeps abreast of them . . ."

"My office also tries to keep abreast of them," interrupted the secretary, none too deferentially, "and I believe we do!"

"Then no doubt, Mr. Secretary," continued DARPA smoothly, "you are familiar with Professor Sejinowski's work at Johns Hopkins in the construction of neural-network computers, modeled on the interconnections of nerve cells in the brain. Left overnight, for instance, a system with just two hundred simulated neurons can teach itself to talk. What if . . ."

"If we begin to pay attention to what-ifs, sir," said Wynans, "we won't get far with the job in hand. I see counterintelligence at work here. I see security penetration and in all likelihood tampering with military hardware of a gross, a very flagrant kind. That's what we have to go after and pin down."

His glance went around the group.

The discussion had refocused, diverting only when moved into the channel of media control. There was no way this could be total but knowing the Saudis' paranoia about losing face (even when caused by circumstances beyond their control), you could figure the king would lay a security blackout on the episode; certainly there would not be the hullabaloo one could have looked for had the damn thing happened in the United States or Europe.

Across the diode-green of Wynans's PC a line flashed:
Schoenfeldt on #3.

Morton Asher Schoenfeldt, a veteran appointee, was secretary of state. Wynans went into another room to take the call.

"Morton. What's up?"

"Is it as bad as it sounds?"

"A bloody mess. We're hoping for some answers soon."

"But until then."

". . . fucking hell to pay . . ."

"You're taking the words out of my mouth. The bottom line is Mayday."

"For me, not for you, Morton. You're in the clear."

"Not at all. Here at State we set the stage, and when you go up to see The Man I'm going with you. I'd like Fogarty there too. I'll be happy to call him if that's all right with you."

"No objection. You know him better than I do."

Or than I want to, the secretary might have added, never having been completely charmed by the individual in question.

Daniel Fitzgerald Fogarty, known as the Harp, was director of the CIA. A former Speaker of the Texas State Legislature, grand sachem of the Dallas Republican machine, he had rapidly proved his grasp of the uses of power. From Langley to the Hill he had made himself respected and feared, the latter perhaps more than the former.

"Will you call me back?"

"In five minutes . . . half an hour at the outside."

Half an hour! That suddenly seemed a long time to wait . . .

It helped to talk to somebody and Morton was obviously hanging with him—up to a point; his tone had been encouraging. Tebuk was bad but not irreparable: that was what he seemed to be saying, so what the hell—wasn't that the way to play it? Maybe the only way?

Tests had gone wrong before. You tried to find out why, to identify the glitch or fix the blame, but looking back, the secretary had to feel that his own conduct had been blameless. He had acted prudently and professionally, strictly within the lines of established precedent.

All nations proficient at weapons making seek to vend their products to other nations. Such is the nature of defense and such had it been in the Pentagon under his custodianship.

There is hot rivalry in the sales competitions, and with good reason. First, of course, there is the original contract, running into a monstrous sum of money, as no one knew better than the secretary. Then comes the life-of-the-weapon deal for spare parts. This, before it has run its course, can amount to several times the original payment.

Crowning everything are the political advantages attached to the long-term relationship. Wynans had been expert in exploiting this: the technicians sent over to explain how the merchandise works and school the buyers in its use often stay on after their jobs are finished; their presence gives their land of origin a new diplomatic and political power base. Nor do they reduce native employment. On the contrary, by cloning new technicians, they open markets for more military sales and still further work and still more teachers.

And more and more money flows back to the homeland, fortifying its trade balance.

Through the years the relationship can be worth more than a state treaty signed before a thousand witnesses.

In Europe, presidents and prime ministers and in the Soviet Union the secretary general have conspicuously used their powers to close a major contract but in the United States, although the action swirls around the President, he seldom actively participates; by tradition and practice the ultimate responsibility rests upon the secretary of defense and the basic rule for him is: never fuck up a sale!

Well, he hadn't fucked up, not really. The SEDAV had proved its worthiness time and again and the army, skeptical at first, had integrated it into the forces. That meant it was ready for the international market where several large sales had already been consummated. Probably the biggest problems now would be, first, cooling the Pudknocker's wrath and, second, devising some means of placating the Saudis.

Morton was right, it was no time to dawdle. Best seize the lion by the tail, get on over to the bunker fast, even tonight if that were possible.

It was, he found: the secretary of state had set up an appointment for 2300 hours—and Fogarty would be with them.

"One for all and all for one," said Morton. "A Jew, an Irishman, and a WASP, the impossible coalition. How can we lose?"

SIXTEEN

CIA Director Daniel Fogarty was an ample man, a big man with a rosy skin, well padded in haunch, paunch, and jowl. He looked like a former football player (which he had never been) now gone to seed. Schoenfeldt, massive and saturnine, with a heavy humorous face and thick blond eyebrows brushed upward like little snouts, was almost as large and yet . . . both had mysteriously undergone some physical as well as status reduction, some shrinking or draining of their essential selves caused by the presence of the person lying on the couch.

Wynans wondered if this had happened to him too. Perhaps not; he was more used to coming down here than they were, to the free-fall in the elevator, the queer air and all, but as usual he was not comfortable, not himself in this environment.

Weaver had shown them in. He had set out chairs for them. Then he had bent close to the President and said, oh so gently, "The gentlemen are here now, sir," and he had lifted the queer-looking cloth wrap or rug off the President's legs. And then he had left and the President had swung his great bony legs down onto the carpet and sat up and looked at these three visiting homunculi with his yellow eyes.

The Pudknocker from the rattlesnake trails and the moonshine stills.

"I figure," he said, addressing Secretary Schoenfeldt, "we'll be hearing from King Hisham not later than tomorrow. Diplomatic pouch. Let me see a rough draft of the answer and we'll take it from there."

"Certainly, Mr. President," said the secretary.

"There will be restitution," said Gantt, "on a large scale along with whatever additional emollients seem appropriate." He looked at Fogarty. "Would you have any ideas on how to handle that, Dan?"

"I believe so, Mr. President," said Fogarty.

"Then kindly proceed, sir," said Gantt.

"Well, sir," said Fogarty, "I punched into our data bank and I believe I have identified a structure that might serve in this, uh, situation. One of my predecessors in office, the Honorable Mr. William Casey, set it up to fund certain black programs. It took shape in the form of an, uh . . . complex web."

He pulled a packet of notes out of his pocket and began rapidly leafing through them while the President watched him with granite patience.

"Maybe," he said after several seconds had gone by, "you might ease round the complexities and jest git to the web."

"Precisely, Mr. President," said Fogarty. "The essence of it—well, you might call it an informal extension of the Agency. Like a shadow CIA inside the Department of Defense. Mr. Casey moved funds around with it, funds that came out of, uh, certain pockets or recesses in the defense, uh, budget. That way the programs he had in mind did not require disclosure. Naturally no illegal action was involved since the defense application was certainly present but in the case of fairly magnum funds disclosure would not have been, uh, constructive and this method moved the process another layer of authority away from disclosure. It would have taken a very heavy investigation to arrive at, uh, disclosure. I felt that some such procedure might be relevant or even desirable in the present, uh, circumstances, should funding be involved. Once the necessary elements are in place, it can render a high degree of protection to the individuals and departments or agencies involved at the, uh, highest levels."

Daniel Fitzgerald Fogarty uttered all this rapidly and coherently in a carefully upgraded Texas accent, and the Pudknocker was nodding approval. Morton Schoenfeldt threw a look at Wynans as if to say, *You see now why I wanted him with us?*

The President said, ". . . thus providing us with a classic face-saver, eh, Mr. Fogarty? The theory of plausible denial . . ."

"Yes, sir," said the director briskly.

"A great idea, Mr. Fogarty. Comes down from the Middle Ages, I reckon—wonderful tool if you kin use it right. But sometimes it doesn't work, Mr. Fogarty—even for Mr. Casey, God rest his soul, it didn't always work. It got two presidents shit-deep in trouble and rousted another one clean out of office. I thank you for your presentation, sir, and I assure you I shall give it diligent thought, but I still hope there is some other way."

He sat hunched over, his thick splayed fingers spread on his knees and his head bowed, showing his tonsurelike bald spot. Gradually he straightened up, aiming a yellow lightning bolt at Wynans.

"Mr. Sec'tary, I assume we're working on a damage assessment. How long will that take?"

The secretary's wits surged back into action at flank speed.

"We should have rough figures in a few days, sir; the final will take a lot longer. A department team will be working around the clock with the Saudis and the ADECT people. Naturally we're looking at a devastating tragedy, sir, but my gut feeling is that what we'll find in due course is . . . sabotage. I still have complete faith in the robot as a proven and effective battle machine."

Gantt's mouth twitched but no reply came out. Could it be that the "theory of plausible denial," just now so sanctimoniously dismissed, was worming its ugly way in after all? At least no one would be able to say later that the President had reaffirmed his support of the SEDAV—nor could any say that he'd withdrawn it.

He got up slowly, stretching his arms in a kind of scarecrow way, and began unbuttoning his shirt.

"Gentlemen, I'm afraid we've reached the time and past the time when I retire. Been upstairs tonight at a shindig of my wife Lucy's, no way to get out of it, and now . . ."

Out of the dimness of the great cellary room, without apparent summons, Weaver had appeared, helping his master to undress.

". . . I intend to contact King Hisham in the morning. He's pragmatic—that's what you find, dealing with the Arabs, that's the way they are. We'll talk. Then I believe I'll write a presidential finding on the matter. That is the most aboveboard method we can use and still keep some degree of secret classification. That finding will go up the Hill to the chairmen of both defense committees and I'll advise them to come down here and discuss it with me if they're a mind to. In committee they will vote in camera, never let a trickle of it reach the floor. That's their kind of black program and they've done it for me and others in the past.

Oh, they'll buck and chomp but in the end they'll fall in line, they have to . . ."

Weaver pulled off the President's socks and pants, then held up the linsey-woolsey robe to preserve circumspection while Gantt stripped further. His big voice reached his listeners somewhat muffled.

"If I were you, Mr. Wynans, I'd prepare for traveling. Ever been in the Middle East? Well, that's nice space thereabouts. A goodwill tour. You might want to visit six or seven friendly countries, including Israel, but Hisham is your man. You should git along with him like kissin' cousins. Pick your own date, so long as it isn't later than next week."

Weaver lowered and folded the robe and the President, ready for the night now in a cotton nightshirt that covered him from chin to knees, strode forward to pay his farewells.

". . . Good night, gentlemen, and thank you for coming in."

The horror at Tebuk and the resulting highly charged and long-drawn-out negotiations were not the only forms of unpleasantness with which the secretary struggled during the next gloomy weeks. There was also new emphasis, conveyed as before through the U.S. Embassy in Moscow, of the undefined plot or scam still being actively mounted against him, in response to which Director Fogarty felt that more vigilance was needed. Additional agents had been assigned to provide this. Fogarty came over from Langley in person to furnish further details, "in case you observe any changes. Actually I doubt whether you will. The personnel employed are absolutely my top people, men and women who have been trained to operate with complete discretion. They are experienced in liasing with the Federal Bureau of Investigation when circumstances call for it, as they do now."

SEVENTEEN

Discretion! A wonderful exercise but one that did not remove the fact that for the present and the indeterminate future the secretary would be thrashing more than ever in a net of invisible eyes and electronic ears with dozens, perhaps hundreds of horrible, armed and fearfully protective goons gliding and sniffing around him day and night. One couldn't be secretary of defense without some of this but . . . good Lord, it couldn't be happening at a worse time.

It struck at the most sensitive center of Walden Wynans's life-style—the privacy which was now essential to his well-being.

He detested being watched. He measured the extent of it as a convict studies the height of the walls that hem him in and observes the routines of the guards in their towers.

Nothing was clearly defined, but as the weeks dragged along and the miserable Washington winter set in with its chills and sleet and the reek of the frigid Potomac in the air—how could the Founding Fathers have picked such a bog for a capital?—boredom leaned its weight on his soul.

The one blessed relief, earlier on, had been his "goodwill trip"—the swing through Jordan, Israel, Egypt, and Morocco (the last now an important policy concern) to Riyadh and King Hisham. He'd not received a palace audience on the date Ambassador Walters, having given due notice of his arrival, had requested, but several days later—a discourtesy he accepted with forbearance.

The king's frigidity lasted through the first interview and on into the second at which point, with matters of restitution and compensation reaching finality, the talk turned to horses, a rewarding diversion. Hisham was thoroughly familiar with the secretary's record in international polo; he didn't play himself but liked the game and had been in the stands at high-goal games in Hurlingham and the Argentine, where it had recently reached new heights of excellence. The king took him down to see his stables with a special stop at the oversize box stall that was the domain of Count Bruga, the chestnut stallion for which he'd paid $20 million at the Keeneland sales without ever having set eyes on him.

That afternoon, with Wynans packing to leave, a messenger in a Rolls-Royce accompanied by two motorcycle postilions arrived with an invitation from Hisham to ride with him next morning; they did some fifteen miles together on magnificent mounts, inspecting the king's irrigation projects, with trucks waiting to provide a change of horses every five miles. After that they were friends, or if not quite, at least friendlier; when he finally departed King Hisham presented him with a diamond and sapphire belt buckle.

A successful trip, and perhaps an international crisis forestalled. Not that there wasn't crisis at home, plenty of it, but continual crisis by some odd dichotomy bred dullness—the endless protocol appearances, the masses of paper to be gone through, the succession of conference tables like oblongs of brown ice with the bald and white and pewter-colored heads along the sides, the sharp pencils, the yellow pads, the water glasses—the boredom, the boredom of it all was what had laid the trap!

At first his resolve with regard to the de Saban girl had been inflexible but boredom had weakened and undermined it until finally, in a gesture of forthright independence, the secretary had thrust it from him altogether.

Jacqueline had left Miss Clampett's. Ilena had been downhearted at losing her company.

"She's a little mad, of course, but so much fun."

"What's she up to now?"

"Going to art school. She showed precious little interest in art while she was here."

Her father smiled. He could readily believe that art was less than an obsession with Mademoiselle de Saban. He'd begun running into her at gatherings where one would not have expected her to be, one such a rather obscure gala at the Cuban Embassy, he himself there only at the urging of Sam Truscott who argued that Angola, still a Cuban client, was coming into the market as a purchaser of U.S. arms.

How to account for her, then? Could her father, the marquis, be using her to gather information for his own diplomatic pouch? Hardly a convincing notion: de Saban's social contacts could provide him any information he might need without further help.

It struck him at times that these appearances of the girl's on the periphery of his life might not be entirely accidental and yet . . . she was always escorted by some young man, some lover or would-be lover who monopolized her attention: encountering the secretary, she would greet him with a smile and a wave, never less and never more. She kept her distance, a coolness which failed to make her less intriguing but suggested that, rather than conducting a campaign to attract him, she might not have forgiven him for his lack of . . . availability . . . that afternoon when they'd driven out together to the polo club.

And then one evening all this changed.

He was leaving a large cocktail party in McLean when he heard the fast clip-clip of high heels behind him on the driveway and her hand slipped into his; he knew it was she before he turned to look, although he hadn't spoken to her at the party.

"I suppose you came in that huge English car with the chauffeur?"

"I did."

She could have assumed the car. What she must have noticed more particularly was that he had come without Barbara.

"Well, send them both away. I'll give you a ride."

"I don't see why not," said the secretary.

Her Volkswagen was tiny, cramped, and frigid, the heater broken and the wheels out of alignment, giving the whole ramshackle pile of bolts a vicious wobble little modified by her odd manner of driving, her eyes flicking left and right, as if searching for some parkway exit unfamiliar to Wynans. She finally found it, pulled into it, and a little way along swerved into a dogwood patch opposite a private driveway flanked by two monumental gateposts on which brilliant pear-shaped globes of light were gleaming, the exposure failing to cause her a moment's hesitation as she wriggled out of her coat, too thin for the weather, and poked a big hard nipple into his mouth. After a little of this—too little actually for Wynans's taste—other garments came off helter-skelter until with charming abandon and a queer, hoarse little moan she impaled herself on top of him; as they made love the car rocked and buckled on its miserable shocks and her sweet juices poured down, saturating his dark trousers (he'd been due, after the cocktails, at a formal dinner) past all hope of immediate or perhaps ultimate restoration.

"If you want," she said later, "we can go to my place, but you'll have to leave at twelve o'clock. That's when my roommate gets out of work."

In due course of time they dispensed with the roommate, then with the apartment; soon she was properly installed in a far more attractive and convenient suite in the Watergate. He was discreet about his visits. He was proud of that. There were even times when he eluded the damned security goons. Nevertheless, coming down to breakfast on a nice Sunday in April, with spring bright in the air, he found that Barbara had ordered service on the terrace. She poured him a cup of coffee and while he was drinking it handed him the "People" page of *The Washington Post,* folded to a blind item she had marked in pencil.

With this she remarked in the carefully detached fashion which she reserved for dire confrontations:

"I see that you are having an affair."

The secretary lowered the paper. Over the top of it he surveyed his wife with a glance ever so slightly mocking but quite bland—a glance such as no guilty man could ever have produced.

But Barbara remained unconvinced.

"It could be, don't you think?"

He shook his head. "They make a lot of trouble."

"Who?"

"Shit-slinging columnists."

"So do people who have affairs."

"Darling . . ."

"All *right!*" she said. "But we ought to talk about this for a minute. I think a lot of other people will be doing that right now."

"What is there to talk about? It's quite absurd, Barbara."

"I'm glad you think so."

"I do think so. And I'd like to drop it."

"If you weren't the person referred to in this item, *I'd like to hear you say so!* Can you say so and mean it?"

And though she spoke so resolutely she looked at him timidly, despairingly, and her defenselessness touched him and he said thickly, "On my honor. I swear it on my honor."

And saying this he swung his chair around and took both her hands. He pressed her hands, then raised them to his lips. Such was his emotion at this moment that he could convince even himself that it had not been he but someone else, some other faithless scoundrel who had been misbehaving with a lady not identified.

"I'm glad," she said softly. "Glad to accept your statement."

But what now, he thought, *what reservations is she hiding?*

And just to tidy the matter up and pack it away forever he had added boldly, ". . . but you could have been a little more trusting, pussycat."

"Perhaps I could be," she said, getting the last word as usual, "if I could also be more forgetful—" an allusion (not all that oblique) to an incident some five years ago, involving a father, a very young woman, and a private investigator.

"All right. Enough. Over and done with," said the secretary complacently. He plunged into his breakfast, poured more coffee, glanced at other news in the paper—for there was other news, mountains of it, all more fascinating than the detestable line and a half of the blind item; on some of this material he drew for conversation, also on comments about the party the night before, a dancing party on Embassy Row that he and Barbara had attended, though for some reason he had gone off somewhere afterward and come in quite late. . . .

Thus he established the climate of *breakfast as usual . . .* and for her part Barbara did not resist, though she did not quite participate either, her wan face ravaged by the bright sunlight that revealed everything, her suffering, her doubts, her effort, since there really was no other way, to trust again, at least to some extent . . .

And Wynans felt content. It had been a close call, but he had acquitted himself well. He had got out of it. And in his well-being and his lusty enjoyment of life he thought again of the strange, timid, hopeless look she had given him after mentioning the item, and he pitied her all over again and realized how much he loved her.

That was the truth, and it was what made his predicament so sticky. His Barbara! It was not her fault that she had aged. Everyone aged; even he himself would age in time. It was most certainly not her fault that he was still so vigorous, that he looked younger than his age. It was unfair to take advantage. It was also stupid. Surely there must be a way to break it off. Hell, he could do it on the telephone. One call would be enough.

However, for the time being he refrained from so drastic a step—this a mistake, as he discovered hardly three weeks after the blind item. Entering his dining room alone (Barbara having gone out to the theater), he found an envelope propped against a wineglass and addressed to him in his wife's hand. Inside was a candid of a girl with her hand on the door of a car, evidently about to open it and get in, he himself in the driver's seat, leaning forward to help with the door. The license plate of the car was readable. It was also traceable: the license of a new silver Club Sport Porsche Jacqueline was leasing to replace the old wreck that had once served so well as a theater of love.

The secretary put the photograph in his pocket. He was very angry. To think that Barbara, whom he trusted, would hire a private eye to trail him and snap pictures of him was disgusting. He soon found that she had also tricked him another way; she and her maid had removed all her things from their third floor suite and put them in a bedroom lower down.

She sent word that she would stay in the house only until she could find a place of her own.

It had boiled down to a hideous stalemate. The one ray of hope lay in the fact that she had not gone public. There had been no more press items, not even blind ones. And tonight, when her absence would have been conspicuous, she had agreed for the first time in nearly three weeks to attend a large affair.

PRESIDENT AND MRS. CLAUDE C. GANTT

request your presence at a dinner honoring

MUHAMMED ALI GUELTA

President, the Republic of Morocco

on Saturday, March eleventh, nineteen hundred and—
at 1850 hours

White Tie   RSVP

EIGHTEEN

"Lean—lean out. No way you can hit that shot with your ass in the saddle."

"I am leaning out, for Christ's sake."

"Lean more. Grab a handful of mane if you have to."

"What mane?" said Sam Truscott. "There is no mane on this hobbyhorse . . ."

For close to an hour the basement had resounded with this type of chatter along with the crash of polo balls struck off a wooden floor and sent spinning against steel mesh. Wynans had installed the practice cage to keep himself in shape during the off-season; now he was coaching Truscott, a beginner at the game, helping him to get some basics in hand before he climbed on live mounts. This evening's session was about over; Sam made a few more tries at hitting a neck shot to the secretary's satisfaction, then got off his dummy animal, dripping wet; the secretary handed him a bath towel which the deputy draped over his naked, skinny shoulders.

"When can we get out of doors?" he demanded as they waited for the elevator. "This sweatbox is wearing me out."

"One chukka on turf will wear you out a lot quicker."

"Well, I'm ready."

"I'll tell you when you're ready. But maybe next week. I called the stable today and the word is, the ground's firming up."

With a discreet bump the elevator settled at the basement level. The secretary was proud of this elevator. He and Barbara had installed it when they'd bought the house some ten years ago; the guides who took visitors through on United Washington House Tours (for charity) described it as "the most interesting elevator in Georgetown," as it undoubtedly was—a wonderful little gilt box full of brass and mirrors. It always worked perfectly, but today something happened; though Wynans had pressed the button for Three, it stopped perversely at One. Then the door opened and there stood Barbara Wynans in a dark mink coat with a plastic shopping bag in one hand. Seeing the two men, she drew back. A look of hesitation, almost of revulsion squeezed her stylish, aquiline face, as she looked at each in turn; she even said something not quite audible, something like "Excuse me—" . . . could that have been it?

But she got in after all.

"Hello, Barbara," said Truscott, "how have you been?"

"Fine, thank you Sam, and you?"

She turned her cheek toward him for the ritual social kiss, at the same time punching for floor Two.

"I get off here," she said. And did so.

"See you later, then," said Truscott to her vanishing figure. The door closed again. During the brief ride she had directed neither word nor glance at her husband, who for his part had stood with his great head high in the air and his eyes fixed straight ahead, his muscular body jammed into a corner of the gilt box.

"I detect a certain chill," Truscott ventured.

"The North Pole," said the secretary, "is a lot warmer. But don't take my word for it. Go there and you'll see."

"I'll take your word for it," said Truscott meekly. Then after a pause he added, "But at least perhaps tonight . . ."

"Possibly," said the secretary. "If so, it's thanks to Mona. Please tell her again how much I appreciate it."

"She was glad to do it. She thinks it's all—most unfortunate."

"Well, it is, it is," said the secretary heartily.

It had been Mona Truscott who had persuaded Barbara to attend the presidential party, "if only for appearance' sake." The two couples had long been close, Sam a college pal and now quite appropriately, undersecretary of defense. Walden Wynans had been best man when Sam Truscott chose to marry a graduate of a Mormon agricultural college and Barbara Wynans had gaily and warmly taken the bride in hand to teach her the ways of the world she was entering. Both women, though they came from opposite sides of the continent and totally different social backgrounds, were rather lonely in Washington; both now had a whole series of activities they shared, just as the men did. The camaraderie within the foursome had become a joy and a source of replenishment for all; maintaining it, rather than any fondness for Wynans, whose conduct she described as "apelike, he should be in jail," had motivated Mona to act as peacemaker.

The men had come to polo practice direct from the Pentagon, Truscott bringing his evening clothes in a carryon which Wynans's valet, Bernard, had unpacked for him. The total dressing procedure, which included showering (in separate stall showers) and massage (by a Japanese masseur, a permanent fixture of the house staff) had reached the final stages: Wynans stood facing a huge bevel-edge mirror while Bernard, on a stool behind him, reached over his shoulders to tie the white bow which Wynans never seemed to do properly (although he could tie a black one all right).

Sam had tied his own. Sam had been a navy pilot and had the air medal to prove it—a considerable medal. Wynans envied that. He unfortunately had no military adornments whatever; during the time Sam had acquired his medal in Vietnam, Wynans had been on a State Department errand in India, playing polo with a high-goal team on the fields of the former maharaja of Jodhpur.

Bernard passed the secretary a morocco box containing his own decorations. He selected the two best: the Order of Leopold, bestowed by the king of Belgium in recognition of his help with certain procurement contracts, and the Legion d'Honneur, Second Class, from D'Estaing, for much the same. Not the best. Not as good as Sam's by a long shot, but they'd do. He stuck them on. Mona had already sent up word that she was waiting outside. It had seemed best for the two couples to use separate limousines, since they might leave the party at different times.

The abominable Potomac climate had turned mean again. Raindrops as hard as grains of rice whizzed past with the speed of bullets.

Barbara looked ravishing. She'd protected her hair with a new scarf with gold spangles on it, probably what she'd gone out to buy that afternoon.

Man and wife sat at a respectful distance from each other as the official car rolled through the wet, brilliantly lighted streets.

The crassness of it, he was thinking, *setting a gumshoe to spy on me!*

And then . . . then without the slightest plan but from some stirring deep in his soul he said aloud, "Barb, I can't stand this. I've broken with the silly kid. It was just some kind of insanity. Can't we get back together?"

But her profile remained just that—the side view of a face intractable as marble, only just a shade too aquiline, begotten and shaped in highly refined circumstances in the town of Devon, on the Philadelphia-Paoli line.

"Goddamn it. Say something!"

"Why?" she said quietly. "We've been through all this before."

"I've been miserable, Barb."

"That's heartbreaking."

"I've waited for some word from you . . . the slightest sign that you . . ."

"If you want signs, call the signal corps."

A cheap shot, unworthy of her. But he persisted. "Have you been happy? Because if you say you have I'll know you're lying."

"No," she said slowly and distinctly, "I have not been happy, if that's any satisfaction to you."

"It's not any satisfaction to me. I haven't had one happy day since—"

"Let's not go into it."

"I wasn't going into it. All I know is that it wouldn't be the same. It probably couldn't be, perhaps not ever but . . . we could make an effort. We could try it out."

At this, she turned toward him for the first time.

A streetlight dumped an odd, crafty look into her eyes. Or perhaps the look was there already . . .

"I'm not sure you're up to it."

"All right. But why not find out?"

He put out his gloved hand pleadingly and she touched it lightly, letting her fingers rest on his for a second or two before moving it away.

"I just might take you at your word—I just might test you."

There was no time to say more. The limousines crawled forward in the storm, police helicopters circling overhead. Electronic decals moved the line through the security checkpoint in Lafayette Square after which Secret Service operators conducted an inspection at the East Gate.

Gantt was not one to relax precautions; indeed, on such nights as this, he intensified them. There was risk, of course. No matter what you did there was still risk, but he was President and he accepted the full duties of the presidency. This included entertaining. Here he had perfected his own style. He had reviewed the fashions of his predecessors and discarded them. He was not about to let 45,000 invited guests troop through his halls his first year in office, the way Nixon had, nor fill the state dining room with long-haired artists and Nobel laureates like Kennedy; he made no effort to cater to the smug, Republican elitists, his predecessors, who had no use for him anyway. Oddly enough these same snobs were the ones who competed hardest for invitations to his galas if only to see whether it was true that Lucy Pearl Gantt, like Abigail Adams, hung out laundry to dry in the Red Room (she did not) or taught Appalachian dancing to the prime ministers of West Germany and Great Britain (she had). Serving sour mash whiskey to the presidents of Egypt and Venezuela and hominy grits to the kings of Jordan and Spain, the Gantts delighted the folk of distant lands who conceived of America as people with strong stomachs and rugged tastes.

Dinner tonight consisted of Norfolk oysters, calf's-head soup, Maryland terrapin, soft-shell crabs, broiled buffalo steak, and cherries jubilee; square dancing began at ten, the guests splitting up into units of eight, each group including a hill-country instructor to guide them through the steps.

The President led off with the Varsouviana. At the first note of the fiddle he crossed the floor and ceremoniously bent his tilting Tin Man body to request the hand of Lucy Pearl, she done up in gray taffeta from Givenchy. They danced with grave and innocent dexterity, three quick steps and turn, three reversed and another turn, her small feet flying to keep up with his huge ones, her eyes flashing with love and pride. The guests gave them a standing ovation.

Wynans went in search of Guelta, who had sat near him during dinner. The two had spent a lot of time together in the last ten days, locked into the DOD's well-established routine for high-ranking military visitors known as "taking a look at the bases." They had inspected the R&D at Eglen AFB in Florida, the R&D at China Lake, the surveillance systems at Offut, the radar watch in the Northern Command. The Moroccan hadn't specified what he wanted most to see, but he had lingered in Detroit and asked for more time at Lima, Ohio, where tanks were made.

Armor! Truscott, who had ridden shotgun through most of the trip, felt that armor was the key, his interest there quite evident even if—as

seemed highly probable—the visitor had heard rumbles of the donny-
brook in the Saudi wasteland.

He popped unexpected questions. He'd been sniffing around.

It was well known that during his Soviet phase he had attended the
general staff school in Frunze, where he might have shed some of his
strict Islamic puritanism but never had. His one indulgence was a
passion for gambling, particularly at gin rummy. He might have held
his own with an inferior gamesman but in Wynans he had an adversary
for whom proficiency in parlor games as in all forms of sport was a status
requirement, instilled in early youth. No cash changed hands; instead
a running book was kept, the balance running heavily against Guelta.

"I don't want to keep playing with him," the secretary told Truscott.

"Then you should either settle up and quit—or start losing."

"I want to lose, but I can't make myself do it. Force of habit, I
suppose."

Now the Moroccan's hand was on his shoulder.

"How about a little game?"

"Fine, Mr. President, I'd like nothing better. But can we put it off ten
minutes? I must dance with my wife."

"Later then. Tonight I'm going to get even."

And with this Guelta moved away.

The country band had given way to a band famous for its renderings
of soft Brazilian rock, the latest craze but one which drove most of the
older people off the floor. Not so Wynans. He had been learning the
steps and enjoyed their sensual, muted beat; he danced with Senator
John Lighty's granddaughter, a wild little blonde, married to somebody
in State. She danced like some kind of mad marionette, bumping him
with her hip if he made a mistake and stamping on the turns; leaving
her with reluctance, he took on the wives of two younger men in his
department, one staid and detached, the other feverishly anxious to
please her husband's superior, regardless of consequences. What consequences? He shuddered to imagine . . .

And then, at last—Barbara, her body, as he put his arm around her,
strange and stiff as if she were trying to pretend that she wasn't his at
all, that there had never been those certain times which she must remember, as he did so vividly, those dances in their own great house in
the days when they had entertained so much there. The bigger groups
had been the best because sometimes, in the crush, they had put their
secret code in operation, neither had to say anything, the only rule was

that they mustn't leave together; she would go up first and he would find her with her clothes off, ready to make love.

God, how sweet those times were, how much he would have liked to bring them back! But alas—small chance of that—for all was changed, and now, instead of a kiss—how did the old song go?—a crock of piss flew over the garden wall.

NINETEEN

When the sheet was tallied on the secretary's pocket calculator—an early ADECT product—the Moroccan had won back all but a thousand dollars of his debt. This pleased him immensely—and Wynans hardly less. He took the president's arm in friendly style, fitting his stride to Guelta's shorter steps as they rejoined the other guests.

The first band had struck up "Good Night, Ladies"; White House parties by Gantt's rules folded at twelve-thirty when the President, omitting formal good-byes, escorted Lucy Pearl upstairs.

Rain was falling, the air warmer now, the drops bigger and gentler; Wynans enjoyed their touch on his bare head. He could see his driver near the head of the line and hurried toward him, glad that Barbara had sent him back after all, it was considerate of her.

"Cross the bridge, I'll tell you when to stop."

A powerful idea had taken shape in his soul: *One more time!* There absolutely must be *one more time.*

You couldn't just walk out and slam the door. He wasn't made that way.

"Right here . . . pull over to the curb. And thank you very much . . . Good night . . ."

He seldom tipped the departmental chauffeurs but, rolling down the tonneau window, he slipped a hundred-dollar bill into the man's hand. No more need be said. If these fellows gossiped about where they dropped their passengers, they wouldn't last long behind the wheel.

Gossip, really, was his dread. That was what undid the best-laid plans—and the best-laid people. It was, he well knew, what had prompted Barbara to set a gumshoe on his heels, with such unfortunate results; any evasive tactics that he might employ, as need arose, were designed solely to frustrate gumshoeing. As for the other kind of surveillance, the official kind—now so much intensified—there was no avoiding it, one simply accepted it, an affliction predicated on his job of work.

The neighborhood was tacky, a jumble of aging houses and roadside businesses. The little deli here closed late and there was a pay phone in it which he had used before. He made two calls, one to that certain apartment in the Watergate, the second for a cab. Waiting, he looked at the stuff in the showcase, the sleek dried herrings, the pastrami, the red slab of roast beef; though he had finished a good dinner hardly three hours earlier, he was suddenly hungry and ordered a lox sandwich. While he was eating it, the old-fashioned bell on the door tinkled and a young Latin-type woman came in and bought a six-pack of beer. She was miserably thin and garishly dressed. She also looked cold. He decided that she was probably a prostitute. There was nothing attractive about her, but in his present mood he wanted to share his well-being with her. While the proprietor was putting her six-pack in a bag, he said genially, "Make this young lady a sandwich, whatever she wants—on my tab."

The woman's expression changed. She looked at Wynans first with surprise, then anger. Without a word she took her package and hurried out of the store, bumping him rudely as she passed.

This behavior seemed hilarious to Wynans. He broke into laughter. He was still laughing when his cab arrived.

"Sheraton-Carlton," he told the driver.

Back across the bridge they went, the secretary quite sure now that he had avoided any tail. Just as a final precaution, however, he spent five minutes in the Sheraton lavatory, then took a second cab. He got out a few blocks from the Watergate and walked the remaining distance, entering through the garage. He used his own card key to operate the elevator, then another card that opened the apartment door.

Sartre, a yellow cat, was sleeping on the living room couch. He jumped down with glowing eyes and spat at the secretary. They were not friends but Wynans tolerated him. He recognized the cat's right to defend his mistress.

"Pretty pussy," he said with distaste.

Seizing Sartre by the fur, he hurled him back on the couch. Then he walked on tiptoe to the bedroom.

Jacqueline de Saban lay nude and beautiful in the center of an enormous four-poster, fast asleep but not alone. Across her legs, with one arm thrown back, curled a slender black girl, also naked. From the condition of the bedclothes it seemed evident that they had been making love, an intimation which disturbed the secretary not at all. Standing at the foot of the bed, he began rapidly shedding his clothes, dropping them on the floor; he did this as quietly as possible but the slight stir roused the black girl, who opened her eyes. The secretary ignored her and she for her part made no move to cover herself or change her position, merely watching him intently and sleepily, with a veiled, silky hostility.

"*Tiens, nous avons un invité!*" she said at length.

Jacqueline de Saban tried to sit up. She had first to remove the black girl's long, pretty thigh from her pelvis. This accomplished, she smiled radiantly at the secretary.

"You are late, *chéri.*"

"I came as fast as I could."

". . . and you have been eating onions . . ."

"A sandwich . . ."

"Did you bring me one?"

"I'm sorry, I did not."

"You're a pig."

"There must be something in the icebox."

"There is not."

"Shall we send out?"

Jacqueline reflected.

"No. I don't really care." And then she added sweetly, "That you are here is enough, *chéri.* We have been waiting. This is Mariangelica, my best friend from Paris."

"How do you do, Mariangelica," said the secretary amiably.

"*Merde,*" said Mariangelica.

She leaped off the bed and rushed into the bathroom, slamming the door.

"What's wrong with her?" said the secretary.

"She's jealous, that's all. She is very sensitive and she adores me but she likes men also. She is absolutely the world's most famous fashion model, of *las Negresses.*"

"Do we really have to have her?"

"Yes, of course, otherwise she would be dreadfully humiliated. . . . Stand a little closer."

For several moments, first with one hand, then the other—"the little paws," as Wynans still thought of them—she had been massaging the secretary's large, thick member—never from the first completely passive and now well on the way to full arousal.

"Mariangelica, come here."

There was no answer from the bathroom. Jacqueline de Saban winked. She pushed away the cat, which had stalked through the open door, his yellow eyes rolling.

"Mariangelica," she called once more.

The bathroom door opened slightly, then wider. Mariangelica emerged with a towel around her head. She had wide thin shoulders, narrow hips, and hardly any breasts at all. Her features were delicate and childlike and her expression serene and scornful. She advanced toward the bed with slow, weaving steps, studying the secretary attentively and, as it were, academically.

"Quel horreur!"

"D'accord, mais c'est mon horreur à moi!"

She took hold of the secretary's scrotum, pulling him down.

"C'est ça que tu pense?" said Mariangelica, and with this she too joined them on the bed.

Though experiencing pleasure, the secretary could not help but feel that events were taking an odd turn. Through the years women had raised a great public outcry against being treated as sex objects, yet here were a pair of young, very attractive women treating him as if he were exactly such an object and in fact as if all he amounted to in the way of being a man and a force in world affairs were now reduced to his penis. He lay on his back watching as if from a great distance while the two girls passed *le horreur* back and forth between them, each bringing her own kind of joy and ferocity to the attack but also . . . sometimes breaking off and leaving him alone while they kissed and licked each other.

He couldn't stand this kind of goings-on, he would not put up with it, and pulling Mariangelica off him by the hair he cried hoarsely,

"Jacqueline . . ."

"Maintenant, chéri, maintenant," said Jacqueline.

She was now very excited. Her thighs were glistening wet and her cheeks sucked in, her upper lip drawn back so that the tiny, unusual piece of cartilage attaching this lip to her mouth, which he had first noticed in that long-ago drive from Miss Clampett's to Middleburg, was visible. With her hands clasped around her own plump breasts she slid adeptly up and down on him, a procedure which she changed, always at just the right moment, rotating her beautiful little buttocks, orgasming once, then a second time with a series of racking shudders but refusing to grant him the same privilege. And all this was not an act, as it would have been with a whore, no matter how splendid and passionate a whore . . . it was real, real passion, real feeling . . . *young stuff,* the wonder of *young stuff,* Wynans's lifelong addiction, a thousand times greater than ever because of his abstinence during all the days when due to his efforts to get reconciled with Barbara he had been staying away.

"*Chéri* . . . I am coming again," said Jacqueline.

"*Bête!*" yelled Mariangelica.

And now, abandoning her role as voyeur, Mariangelica was straddling him above the shoulders, holding herself open with long tapering fingers while she jerked her wet stubby clitoris on his tongue.

Sartre too was on the bed. Sartre was mewing, was rubbing and grubbing around the three of them. . . . *Jesus,* he thought, *do they let the cat into these orgies?* . . . but then he realized the noises didn't come from Sartre but from Mariangelica. As she came, he pushed her off him and took hold of Jacqueline. She had swiveled around, without releasing him, so that her back was turned to him; hunching very fast now and with his hands on her hips to give her added weight, he drove up into her, feeling himself released at last as he exploded in spasms that seemed as if they would never end and gave him, while they lasted, a feeling as if his cock was fused with his backbone. He was still experiencing this feeling when the cat bit, then scratched him. He knocked Sartre onto the floor, where it let out a screech and disappeared.

For some minutes the room, a scene of carnage, became as still as a graveyard, the three bodies hardly touching on the enormous bed, the cat nowhere to be seen.

The secretary was the first to stir. He was getting cold; what was more, either from the lox or from the love, he had a fearful thirst.

He hoisted himself up. Only a few days earlier he had sent round a case of Tattinger, a gift of atonement for recent neglect. It couldn't be all gone. He put on his trousers for warmth, then padded through the living room into the kitchen. The wine was still there all right, but none of it had been chilled, nor could he find an ice bucket; he substituted a large pot. This he filled with ice cubes, setting the bottle tenderly among them and three glasses on top of it all. No sound yet from the bedroom but . . . from somewhere a noise that was not . . . natural.

As the secretary left the kitchen the front door opened and a stocky baldish man walked in and looked around as if he owned the place; then, noticing the secretary, he said quietly, "Excuse me, sir."

"What do you want?" said Wynans.

His first thought was that this was one of the house security men who had wandered in by mistake; they all had passcards.

But the intruder was not as calm as he'd first seemed. His lower jaw was quivering and his words were not clear.

"Hmmm . . . mmmm . . . Investigative Service . . ."

He was holding out something at arm's length for the secretary to inspect—a badge in a leather case.

Wynans dropped the pot on the floor. He hit the man and knocked him down. The fellow rolled against the wall, then got up on all fours: he scrambled among the ice cubes and broken wineglasses, looking for his badge.

". . . Get out! . . ."

Wynans now knew very well what this was. He also knew that if there was one thing he didn't want it was that flatfoot in the bedroom. He grabbed the fellow by the coat as he rose to his feet and was about to heave him through the door, which still stood open . . . and would certainly have done so had it not been that at that moment Barbara walked in, wearing her mink as usual along with the same spangly scarf she'd had in the car.

"You would do something like this," said Wynans with disgust.

"I gave you fair warning," she said coolly.

"Like hell you did."

"I said I'd test you, so I have. You flunked."

"Do you mind leaving?"

"Not at all."

But instead of leaving she moved toward the bedroom.

Wynans grabbed her. This turned out to be a mistake since the sleuth, bleeding from the nose, got there ahead and snapped pictures with an Instamatic. Then he and the false treacherous wife left together.

Jacqueline was weeping.

"Oh, I'm so sorry, *chéri.*"

"Don't be ridiculous," said Wynans.

"But what will happen now? It will cost you some terrible price and it is all my fault."

"Not at all," said Wynans. "It doesn't matter in the least. It was just very, very rude and absolutely beneath contempt for her to do what she did and I apologize for her. She'll gain nothing by it, she just did it out of spite. She had no business coming here at all."

"*Bien sûr!*" said Mariangelica, who evidently understood more English than she let on. She was now fully and very stylishly dressed and ready to go out. She kissed Jacqueline on the cheek. "Will you call a taxi for me?"

"The number is beside the telephone," Jacqueline said in English. She embraced Wynans.

"You will blame me now and you will stop loving me."

"I will not."

"Oh, yes. Now you don't think so, but I know about such things, I can tell. You will decide it was all my fault."

"It was not your fault and it absolutely doesn't matter. You must take my word for it. It may be just as well it's all turned out this way. It's just one more problem nobody has to think about."

. . . for it didn't matter and that was the truth, he told himself again, dropping off to sleep exhausted and satiated, his hand throbbing where he had hit the detective but his mind lulled and drugged with a number of glasses of champagne and one more sweet quick bout with Jacqueline. He lay in the disordered bedroom, in the canopied bed with the little French nymphet curled up against his back and Sartre slumbering at their feet. Far back at the edge of his brain was a black area which he could contain now even if it would expand later into the knowledge that his life had suffered a drastic shock, that its commendable order and regularity, so necessary to him, would immediately be altered, its underpinnings knocked awry and all sorts of new and painful adjustments made which would leave everything different.

Scandal had threatened before. It had nibbled mousily on the rind of his reputation but there it had stopped. This time, Barbara had the upper hand. She would be mean and she well knew how to be so, just as she well knew how to be sweet, to be gracious, to make people like her and see her side of things. Suddenly a vile thought clove through the vapors of the secretary's brain; it made his body twitch and nipped his mind back to consciousness like the touch of a red-hot poker.

Could tonight's incident somehow relate to the warnings the embassy had conveyed—the rumble of some devious Moscow campaign to unseat him? And could it now, randomly combined with the Saudi fiasco, accomplish this very purpose?

The secretary pushed the thought away. Such fantasies beset the human mind only when untoward events have frayed its accustomed fastenings . . . or thus the secretary's common sense informed him, but for a long time in the downy bed of love he lay awake peering at the future with few conclusions that were reassuring.

Jacqueline rose late. After a night of sexual extravagance she always experienced a rush of new energy and an impulse for righteous deeds. First she made a mandatory phone call, following which she cooked herself a big breakfast, then cleaned her apartment from wall to wall. She had just finished when her father called, inviting her to lunch at the Madison.

He wasted no time making clear the purpose of the meeting.

"I have decided that Washington is no longer a good place for you. You are to go back to Paris and live with your mother."

She gave him a hard, furtive look. Had he picked up some gossip? That was quite possible—in fact she had felt it inevitable—though surely the drama of last night would be exempt, at least for now. News traveled fast in the Capitol but not that fast.

"I thought you brought me here to remove me from the evils of Paris."

The Marquis de Saban took a sip of wine. He had begun the conversation in English. He now switched to French.

"I disapproved of your companions there, particularly at that place in the Rue des Anciennes Comédies or wherever it was. Political riffraff."

"Students, Papa. Intellectuals. Some of them were very nice."

"Radicals," said the marquis, "Communists—proselytizing you for their own purposes as they do with young people the world over, young people like yourself fretting against authority and looking for excitement in the streets."

"And the right type, I suppose, were those snobs at Miss Clampett's?"

"Miss Clampett's benefited you in many ways. It was a good experience. I did not object to your leaving in order to study art, but you have not been studying art. I checked with the institute. You have not attended classes."

"They were dull."

"Many things that are worthwhile are also dull. Like keeping one's accounts, for instance. It is impossible to understand how, on your allowance, you can afford that expensive apartment."

". . . unless I have had help, Papa? Is that what you were going to add?"

The Marquis de Saban made no reply. He concentrated on his *entrecôte à la béarnaise,* broiled to exactly the right rareness inside, black without.

Said Jacqueline brazenly, "I *have* had help, Papa. You are quite right."

The marquis's only reaction was a slight additional color, by no means approaching that of the steak, darkening his already swarthy cheekbones. How handsome he was! Few women could resist him, a vulnerability which his daughter, at a particularly fragile age, had shared: it was this that thereafter gave her a certain independence, a power she used rarely and only when backed into a corner.

"You can stop my allowance at any time, Papa, as you know. I suppose I can stand that. But I'm not going back to Paris. I love Mama but I can't put up with her ways, the priests and nuns padding around and the windows locked so as not to let in a breath of air. That was why I started going to the Rue des Anciennes Comédies in the first place and I'm very glad I did."

The remainder of the meal passed with little communication, though on leavetaking the marquis, brightening, offered to drop Jacqueline wherever she wished. She declined. Hailing a cab on Connecticut Avenue, she drove out 16th Street toward the Army Medical Center, getting out near Rock Creek Park. She walked east along Missouri to one of those red brick buildings, part stores, part dwellings, rapidly disappearing from the Washington scene. Here, over a computer service shop, lived her control. He had a new housekeeper now, who did not know her, but Valentin Rudenko heard her voice and called from the back room for her to come in. He was propped up as usual with a mountain of pillows, his long hair a mess but his pale jowly face freshly shaven. As usual also there was a bottle of vodka cooling in a bucket by the bed. He made no effort to get up but waved to her indolently, his eyes full of welcome.

"So you are a success. My God, what goings-on! Like an Italian opera. How do you feel? Sit down, sit down!"

"I feel lousy, if you want to know," said Jacqueline.

She pushed newspapers from a stiff chair and seated herself gingerly on its edge.

"Have a drink."

"No thanks."

"Darling," said Rudenko, "once more I assure you—your name will not surface. Not in the newspapers, not on television. It will not be mentioned in court proceedings, if there actually are such proceedings."

"Is that the law?"

"It is not exactly the law, but it is the way such things are handled. That is how it is done in the United States. Take my word for it. Here—"

Groping for the chilled vodka, he poured her some in a glass which did not look very clean. She could not bring herself to drink from it.

"Listen, Tino," she said, "I want to get out of town."

"Certainly, darling," said Rudenko. "Why not?"

"But I mean right away. Or as soon as possible."

"It shall be arranged." He studied her affectionately. He seemed very pleased. "And I am delighted—happy indeed that you have changed your mind. That you wish another assignment, in short."

"I don't wish it," said Jacqueline. "You know what I said before. But I'll take it. I'll do just one more, with the solemn understanding that this is the last. You give me your word on that, Tino. Is that all right?"

"Of course!" said Rudenko heartily. "Something will be found. Something very interesting, very suitable for you. I have an idea about it already."

"Will I be working alone?"

"I think so. Isn't that how you like it?"

"No. I'm sick of working alone. It's not a game when you work alone."

"It's never a game," said Rudenko sternly. "It's reality, my dear." He reflected. "We do have one person in place, one who could serve as backup but we cannot put him at risk for this. Besides, his tour is almost finished. You will be alone but it will be a perfect setup for you. Wait and see . . ."

And with this he reached for the glass she was holding and drank it off.

"Your instructions will be in the drop. You can expect them by week's end. Then you can return to Europe with your diplomatic passport. You will be given a new one there and a new identity, even in all likelihood a new appearance. You will love it."

"I shall detest it," said Jacqueline, "but I will do it this one time. The finale! As long as we understand that."

"We do, we do! You are priceless, darling. There is no one like you!"

He flopped back on his pillows and lay beaming at her, his disorderly hair like a theatrical wig, his face the bluish white of some underboiled potato.

TWENTY

ynans v. *Wynans,* heard in Superior Court, District of Columbia, shortly before Washington closed down for the summer, was resolved on the ground of irreconcilable differences, a property settlement having been effected out of court.

None of this surprised anyone with access to the gossip hotline nor did the resignation of Secretary of Defense Walden Wynans, which soon followed, come as a shock. Entrapment it well might be, but there had never been any doubt of the outcome in view of Lucy Gantt's feelings about moral turpitude among the President's appointees.

For ADECT, there was trouble afoot and only John Lighty left now to battle single-handed against the opposition in Congress and the screechings of the left-wing press at the concept of robots making war. In April, one more round of disarmament talks had broken down over this issue and even the argument was losing adherents that if the Russians hated and dreaded SEDAV so much, and had made such efforts to steal it, it was obviously just what was needed to keep the peace . . . along with *glasnost.*

No doubt Walden Wynans's successor in office, Sam Truscott, would stand fast. No political appointee he but a department career man, able and prepared to keep the caissons—and the robots—rolling along. It seemed the worst of luck that he should now be faced with a new emergency—an inexplicable and sickening outrage by the TY60 or some yet unexposed rogue tank, immediately involving both defense and ADECT in an investigation and probably a subsequent cover-up of magnum proportions.

So far only the inner core of ADECT staffers had the details of the incident—these being handled strictly on a need-to-know basis. To this elite group Jason added, on his own and off the record, Imry Kraskov, with whom in recent months he had established a close personal relationship.

Both were rather lonely people—Imry less so, due to his charming wife, but at the plant still somewhat outcast; Jason, naturally more sociable but positioned by fate at the eye of the whirlwind, the vacuum in which the spin of events isolates high office.

He was comfortable with Imry. With him he could play hooky from the company's merciless six-day work ethic—sneak off for a swim at the Decathlon Club, a game of chess, or a shopping spree at the computer swap fair at the Santa Clara Fairgrounds where as a boy he had amassed a closetful of weird junk: a blue ADM terminal, a digital decoscope, a TRS-80 . . .

Imry was full of energy.

"I would have given my soul for a Trash-80," he declared, his eyes gleaming, "I could never get one. But I had an IMSAI, can you believe it? I found it in a garbage can at the university. No one in Russia knew what it was . . ."

There were other bonds.

Both men had been hostages, though such different kinds. One night as they sat drinking before dinner in Isabella's gay little kitchen, the Russian spoke of his debriefing at the hands of the CIA—the year in solitary confinement—"they built a special cell for me"—the all-night interrogations, the ten-minute "health walks" in the yard.

He was talking a language Jason understood.

"Did you have dreams after you got out?"

"I prefer not sleeping to sleeping and having the dreams, even now . . ."

"For my part," said Isabella, "I prefer you awake. It's much more romantic."

She kissed him playfully, winking at Jason. "And now, don't you think it's time we ate?"

"We shall, we shall," said Imry, putting his arm around her. "What has happened to the soup? And for God's sake pour our son a little wine."

Jason was not sure when the father-son terminology had come into their dialogue but it was not alien, in truth, to the pulse of this relationship, his finding in the older man a warmth and rapport denied him in his real family.

He also admired the quality of Kraskov's mind; several times he had come to him with issues which had baffled the people at ADECT but which Imry had seen straight through at once.

Such an issue was this latest robot mischief. ADECT investigators had been in Hawaii for a week, trying to pin down the details. Jason and Garay were leaving that evening to join them.

Said Imry, "Naturally, the initial step is identifying the tank . . ."

"That's known."

"—and getting it released to us . . ."

"That's harder."

"But it might be done?"

"We're working on it."

"You say this incident occurred in midafternoon?"

"At a parade. With hundreds of people present."

The Russian hesitated. "Do you see any connection or similarity between this and the attack on your father?"

"Not the slightest."

"I don't suppose you care to recall the night . . ."

". . . when I found J.C.'s body? I don't mind at all."

This last was far from true. Jason could never talk about that night without sorrow and fury.

"You saw the house lights on and you drove in. You got out of your car."

"Yes."

"And you started toward the robot."

"I did."

"As you drew near it, did you notice anything particular?"

"The systems were on GO."

"I don't mean with regard to the machine. I mean some change in your own sensations, the way you felt, you yourself—physically. Mentally too. What I'm getting to would be more of a physical thing."

"Yes," said Jason slowly. "I felt—like a chill. Like . . . a projection. I can't explain."

"A projection coming from the machine . . ."

"Projection might be the wrong term. It wasn't all that definite."

His voice wavered in spite of his effort to control it, to maintain a calm he didn't feel. He had never talked to anyone about his feelings that night . . . above all those that concerned the robot.

"Would *aura* be a good word for it? Does that seem to fit?"

"I think so. Something . . . peculiar. It affected me . . . I don't know. It was weird."

"And frightening?"

"It scared the hell out of me. But right then the dogs . . . I saw the dogs there, all shot up. So I concluded that the killer was inside the house. That was when I went back to my car and got armed. Then I went on in. All this is in the record, Imry."

This last came out with a trace of impatience. It was hard to tell what the Russian was getting to.

"As you know, I was never invited to see any records. I was just wondering about the . . . emanation. You most likely would have found it at Tebuk where the distances, the huge dimensions, kept it from being noticed. Or considered relevant. And if you check out this new incident you may run across it there. If so, it would indicate that the robot or robots involved have been tampered with."

"You'd better make that a little clearer."

"Well, I think what we're talking about here is a side effect. Some kind of intense electromagnetism. Or something of that nature. No experiments have explored it just as there are phenomena in astronomy, for instance, that have never been explored because they seem to exist outside established scientific law. If we were dealing here with human instead of man-made brains I suppose you'd say *vibes* instead of *aura,* for want of a better word. They seem to happen when a robot's systems have been overloaded. As in certain combat situations."

"I'm reading you. But in Hawaii the robot that freaked out wasn't in a battle situation. It was trundling along in a parade. Why would it give out any special vibes?"

"Because it might have been reprogrammed. The reprogramming— or tampering—could have produced that aura. I just mention that as something you might check when you're there, that's all."

More was said, but nothing of much consequence, and presently Isabella called them in to supper.

The two men, the old one and the young, had been at work in Kraskov's garden, building a stone wall along a flank of it: both were tired after the work and the break which they had spent in such queer, rather strained talk. They felt improved after a washup and change of clothes, followed by one of the Polish stews which Isabella composed of goose, lamb, rabbit, sausage, peppers, leeks, and other exotica. They ate and drank under a preposterous bear's head Imry had bought in a taxidermist's shop and mounted on the wall as a "memorial to my origins."

The summer dusk was cool and pleasant and the three of them enjoyed it and the view from the Kraskovs' porch across the great electric spread of the Valley as they sat and waited for the stretchout that would come to take Jason to the airport.

TWENTY-ONE

here had been times in the past when he and Ken Garay had made the hop to Oahu by company jet as a weekend pleasure jaunt—Friday night takeoff, back to work bright and early Monday morning—but this time recreation was not the goal.

"Should we ask Truscott for some clearances?"

"Not appropriate till we have more facts."

"One call from him could cut through a lot of red tape."

"Save him for later. Right now let's go in quiet as mice till we know where all the pieces are."

An ADECT team assigned to the investigation had preceded them by several days, the group consisting of Phil Townsend, program manager, T. R. "Tommy" Noo, assistant systems engineer, and Debra Fine, public relations. They gathered for a breakfast meeting with the new arrivals in a lanai suite overlooking one of the Makaha Sheraton's swimming pools, Ms. Fine setting the tone of the occasion when she said,

"It's an army matter, Jason. That's what we have to keep in mind above all. The brass might sit on it forever. I'm not sure they want to, but they might. The decision will come down through channels which for now means no decision. There's been nothing released to the wire services or TV. All that's come out so far has been this item in the post newspaper. Here—"

ACCIDENT MARS SCHOFIELD FESTIVITY.

And as Jason ran his eyes over the few lines of print she added, "Ken suggested that we give home addresses rather than the company when registering at the hotel. I don't think anyone outside the barracks knows we're in action."

"Which, if I may so suggest, is how I'd like it kept," Garay put in. Townsend nodded.

"We've done our snooping under handicaps, let's say, but at least I have a few conclusions. Also, by sheer luck, some films. Would you like me to run those past you?"

"I would indeed," said Jason.

"Okay. First, nothing occurred to trigger an attack by the robot. Only a high profile enemy signature could have done that—a tank's, for instance. And only if the robot had been combat-programmed. In some way that we don't understand this particular SEDAV had been deliberately set up to perform an act of violence."

Jason glared at the quiet, monkish-looking program manager. A feeling like the resumption of an illness pulled him tight, Townsend's theory running so close to the conclusion held by Imry Kraskov.

"And the films?"

"Tommy got hold of those. You tell it, Tom."

Jason turned to Noo, a Harvard-educated mainland Chinese, a scratch golfer, and experienced practical joker, but not joking now.

"Some bystander took them, Jason. A hand-held Minolta Super Eight. Someone watching the parade. I bought them with your money, quite a lot of it. It was a case of our getting them or the army getting them before we did and locking them up. Okay?"

"Of course."

"The whole sequence only runs about thirty seconds. I had one frame optically printed, so you could see—"

A certain master sergeant's service record was included in the folder Noo and Townsend had prepared: it provided a coherent picture of that soldier's upward movement in the United States peacetime army, also suggesting, within its limited scope and official language, the sort of man who had lived inside that military shape. The truth was that Marlin

Purdy was the most unlikely person you would have picked to suffer an accident, if that was the correct term for what had happened to him.

Master Sergeant Marlin Purdy had never been a bad luck kind of soldier. Quite the opposite. If there was one thing that had set him apart it had been his easy rhythm and his confident, lucky way of living his life and avoiding confrontations of discipline and order, always a danger to soldiers of high spirit and superior intelligence. At age thirty-two he had made his current rank, a considerable achievement and just the level that suited him. He had almost twelve years' service on his record with a reenlistment anniversary coming up, and in addition to the highest and most respected rank available to a non-com he had a good-looking, active, sensible wife in Ailsa Versie Purdy, a Virginia woman he had met while training at Fort Benning, she busy now with all kinds of post affairs and with her children by Marlin, Cleve, nine, and Tina, four.

No twelve-year man in his right mind would do anything but roll over for enough remaining years to get full retirement benefits and pay as a twenty-year man. Or go on to thirty or whatever. So Ailsa saw it and it certainly made sense. But Ailsa, in her husband's opinion, might not be looking far enough ahead. She didn't see the two of them along with the kids bobbing out into another world, he considerably older, the pension in place and all, but doing what? Pinning on a tin badge and sitting up all night as a bank security guard? Living in a mobile home in Florida and fishing off a pier?

There were changes out there in the white world. There might be opportunities which he, at his present age, could lay hold on better now than down the line. In the night talks when they discussed all this their voices blended, his deep and assured but probing, testing her feelings, she responding warily, by no means convinced, shrinking away from what seemed a wild and dangerous leap into the unknown.

At times they would be close to quarreling. If that happened they would draw back. They would let the issue subside until by itself it rose again in the dusk of large soft Hawaiian nights in the small clean house and they would resume it tenderly and warily, their voices becoming like two strands of a single voice.

"Some things out there never change. You think they change?"

"I think there's changes here an' there, maybe not everywhere. You can't keep on thinkin' in the old ways, Ailsy, when new ways are opening up. That's what I have to find out."

The decision was for Marlin to get all this straight in his mind. He was to use a coming furlough to obtain some answers.

Heretofore he had always dressed very casually when off the base but now he bought himself an expensive lightweight gabardine suit to travel in, also appropriate shirts and shoes and a carryon suitcase to put it all in. Going back to his home turf, he intended to go in style. He reserved a nonstop coach seat out of Honolulu to Dallas where he changed planes for a late evening flight to Montgomery, Alabama.

The travel agency had booked him a room in the Marriott Hotel in Montgomery and when he signed in he gave his home address as Shorter, Alabama—the place where he had been born.

Shorter is a crossroads town near the Tallapoosa River. Here his father had fished and preached longer than most other places, a happy period for Marlin. After a night's sleep and a good breakfast at the Marriott, he rented a car and drove down there.

He wanted to look at the river and stroll around the streets, also to inquire for one person, Charles Pogue, his teacher in elementary school, who had encouraged him to make something of himself.

Charles Pogue's niece worked at the 7-Eleven. She walked outside with him and stood a few moments in the main street that was still part of the highway.

"I guess they didn't want him teaching the white, after the schools got integration. Charlie didn't want to leave. This was where he belonged."

"I know," said Marlin.

He drove along the river a little way and parked, then walked down through the willows to find a dry and sunny place. There were memories in the big brown reach of the river and its good muddy smell; he felt at ease and happy being near it. After a short walk he found the kind of place he wanted and there he sat down and made a sandwich with the food he'd bought and drank his beer; he was dozing, stretched out in the sun, when he heard someone bashing through the willows behind him.

Presently the noises stopped and a tall stooped man with a little spiky beard came into view. He had some kind of a skinny brown hound with him on a leash, the hound as bent and angled as he was, both man and dog dead still now on the bank, seriously studying Marlin.

"You got a permit to fish here, boy?" said the man.

He had a voice that could have wormed the hound.

"I'm not fishing, sir."

He instantly regretted that "sir," coming after "boy." Service conditioning had pushed it out of his lips.

"That yore trash?"

He pointed to the empty Bud Light bottle and the leftover bread, still in its wrapper, on the ground beside Marlin.

"My lunch—or it was," said Marlin, the secret layer of control that had taught him how to move in bad places coming to his aid now. "I plan to remove it."

No "sir" this time. He had clamped down on that, for better or worse.

"You better remove yore ass along with it. Thisyere's private property. Thet yore car up on the trace?"

"It's a car I rent."

The man reflected, spike beard ganting up and down.

"Move it," he brought out, "an' next time you plan on strewin' trash around, go elsewhere. Thisyere's posted land. You trespassin'."

There had been no posting that Marlin could see or had seen but when he got back to the Buick Skylark he found a rear tire slashed. There were tools in the trunk and he put on the spare and drove out of town.

So much for Shorter.

His plan originally hadn't involved the detour to the river: obviously a mistake. He was headed now for Selma, where the Edmund Pettus Bridge, an old steel humpback, spans the high banks of the Alabama River.

At the Pettus Bridge in 1965 the thing happened that Big Marl used to talk about. Big Marl wasn't in that first march, the one when the Reverend Martin Luther King, Jr., had told those who volunteered, "I can't guarantee you won't get beaten." And they had been.

Big Marl was in the second march, the one that got across. He was very proud of that.

Master Sergeant Purdy had decided Selma was a good town to check for changes. Anyway it was a nice day for a drive and he enjoyed the once familiar countryside, easing along in the new, responsive rental car. He took Highway 14 out of Montgomery and at Autaugaville he pulled into the parking lot behind the Greyhound bus stop and went inside, looking for a soft drink dispenser. The ice-cold Pepsi felt good in his hand but the station smelled of urine and gas fumes; he took the bottle out front where he fell in conversation with a middle-aged, primly dressed lady waiting on the bench there.

She asked where he was from and he told her, Shorter.

". . . originally. But I've been in the army. Still am."

"Home to see the folks, then," she suggested.

But no, he said, his folks were long gone from Shorter. He was on his way to Selma. And then, somewhat to his own surprise, he revealed a secret of his past.

"My pa was on the march."

"First or second?"

"Second."

She nodded gravely and kept nodding more times than necessary, her manner indicating a proprietary acceptance of his confidence—all that she would ever need to know about him.

"Well, good luck. You with your fine clothes and fancy car."

The great bus, a gleaming steel chariot, swung off the highway, its airbrakes hissing. The door opened and some people started getting off.

"Why would I need all that much luck?"

"If you don't remember, no use my tellin' you."

"I remember well."

"Okay then. Go with what you know. Reverend King had a dream but he's gone to the Almighty a long time now."

The bus driver switched off his motor. He got out of the bus and went into the men's room.

"Have a good trip," Marlin told the little lady. He took her case from her, carried it the few yards to the bus, then handed it up to her where she stood on the high step looking back at him, her small fierce eyes imperious with caution.

"Be careful, is all."

He handed her the case and she disappeared inside the bus.

The driver came out of the men's room. He leaped up into his seat and yanked on the lever that closed the door. As the bus pulled away Marlin could see, behind the tinted windows, an agitated motion—his friend waving good-bye to him.

So much for Autaugaville.

In Selma the Burger King, like most such places, had a beefy, buttery warmth and cheer and a friendly bustle; Marlin had the King Burger with everything on it, plus a salad, fries, and coffee; he paid his tab and walked up Broad Street. Tomorrow he would check out the project.

Mamma's Place looked dingy but The Yellowhammer's neon—a bird popping up and down as it drank from a cup—implied the availability of liquids if not conversation. Also there was space at the bar and he took it. Every face which now turned toward him was white and he knew that he was into something he hadn't expected—anyway, so soon.

The bartender was a big white woman with yellow birds on her opulently filled shirtwaist.

"Can I help you?"

"Bud Light," said Marlin.

She made no move to draw the beer or produce a bottle.

"Just a minute, please."

She peered into the dimness of the wooden booths lining one side and the back of the room and from one of these a wispy white-headed man in a white silk suit too big for him arose and sauntered down toward Marlin, smiling pleasantly.

"Evening," he said. "How's it going?"

"All right," said Marlin.

"Did I hear you place an order?"

"I asked for a Bud Light."

"Uh huh," said the white-headed man, "I thot tha's what I heard."

Still smiling, he looped his leg over the barstool next to Marlin; he bent toward him and spoke as before in a friendly, confidential tone.

"I guess nobody told you, but we can't oblige you here. This is a membership club, friend. A membership is required before we can serve you."

"I see."

"Sorry about that. See you around."

He took his leg off the stool, but Marlin shot out a big hand, detaining him.

"How much is a membership?"

As he said this Marlin too was smiling, opening his mouth wide—a smile that he deliberately sought to make Uncle Tomish, as if on cue he was ready to hump into a cakewalk or slobber up a watermelon.

"A membership is twenty dollars and take yore fucking hand off me."

"That's a lot of money for a Bud Light," said Marlin quietly, "but I'm calling you."

He laid a twenty-dollar bill on the bar. On top of it he put his service ID card.

The white-headed man was shaking. He took out a handkerchief and rubbed at the place on his sleeve where Marlin had taken hold of him. Then he turned and went back to his booth. Evidently, however, some kind of signal had passed between him and the barlady because the latter handed his ID back to him and rang up the money. She drew his beer and set it before him.

"The twenty was for the membership. The Bud is two-fifty."

He paid her, leaving a fifty-cent tip. He drank the beer slowly, enjoying it. After that first one he had another. People were leaving the bar. One young honky in a booth grinned at him and gave him a thumbs-up sign but the place was virtually empty when he left. He walked the few blocks back to his car and drove around a while, looking at motels, finally picking an expensive one. It was a chain motel and there was no trouble whatever about registering. At least that much had changed since King's march—and his murder.

Next morning he strolled around the project, talking to people he ran into, getting the lay of the land.

A lady cooking biscuits in the basement of Queen of Peace thought progress had been made. She asked what he was selling. Wasn't he ashamed to set foot on church grounds?

"Do I look like a salesman?"

"Like a pusher. Go on back where you came from—we don't need your peddling—or your crack or smack or whatever else."

Later he found a white cop half under his parked car, poking with a flashlight, his black partner writing a ticket.

"Your vehicle?"

"I rent it."

"You're Marlin Purdy?"

"I am."

"Open the trunk."

"What's my offense?"

"Just open the trunk."

The ticket was for overtime parking. The meter allowed two hours. He had put money in two hours and eight minutes earlier.

He accepted the ticket with the comment, "You cut me down pretty close."

"He's askin' for it," said the flashlight cop.

Ticketer shook his head.

"He's clean. Just so he stays that way."

He folded his ticketbook and got back into the squad car and the two of them drove away.

The words "just so he stays that way" jangled in Marlin's mind with the way The Yellowhammer had emptied out after he got his Bud. Had the project lady really thought he was a pusher? And if he'd been one, would he have been stupid enough to stash his wares in a glove compartment? Or a slashed radial?

No, he wouldn't. Even squad car cops knew better than that. But they might have made a play of looking in such places *while they planted the goods somewhere else*!

After dinner, which he ate in a Chinese restaurant with a solidly black clientele, he borrowed a flash at his motel and went to check. It wasn't taped to the frame or even among the engine parts but in the concave dish of the rear seat courtesy light—four ounces of street grade heroin, wrapped in plastic. He'd confiscated enough of that from addicted recruits to know what it was. He took the dish over to a hose bib and washed it thoroughly, letting its contents run into the motel lawn. He burned the plastic and buried the ashes. He returned the flashlight to the motel desk, then went up to his room and slept till morning.

No city police hassled him on his way out of town but on Highway 80, heading for Montgomery, the AHP stopped him twice, once for jumping a red light, the second time for driving sixty in a fifty-five-mile zone. He was guilty both times. He'd committed the offenses to embarrass the stakeouts when they found he was *not* transporting drugs; the enjoyment was worth it, even though after the speeding rap they spread-eagled him against the side of the Skylark and gave him a body search.

He was back at Schofield a week before his leave ended, his conjectures about the country of his youth settled now for good and all. He would have rolled over his enlistment for ten years or more if six had not been the limit for each additional hitch. Ailsa was content and their lives now had a new and expanding security . . . until Armed Forces Day.

At Schofield Barracks, Armed Forces Day was not ordinarily an occasion that blew your mind. It was a holiday so it was welcome. Unless you were one of the poor trolls assigned to special duties you could get off the post and into the bikini beaches and porno pastimes downtown.

"Special duties" meant *the parade*. Organizing it. Cutting the specs for it. Working as an MP along the route or in the parking lots. Cleaning up after it or, worst case, *marching in it*.

In the parade you mustered in by companies, generally five companies of ten ranks each, marching four abreast, though the screwball post commander, General Ryland Fortune Gibbs, might turn out ten companies or more at short notice, fucking up any individual plans for a day in the sun scouting the proclivities of the incredible bodies packed thigh to thigh along the golden strands of Waikiki.

Well, the bodies would always be there. That had been proven. And today was supposed to be different—a new kind of Armed Forces Day and a parade worth staying on the post to see. There were to be six companies, plus the band, plus two companies of marines, and a detachment from the navy, Gibbs feeling it appropriate to remind one and all that in addition to the dreadful fire-blackened shot-to-pieces ancient battleships lying shattered—a tourist attraction—in Pearl Harbor, there was also a modern navy on Oahu, alive and well.

Having navy in the order of march, you couldn't very well ignore the air force, so there was another added element and another flag to be borne aloft when the colors were trooped: the Stars and Stripes, the army flag, the three service flags, escorted by an honor guard of riflemen. A real array. And on top of all, the new weapons.

There had been no formal announcement about the weapons but the word was out. All week air force cargo planes had been flying them in, some said fifty, some said more. Robots. Drones. Whatever you wanted to call them: wild little machine killers with brains of their own, so smart, deadly, and ingenious that their voracious technology would change the face of war and perhaps even make nukes obsolete.

They would be in the parade. They would not demonstrate or anything but just looking at them could be . . . interesting. A conversation piece.

Even the kids had picked up the scuttlebutt and were asking questions.

The start was set for 1400 hours.

The day was perfect. Gray and pink and tangerine caissons of cloud rolled across the sky above the post and the boundless ocean down there unseen to the west—the kind of day when you could imagine band music even if there wasn't any.

The Purdys got ready early. All of them particularly enjoyed days like this when they could do things together instead of Cleve going off to play Little League in Waimea and Marlin having to drive him there and Ailsa working in the thrift shop or women's community choir club. They skipped lunch; there would be plenty of vendors selling food and pop along the line of march. So here they were, walking over in a group, Cleve wearing a new T-shirt with a jumping swordfish stenciled on the back and Tina, ever the restless one, breaking ranks to run on ahead; when Ailsa, impatient, called her back one last time, Tina decided to snub her mother by walking with her father, shyly and hopefully reaching up her hand for him to hold and so he held it, shortening his stride to fit her skipping skittery steps. She was something else, this kid, her wild clear eyes, her braids tied with tassels of red ribbon, the brown sneakers she loved and would not give up though the toes were wearing through: she had a mind of her own. It was she, once more on the loose, who dove in among the spectators, picking a place for the family to stand, a good place, only a hundred yards from the reviewing stand containing Gibbs and his staff and the visiting marine and navy brass.

Pretty soon, down the line out of sight, a signal squawked in the walkie-talkie of the band sergeant major and simultaneously that of each company captain; the moment had come and the band, still far away, played the three chords of "Sound Off," then stepped out, playing, and the men and vehicles moved forward in the order of march and the parade was on.

Beside the robots which were yet to come—the grand finale!—General Gibbs had gotten hold of some weapons never beheld at Schofield before and to be seen little thereafter, monstrous belly-quaking objects any one of which, it seemed, could win an ordinary war by itself: the Lance Missile (M667) on its enormous tracked carrier, a driver at the wheel and the missile gunner riding alongside the Lance, needle-nosed, shaped like a rifle round except two hundred times as big, the power to destroy a battleship or half a city packed inside its dull burnished hide but guaranteed, old chum, to be nonnuclear; the Hawk Missile (M727), three of them playfully clumped together, their configuration resembling nothing so much as the paper darts of torment in school classrooms, blown up to incredible size, but their kill potential only a wink behind the Lance's; then . . . well, then the mad stubby Chaparrals (M73/A1), just oversize steel arrows, Indian style, you might say, but oh, my . . .

These pterodactyls had a function in the march besides display; their passage buffered out the main band so that the reserve band could step into the vacancy, its strum setting the measure for marching companies before the entry of the SEDAVs, a basic rule in any parade being that you couldn't have two bands within earshot of each other or the offset cadences would set soldiers to falling over their own feet.

The reserve band swung along with style. It contained a bagpipe unit, adding Highland squeals and foggy Dundee cadenzas to the sturdy Sousa beat of "Hearts and Flowers," a tune suggested by the ladies of the post enhancement committee who—in the classic spirit of Hawaiian welcome—had dressed the oncoming SEDAVs with big hibiscus leis.

The guests of honor!

Weird guests. After the mighty Lances and the fearful Hawks and arrowheaded Chaparrals they looked . . . insignificant. Just a bunch of creepy mean little iron bugs, sniffing along, hugging the ground with the ridiculous leis flapping on their slant steel snouts. No one was riding on them or driving them and only a midget could have got inside them anyway. And they were crawling! Slowed to the infantry pace of the marching men ahead, they hardly seemed to move at all, spaced at such intervals that certain children, probably there without their parents, started a game of dashing out, daring each other to cross between the units.

Cleve Purdy watched this byplay with an elder brother's superiority but to Tina it seemed cool and when a girl she knew on the opposite side of the avenue taunted her to come over she got her four-year-old legs in motion and started, albeit fearfully, to cross.

Ailsa made a grab at her but not in time, the touch upsetting her.

"Marlin!" Ailsa screamed.

Marlin Purdy hurtled through the bodies packed in front of him, already stooping to grab his daughter. He reached her and with one powerful movement threw her clear, tossing the forty-pound child the way a big league infielder might barehand a grounder. There was plenty of time, the robots were going past in this ridiculously slow way, only something happened to the time frame. It had collapsed and the snout of a SEDAV painted rice-paddy green was on top of Marlin, then *over* him—and then it continued on its way.

The next robot in line, its sensors differently programmed or working better, stopped in its tracks and all behind stopped in orderly array, the crowd parting to let the ambulance through and the MPs forming a protective cordon as the paramedics packed out the victim of the accident, so pulled apart they had to use two bags for him.

. . .

"We know where the parade started," said Engineer Noo, "also the termination point on Waimea. So we had two positions. The third had to be the exact spot where Purdy was hit, which the MPs had chalked. Factoring in the length of each robot, the programmed spacing and the parade speed of 3.4 mph it took a vehicle 8.4 seconds to replace the one in front of it."

He laid out a piece of engineering paper on which he had drawn a graph of this calculation.

"The SEDAV that hit Master Sergeant Purdy was four feet ahead of its programmed position when it killed him. In other words, *it speeded up to make that contact.* That is our conclusion and the end of our report."

Jason wasn't listening. His arms were folded on his chest, his head bent forward. He remained in this position for an uncomfortable interim, as if locked in it.

Noo and Townsend looked at each other, then at the floor. Garay was the first to move. He rose and crossed to Jason, touching his shoulder to break him out of his spell.

"Boss, could you and I speak privately?"

Jason's head came up. He glared at the lawyer but followed him out onto the balcony of the suite.

"Look, Ken, I know what you're going to say. You can save yourself the trouble."

"Can I say it anyway?"

"Go right ahead."

"Any way you look at this thing it's a nightmare."

"Granted."

"—and for the company a trip to hell in a basket."

"The company isn't what concerns me right now, Ken. Or damage suits. Or anything of that nature."

"Maybe not, but it does me. Can't we, this one time, hang tight like the barracks command obviously intends to do?"

"We probably should. But I'm going to ignore your advice. I'm going to come up with some answers—whether the DOD likes them or not. And no matter how many heads have to roll before I'm through."

"One of them might be yours, pal."

"I don't give a shit about that either."

Turning on his heel, he walked back into the suite. Townsend was lying full length on a couch, his eyes fixed on the ceiling. Noo sprawled in a chair, an unlighted cigarillo dangling from his lips. Jason addressed the engineer.

"Tom, I'd like a copy of your work sheets." And to Townsend, "Has the CO at the barracks seen this report?"

"Yes. That was a condition for letting us on the post. General Ryland F. Gibbs. They say he's an oddball but plenty tough."

"See if you can set up an appointment, anytime tomorrow but the sooner the better."

Garay hesitated. This was treacherous ground.

"Am I allowed to tell him what this meeting would be about?"

"It's about getting the vehicle released to ADECT for examination."

"Yes, sir," said Ken Garay, "whatever you say, sir."

Noo was going through his briefcase, sorting out a number of thick files.

"—the work sheets are on top."

"What's all the other stuff?"

"Well, sir," said Noo, with some embarrassment, "just for comparison—I brought along my personal studies on the other incidents. The accident to Mr. J. C. Streck. And the Saudi job. I can pull them out if you don't want . . ."

"Leave them in," said Jason. "Comparisons—that could be a good idea."

Taking the case with its unexpectedly bulky contents, he went into his bedroom, closing the door behind him. It was long past the dinner hour, even for Hawaii; the rest of the group ate off room service trays, then scattered to their separate quarters.

Day was in the sky and the sounds of early golfers audible on the nearest of Makaha's two big courses before Jason's light went out. Even then sleep was slow in coming. Engineer Noo's computations had been interesting and, he felt sure, accurate; they put bygone catastrophes in tense perspective but failed, as had all such attempts in the past, to establish an interrelationship. Noo had included, however—apparently as an afterthought—some notes by Debra Fine who, with her publicist's instincts tuned for copy, had interviewed people standing in line near the Purdy family at the moment Marlin was run down.

". . . I heard a noise like a—"

"No, it was a howl."

". . . I had a feeling, a shock . . ."

". . . a cold sensation. I don't know how to describe it . . ."

". . . terribly intense. It ran right up my spine . . ."

"Yes, I did feel something. I'm not sure . . ."

"—bad, bad, bad . . ."

"It wasn't like the other little tanks. I mean it looked the same, but it was . . ."

". . . evil . . ."

". . . A noise. Scary. No, not the baby, I mean—"

"—the Thing—"

". . . I couldn't move . . ."

". . . yell . . ."

". . . see it, but I felt . . ."

". . . something wrong, that something terrible was going to happen . . ."

Such were the voices heard after the event: hindsight impressions recreated and exaggerated, should you be inclined to thus regard them. But all had this in common: all suggested, though they did not confirm, Imry Kraskov's theory of "vibes"—an idea of an electromagnetic aura thrown out under certain circumstances by a battle machine that had been, in Imry's phrase, tampered with . . .

TWENTY-TWO

General Ryland Fortune Gibbs sent a staff car to bring Garay and Jason to the barracks; when the sentry at the Macomb Gate flashed word that they had entered, he came out on the steps of his headquarters to meet them. With his executive officer moving ahead to open doors, he escorted them into his office, made them comfortable, and sent for drinks.

He was a tall rangy man with a long wrinkled face and the eyes of a weary bird of prey. He wasted no time getting to the matter in hand.

"As to your request, Mr. Streck, that I release this vehicle to you for study, I can't accommodate you. There are several reasons, any one of them conclusive. Let's just say I don't have the authority."

His tone was gentle, regretful. His predatory gaze moved appraisingly over his visitors.

Said Jason, "I'd hoped we could work something out."

"It seems a pity," said the general.

To hell with him and his pity, thought Jason. *A toughie indeed—certified there on his uniform: Bronze Star, Legion of Merit, Combat Infantryman's Badge, a cluster of commendation ribbons. A hero! I could have known he'd stonewall like all the rest of them.*

But the general continued:

". . . speaking off the record, the report of your investigators quite parallels our own. The speeds. The measurements. To coordinate them beyond a reasonable doubt, however, one needs the precise starting point of the lead robot on Waimea Avenue—something we're not as sure of as your people seem to be. Malfunction certainly isn't ruled out, but the real reason is a lot simpler. The devil has taken over your robot. I'm as sure of that as of my faith in the Lord God Jehovah. Do you know what I mean?"

Jason searched the man's wrinkled, vulturous face for some trace of a smile. Not finding any, he managed to bring out, "I'm afraid . . . not exactly, sir."

"Then you're not a student of Satanism."

"No, sir."

"It's a force in all human concerns—but above all in your special trade. Let me give you one example—"

He punched a key and a word appeared in capitals on the giant screen at the opposite end of the room:

HEPHAESTUS

"Perhaps you know this fellow? The armorer of the gods. An ugly bastard, lame in both feet. His mother was ashamed of him; she threw him out of Olympus—and when he crawled back up his father did the same. But he survived. He built a forge on Lemnos and made weapons. All his life he lived in soot and smoke in the glare of his fires. An incredible artisan of swords and spears, he put his hate in all of them—closest thing to the devil that the ancient Greeks conceived. Naturally, not having our Christian God they didn't have Satan as we know him, but they felt his presence, and today it's more evident than ever. You share the craft of Hephaestus and also another of his characteristics—"

The general looked at Jason's stick. It was as if he had added, ". . . his lameness." Garay was shocked by the reference but Jason seemed to take it in stride, spellbound by the general's weird exposition.

". . . smaller creatures," he was saying, "always abound, the gremlins that played hell with World War II aircraft. I won't even mention Vietnam—the devil's playground from the start. He has many ways of amusing himself and weapon games are among his favorites."

Ken Garay's voice cut into the hush of the room:

"General Gibbs, are you speaking seriously?"

The general erased the word *Hephaestus* as if the interruption had made its exposure indecent.

". . . as seriously as one may in discussing affairs of this nature."

Said Jason, "And you identify the parade incident as a Satanic event?"

"No doubt of it. Old Horny was riding the heads of your engine, he was splitting his sides laughing when he ran down the master sergeant. His one regret was that he didn't get the baby too—"

Jason and Garay avoided each other's eyes. Finally the lawyer brought out, "Would you have any advice, General, on how to handle such situations in the future?"

General Gibbs's head tilted back, his old vulture eyes fixed on spaces inviolate and remote.

"Trap the son of a bitch," he grated out. "Lay a snare for him, that's how. Make him expose himself. He can't stand the light. Only be sure you have protection. Here, let me show you something—" He took an object from his pocket. "This is what I carry. *He's* been after me since the day I was weaned but he can't lay a finger on me, not in combat or elsewhere, as long as I have this on me. Get yourself something like it. Get it right away."

And so saying he held up his talisman—a small book curved to fit over the pectoral muscle, its covers made of iron, its title, in worn gold letters, still readable: *HOLY BIBLE.*

"He's had a lot of combat. You can't go through that without getting your weather vane a little bent."

"His wasn't bent too badly. He said one thing that made much sense."

"I must have missed that."

Jason smiled. He and Garay were having sandwiches alone at the pool while the rest of the group packed to leave.

"Trap the son of a bitch is what he said."

"—talking about your classic, brimstone-breathing Satan . . ."

"Right. But it applies to our own breed of devil just as well. A trap is the one move we haven't tried—staging a planned experiment to track this machine under supervised conditions instead of dealing randomly with each breakout as it occurs."

"A free-choice test . . ."

"Exactly."

"How can we do that if the army won't release the vehicle?"

"They don't have to release it. Not if they run the test themselves—and let us observe it."

"Looking for what?"

"I'm not sure. Let's say whatever turns up. We're still between the devil and the deep—Gibbs's medieval Satan and our own technology. Last night I went through all the material: the research on my Dad's death, the Saudi thing, and now this. I think I see a pattern that I hadn't noticed."

"Do you want to clue me in?"

"Not yet. Maybe soon."

"Well, soon would be better than late. Remember, the clock is running: the thirty-day grace period before Gitlin starts buying up the company. And ten days of that is gone already."

TWENTY THREE

Through DOD channels a special order had come down for 500 SEDAVs for export, these to be modified in a particular manner to fit them for mountain as well as desert warfare. The deal, while highly profitable for ADECT, was no great matter but you had to be a dunce not to know where these robots were going. They were going to the Republic of Morocco, ever more important now in world affairs since the completion of the bridge-tunnel from Gibraltar to Africa, and the discovery of titanium in the lower Atlas slopes. The word had come down that President Muhammed Guelta would again visit the United States, this time to accept delivery in person, Guelta now busily collecting military hardware as other men might gather postage stamps, pioneer word processors, or vintage comic books.

Jason had the Lear fueled for a trip to Washington.

"Mr. Streck of ADECT asking for an appointment. Says it's important."

"Important for him or for me?" snapped the bald-headed, elegantly dressed old man behind the desk. And he added truculently, "Didn't we just write to him about that SEC matter?"

"Yes, sir," said the intercom voice patiently. "He said he'd received the letter, but he still wants to see you. He rang up twice yesterday, but you'd been called to the Floor."

"Tell him to come in at eleven. But warn him, he'll have to wait."

"Thank you, sir," said the voice.

Senator John Lighty seldom let his duties bother him but today had been unusually difficult.

He'd had nothing to do with President Guelta's return visit. That had been cooked up at State or perhaps even earlier, at the Pentagon, when former Secretary Walden Wynans had been hosting him around . . . and now Senator Alvin Friedkin, chair at Foreign Affairs, wished to avoid service on the reception committee, so the duty had fallen on him, Lighty.

The Friedkin call had come in while he was still dressing, delaying him, so that by the time his limousine, after its charge up the Hill and a turn to the right, deposited him at the new office building he'd been too late for his usual swim and Jacuzzi; he'd picked up his messages, then gone straight over in the subway to breakfast in the Senate dining room, where the men and women at the press table had fallen upon him like hyenas, demanding explanations, clarifications.

Why all this official warmth to a notorious human rights violator?

Did he know that police were clashing with demonstrators in front of the Moroccan Embassy?

No one paused to inquire why the senior senator from California should react to misery in the hamlets of the lower Atlas mountains. There was no need to. America was still chatelaine to the woes of the entire world.

Nevertheless, the day was lovely and few visitors lined up as yet to get into the gallery; it would be pleasant to take the overland route back to his office—but he had hardly left the Capitol steps when the presidential beeper rasped his nerves. Gantt's protocol officer, Merton Gossage, asking for a conference.

More about the damned SEDAV sale! Lighty had no patience for Gossage's gabblespeak. He invented an excuse—if the Pudknocker himself wanted to chat he'd soon make it known.

Meanwhile in the senator's staff room a home state environmental deputation waited for him with a gift—a redwood gate sign (useless to a condo dweller such as he) with his name decoratively carved thereon. Lighty thanked them lavishly and delightedly, signed their autograph books, posed for their Instamatics, and with tender pats and smiles and nudges herded the whole kit and caboodle out into the corridor, setting himself free to caucus by telephone for votes critical to a subcommittee meeting that afternoon in Room 224, Russell Senate Office Building, he himself presiding.

He drew in a long breath. The morning was slipping away . . . but his gold desk clock still lacked thirty minutes till eleven. Why not go up to the solarium for a half hour?

No sooner than done. He was less than fifty feet from the elevator and a clean escape when good night, Annie, bar the door—here came Jason Streck, thumping along on his thick stick, his red hair aflame as always but an indefinable trouble or anxiety in his handsome face that Lighty had not seen before. And immediately the bonds of old-time neighborliness and family closeness asserted their force and the senator forgot his longing for a few minutes in the sun; he moved forward quickly, took his visitor warmly by the hand, peering at him with genuine liking and concern.

"Come in, lad, come in for God's sake. What took you so long?"

He should have been more responsive to the young fellow's calls, less irritated by this interruption in his busy schedule. He went back a long way with the Strecks, clear to when he'd been a congressman, his beloved Amy still alive then—Amy whose liking for Gertrude Streck, Jason's mother (so different from the later Streck wives) had led first to dinner exchanges, then a solid friendship between the families, the Strecks on Mercy Street, he and Amy only a few blocks away on Linden. That had been the golden period of exploding technology in the Valley: J. C. Streck, not long out of the army, bashing his way into the office machine field but looking over his shoulder at defense. A brilliant son of a gun, he had some of David Packard's ability as an organizer, a share of Jerry Sander's flamboyance, but also a loneliness, a queerness—you never knew quite where you stood with him.

No matter. His hand didn't stick in his pocket when campaign funds were needed.

Lighty was duly grateful. He'd also evened the score—done it, in fact, in a single conversation. The two of them had met one summer morning in the Santa Clara post office and stood there, each with an armful of mail, chatting, and as they walked out Lighty had said—ah, how clearly he remembered that now, more than twenty years later—"I have an idea for you." And then, as they stood on the steps in the sun, he'd suggested that J.C. send for DARCOM's *Guide to Unsolicited Proposals*.

". . . there's heat focusing on a robot combat vehicle . . ."

There'd been no further talk. Nor had J.C., to do him credit, ever requested an improper favor or so much as referred again to the post office meeting. But when, at long last, the contract was let, it went to ADECT. The appropriation had been in the area of $4 billion.

". . . and I deeply appreciate your help with the SEC commissioner . . ."

"Ah, that Tod Magrame," snorted the senator, "no telling what he'll do, a hard-working fellow, keeps his own counsel. Let's hope he sees it our way . . . But the bloody corporate raiders! I understand your fix, my lad—I do indeed. I'd do away with them by legislation if I had my way. So what else is on your mind?"

The senator's formula with petitioners consisted in waiting for the right moment to inject the magic offer: "What can I do . . ." But in this confrontation the right moment seemed swept aside.

Jason was certainly revved up. Taking stock of him the senator could see confirmation of the man-of-the-world maturity and thrust he'd observed and liked at J.C.'s funeral as J.C.'s son squared off to face new tasks, entrench himself in a large ambition. He'd done well, very well: The takeover threat now poised over ADECT was unfortunate, unfair, but there seemed little correlation between that threat and Jason's new idea about further testing of the SEDAV.

Tests were all right, of course, very necessary, but to keep on with them sometimes did more harm than good.

You were never going to come up with a war engine that was foolproof. There'd never been one in history.

"Let me get this straight, son. Your idea is to work along with the ceremonial exercise that's to take place next week."

"Yes, sir. The one at Fort Irwin."

"You're aware that the person to be honored there is your old friend Muhammed Guelta?"

"That's irrelevant. I try not to let it bother me."

"I'm afraid I think better of your fortitude than of your proposition."

The senator said this with a certain finality, but Jason pressed on.

"Uncle John, we need new evaluations. Too much has been happening. I mean, we can't sit by and close our eyes to . . ."

"Ah, yes, yes, I know, I know," said Lighty rapidly. "Most regrettable. The committee discussed some of those incidents. We keep track, indeed we do. But let me stick my two cents worth in here—if it's evaluations you're wanting—"

"Yes, sir?"

"Why not wait until the army makes them?"

"The army won't make them."

"That's a pretty large assumption."

"It may be, but for instance—the case of the Bradley Fighting Vehicle?"

"That was before I chaired the committee."

"—however, sir, you might recall that when a shell hit the Bradley the ammo stored inside blew up and destroyed the vehicle. Always! Without exception! But the army went ahead and bought five thousand more Bradleys *after this had been proved!*"

"The SEDAV isn't the Bradley," said the senator, his expression hardening, "it's a far, far better weapon."

"Of course, sir. The trouble with the Bradley was quite evident. It was the same with all Bradleys. That's different from the SEDAVs. We're not sure, but perhaps only a single robot goes on these killing sprees."

Lighty nodded. He smoothed the skin creases which served him for eyebrows, the eyes themselves, sometimes so merry, now hard as slate. "I seem to remember your robot's brain: the twenty-six interfacing minicomputers. Wasn't that how the specs read?"

"Yes."

"And wasn't there an error-detection function stored there?"

"We build that function into every system that comes off the production line."

"So a certain incidence of failure is a precalculated factor."

"We call it graceful degradation."

"So what's interdicting that, in this one or these several machines, isn't that the problem?"

"Part of it, perhaps. Not all. There's a force operating here that we haven't identified, nobody has. General Gibbs at Schofield thinks he has the answer—the robot is possessed by the devil. I'd buy that quicker than the CIA's idea that some agent is working our gear with a remote setup based on a telebeam."

"An agent?"

"A spy. I suppose they could have planted someone, but to me that's absurd."

Senator Lighty shifted his well-padded frame uncomfortably. He wriggled in his posture-supportive, custom-made office chair as if some-one had stuffed it full of tacks. *Spy* was a word one didn't use, the irresponsible coinage of TV soaps and grocery-store paperbacks.

"So what's next?"

"Well, sir, I have my own idea. It's far out, not one engineer at ADECT thinks it makes sense. But it's all we've got and I want to go with it; the game at Irwin provides perfect conditions. Rather than take up your time with an exposition, I make only one request: that ADECT be permitted to participate in that exercise."

The senator swiveled around, his back to Jason, staring out at the great vista of the city, the river, and the Virginia countryside below. He spoke over his shoulder.

"—meaning you want to be there yourself?"

"Yes, sir."

"And bring staff with you?"

"Half a dozen people at the most, all with top clearances."

The senator sighed. Time was flying. He moved his chair back to its normal position and stepped on the secret button that caused his inter-com to buzz—an interview-termination signal. "In a minute," he said into the device to which no one was listening.

"Let me put on my thinking cap, my boy. Mind, now, I make no guarantees, but I'll look into it. I'll look into it most thoroughly and we'll take it from there. Would you have time for a bite of lunch with me? No? . . . Too bad. Well, some other time then. And thank you for dropping in . . ."

And with the same fond pats and nudges and squeezes he'd used on the environmental group he ushered his visitor out and sat down to attend the business that had piled up meanwhile. And as he telephoned and caucused and later, rather hurriedly, had an abstemious midday meal at his desk, he kept thinking about young Streck and his odd request. A hurdle, not really all that easy to bypass, though bypassing hurdles was one of the senator's specialties. The concept was what made the trouble, the notion of a killer robot at loose ends in a war game. Not something you would gab about, but of course no need to.

But the boy, now. Yes, the young chap. He was certainly under pressure. The bloody business he was in.

The senator had lived and worked with weapons suppliers for many years. He'd seen how they screwed up . . . or burned out. Too much competition. Too much money. Too many new ideas. The wild armor-ers, a breed apart.

He pushed as politely as he could through the reporters, photographers, and tourists clustered at the doors of Room 224, made his way to the great high bench and the central seat there whereon he laid out his notes and looked down into the pit where the witnesses to be questioned today were clumped like cattle in a pen—which of course was just what it was called. The Bullpen. Well, fine. The hour had come—1400 as the Great Pudknocker had ordered time to be measured.

The senator glanced around, then tapped twice with his gavel; the hubbub dwindled, and at the third tap stopped. And then a curious thing happened—upon the men and the one woman seated along the high committee desk descended a peculiar aura or presence, the habiliment of those who deal in weighty affairs. Such is the marvel of this visitation that no matter what miserable oafs or rascals the recipients may by nature be this grace is lent to them so that for a few hours on appointed days they may appear and perhaps, if the wind is in the right direction, veritably become wise and farseeing and scrupulous and of course (as they truly are) wielders of destiny.

The firm tenor tones of Chairman Lighty took shape in the silence:

". . . The Armed Services Committee of the United States Senate meets today in open session to hear the report of the special subcommittee on the proposed sale of one thousand T-38 surplus Talon trainer planes to the People's Republic of China . . ."

TWENTY FOUR

The little helicopter flew awkwardly, strong cross winds making its course crablike. Stubbornly, persistently, it thrust its stubby, camouflaged body against this unseen power, its nose pointing northeast, its intended course northwest by north. For a while it trundled above Interstate 15, its clippety-clacking flight audible to the traffic below—the passenger cars, rec vehicles, and buses heading back to Los Angeles from the all-night Vegas gaming tables.

Down there the drivers had their headlights on. They needed them. Whatever sun crept into the cloudy sky from behind the dark, measureless Sierra, far away, the copter pulled into itself, making its own little piece of day in the low clouds.

The five men in the cabin took no note of this. They sat hunched together in a space rendered too small by the bulky garments they wore—service issue parkas they had not bothered to take off. They passed around a thermos of coffee—lousy coffee. They drank it out of boredom, all except the pilot who was busy flying the bird.

"Fucking wind," he said.

"Is it always like this?" asked the congressman.

The pilot didn't answer, so the briefing officer filled in for him.

"Mostly it is," he said. "The desert, sir. Usually a lot of wind on the desert, sir, except in summer, when you need it. Then you don't get it at all."

"I see," said the congressman.

Nobody knew exactly how the congressman had come aboard. He had just been there on the pad at takeoff. Jason had asked for a briefing trip and Colonel Jared, acting as liaison between the ADECT group and the army, placed the request with his opposite number at Fort Irwin. Action had been affirmative. When you had the blessing of a hierarch like Senator John Lighty, the action on most anything you wanted was affirmative and Jason had that blessing. Somehow, though, the congressman had heard about the trip and had decided that he too wanted to be briefed even if he could not be blessed; his name was on the manifest that Public Affairs at the fort had sent up for the trip. He was there at first light and he got in, a serious man asking questions about the wind.

It really made no difference. He was a proper congressman but the trip was still Jason's trip. The congressman was supercargo. Those things happened when the army was involved.

At Barstow the flight pattern changed. The copter was lower and the land below was rougher. This was desert now, a thousand-square-mile piece of sand, cactus, basalt and granite rock, and yellow squat creosote bushes spread across a desolate corner of San Bernardino County, California. Over the dunes and rills and wadis and the bristly black escarpments and the cactus wastes, the bird, as the light rose higher, cast a frail and wavering signature, whisking its shadow across the white buildings of the Fort Irwin cantonment to the left and further, lower, into a wild declivity known officially as the Central Engagement Corridor.

"Is that it?" asked the congressman.

"That's it, sir," said the briefing officer. "The shooting gallery."

The bird kept tilting down. Soldiers now could be seen at work. *Soviet soldiers.* Through their binoculars the men in the cabin could clearly make out the black berets of the USSR field armies with their silver-circled red star. The soldiers were laying miles of concertina wire, emplacing land mines, digging out artillery positions, moving around in Soviet MTLB troop carriers, running target drills with Russian AK-47 rifles.

"They look very real," said the congressman.

"They are real, sir," said the briefing officer. "The Sixth Battalion, Thirty-first U.S. Infantry, and the First Battalion, Seventy-third Armor of the Thirty-second Guards Motorized Rifle Regiment. They think Russian, drill Russian, and fight Russian. The tanks are Russian or Sheridans modified with plastic kits to look Russian. They train two hundred days a year, sir. They are the best-trained Russian soldiers in the world."

"Where do they get the manuals?"

"I don't know, sir," said the briefing officer. "All I know is, they have them."

Colonel Jared winked at Jason. Both had witnessed the Fort Irwin operations long ago when ADECT, for a brief period, had been second-source supplier for some tank fire-control systems. In those days only a few selected U.S. Army units had come in for special training, matching their skills against the Sovietized Fort Irwin battalions. Now the trainees arrived massively and routinely from all the army's seventeen active duty divisions and all its National Guard and army reserve components.

In the early days, with little enthusiasm, but as a corporate duty, Jason had gone downrange to observe battle exercises from an armored troop carrier with a public affairs officer alongside; he remembered with sickening vividness the noise, stink, fear, fury, and confusion he had then experienced—less perhaps by much than that of a true modern battlefield but closer than he had wanted to come to it. A hell of a lot closer . . .

There were new elements now and new weapons. There were chemical gases and shoulder-portable assault guns and mobile chaff-emitters, Smokey Sams and terrain-masking flares and star clusters to confuse the air elements. And on the contested ground the robots. SEDAVs would be in the attack force.

Tactics could never be pinned down to a tight, preplanned scenario, since the whole point of the engagement was improvisation, but study of defense preparations gave useful clues.

"You can do more damage with one canister of Rockeye than with a TOW missile," said the briefing officer. "Air-to-ground is important as support, but as we tell the trainees, you can shoot down every aircraft in the Warsaw Pact—but if one Soviet tank commander is there with a tank when you land, then, buddy, you've lost the war. . . ."

"Good thinking, Lieutenant," said the congressman. "But won't the shooting tomorrow be with laser beams?"

"Absolutely, sir," said the briefing officer. "The live fire will be confined to eliminating drone planes. We are approaching the live fire exercise area now, sir—ahead about two o'clock. Drinkwater Dry Lake that area is called, sir. Those structures behind are the ground interrogator stations."

Other, recognizable structures, once familiar to Jason, emerged below, perched precariously in the wind-driven sand on humps and bumps masquerading as hills, gouged out of the earth when, a billion years ago, the desert had been the cradle of a doomed, retreating ocean. Tiefort Mountain, straight ahead, mounted the huge Zeiss lens with which every turn of the battle could be videoed, with the VHF commo beside it; further on rose the fish-shaped swell nicknamed The Whale from which privileged visitors did their viewing while the media banged around in armored vans among the training units.

The Whale was where it would happen.

Jason had a sudden, strong conviction about that. *Hold on,* he told himself. *Don't rush it.* But the notion wouldn't go away and there was logic in it, for The Whale was different now from when he had last seen it—drastically altered.

Fort Irwin had never discouraged visitors—if they were well connected. An early-day CO, lunching with Jason in the officers' club, had been emphatic about that. "Sham battles, like parades, are ritual—they're drama, which is what the army is about. Read history. Roman generals had the legions march through Rome to assert their identification with the gods. Frederick the Great defended his incredible reviews because, he said, 'They bind my soldiers to their king.' "

This CO, in his time, had equipped The Whale with what he considered adequate amenities: a couple of rows of canvas chairs, some map boards, some GI binoculars, and a loudspeaker system hooked to the TOC, Tactical Operations Center. Now there was a grandstand—obviously new, since an infantry work detail was still busy building a sandbag revetment around it. It was not a grandstand like any other. This one was inset into The Whale's flank like a bunker. A jutting cantilevered concrete roof, layered with slabs of steel, overhung its observation window, reducing this to a slit. A tram connected it with the valley floor.

The congressman seemed little interested. This time it was Jason who had a question.

"What's all that for, Lieutenant?"

"We haven't been informed," said the briefing officer. "For some certain group. Whoever comes along, I suppose, sir. Would it be President Guelta, sir, or someone else? Whoever it is, they'll have a good place to see the show."

"They will indeed," said Jason.
The Event. That was where it would be.

Working with machines designed to perform very sophisticated tasks, he had long ago rejected the general idea that a computer could do no more than what was put into it. You didn't need Professor Sejinowski's neural network inventions to know that. Once programming had established a purpose, the computer's logic could and would expand that purpose as if by a "logic bomb."

There were many examples. Oxford biologist Richard Dawkins, for instance, had punched EVOLUTION into his sixty-four-kilobyte computer, then designed games to replicate the processes of natural selection. Needing biomorphs, he told his machine to expand a dot into a tree by adding Y forms to make branches. Each tree had its own genetic formula, an equation built of nine allotted genes. Dawkins had hoped for "cedars of Lebanon, Lombardy poplars, weeping willows, seaweeds, perhaps deer antlers . . ." Nothing in his "wildest dreams" prepared him for the pictures of bees, lamps, spiders, scorpions, foxes, bats, sabers, and Spitfire planes that his computer turned up when left to run all night.

His PC had gone beyond his INSTRUCTION and taken its thrust from his INTENTION . . . and in so doing—the only clue to its madness—it had acquired what Imry Kraskov called an "aura."

The purpose of SEDAVs was to make war. To this end and no other, they had been equipped with treads, armor, power plants, cannon, and sensors that could read terrain, identify enemies in the air and on the earth, and decide in the flick of an instant when to attack, when to flee, when to deploy, when to take cover. Such was the sum of capabilities provided in their data cassettes but one—one robot and one only—had brushed past diagnostic restraints, tossed aside obedience to military procedure.

One SEDAV had made the quantum leap from instruction to intention.

The TY60 knew it had been born to kill!

Arrogant in its deadly autonomy, it had acquired the cunning of an outlaw but only in order to demonstrate how splendidly it could serve the undeclared intention of its maker.

Once, at the very beginning, it had killed alone, by stealth, at night, its target an old man (though to be sure a celebrated one) helpless and unarmed. A sloppy business—but as the robot honed its talents it moved into the spotlight, linking its adventures to grand occasions, spectacles of historic moment, with a large cast of witnesses: the Saudi fly-off with the king watching, Marlin Purdy at a holiday parade. Unless it were now to break with its own precedent it would stage its next performance at the most conspicuous site available at Fort Irwin, that queer-looking slit where the VIPs would sit to see Texas fight the Opposition Force (OPFOR).

The copter clattered past the base of the mountain. It lurched to port, then continued down the groove between the sagebrush-studded hillocks, a course which the briefing officer described as "the valley of death." Drama again.

"... to Soviet tacticians, the forward elements are always expendable. The same with recon. In a meeting engagement they'll sacrifice an entire division if need be, then slam another right through the wreckage of the first. Men and matériel are totally expendable. It's right there in their manuals, in black and white. ..."

Through the rest of the inspection trip, the briefing officer's chatter, then the lunch at the officers' club and the flight back to Las Vegas Jason weighed what would happen at The Whale when the battle was in progress. He projected it in terms of graphics, breaking it down step by step in his imagination. That, and what he would do next. He worked hard on his plan, and gradually it took shape.

It was not complete. It would never be complete. The details would depend on circumstance, but it was something to start with.

At least the scene was set and the trap baited. Possibly the TY6o could be taken alive, as it were, its black-box brain intact and submissive to reverse engineering later, in ADECT's big lab. Such was the game ahead. Meanwhile, he had to keep his head on straight somehow in the bustling agenda that his own PR people had laid on for him in Vegas.

"Don't forget the press conference," said Debra Fine. "Fourteen hundred hours, at Caesar's Palace. Secretary Truscott is chairing it himself. There'll be a hundred media people present. You don't want to be late."

"I think I'll skip it," Jason said.

Said Debra Fine, "You can't. Not without discourtesy, and we don't want that, do we?" What with long association and the egalitarian ADECT ethic she sometimes took a nannyish tone as if Jason were a recalcitrant five-year-old, an approach he did not relish.

"One of the assistant secretaries called personally to make sure you'd be there and I said you would. I've stalled the personal interviews. *The New York Times*—I got you out of that; I think she has some antagonism. But *Armed Forces Journal* is legitimate and I think you should go along. Also *The Christian Science Monitor.* They want a statement on the IFF thing—Identification of Friend or Foe. What does a SEDAV do if an enemy wants to surrender—can it recognize a white flag?"

"Certainly. Anytime a soldier wants to wave one. Then all the man has to do is walk up and hang a grenade on the robot."

"Very funny, but I doubt if a United Nations referendum would buy it. I've written something for the *Monitor;* I think it will do. They don't sling mud. Do you want to do any foreign papers? *Manchester Guardian*—very influential, could help sales."

"Please!"

"All right, all right. But look—the strip is really crowded this time of day. You'd better hurry."

Observers cleared for Fort Irwin could not be billeted there. There were no quarters for them. Both Barstow and Ontario provided respectable hostelries but for VIPs with access to the army's helicopter shuttle the logical operations base was Las Vegas, a location which also concurred with Muhammed Guelta's well-established taste for games. He was in the Gable Suite at the MGM Grand where the Secret Service, in cooperation with State Department security, leased all rooms above and below. No assassin's bullets would slant up through a floor or crunch down through a ceiling: an advisable precaution. There were still plenty of displaced royalists and others with a personal grudge who had no love for President Muhammed Guelta.

The hotel provided a private gambling room for his personal use, and an alert travel agency had sent in a list of the city's better brothels, indexed on a scale of one to ten for safety, cleanliness, and showmanship.

Jason and the ADECT group were at the Flamingo. There had been no room for them at the Sands where Secretary Truscott with the undersecretary, several assistant secretaries, and their staffs bedded down with the people from DARPA, TRADOC, and State; the Dunes held a large reservation for an unidentified VIP, his arrival time not yet confirmed.

Jason changed his clothes and went to the press conference.

From the moment he sat down he suspected that giving in to Ms. Fine had been a mistake. Ten minutes later he was sure of it.

A Pentagon media person monitored the questions, redirecting them to the panel members whom he felt best could answer. The first few raised no hackles. *Newsweek* wanted an estimated cost of the Fort Irwin sham battle related to proposed defense cuts—what were the figures? *The Economist* (England) had stats on new monopulse coherent radar devices and why had these not been shared with NATO forces? (They soon would be.) *Los Angeles Times* complained that battlefield command-and-control electronics had interfered with civilian frequencies and would this be remedied? (Affirmative.)

Secretary Truscott denied, for *El Italia* (Milano) that he had appointed a committee to investigate injuries to an Abrams tank crew from live fire practice at the fort.

". . . no soldier to my knowledge has ever been hurt in such practice. We have steel-on-steel hits but we simulate these with Hoffman charges and black smoke canisters to make it look as if the tanks are burning. A tank crew is in no more danger in those situations than if they were setting off firecrackers in their own backyards. . . ."

Not exactly truthful, but who cared? The DOD had a right to some license and besides, he couldn't be expected to know everything. . . .

So far the procedure had been routine. But suddenly a lady in the back row threw a teaser.

Q. A question for arms supplier Jason Streck of ADECT Corporation, California. I am Sheila Bregstein, *The New York Times.*

The moderator, evidently familiar with this lady, looked uncertainly at Jason.

A. Go ahead.

Q. Didn't you yourself along with a delegation from your company recently visit Hawaii?

A. We did.

Q. Was that a business or a pleasure trip?

A. A little of both, I suppose.

Q. Thank you. And on that trip didn't you spend some time at Schofield Barracks, Mr. Streck—wasn't that the business part? And didn't it focus on a tragic accident that had taken place there involving one of your SEDAV robots and a master sergeant that the robot killed?

A. We'd heard about the accident, yes. We were concerned about it, naturally. We are always concerned about any real or alleged malfunction of an ADECT product.

MODERATOR. Thank you, Ms. Bregstein.

He recognized another correspondent, but Bregstein kept the floor.

Q. I direct my last question to Secretary Truscott.

MODERATOR. You are out of order, ma'am.

Q.—in view of what we've been hearing about this robot's instability, is tomorrow's exercise actually being staged to advertise our ties with Morocco? Or is its true purpose to determine whether SEDAV will continue to be made and sold or whether, like some other baroque weapons in the past, it will be canceled?

MODERATOR. Next question.

Truscott never answered Ms. Bregstein but at adjournment her inquiry still hung in the air, exposed and quivering. Now it had been asked in public, which should not have happened.

Jason did not propose to concern himself with it now. He put on his swim shorts and went to the pool where, though the afternoon was now more than half spent, the desert sun still cast a warm spell on the colored umbrellas, the dyed azure water, and the waiters in bright jackets serving mai tais and piña coladas while they pranced and sashayed, as in some existential ballet, around and over the oiled bodies stretched in their paths.

Jason ordered a Bloody Mary. He felt entitled to that. He trusted it to remove the dreamlike haze from the scene around him, unreal after his morning spent above the wind-scoured sand bristling with military hardware. Idly he watched the swimmers, the long-legged showgirls demonstrating the eight-beat free-style strokes they'd learned in younger days—and one woman with the best body of all (he had seen her getting in) who could barely keep afloat. She wallowed along with an action that fell somewhere between a dog paddle and a breast stroke and looked as if at any moment she might give up and go under, perhaps for good.

Did she need a rescue? Maybe . . . but having been up since an hour before dawn Jason felt this duty should go to someone else.

Another Bloody Mary might be a better idea. He raised a finger, pointed to his glass . . . but when he looked back the lady was rescuing herself. This she did beautifully. She came out over the side in a single rippling motion, in a rush of water, gleaming like a fish. Then followed business with a towel—another triumph. There was a tender eroticism in the way she touched and smoothed and stroked every bit of burnished skin not covered by the tiny stretch suit.

Too great a body for a hotel pool: a body for magazine covers, for the cinema! It drew, from every male in the area not suffering from sight impairment, the voyeurism that was her natural environment.

Now—act two. At her sunning place were makeup needs—a comb to discipline the mass of her rough-looking blond hair, lipstick, eyeliner. Fantastic! And then—

Act three. She put on clogs and a terry-cloth robe, produced from somewhere a notebook, a pen. She was standing beside Jason's table, smiling at him as only an authentic beauty can smile.

"Mr. Streck! Excuse me . . . I am Ariane Artaud. *Paris Soir.* "

"I'm sorry, Miss Artaud."

". . . I spoke to your public affairs secretary this morning, she said . . ."

"Whatever. Unfortunately, at the moment, I . . ."

". . . she'd try to set something up. Then I saw you at the press conference, but before I could reach you . . ."

". . . am not giving any interviews."

"Mr. Streck, please listen to me . . ."

She moved her notebook as if to keep the sun out of her eyes but in effect also screening her mouth. "Here it is very easy to audit a person with some device, and it is possible such a device is now being used. Here at the pool. Or my lips read. Could I talk to you privately somewhere, just for five minutes?"

"I'm afraid not, Miss Artaud. Perhaps tomorrow."

"Tomorrow there will be the battle exercise. We will all . . ."

"Good-bye, Miss Artaud."

". . . be leaving. Mr. Streck, I beg you. All the other people on the panel were officials of some kind except you, and I thought . . . I couldn't keep myself from hoping that perhaps . . ."

The waiter was finally arriving with the Bloody Mary. Jason signed for it and without another glance at Ms. Artaud picked up his glass and walked away.

Back in his suite, he said to Debra Fine, "That tall blond number from the French paper . . ."

"She got after you?"

"Did she ever. At the pool."

"Sorry, my fault. I sent her down there just to see if you'd show up. And to get her out of my hair."

"I said no interviews, Debra."

"I know. But this one . . . well, I thought she was different somehow. Troubled. Also she's attractive, or didn't you notice?"

"I'm supposed to notice? I'll tell you what I think about this chick. She's working some kind of racket. Ask Abe to check her out. The whole media act around here is for the birds. When did we ever have pressure like this? Interviews, for Christ sake—nobody outside of the trade journals ever wanted interviews. The *Times* dyke picked up a leak about the Schofield thing. That's what it is. She's got that and she's trying to build it into a major story at our expense. . . ."

"Possibly," said Debra. "But if you'll stop yelling for two seconds I'd like to mention another angle."

"I don't need any other angle. No interviews. And no press conferences. Deal me out. That's final."

"Whatever you say. But this is an approach that can work for all of us. Your own story. Your background as a former hostage."

"—which is gone. Forgotten."

"—and might well be recalled. A human interest piece that would grab space everywhere. Once upon a time you were Muhammed Guelta's prisoner. Now he's your customer. You've wiped out your personal bitterness and he's into an alliance with the free world nations. So tonight you'll be photographed shaking hands with him."

"Never. I'd rather not be in the same room with him—unless I went there to kill him."

"But you *will* go to the party?" said Ms. Fine anxiously.

"Yes. I'll go to the party. That and no more."

Said Ms. Fine in her most nannyish tone, "We shake hands with customers, don't we? Unless you wish this to become a precedent—"

Jason opened his mouth to reply, then changed his mind and turned away, almost colliding with Ken Garay entering from the adjoining suite.

"General Ryland Gibbs calling you from Schofield Barracks."

"Does he know we can't scramble incoming calls?"

"I've so advised him. He feels a secure line isn't needed."

Jason went to take the call.

TWENTY FIVE

Ryland Fortune Gibbs's voice was warm and hearty.

"Young fellow! How are you?"

"Fine, General, just fine. Waiting for tomorrow."

"You've been in my thoughts and in my prayers."

"I'm grateful. I'll need all the help I can get."

"And tomorrow's D-Day."

"Yes, sir. I was out at the fort today, doing some reconnaissance."

"And you're prepared?"

"I feel confident, General."

"You're up against Belial, my friend."

"Yes, sir. I'm ready."

"All right. Fine! But remember that little book I carry? That's important! Have God on your side. Use all His instruments."

"Instruments, General?"

"Absolutely. Holy water works in some cases, or the Host. But still better, a man of God at your side."

"We're talking here about a priest?"

"Right on. I've called one in Vegas. You'll be hearing from him shortly. He's your sword and buckler, right there."

"Well, thank you, General, that's a good point. And thanks for the call."

"Nothing at all, my boy. I know you'll prevail. And God be with you."

The line went dead.

Back in his own suite, dressing for the evening ahead, he reflected on the general's call and felt warmed by it. Mad as a hatter Gibbs might be, and no doubt was, but there was something grand about him, some traditional splendor he shared with the old wound-seamed, God-fearing leaders of history who had ridden out to slaughter Indians and Mexicans and Spaniards and Huns with scripture on their lips and sabers in their fists. But that bit about sending him a priest, what was all that? One thing he didn't need was some busybody in a cassock fussing around him at this point; he would tell Debra to discourage the padre should he be heard from.

The big main floor lounge at the Dunes was crowded and noisy. He ordered a highball at the bar and found a seat from which he could take in the scene.

The Moroccans had hit town in force—they were all over the place.

Possibly they didn't like the booze at the MGM Grand or weren't supposed to be seen drinking there . . . and was colonel now the lowest staff rank in Guelta's army? Colonels proliferated, turned out in belted British World War II-style tunics with red collar tabs which Jason remembered so well and with so little pleasure. They were mostly small men and not conspicuously attractive or well-mannered but many of them seemed to have found girls already. That wasn't difficult in Vegas. It wasn't difficult at all.

Jason drank Pinch and Perrier, distracted by a quarrel in progress at the bar. Certainly a quarrel—or at least a peculiar dialogue between a man and a woman, the body language of the participants establishing its tensions. The girl was unmistakably the irritating *Paris Soir* reporter, although her bare burnished shoulder was turned so that he couldn't see her face. As for the man, he was another of the colonels, though chubbier than most. He had on oversize, designer dark glasses and he was very intense about the quarrel, the girl very remote, very scornful. Jason forced himself to look away. He had distrusted the girl but he had no wish to spy on her.

A correspondent from *Popular Mechanics* who had been at the press conference now elbowed in. He'd recognized Jason and he wanted to talk about the regenerative-drive steering brakes incorporated in SEDAV, but it was hard to concentrate on regenerative drives with the girl so near and the quarrel going on. Jason bought the correspondent a drink. He signaled for the check but before it could be brought a disturbance violated the euphoria of the bar—the sound of a loud, hard slap.

The son of a bitch hit her, Jason thought.

Then he turned.

The Moroccan was on the floor.

The girl kept her place.

People were moving away, giving them both plenty of room. A drink had spilled on a lady with a sequin lizard in her hair. She mopped herself furiously with paper napkins.

"Someone will have to pay for this," she yelled.

One of the barmen spoke on an intercom. He raised the service flap and came around the elbow of the bar; he looked studiously at the Moroccan on the floor but was careful not to touch him.

"He hit his head," said the correspondent. "He must have hit it on the rail when he went down. Oh, man, did he ever go down."

"Barman!" said the girl from *Paris Soir.*

"Did you hear that slap?" said the lady with the sequin lizard.

"You could have heard it out in the street," said the correspondent.

"Barman," said the girl, "may I have some ice, please? I'm afraid I've hurt my hand."

Security persons were tending to the Moroccan. They had him up. One of them located his designer shades where they'd fallen, still intact. Security put them back on the colonel's nose. He didn't look well, with or without them.

"Ice in a bowl," said the correspondent to the girl. "That's the ticket. It will keep down the swelling."

He had elbowed into the vacant area between Jason and the girl. He had great gifts as an elbower. The girl regarded him with distaste.

"Do you mind not coming quite so close?" she said. "Or not being where you are at all? Thank you. . . ."

The correspondent elbowed away.

Security supported the Moroccan, whose legs were not functioning well. They marched him to a fire exit. There was protocol in the way such matters were conducted at the Dunes. Meanwhile, a busboy mopped up the spilled drink and brought a bowl of ice in which the girl immersed her hand.

"Do you really think it will swell?" she asked Jason, quite as if they had already been discussing this.

"I wouldn't know," said Jason.

The girl spoke in a low, rapid tone.

"I apologize for the way I approached you at the pool, but . . . please understand . . . I have to talk to you, it's really terribly important. Not for a newspaper interview at all—that was untrue. . . . Will you listen to me for five minutes, Mr. Streck?"

All this she brought out coherently, but having said it, with her hand still in the bowl of ice, she began to shiver, imperceptibly at first, then with a growing vigor, shaking and shivering from head to foot as if a deadly chill had struck her to the bone.

The barman brought her a small white towel. She thanked him and, still shivering, dried her hand with it, after which she, Jason, and the barman all studied the hand with interest. It showed, so far, not the slightest indication of a bruise or of swelling but the hand, the hand itself compelled attention, a firm, roundish, willful hand, its compactness and strength and short small pointed colored nails somehow putting one in mind less of a lady's hand than of . . . a little paw. . . .

The barman set up the Pinch and Perrier, and for the girl a margarita. "On the house," he said.

Abe Kohn, watching from a table across the room, was not close enough to share the fascination of the hand but he had seen in general what was going on and he liked none of it. He watched because watching was his nature as well as his job. He had been trained for it through an arduous lifetime and he had instincts about it which he relied on because, when tested, they had usually proved sound. One such instinct had advised him earlier on that security at Las Vegas was a mess. He wished tonight was over. What happened tomorrow at the fort might be different. He hoped to God it would be. At least it was the army's business to see that it was. But tonight! A catered party in a hotel. No way you could provide more than token security, if that, in such an event. Leaks and loopholes everywhere. The kitchen help. The music, the entertainers, the waiters. All of it, but the waiters the worst—many of them not regularly employed at the place but brought in to help out for a special occasion, hardly checked if checked at all, and in addition, the guests themselves, VIPs to be chaperoned, hordes of questionable women all over the place, foreign military people in on short-term special visas, absolute dynamite on every hand. A farce. He was thankful that, except in the limited scope of company surveillance, he had no essential part in it. The problems belonged to the FBI, the Secret Service, the local authorities, and the hotels.

Better theirs than his.

He had sat alone for some time, sipping a soft drink, keeping watch.

He had seen the girl backhand the colonel. She packed a punch, quite a few of them did, young and beautiful like that, more than you'd ever expect. The Moroccan had gone down like a slaughterhouse pig.

Kohn sipped his cherry Coke and when next his gray and level glance traveled over to the bar he saw that Jason and the girl were now deep in conversation.

He waited and finally the break came. The girl got off the barstool. Going to the Ladies perhaps, but no, she was in the lobby, heading for the elevators.

Kohn rose. Jason, catching his eye, motioned him to stay in place. He came over and Kohn pulled out a chair for him.

"Don't you ever get tired of sleuthing, Abe?" he said. "I could see you in the mirror, and you didn't look happy."

"I'm happy as long as you're having a good time, boss."

"Well, thanks. The gal, now. This is a long way from what you might suppose. And don't tell me she's an agent, because I know that. Also right now she's about to be an ex-agent. Or like maybe dead."

"Let's hope not," said Kohn gravely.

"Now, Abe, don't rib me. This may all be one more steaming crock of something. An act from start to finish—the way she's come on. Socking that colonel. The whole bit. But the fact remains that she's in trouble. Or so she says."

"So she says. . . ."

"I know, Abe. Mind you, I don't give a shit. But it might be worth taking a look. She wants to talk. She wants that badly, but before she talks she wants some guarantee. I mentioned the government witness protection program. Any way she could apply for that?"

"No."

"Why not?"

"An individual can't apply for witness protection. Only an agency can apply."

"Okay, an agency. What's wrong with that? Don't you have contact among the people here, the bureau people? Or the ones from Langley?"

"Jason," said Kohn, "when you're talking witness protection you're talking about a hundred-square-foot spider web. It's a great idea, but it doesn't always work. Some witnesses haven't received what they've been promised. Others have been traced and they've wound up dead. Like you mention about her. It could happen. I'm not telling you it couldn't."

"Abe—"

"Let me lay it out for you. The Justice Department is the authorizing body but the U.S. Marshal's office administers the program. When an agency applies it has to have solid evidence that the nature of the testimony would pose a credible threat to the life of the witness and/or the witness's family, if there is one, in which case—"

". . . I hear you, Abe, but there are shortcuts, right?"

"I don't know."

"Come on, Abe. There are always shortcuts, and no one knows them better than you."

Kohn's glass was empty. He tilted it, then sucked thoughtfully on a piece of ice.

"Where is she now?" he asked at length.

"Up in her room. And she's going to stay there till she hears from us—from you . . . and she's scared pissless, Abe."

"She didn't look scared when she hit that Moroccan."

"Well, she is now. And she's young, Abe. She's goddamn young for what she's been doing."

She's young, thought Abe, *and you're not so old, buddy, that your balls aren't tied in knots until you can get in the kip with her.*

"I can give her a guard up there to keep an eye out. A guy with a gun and a badge. If that's what you want, for whatever good it will do."

"It might do a lot of good."

"About the program, I'll see. I don't make any promises."

"I'm not asking any. I appreciate this, Abe. Will you check with me later? Right now," he went on, not waiting for a reply, "I have a feeling this could be a long evening."

"That it could be," said Abe Kohn.

TWENTY-SIX

Rumors had circulated for the past two days that President Gantt himself would arrive in time for the party honoring Muhammed Guelta—a great gala at the Sands to be conducted along the general lines of the ball in the Tuileries the night before the Battle of Waterloo. It took a very large occasion indeed to prod or coax the Old Pudknocker out of his bunker but off-year election demands had accomplished this; he had been campaigning in California on behalf of gubernatorial and Senate candidates so it would have seemed logical and not too risky for him to pop over to Las Vegas for one night. Evidently, at the last minute, he had decided against this but not in time to forestall frantic preparations on the part of concerned individuals with government IDs who had been seen inspecting manholes, crawling through ventilator pipes, patrolling roofs, and screening hotels, restaurants, and casinos, Uzi submachine guns at the ready: there had been station wagon and limousine and van loads of them, strong, silent selfless chaps, conspicuously inconspicuous. They were not cops or sheriffs or soldiers and above all they were not servants, although when they showed up unexpectedly, as at times they did, at private gatherings, they did not have to be introduced to anybody and in fact it was poor taste to do so. In Gantt's absence they supplied added protection to the other notables present.

Secretary Truscott was the genial host tonight—not perhaps as skilled in the function as Walden Wynans had been, but presentable enough in his lightweight dinner jacket, lined up with the head of a foreign state beside him to receive the guests moving in a slow dense decorous file into the largest dancing room available at the Sands.

Jason had secretly dreaded facing Guelta, not sure that he could depend on his own conduct, yet when the moment came he was in complete control of it and of himself.

We shake hands with customers, don't we?

Since their last meeting the Moroccan president had put on thirty pounds. He no longer wore the trim belted uniforms that had become him so well; instead, in his role as proponent of Muslim unity and power, he had adopted Arab gear, folds and rolls of thick cloth trappings which, along with a black net of new facial hair, made him look like some sinister, oversize beekeeper.

The confrontation was brief. His hand was moist, heavy, and limp. His eyes were dull. No words were exchanged. He bore little resemblance to the man who had once pushed a telephone toward Jason saying, "Let's make the call and get through with this nonsense."

If he'd obeyed that command, would his life have been the way it came to be? Would his father, directly appealed to, have paid the ransom, and the break between them never happened? And in that case would he, Jason, have behaved as he had—behaved as if the breach in their closeness had been his fault rather than J.C.'s, the guilt of it something he'd had to set right by proving himself once more in the corporate grind when to be his own man he should have moved away?

In the past he'd gone over these thoughts endlessly, knowing there was no resolution to them, until time itself had made them meaningless.

Guelta was nothing to him now. A nonperson, replaced as an adversary by a robot tank. And tomorrow that issue at least might with luck be settled for good or for bad.

Jason left the line, proceeding to the ADECT table where he sat down at the place reserved for him.

With a crash of brass and percussion, the Sands's big-show orchestra opened the floor for dancing; waiters at every table were popping champagne corks while others scurried around, serving caviar and chopped egg canapes from a buffet where the centerpiece was a four-foot SEDAV carved out of ice, perfect down to the smallest detail. The individual aspic salads were also SEDAVs as were the strawberry ice cream molds, a grand piece of decor . . . but then everything about the party harmonized, it was so appropriately a corporate party (though this had not been its basic design) as well as a military one: uniforms everywhere, the Moroccan colonels, and now it appeared captains and majors and general officers mixed around with the command staff from the fort augmented by political and business pashas from Los Angeles and San Francisco who had flocked in, drawn by the irresistible lure of a gun show plus the chance to mingle and perhaps be photographed with high department brass.

But the corporate feeling—that was what prevailed, perceptible and comfortable even if a long way from the magnificence of some ADECT parties Jason could remember from the Valley boom days—jeweled pins and earrings for the ladies, gold money clips for the men, the Grateful Dead on the bandstand, and a Ferarri Puma as a door prize.

The main difference between a Silicon Valley party and tonight's was that wives would have been invited in the Valley but here were not. Jason suspected that no wife would have been present here unless bound in irons or rolled on a gurney. This was a camptown fiesta, nor could all Sam Truscott's geniality or the Pentagon's money make it anything else.

Muhammed Guelta would not know this or probably care if it was explained to him. He'd had one White House gala and come through with flying colors but the glitzed-up hoedown now in progress might conform better to his concept of high-living America; as for his retainers, they were free-form dancing like mad bemedaled imps, though some of them would have needed a crane to raise them tit-level with the long-legged showgirls who were their partners. They gobbled up the good fresh shrimp from Mazatlán and the rubbery Cornish game hen from Stouffer's and they drank, contrary to every doctrine of holy Mecca, whatever the five full-time barkeeps working at top speed could stuff into their glasses.

Jason's good mood held steady. At the ADECT table, Debra Fine sat with him when the others went out on the floor. He liked Debra. She knew this, and no doubt the knowledge had fortified her independence, but she was nice, very nice. She probably had a boyfriend (no husband, he was sure of that) stashed somewhere; he'd never inquired nor had she volunteered any information. She showed no restlessness at just having to sit while so many others were dancing. Obviously a gentleman did not indulge in aerobic activities to music when partially supported by a blackthorn cudgel. So they sat. They talked and drank and he enjoyed the warmth of her and the quickness of her thoughts—but when a young officer from one of the DOD groups, whom she seemed to know, came over and sat down with them Jason turned her loose by leaving. He went to the bar, as he had earlier at the Dunes, and it was here that Abe Kohn found him awhile later.

The security man inquired whether he intended hanging out at that location for the rest of the evening.

"You have another location in mind?"

"Cherry Coke over ice," Kohn directed the barman—and to Jason, "I have. Like someplace we can put our feet up and rap about *Paris Soir.* From what I hear—but this is just hearsay—she may qualify for the program. My friends have been talking to her."

"Great, Abe. I appreciate this."

"Don't mention it. But let's move. It's getting stuffy in here."

Jason was familiar with the kind of rhetoric Kohn employed when his conversation might be audited by electronically assisted ears or little spools of spinning tape.

"Let's go."

Kohn finished his revolting soft drink and set down the plastic glass stenciled around the rim with the word *SEDAV.*

Jason followed him out and together they walked across the street to the Dunes.

"So, here's the rundown on Mademoiselle de Saban . . ."

Kohn made the statement as soon as they were settled in Jason's suite and Kohn, to satisfy his stubborn, methodical cop's soul, had swept it once more for bugs.

"So now we're calling her Mademoiselle de Saban?"

". . . or Ariane Artaud or Lili Werner or several other AKAs. She has quite a résumé. Rich French family, broken home. Papa a diplomat. Brought her to D.C. when he found that she'd been screwing some CP card carriers and Red Brigade grads. He put her in an elite school to cure the adolescent yips but she kept contact with political action, Soviet style."

"Not exactly Mata Hari then, is she?"

"No. But there's a switch. She was the decoy in a scam to discredit

Secretary Walden Wynans, a logical target because he was SEDAV's initial supporter and biggest proponent. The scam worked."

"Okay. But how does it relate to that fracas in the bar?"

"That's where the interrogation started."

"So?"

"The colonel is under arrest. He's a Soviet mole who'd been pimping for Guelta. She was supposed to make a hit on Mr. Big of Morocco during or after a sexual encounter; when she refused the colonel threatened some unpleasant things. That was when she knocked him off the barstool."

"Very gutsy."

"—or just self-protective. Whether she killed Guelta or refused to be part of the plot her survival chances were like zero. Breaking cover had become her only option."

Silence prevailed, Kohn chewing ice from still another cherry Coke, Jason stretching and fidgeting as if what he'd been hearing had induced in him nothing but dullness and lassitude. At length he said:

"We'd better go back to the Dunes."

Kohn nodded.

He stood up, at the same time reaching in his pocket for a hotel key which he dropped on to one of the Sands's mahogany cocktail tables.

"That's where she is, in case you want to talk to her. I have a guard up there, as you requested. Tomorrow she won't need him; the U.S. Marshal's office will be taking over."

Jason stared at the key. Kohn turned his back, starting for the door, but without looking he had not the slightest doubt as to what would happen next. Jason scooped up the key. He walked down the hall, filled with an impatience that defied all common sense. At the elevator ramp he glared angrily at the light indicating that an up car had just passed his floor—and on *her floor,* hurrying along, he made a wrong turn and had to retrace his steps, the numbers on the doors conspiring to frustrate him, the endless numbers, the endless doors, the heavy carpets, the long halls. And then—*her* door.

The guard looked at Jason but said nothing. Kohn must have given him some instruction about this—that he, Jason, should be admitted. Christ, that Kohn . . .

Could she, like the guard, be *expecting him?* He put the key in the lock. Even the tiny rustle of it was . . . scary. He knocked, then turned the key and entered.

She was sitting on the bed with her legs crossed under her, writing something on a pad, her mop of rough pale hair obscuring her face.

Her body jerked. She pushed back the hair, staring at him in terror. Then her expression changed. She leaped off the bed and came toward him, he still standing a few feet into the room, the door stupidly left open behind him; she shut the door, then turned to him. She had on a silk shirt that hung open to the waist, nothing below. They slammed against each other, kissing as if bereft of their senses, but when he touched her sex she pulled away.

"It's late, you know . . . it's awfully late . . ." Late—what did that have to do with it? He unfastened his belt, his pants slipped down. They tangled around his knees, he threw off his coat, he struggled with his tie, his shoes, which refused to come off, then did—all this time standing before her naked, his penis erect, smooth, twitching, and she . . . she who had watched his contortions at first with a kind of remoteness, as if none of it had anything to do with her—*what was the matter with her?*—now lay on the bed, on her side, her face hidden, her body making jerky movements—*was she laughing at him?*

He threw himself on her. She wasn't laughing, the coiling and jerking was like the way she'd shivered and shuddered in the bar after she'd hit the pimp, only now it was something else, she was starting to come, her legs opened, her hand was on him guiding him in as she climaxed in wild, hard thrusts, her muscles tightening around him, her movements never stopping.

"Way up, way up inside me. Oh, that's so good . . ."

So it went. Later they slept sweetly, her body wrapped around him like a rope, nor did they wake for love again until morning, for late—as she had stated—late indeed it was and a hundred miles away, as the copter flies, two opposing armies were moving out in the eerie desert chill, taking their stations for an operation quite unlike the one in which Jason, the talented arms supplier, was so well engaged—this other a force-on-force confrontation which would last the rest of the night and all the coming day.

TWENTY SEVEN

ble Company of Task Force D, a training unit from a Texas army post, stood to arms in a pocket of darkness. They were a sorry bunch—dirty, hungry, irritable, bone weary, and nervous. The arid air had chapped their hands and the sun had cracked their lips and in their eyes was the sullen blankness that comes from many nights with little sleep and many days of moving and fighting and fighting and moving.

The day now beginning was their next to last training and the most critical.

The battalion commander had made that clear. He had laid out their mission—a "movement to contact"—which meant to find the enemy and attack him.

The enemy was supposed to be approaching a place which the battalion commander had marked on a map. Every company had similar maps and each had a different but related part of the same mission.

Find the enemy. That might not be so easy when all you had to go by was a pair of map coordinates, but as the battalion commander pointed out it would be easier in daylight and it would now be daylight very soon.

Able Company's main concern at the moment was not getting lost and their next concern was not running across some enemy unit that might have anticipated their move and be lying in ambush somewhere along the way, ready to cut them to pieces.

The enemy was the OPFOR, the Fort Irwin permanent cadre, or in other words—*Soviets.*

OPFOR's regimental array was deeper than yours. He shot with deadly accuracy, whether with missiles, rockets, mortars, howitzers, or rifle rounds. He knew how to breach wire, wriggle through mines, jam your signals, and infiltrate your positions. He moved fast and deployed with assurance. Every boulder and knob and wadi and rill and creosote bush in this desolate and menacing chunk of desert was ready on his brain for instant screening. Beat him, you poor dumb bastard, or you'd flunk the course. Or, in other words, you'd be dead.

Well, not really dead. There had from time to time been real deaths. That happened mostly from tank and truck accidents. Collisions. Running over sacked-out sleepers. Tumbling off high places. Parachuting in high winds. Seldom from live fire.

Able Company had already had live-fire exercises. They had laid behind mattresses of mines and wire and bashed Soviet soldiers who attacked in the form of wood or metal silhouettes weaving and lurching on huge unseen belts, straight or sideways or in columns but always unexpectedly while their shells burst around you and their gunships blasted you from above.

Able Company had done all right with the live-fire drill but today would be an even greater challenge. It would be where they divided the men from the boys and success from failure.

The column moved out slowly in the dark. It crossed a series of rills, a term taken from astronomy where it defined the grooves in the moon, a landscape not unlike that with which Able Company was now grappling.

The tanks and APCs rattled along, the drivers in their night-vision goggles seeing a clear but absurd green-glimmering world, an existential concept, mocking and dangerous. The land climbed and the sun rose pale and veiled behind Soda Mountain to the east. Here General John C. Fremont had once camped and, later, twenty-mule teams had hauled borax (the picture of those mules stamped on the boxes in old-time grocery stores). Soon it was possible to take the goggles off, dig into a ready-to-eat field ration in its plastic container and complete a linkup, as ordered, with Charlie Tank.

Charlie was there.

Able Company's captain got out of his APC, map in hand. He ordered deployment and the TOW crews dismounted their missiles from the carriers and dug them into the face of the hill. The tankers and infantry got to work digging foxholes in the flinty volcanic earth and planting blue simulated ceramic mines where they would do some good.

The kill corridor lay south and the swell of the hill would shelter the gunners from OPFOR fire at least until certain new weapons were brought up along with instructions phoned in from TOC on what use to make of them.

There had been scuttlebutt about the new weapons—the robot tanks. They had been described in newspapers and shown on television. Nobody in Able Company had ever seen one for real but all hoped that the company would be assigned some since it was rumored they had limitless tactical powers, they could win any battle on their own. Gossip had had it that OPFOR would get them first but this was worst-casing it: OPFOR had too many advantages as it was. Surely the task force—now in its various linkages, along the ridges south-southeast of Tiefort Mountain—would be the one to get them. Or so Able Company hoped when they were not too tired to hope or think at all.

They chipped and they dug. They ate cold food and drank alkali-tasting water from their canteens and the captain glassed the attack corridor with his binoculars. He knew he had the right coordinates. He had made his linkup and it was not his fault that the movement to contact had not resulted as it was supposed to. Not as yet. The enemy would be along. He would certainly be along in due time and the robots would be too. They had to be because their presence was the main feature of today's exercise. Certain VIPs would be on hand to witness the exercise but this was nothing that a captain from a Texas training unit had to bother his noggin over.

Everyone knew that VIPs visited Fort Irwin. The fort was a kind of army Disneyland with much appeal to visitors, though there was nothing Disneyish about what took place there.

What took place was training, not staged for the entertainment of the VIPs. The VIPs were there by courtesy of the commanding general and certain politicians and that was all.

By swiveling his glasses in a ninety-degree arc the captain could see the new bunkerlike grandstand notched into The Whale—an eyesore—and to the captain, an irrelevancy. He reflected on his position. He was understrength, he knew, but at least he had some Dragons and Vipers for short-term battles. That was mainly what he thought about. He also had some wishes. He wished the Dragon had been a better weapon. He wished he had time enough to build a decent mine field. He wished he could roll more wire but it was dangerous to leave soldiers exposed out there on the sand, in the sun, where they could be spotted by enemy snipers. Some were and they got killed so the captain recalled the rest of the detail and set them to digging.

The captain put some water in his canteen cup and mixed coffee powder with it. He drank the coffee slowly, then refilled the cup with water; moistening his fingers, he tried to ease the aching in his sun-strained, wind-irritated eyes, then lay back against a rock, drowsily watching Charlie Company digging and chipping. The rock was warm and the captain must have dozed off for a few minutes for when he looked again he saw that the men making foxholes had stopped their work, they were staring at the sky, and the captain, shading his eyes, looked also, and perceived a flight of specks up there, rapidly approaching, their clatter identifying them as helos, a regular swarm of them. At first they seemed to form a random pattern but it soon became clear that this was not so, they deployed as an escort for a large, Sea King-type bird, some above it, some below.

A staff sergeant climbed up to the captain.

"Can you see it, sir? On the Sea King, sir—the seal. Is that for real, sir, is *he* coming in?"

"Is who coming in? What are you talking about, Sergeant?" said the captain, not yet able to fix the big bird in his field glasses, but as he spoke the big helo obligingly stabilized and he indeed perceived some kind of unusual insignia on it—an escutcheon or something—and in a moment he was able to make out the words:

UNITED STATES OF AMERICA

The captain lowered his glass. All the weary dirty soldiers in the steep little redoubt were standing now, staring and waving, and a few were cheering—and then all were cheering—and on Dan Company's hill they were doing likewise, cheering and cheering, the insubstantial quavering sound hardly audible in the thump of the convoy's engines, now almost overhead, because now everyone could see it, *the Presidential Seal,* it was true, by Jesus, yes, the Old Pudknocker himself was up there, he had left whatever else he had been up to and flown out here to the boonies, the old son of a gun, to watch Texas fight OPFORs.

The frail hoarse ridiculous cheering went from company to company along the defense perimeter in the rimrock, and in the faces of the men who raised this preposterous sound could be seen the bemused childish expression of people who have won a lottery or collected a wager on a big race as they watched the bird with the seal on it tilt softly, grandly down and settle, light as a feather, on the dry salty bed of Bicycle Lake.

TWENTY EIGHT

President Claude C. Gantt stepped out of his helicopter and walked with his stiff angular stride past the honor guard awaiting him. He saluted the guard, then entered his bulletproof tram and was whisked up The Whale. Muhammed Guelta had preceded him into the bunker-grandstand and the two men shook hands cordially while press cameras snapped and the single video crew allowed in the stand that day went through its annoyance and departed. A lunch of sandwiches, coffee, and soft drinks was served while below in the main attack corridor artillery was firing and fighter planes were screeching down to support the OPFOR armor advance against the training task force.

The commanding general of the rotating units and the brigadier general commanding the National Training Center took turns briefing the notable onlookers.

Guelta seemed puzzled.

"Do you not use laser beams to simulate live rounds?"

"Yes, Mr. President," said the brigadier general, "we do—the Multiple Laser Engagement System, or MILES. Those small black boxes you can see on the tank cannon and the machine guns emit the beams—a tight pulse which must strike a detector on the target man or vehicle.

Microchips in the detectors record hits and misses. If a man hears intermittent beeping from the box in his detection harness he's been near-missed. If it turns into a kind of shriek he's dead. Dead men must disarm their weapons to stop the beeping. Then they're out of the battle. Trucks and tanks have revolving lights instead of beepers—interrupted for a near miss, continuous for a kill."

"But the detonations and the smoke—"

"The lasers are triggered by blank rounds. They won't go off unless one is fired."

The Moroccan pulled thoughtfully on his beard.

"I am in the market for such a system," he said quietly, a remark to which no one paid attention. The business of the day was not to sell lasers.

Claude Gantt leaned forward in his upholstered chair in the center of the front viewing row, his attention fixed on the sweeping battle below. With his interest in defense and his mastery of its detail he could have delivered the briefing as well as the commanding general or perhaps better. Modern battle, real and simulated, had always fascinated him for its density, its complexity, its ever-changing, fluid currents; he had studied the Fort Irwin training procedure and even suggested some variations which in due course had been approved and incorporated in the exercise but this was his first personal visit to the site itself and he was prepared to enjoy it.

Far better meeting Guelta here, letting him have a look at the new warfare and what the robot tanks would do—those new and fascinating toys for which Morocco would pay such a high price—far, far better here than sitting through another state dinner with him in the White House.

Guelta was not the type of guest who made an evening merry. A pompous bore abroad, an infamous autocrat at home, he nevertheless had a geopolitical dimension that forced concessions as did his Bedouin guile, his camel-driver shrewdness.

He would do much with his SEDAVs—a lot of it to no one's taste. But never mind. Letting him have them enlarged and extended the U.S. presence in Africa. He was big enough to be in the game.

The President of the United States stretched his boondock legs out as far as space allowed, although not quite far enough to get the stiffness out of them: the military contractor who designed this nook had not built it to accommodate legs of this type. Still, it was a good place from which to view the action—strong and well revetted, more than reasonably secure; Gantt wondered why he didn't feel more at ease in it. He had a peculiar prickling in his nerves, a sense that something here was not quite right, that there was danger in the air. This discomfort was a piece of his professional equipment, an early-warning system to which he was highly sensitized. It had saved him often as a young man riding the high country where grudges were treasured like family jewels, passed along like genes, and violence could erupt suddenly and fatefully when least expected; it had supported him no less effectively after he'd risen higher and the perils were more subtle, better concealed but no less deadly.

It was bothersome at times, being so sensitive, so aware—he would never deny that the secret signals had been wrong occasionally, had alerted him without due cause, but that was a small price to pay for such a built-in security device. Better safe than sorry, as Lucy was wont to say.

Down in the attack corridor, a spearhead of OPFOR armor was moving forward, planes and gunships screaming above it, simulated rocket and shell fire preparing the way and the President watched, understood, and made mental notes on it all . . . and yet all the time there was that faint insistent shrilling in the back of his head and his large bony hands, holding the binoculars to his eyes, were a little colder than they should have been. Nothing unusual about that, of course; he lowered the glasses and felt for a pill which he popped surreptitiously into his big fanged jaw.

This was about all he could do to ease his portent; protocol demanded that he stay fixed at the side of the worthy Moroccan through thick and thin, though in all truth he would have preferred to be in the control tower over on Tiefort Mountain where the huge vibration-free gyro-zoom video lens tracked the action for the observer-controllers and their computers. There he could see the whole battle, here only part of it, the movement of OPFOR to turn the flank of the U.S. motorized rifle regiment on the ridge.

OPFOR came on steadily, the hatches of the Soviet T-72s closed, their cannons spewing fire. The biggest tank guns in the world, those—125 mm (the heaviest U.S. were 120); the roomiest, most agile turret—more room inside than the M-1 or the West German Leopard 2; the "live tracks" (turned by sprockets under the fabric skirt), and on the engine deck the tried and true Soviet twelve-cylinder diesels, supercharged so as to drive this forty-four-ton mastodon forty-five miles an hour in peace or in war, on level earth or up stone walls. An engine of nightmare!

Evil monster from a space-age fairy tale! All this Gantt knew from the stats, the little marks on paper that he memorized so easily. But to see them in action was a gut-shaking experience . . .

Following them came the BMPs—the Russian version of an armored personnel carrier—savage, bristling rows of them, rolling track to track. Shells rained on them all from the artillery in the basalt and granite clefts above, land mines took a fearful toll, kill lights rotated in the black sooty emission of smoke canisters, but still they churned on and when they were hit backup armor and more armor drove relentlessly through the wreckage. For this was the classic Soviet assault tactic, proven and approved from Stalingrad and Kursk to Afghanistan and the Mongolian border: give no quarter, ask no aid, plough ahead no matter what, for every man, weapon, and vehicle was expendable, and there were more to throw in, always more and more and more.

A T-72 diverted to attack the flimsy wire concertina Able Company had worked on so laboriously in the weary heat of noon, its obliquely slanted and heavily armored frontal plates ("glacis") shrugging off armor-piercing rounds from Able's hand-held antitank weapons as if they'd been birdshot. A point-blank cannon hit laid it low but a T-80 and a T-60 soon replaced a direct ascent of the seventy-degree rock wall of the redoubt; if the tanks' clawed climbing tracks could chew into the steep grade and get traction, Charley Company would be out of the fight . . . and the battalion commander eligible for reproof at the After Action Review later that day.

Would that be the scenario?

Well, not quite yet. For now, from their bivouac in a hidden elbow of the desert, came the SEDAVs.

Jason saw them at the same moment as Able Company. He was in a Hummer—an updated version of a jeep—bouncing through rutted tank trails running down from the fort cantonment into the battlefield. (There are no roads.) There was terror and madness in the air, a brain-boggling, stomach-clenching confusion in the roaring attack and counterattack of behemoth steel engines, the shuddering of the earth under their treads, the choking smears of smoke, the fire of dismounted infantry maneuvering with hand-held weapons while they tried to avoid "friendly" as well as enemy firewalls, the wild plumes of white whirling dust, the explosion of mines, mortar rounds, and bombs, the howling flight of fighter planes overhead—all this formed a hideous melee into which his small tub on wheels, flying a yellow guidon from its aerial, plunged without hesitation, without orders or a coherent direction plan.

The Hummer had room for four passengers in proper seats, or four more if you used the pull-down ledges to the rear. Now it carried a total of six: the controller-observer (detached here for special duty as a guide), a small chaplain in a funny uniform, Colonel Jared (ADECT's link with the army), the congressman from Georgia, Jason himself, and a Spec 4 driver, who had his hands full avoiding destruction while he skirted the edges of the OPFOR advance, firmly convinced that he was driving a jeepful of lunatics.

There'd been a problem relating to the congressman. The lieutenant confirming allocations at the Fort Irwin cantonment hadn't wanted him aboard.

"I don't have you on my list, sir."

"Then somebody's goofed," said the congressman.

The lieutenant consulted his clipboard.

"I believe you're assigned to the computer center, sir. All the action is beamed in there instantly. The viewing is much more comfortable there, sir."

"No doubt, Lieutenant, but I'm to go downrange and that's how I want it," said the congressman.

Jared leaned over and said something privately to the lieutenant, who shrugged his shoulders. One did not, when a colonel spoke, assert an opposing view.

The chaplain had been another added starter. He'd arrived unannounced that morning in the lobby of the Dunes: a small, eager, cocky person got up as if for a costume party in musty, old-style combat fatigues, with a silver cross on his collar.

"Mr. Streck! An honor, sir . . . I'm Father Armando. General Gibbs ordered me to contact you."

"How come you're in uniform, Father?"

"First Cav, Vietnam, seventy-one. I just pulled it out of the trunk . . ." He spread his arms, proud of the period jungle-green suit.

"I see."

Armando moved closer, raised himself on tiptoes to speak into Jason's ear.

"The general told me what you're up against. I've come prepared."

Jason stared at him stupidly. Five minutes earlier, in this lobby, he had said good-bye to Jacqueline, AKA Ariane Artaud or Lili Werner or whatever—walked with her to the great doors of the hotel after one of the most memorable nights of his life, her arm in his, his stride holding steady with as little help as possible from the blackthorn. At the door they had kissed briefly, in the manner of people who might meet again in a few hours, and he had seen her get into a tan compact like any other tan compact except for the lettering U.S. Marshal on the forward doors. She'd waved and then the car had whirled her away into the witch's cavern of the witness protection program, from which few travelers return.

Waves of desolation were still sweeping through his veins as he studied the thickset soldier-priest with his smiling face and his idiotic message. Father Armando's nose was flattened and one ear cauliflowered. He looked more like a miniature ex-pug than a servant of the cross. Jason's first thought was to send him away, with thanks and apologies to General Gibbs . . . but there was something about this Armando that made him pause: his utter confidence in himself, his eagerness to be accepted. He radiated goodwill. You couldn't just tell a chap like that to get lost. It would be unkind and perhaps . . . bad luck. Gibbs himself wore an iron Bible in his pocket—a holy object, no doubt, but a good luck charm too. And it could stop a bullet!

Fortune's wheel today spun in a narrow track. Jason knew he would need all the luck he could get.

He had taken Father Armando to the hotel desk and written him a pass for the helo trip to Irwin.

The congressman regarded the priest and the surrounding environment with equal distaste. He was already pale and sweating and evidently in the throes of some private malaise.

Spec 4 wanted to know where to go; Jared snapped an order no one heard. And off they went.

Spec 4 faced straight ahead and drove, struggling in the rutted trails; the set of his shoulders as he fought the wheel conveyed no approval of the direction. In fact, with OPFOR's steel cavalry thrusting west between Langford Lake and Red Lake Landing, there was now no way to head but southeast, and fast.

The lakes weren't true lakes in any sense—rather irregular spreads of soft-surface alkali where geologic water had once been and where the rare desert cloudbursts still clotted. They could be traversed better in a tracked vehicle than a Hummer, but that was not the trouble. The trouble was OPFOR—a wall of moving steel. Jason hadn't foreseen this. Brigade's intelligence assessments were available on the Hummer's radio but so jammed that little could be made of them. They shed no light on his hunch that if TY60 went on a killing spree the action would be at The Whale.

Perhaps the heavy armor flowing like lava up the corridor would pause and leave a gap. Or fall back. Obviously it was meeting strong resistance. The ground was littered with decommissioned tanks (in real combat they would have been burning), and to the west artillery fire lighted the ridge.

He couldn't see what the SEDAVs were doing but he could hear their howl, a whooping, high C note, distant and insistent, pushing through the door-slam *whump* of howitzers, the thudding of heavy machine guns, and the scream of ground-skimming planes. Flares were going up. In the coiling black smoke, the yellow flare bursts, the whirling sand, the scene in its moonscape frame looked like a medieval artist's concept of hell.

The howling issued from the west, a shift which meant even wider deployment if the Hummer was to approach The Whale. He leaned forward to yell at the driver who had now stopped and sat leaning on his wheel, watching Jared. The colonel had jumped out and run over to a Texas soldier sitting with his back against a rock.

The soldier was bearded and incredibly dirty. He had shed his helmet, shirt, and boots. An unlighted cigarette dangled from his scabrous lips. He stared vacantly at the men in the Hummer.

Jared stood over him, asking for something. The man shook his head. He reached for his AT-4, propped beside him, but Jared shoved him back. He did this in an unbecoming, unofficerlike way—with his foot. He seized the weapon and ran back to the car with it, sliding into his seat. Spec 4 gunned his engine and away they went, but still—Jesus!—headed the wrong way. Jason leaned forward and yelled in the colonel's ear, "We have to get over to The Whale."

Jared didn't answer. He was fearfully excited and there was a waggish ferocity about him that took Jason by surprise. He held up the AT-4, the light antitank weapon the United States manufactures from a Swedish parent.

"Live rocket load—should have been turned in yesterday. Man should be court-martialed."

The Hummer now was pitching like a skiff in a rough sea. It was crossing one of the wadis—easy enough to travel downgrain, hell and all if you were at a cross angle, the only course Spec 4 could take.

The congressman from Georgia had his head almost in his lap. When he raised it his face looked green. He spoke to Spec 4 who stepped on the brake.

The congressman jumped out and immediately fell to his knees. He vomited copiously into the sand, then straightened up, wiped his mouth, and retched two or three times more.

The Hummer had stopped near a medical unit, three ambulances sheltering in a clump of creosote and cholla; toward these the congressman walked unsteadily, a hand raised in supplication.

"Let them take care of him," said Jared disgustedly.

He got back into his seat. As they drove on he was cradling the AT-4 in his lap, rubbing dirt from it with his sleeve.

And now the little car held five men instead of six.

The firefight in the west was slackening and it was clear that the OPFOR thrust had been repulsed. Behind a volcanic outcropping some T-80s were dug in as artillery, their cannon elevated as they fired long-range at the ridge, but in the corridor the Soviet armor was slowly redeploying or pegged down in motionless files, engines idling, crews waiting for new orders. The smoke was thinner here and the pandemonium of battle slightly diminished but the howling of the SEDAVs still drowned all other noises. Amplified by the packed sand, the naked rocks, the coppery bowl of the sky, it shattered the eardrums—the acoustical signature of the new, robot-style war.

The observer-controller was no help. He had more pressing concerns; first to keep the Hummer from getting in a wreck, for which he would be blamed, or from interfering with the action in the field, which would be even worse. Once both contingencies came near happening simultaneously. They had been crossing an open area after a particularly jarring wadi when a bullhorn voice accosted them authoritatively: *"Visitors in Hummer. Stop* NOW. Repeat, NOW. Back in your own tracks! BACK FURTHER! *You are in a mine field!"*

A careful hundred-yard backtrack, bullhorn-guided by some unseen guard, got them off undamaged to lurch again into battle but still far from where Jason wanted to be, *had* to be.

Jared had refused to head southward through the attack corridor when it would have been easier to cross; it would be harder now, perhaps impossible, but the try had to be made.

Jason yelled orders at Spec 4; Spec 4 looked at the colonel and Jared, with a waggle of his finger, countermanded the orders. Then Jared and Jason, bouncing around in the Hummer, got into a shouting match with Jared finally declaring, "Mr. Streck, let me remind you that I am in charge here."

Ho, what bullshit! He was not in charge. He had never been in charge. At worst, the line of authority had been left undefined. The NTC had received a Pentagon instruction (Jason had a copy of it) requesting co-operation with the ADECT representatives of "such nature as to enable them to view and record the exercise as they may see fit without interfering with its progress," only further along adding that "Colonel Jared will serve as liaison, and all reports should be cleared through him."

He sure as hell wasn't clearing reports now. He was trying to run the goddamn show.

Jason had never felt any comradeship with Jared. He was an odd duck. Dig under the facade of a West Pointer and you found an odd duck, one who didn't think or act like a normal person but according to some secret manual. They were all like that, his own father had been like that. He'd shared no confidences with Jared—hadn't really trusted him since the time he'd been so stubborn, refusing to return the TY60 after it had been shipped out.

All right. He was fed up. He felt confident that within the mandate "to observe and record . . . as they see fit" he could unload Jared; at least he had this right, although most likely it would not be possible to prove it.

And then, out of the blue, the opportunity arrived . . .

The Hummer had reached a checkpoint, flagged down by a sergeant standing in the trail between a truck and an APC. Two soldiers were handing out equipment from the truck. The sergeant saluted the Hummer.

"Gas masks required from here on, sir."

For gas attack simulations, both armies could fire CS riot-control shells, hardly lethal but fiercely irritating to the eyes and sickening to breathe. The OC was explaining this to Armando as Jason addressed the sergeant.

"Do you have contact with the TOC?"

"Ground line and FM. Do you wish to send a message?"

"Yes. Ask them to get a vehicle here to pick up the colonel. He's going back to the cantonment."

"Hold that, sergeant," snapped Jared. He drew Jason aside. He clenched and unclenched his fists as if restraining an impulse to throw punches.

"What do you mean, I'm going back?"

"I'm requesting that you do."

"Why, for Christ's sake?"

"It's nothing personal."

"I'd say it's goddamn personal. And I resent it, sir."

"We don't have to make a big deal out of it. I can conclude my mission from here on without your services. No criticism is intended."

"So now it's a mission. I thought it was an observation tour."

"You can use any terms you like."

"You said mission. That's a military term and we're on a military reservation, Jason—er, Mr. Streck. I'm not subject to your orders here. I take my orders from the army, from my superiors. You're not my superior."

"I haven't given you an order. I've made a request. I'm sorry if you've taken offense."

Jared's knuckles were still tight but he seemed now able to weigh the situation more objectively. He spat venomously on the lava sand, messing the spittle around with his foot.

"I'm entitled to a full explanation of this."

"You shall have it. Later."

The sergeant was on his way back from the truck.

"I've raised the TOC, sir. Vehicle's on the way."

The Hummer took off again, four men in it now, these four all wearing black, long-snouted gas masks which made them look like enormous conspiratorial rodents on a spree.

The driver drove, the observer-controller observed, the priest sat silent and composed, and Jason gave the orders. Bouncing and jerking, they wove through the stalled armor in the corridor, sometimes losing ground, but always making it up again, the O-C's yellow guidon giving them passage rights. And down the wind, sometimes near at hand, at others faint and distant, came the strange, shrill terrifying howling of the robots.

TWENTY NINE

Able Company's captain was jubilant. The ridge had held. His hasty mine carpet, so lacking in depth, his pitiful wire concertinas, his machine guns, his tired soldiers, his blind desperation, and Charlie Company's mortars had held off OPFOR's spearhead just long enough for the arrival of the new, wondrous beetles. Oh, what a sight that had been, their charge from under their camouflage nets in the rocks and the wadis. How splendid their assault as they leaped on OPFOR's Soviet monsters, harrying them, ramming them, scuttling in head-on—too low for the most depressed range of their 70- and 80-mm cannon—to put them out of action.

Able Company's captain felt great affection for the brigade commander who had laid out the battle plan. Texas itself would honor that brigade commander and some of the honor would spill over onto Able Company. Every goddamn man in Able Company was now some kind of Davy Crockett, courtesy of the brigade commander and the lovely robots.

The Valley floor was strewn with blinking wrecks—tank casualties, doomed to sit helpless until the observer-controllers with their little green keys turned off the rotating lights, restoring them to life. The captain took pleasure in that too. He had forgotten his aching bones, his cracked and blistered hands, his chapped lips, his weariness, his hunger; he stood tall in his defended redoubt, watching medics evacuate the "wounded."

Half a mile further along, hardly visible in the funky murk of low-hanging smoke and CS, half a dozen SEDAVs blazed away at stragglers from the retreating armor column. The captain noticed one SEDAV which had either sustained a hit or was out of control for some other reason because it was blindly and aberrantly trying to force its way up *toward The Whale*!

President Gantt had watched the OPFOR vs. Texas engagement with pleasure. He was proud of his army and the improvements in the conventional forces of all three services under his regime; when the SEDAVs made their flank attack he had a telephone brought to his seat and called Walden Wynans in Washington to tell him about their success.

"They're the stars of the show, Walden."

"I'm delighted, Mr. President."

"We'll review the whole program. There's been opposition, as you know—some recent doubts. But today's doings should lay all that to rest."

"I hope so, Claude. And I'm glad I contributed."

"Without you and the senator there wouldn't be any SEDAVs. He's right here. He wants to speak to you—"

And with this he handed the instrument to John Lighty, seated between himself and Sam Truscott, who said a few kind words.

Feeling in the Pudknocker's kitchen cabinet ran high that, having suffered conspicuously for his disgrace, the former secretary was due for restitution—possibly as a major ambassador.

Catering people passed canapes and champagne. Armor deployed and redeployed, artillery crashed, and CS gas wafted about below. Gantt fidgeted. The ominous disquiet he'd felt earlier still afflicted him; he'd better move along. But easier said than done. *If he could just get through the next few minutes . . .*

The President rose. He walked back to the toilets, located up a slight incline to the rear—a move that saved his life.

. . .

The going was bad, the angle steep. The robot would gain a few feet, its tracks spinning, then slip back, but it persisted, little by little making headway in its senseless undertaking. The hardest part was negotiating the base of the abutment. After this it picked up speed, amusing the captain who followed its ascent with his binoculars, fully expecting to see it spin out and roll back down. This did not happen. Instead, the preposterous machine gained height. Backed into a crevice, it elevated its cannon and . . . *it fired! The captain saw the rocket strike the bunker-grandstand.* Dirt flew, sandbags shifted, a chunk of prestressed concrete broke loose and bounded away like a pebble.

The captain refocused his glass. He could not believe what he was seeing.

What was the matter up there, what were the guards doing, the security squad, the Secret Service . . . where was the counterfire?

Surely the revetment had been built to be proof against any such attack . . . and then he realized that the terrain itself might have been considered protection enough, the planners assuming that in the middle of a 20,000-square-mile military post, *there was no danger.*

The President's grandstand had no fire power. Side arms carried by the Secret Service and the FBI would be about as effective as slingshots against the homicidal, armor-plated creature that had just cut loose at the VIPs they were supposed to entertain.

The captain jammed his field glasses back into their case. Yelling to the soldiers within earshot, he led them back to where his APC was parked. He took the driver's seat himself. He was glad he'd broken the rules, failed to turn in all his RMP rounds after the live-fire exercise.

In the bunker the lights went out. A beefy Secret Service agent threw himself on Gantt, pushing him to the floor and lying on him.

"For your protection, Mr. President."

"Get off me, you son of a bitch," said Claude C. Gantt.

Jason picked up the Mayday call on the Hummer's shortwave. Every OC vehicle in sight was racing toward The Whale along with the medics and fire emergency squads. The Hummer was now in the south-middle of the corridor and he could see the SEDAV scrambling out of its niche, zigzagging downward, at first handily, then in a crippled, lopsided style, the treads on one side working better than those on the other.

Able Company's captain had connected with at least one hit. He fired his last armor-piercing round—a near miss.

He was out of ammo.

The men and women in the shattered observation post sat quiet. Someone had located an emergency generator. Soon lights would be on and the wounded could be tended, the dead separated out. The others waited. There was no disorder. The casualties had been caused by ricochets and falling debris rather than fragmentation but the choking dust made it hard to breathe.

Help would come. The call had gone out. If the tram wasn't damaged relief would be there soon. And even if the tram didn't work at all some way would be found. They would be reached.

They waited. When disaster strikes, people somehow find the strength to deal with it. Even very lowly folk do this and those in the bunker-grandstand were not lowly folk. They were the elite, the leaders. Tempered in crisis, terror was by no means new in their lives, but today it was unseemly.

No bugle had summoned them to defend themselves or rally to the flag. This was supposed to be a friendly outing, a Shrine picnic, a cruise on the Good Ship Lollipop.

The anatomy of terror had failed to conform. That was the nature of the beast.

The Old Pudknocker lived. That was the main thing. Even now he was busy. He personally helped the shaken Secret Service men carry a great bundle of blood-soaked and excrement-impregnated Arab robes encasing the unconscious form of Muhammed Guelta back to the service area converted into an emergency first-aid station.

When the President travels, dread trots at his elbow; countermeasures are preplanned. Ambulances stand by, doctors and paramedics ride in his entourage, hospital routes are charted, staffs alerted, surgical teams are quickly available. General Noel Harpsfield, Gantt's personal physician, noting Guelta's blood loss, injected Ringer's lactate intravenously and shocked him with 200, then 300, then 360 joules to steady the arrhythmic, failing heart. Blood pressure was undetectable; immediate application of Mast trousers restored it only slightly. The Moroccan's eyes were open but unfocused, his nose already high and thin the way dead men's noses get. He died twenty minutes later in the ambulance on the way back to the cantonment.

. . .

"Good-bye, sir," said the observer-controller. He got out of the Hummer, now slowed to a crawl, and jumped into another guidon-flagged vehicle, heading toward The Whale. So now, where once six men had ridden, there were three: Jason, Armando, and the Spec 4 driver. They drove on.

A shortwave from Able Company's captain and the Mayday alert from the bunker was the only notice the battlefield got of what had happened. Few had seen it. To do that you had to have been positioned above it, like the captain who flashed:

Damaged robot heading west.

TY60 itself, dragging through the confusion in the fire corridor, was just one more partially disabled vehicle among many others. Jason, glassing The Whale and the area below, saw it because he was looking for it, then lost it again, but raced on by haphazard calculation designed to bisect its retreat.

West had to be right. To the north was trackless desert, further on Death Valley with its hotels, gas stations, and tourist stops and to the west NASA's huge Goldstone Tracking Station, closely guarded and patrolled, behind which the sun was now setting. The only escape route was here, the rough terrain between the cantonment and the alkali beds of Langford Lake and the so-called Langford Spring, and then on and on to craters, caves, old abandoned mines—the Olympus, the Daisy— and beyond these the mazes of the Paradise Mountains, roadless and rugged, cleft with gnomish fissures, volcanic cul-de-sacs, and dried secret streambeds dead-ending in sheer rock. His thought was:

Cut the bastard off now or we lose him.

The thin September twilight fell fast in the desert under the cantonment cliff. Chill sprang out of the ground. Spec 4 turned on his headlights . . . but now there were other vehicles coming on, late pursuers who had followed Jason's course or picked up the robot's trail on their own. Hell and all to pay if they caught up now.

Twice, in spite of his haste, he had the Hummer stop and got out to look for a single trail where hundreds of tanks, large and small, had savaged the desert floor: the signature print of a robot running wild, running crippled. . . .

There seemed to be no trail at all. The lights behind were closer, gaining as the vegetation thinned, the rills became fewer; mixed with the spicy, acrid smell of crushed chemise and creosote rose the reek of burning diesel—the stink of the robot's turbo drive. They were close, very close, and standing in the Hummer Jason got his first glimpse of the fleeing thing, its plates catching glints from the Hummer's beams, its aerial wagging like an insect's feeler.

Spec 4 slammed to a stop.

"For Christ's sake, move it!" Jason yelled.

"No, sir," said Spec 4.

"What the fuck is wrong with you?"

"I doan go no further, sir.

Up ahead, the robot slithered off into the gray sand, the darkening air.

"This vehicle doan leave the reservation. That's mah orders. I'm responsible for this vehicle."

Spec 4 took out a pocket map, unfolded it, pointed to a long straight line marked with Xs.

"That's the boundary, sir. The Barstow Road."

"Give him an order," Jason said in the priest's ear.

A chaplain was an officer and Spec 4 listened to officers.

Said the priest:

"Okay, Specialist. You're relieved. Stand down."

"Yes, sir. Thank you, sir," said Spec 4.

He didn't move.

"Get out," snapped Armando.

"Very well, sir."

Spec 4 raised his long, bony body from behind the wheel. He stepped out of the Hummer, then reached in and took the engine keys. He stood quietly, the keys in his hand, his hands at his sides, looking with bright, wary malice at the chaplain and the important lame civilian who walked with a stick and his expression said, *you want the keys, come and get them.*

Armando, the man of God, hit the tall driver with a left to the stomach, then a right to the jaw. Spec 4 went down on his side, then rolled over on his back. He had cut his forehead as he fell. He tried to rise, then flopped back again. The keys were in the sand. Armando picked them up and handed them to Jason.

"I'm sorry, sir," he said. "I overreacted."

"You did just fine, padre," said Jason.

He leaped in the Hummer.

"Get in, get in."

"No, sir," said Armando. "I must help this soldier. I may have hurt him."

Jason jammed the car in gear and shot across the road. The vehicles behind were close enough now to deluge the Hummer and the surrounding scene in a pour of fierce metallic light. An old trail, half overgrown and hardly visible, angled off to the west and he followed this blindly, recklessly, crossing dead streambeds, or dodging around boulders, his purpose now to divert the chase from where the TY60 was holed up, back by the Barstow-Irwin hardtop. After a mile or so he pulled over and let the bunch behind go past: two APCs, a Hummer, another Hummer, a field ambulance, and, absurdly, a signal corps TV unit. An MP sergeant on a motorcycle drew up beside him.

"Trouble?"

"Out of gas."

The MP waved off a salute and sped away. Jason waited till his taillight disappeared, then turned back the way he'd come. He drove slowly now; calm pervaded him—TY60, at the end of its tether, was at his mercy. Though it might kill like a jungle animal, it still must have current to drive its systems—current that the radio beam in his hand-held projector could cut off.

If he could get close enough. That was the trick now. To make no mistakes, to find the right place, to use the beam correctly. When he'd crossed the road he'd committed certain landmarks to memory: a big cholla cactus with a thick raised phallic limb, also a basalt outcrop where the firebreak made a turn. Both were there . . . but there was another cholla close by, or one that looked the same and . . . the outcrop seemed to be gone . . .

He stopped the Hummer. Best now just to use a flashlight . . . or no light at all. There was still enough afterglow in the sky to see by, maybe, when his eyes got used to it. Waiting for this to happen, he climbed out of the car, flash in hand, making sure he had the beamer ready. He stamped and kicked to loosen the cramps in his legs, feeling the desert reach out for him, a queer bone-penetrating cold as if he'd stepped into a meat storage locker. It was harder to see than he'd expected but he felt his way forward a few steps, then stopped, conscious of movement ahead: in the beam of his flash a big old desert jackrabbit went past, then two little gray deer and a bobcat, neither deer nor jacks fleeing from the cat, their natural enemy, for the cat paid no attention to them, going its own way, running like them from something else . . .

Rocks, cacti, greasewood—anything could look like a tank in the half-light, in the desert cold, when your nerves were jumping . . . but then something that wasn't quite a shape became a shape and moved and Jason, so self-assured a few seconds earlier, ran in blind panic, tripping, falling painfully, scrambling up, running to the Hummer, getting in, switching on the lights.

The robot was there, all right! Not fifty yards away. He'd almost walked into it. And facing it, incredibly, he now saw Armando . . . and Armando wasn't running, by no means, Armando was walking slowly forward, shouting or chanting, his lips moving, though what came from them could not be heard. He had made a cross with two sticks lashed together and this he held high, his stocky body stiffly erect, his face in the stream of light as plaster-pale as a saint's in a church niche, walking fearlessly forward to his death under the treads of the machine . . . or to cast out, by the power of Christ, the devil that according to his instructions must inhabit it.

"Go back, go back!"

Could the priest hear him? He paid no heed . . . but next moment everything changed; the robot's sensors detected a new threat environment—it swung around, the treads on the damaged side hardly turning at all, the right side dragging the hull forward in that sidling, slouching thrust its trail had made familiar. The vehicle, not the man on foot, would be the target—and TY60 was out of ammo.

Jason took the telebeam projector out of his shirt pocket, leveled it, and punched the release button. Nothing happened. He punched again, again, and again, then threw the plastic gizmo at his oncoming destroyer. The heat of the tank seared his skin as he reached into the Hummer for Nolan's AT-4; resting the barrel on the windshield, he fired point-blank at the robot's heavy nose plate, the worst possible place, but at this range it didn't matter. The fearful impact of the hit tumbled the robot on its side, *its good side,* the treads churning as if scooping out a grave. It writhed there momentarily, then burst into wild blue and orange fireworks, a wondrous arc that lit up sky and desert, setting fire to the brush, crystallizing the sand with its ferocious core of heat. Armando, still carrying his homemade cross, came up and the two men stood together, watching its last, ceramic-treated plate disintegrate and the secrets of its devious, man-made intelligence contract into a little heap of reeking slag.

They found Spec 4 back by the road, his back against a rock, listening to a ball game on a pocket radio. Jason had him try a sweep of other stations, all routined with their regular programs; evidently news of the attack on the President and his party, which the entire world from pole to pole would have learned instantly had it happened anywhere else, was still locked in the discretion of the Fort Irwin post.

Spec 4 switched back to the ball game.

"Low and inside, strike one."

"You saved my life," said the priest.

"Don't you believe it, you hung in there, Father."

"By the grace of God," said Armando. He kissed his cross of sticks, then laid it reverently in the sand.

"Change-up, strike two," said the announcer.

They drove back as they had come along the tank trails, avoiding the road on which a line of cars had suddenly appeared, going wide open, an ambulance behind them shrieking for passage; further ahead, at the base of the mountain, was another vehicular jam, turret lights spinning, wafflers growling, and in the corridor the Old Pudknocker's great red, white, and blue bird taking off, its escort Cobras circling above.

From the radio came the crack of a bat, the roar of a crowd watching an evening game in some distant, unidentified city . . .

THIRTY

Senator Lighty, at the President's request, chaired the special commission appointed to investigate the tragic occurrence at the army's National Training Center, Fort Irwin. The hearings lasted for five months. They comprised 111,000 pages of testimony and established a precedent seldom equaled for the meager sum of coherent fact that they produced.

There were, to be sure, some gains. Major General Emmett Xavier Mulcahy, commander of the NTC, was cleared of all charges of negligence in the overall operation (this largely anticipated in view of the general's unblemished service record and wide popularity) and Major Strickland Hayes, Mulcahy's deputy, also came off well in spite of criticism leveled at him for placing the chief executive and his distinguished guests in "hazardous proximity" to the activities of a robotic field weapon which had "previously demonstrated performance instability . . ."

At a lower level the army, acting on its own, court-martialed and sentenced to five years in prison Staff Sergeant Jay Tom Hinshaw, twenty-one, of Blackstone Corner, Ohio, and Specialist Yakima Littlefeather, twenty-six, of White Sands, New Mexico, for failure to account for rocket ammunition used in the battle exercise long after all live rounds, of which they were in charge, had been ordered recalled.

Jason Streck appeared as an expert witness before the commission. When sworn in, he defined his profession as "defense materials supplier," but some of those in the hearing room later expressed the opinion that this phrase would not be an accurate description of what he did much longer.

They, of course, proved right.

To understand the forces gathering around ADECT at this time a student of the procurement process must keep one thing in mind: the basic law is change. The center cannot hold; a great defense program, complex, vibrant, and exotic, bursting with energy, seeded with duplicity, packed with brilliant people and ideas, and apparently designed for the ages has actually about the life expectancy of a party balloon at a pistol convention, its existence hanging on one stroke of an administrative pen or a line item veto in a congressional budget.

Naturally there is a lot of talk before the cutoff. Many hundreds of pounds of printed sheets are passed around. People gather to pore over military blueprints and assess political and geopolitical issues. The ritual has a certain elephantine grace which satisfies its participants, though its result is determined at the start: the thing—tank, plane, bomb, rifle, or whatever—the bloody thing must damn well go!

The supplier himself may be the last to get the news. By then he is generally well prepared but nothing is official until the contracting officer passes down the word. He may do this personally or delegate it to an appropriate subordinate . . . generally, if army equipment is at issue, the department's field tech rep at the designated plant. Thus a time arrived when Colonel Nolan Jared faced Jason with this issue as the agenda.

Jared had no repugnance whatever to the role of executioner especially since his humiliation, as he regarded it, by Jason at Fort Irwin was still raw in his mind; the only problem was to get to the point fast but with appropriate tact and on his way up to the tower office he devised an opening which he felt accomplished both objectives.

"I don't suppose, sir," he began, "that what I am about to say will come as a total surprise to you but I must add that I would rather have blown out my brains than have this duty fall on me."

Jason raised a protesting hand.

"Colonel, I appreciate your sentiments. However, should the first option still attract you, by all means feel free to proceed with it."

He said this with glacial frigidity—then broke up, Jared laughing with him, and the final settlements between the Department of Defense and Advanced Electronic Technology were terminated without bloodshed.

The doors of the plant still opened early and closed late. The parking lots were filled with cars as usual and all day in the great decorous rows of campuslike buildings work went on. There were other divisions, after all, making other products, and still hundreds of robot tanks to be delivered. The phaseout would take many months, everything was the same and nothing was the same, the hemorrhage of talented people leaving for employment elsewhere increased each week and Jason gave them his blessing, although many of the walkaways had unexpired contracts. There was no need to fill their places—not until new directions could be decided, new plans moved off the drawing boards.

Retooling would take money, lots of it—and for the first time in its history, money was a problem at ADECT.

The shell that hit the observation bunker at the NTC had blown away the takeover threat at the same moment; ADECT stock selling at $40 that day was at $16.50 a week later with few takers. The crunch was on, even when the DOD (traditionally tardy) paid the recoupment estimates, the funds received would go to the shareholders—they could not be used to finance current operations—and bankers who had once torn their pockets to be first with a credit line were dissuaded from foreclosing only because when confronted with the unasked question, "Do you really want to own a tottering electronics company?" the answer had to be no.

The Old Guard stayed in place: Ken Garay, Abe Kohn, Debra Fine, Dr. Noo, Engineer Townsend, Tom Heyn, and a long list of others stood up to be counted; they were Jason's people, and come hell or high water, good times or bad, they would be with him, as would Imry Kraskov. By staff rank Imry had never been part of this inner circle, but his personal ties continued to be close even though there was little time now for leisurely cafeteria lunches or weekend outings. Imry had reported regularly, to Jason alone, on his progress with the robot's self-destruct component; this complicated, secret work was almost finished and it seemed monstrous to pull him away from it but the break had to be made—before long Imry had come up with plans for a new business machine, a very small, ultrafast electronic printer, which, if it proved up, could be as much of a breakthrough as the early-times Osborne PCs.

He concentrated hard on this and Jason, in the pressures which the company changeover put on his own time, left him alone; it never occurred to him that all was not well with his friend until Isabella arrived unexpectedly (and inconveniently) at the plant one day and asked to see him privately.

"I'm worried about Imry, Jason. I'm afraid he's going to be ill."

"What makes you think so?"

"There are limits even to his kind of strength. And he's not sleeping."

"Is that so unusual? He talked to me about that, you know—his dreams . . ."

"Oh, yes, he dramatizes them, I think—and they come much more seldom now. This is something else . . . You know the crazy hours he keeps, sometimes not coming home till one, two in the morning. You don't suppose—this may be a silly question—but this new machine he's working on, could that put him in danger of some kind?"

"I can't think of anything less likely."

She looked at him skeptically.

"Isn't there big competition for such inventions? I've heard of stealing, and sabotage . . ."

"Yes, Isabella," said Jason patiently, wondering if the source of her concern wasn't some hidden marital problem rather than any peril to Imry from outside sources. "Even spying. You're quite right. That goes on, but it's not obvious. And not violent. If that's your worry . . ."

"It is my worry."

She lowered her head. When she raised it he could see the fear in her eyes. "Would it be possible, even if it sounds ridiculous . . . I mean, could you ask him to go home at a normal time? Not to be driving around out there in the streets where . . . something could happen?"

"I don't make that kind of suggestion to Imry. If I did you know what he'd say."

"But for his own protection . . ."

"Isabella, he'd tell me to go to hell. And he'd be quite right. Nobody tells a man like Imry Kraskov what hours to keep or how to do his work."

"I see." She rose, picked up her handbag, smoothed the skirt of her trim tailored suit. "I'd hoped . . . but never mind. Thank you—for nothing. I'm sorry I took up your time."

Her anger surprised him. She was obviously deeply upset. Was she ill herself? Or suspicious that Imry was seeing another woman? From what he knew of their marriage, the latter notion seemed silly.

Gallantry was now in order, if only as a way to end the interview. Jason came around the desk, took the lady's arm, and escorted her ceremoniously to the escalator.

Had he seemed unsympathetic? If so, he apologized. He'd have lunch with Imry, he promised—try to find out what was bothering him if anything, even suggest a leave of absence if that would help . . . And he would call her . . .

Back in his office, he touched Abe's code number.

"Abe, could you shake loose a man for special duty?"

"Sure," replied Kohn's raspy voice. "What's up?"

"I want an escort for Imry Kraskov."

"Where and when?"

"Anytime he leaves here late—which seems to be his routine. His wife is worried about him."

"Lots of wives are worried. Any other reason?"

"I thought of that too, Abe, but I discount it. This is just a hunch. If he's bothered about something, she's sensed it. Might be well to check. He's important."

"Okay. But surveillance—he'll have to know. What will I tell him?"

"Tell him it's current policy . . . or anything you like. Just so he knows he's not out there alone."

"Whatever you say, boss."

Jason thanked him and cut the connection.

The matter was taken care of. He put it out of his mind until one morning some weeks later when his bedside phone rang long before his usual rising time. A woman's voice jolted him awake.

"Jason, Imry hasn't come home."

"What time is it now, Isabella?"

"Almost five-thirty."

"Well, he's probably still at the plant."

"He's not. I've been calling on his direct line. I also talked to the night operator. He checked out a little past one."

"Isabella, Imry has surveillance, a guard late at night. Hasn't he told you that?"

"Yes, he has. But this is unaccountable. He's never stayed out all night."

Her voice was shaking.

"Isabella," said Jason firmly, "he'll be there. I guarantee it, so relax. I'll call you when I get to the office."

He hung up. *This woman, now she's really going bonkers,* he thought.

He still had an hour to sleep. He intended to use it but he'd hardly dropped off when the phone rang again. This time the caller was Abe Kohn.

"You'd better get down here," he said. "Our pal Imry Kraskov has been snatched."

THIRTY-ONE

Sitting with Kohn in the tower office was D. L. Reilly, a blade-thin, white-haired police captain from the San Jose Police central station who summarized for Jason some facts previously communicated to Abe.

". . . he signed out of the plant at 1:32 A.M., driving a black Honda Civic '87, and turned north. At approximately 1:39 he entered the approach ramp leading off Monroe onto the Lawrence Expressway where a black Thunderbird, Cal license 3 Mot 478 lugged in and cut him off. Thunderbird reported March 6, this year, as stolen vehicle, owned by Willis Yander, Novato, California. GMC longbed panel truck, owned by Budget Auto Rentals—no record of current rental—blocked rear of Civic. Abduction suspects were wearing stocking masks and dark-colored jogging suits, one carrying a sidearm, exited truck, removed Kraskov from Civic, where he had remained in driver's seat, and conducted him to Thunderbird, getting in with him. Thunderbird entered expressway traffic heading northwest. Truck and Civic both reported as abandoned vehicles by Mrs. Evalyn Gosch, resident renter at 3673 Monroe Street, a four-unit apartment building. She is a nurse employed at Kaiser General, San Jose. She got off duty at 12:58 and got home in time to observe the incident, she estimates at about 1:46."

The captain picked up a computer tear sheet from the desk and handed it to Jason.

> He never had a chance, the man in the little car—the stout man. First the black car in front, then bingo bango, the truck behind. The men in the truck got out and one had a gun. He had a mask on his face. It was certainly no accident. I'll say that and I'll testify. I've seen accidents right here, they need it wider here, but this was just like a movie. They got him. I don't want to be mixed up in it but I'll testify to what I saw. The name is Gosch, G-o-s-c-h. I'm the person who phoned in . . .

"Can we keep this?" Jason asked.

"Yes, sir. That's a copy. If there's anything further I can do, gentlemen . . ."

He rose, as did Kohn and Jason.

"Just keep in touch," said Kohn. "Mr. Streck and I appreciate your coming in."

"Anytime, gentlemen," said Reilly. He shook hands with Jason, then with Kohn who walked to the door with him, where they shook again.

"We keep them greased up pretty good, Christmastime and so forth," Kohn said coming back. "The Ess Jay Pee Dee."

"Fuck the Ess Jay Pee Dee," said Jason. "What kind of shit is this?"

"Not good, I grant you."

"Where was our security? I asked for an escort for Imry."

"Plant guard Harry Ellard had the duty. He was called away. He got word that his wife was sick."

"You didn't have backup?"

"Double the number of people I got and I'll have backups. I'll also double your costs. And if you're going to blow your stack, I'll tell you what will really make you blow it. Ellard's wife was all right. She was up making coffee when he got home. The call was a decoy. And it was timed to perfection."

Then the snatch was a highly professional operation, planned by someone with inside sources of information! Jason felt sick.

Mrs. Purviance was on the intercom, announcing an appointment set up earlier by Kohn.

"Two gentlemen from the FBI to see you . . ."

"Send them in."

So far, no one could complain of laggard action.

Kohn introduced the younger of the two visitors, Rufe Miglio, deputy director of operations, San Francisco, a tanned, athletic man in his mid-forties with an Ivy League flair about him. His older and heavier-set companion was the ops officer assigned to the case.

Chairs were pulled up, coffee brought. The door closed behind Mrs. Purviance.

Miglio spoke first.

"Before we get down to details, Mr. Streck, I must advise you that you can expect a ransom demand later today, tomorrow at the latest. I suggest that you ignore it."

Jason's mouth tightened.

"Is that a bureau policy? No negotiation with terrorists?"

"Not in all situations, sir, but in this one, yes."

Said Jason, "I won't go along with that. This company will negotiate any time the life of an employee is on the line. I've been a hostage myself. I know what it's like. We'll pay whatever it takes to free Imry Kraskov."

"Money won't help now, Mr. Streck. Kraskov is no longer in the United States."

Jason and Kohn exchanged glances. If true, this was appalling—it was also, on the face of it, incomprehensible.

"You have proof of that, Rufe?" said Kohn.

Miglio reached for his briefcase. He pulled out a sheaf of oversize photos. These he laid on Jason's desk.

The shots looked as if they had been badly printed or taken in a weak light. One could see, as through some material that seemed to obscure the lens, the figure of a seated man in profile. He looked to be of medium size. He was bent slightly forward, as if reading or dozing.

"What are these?"

"Those, sir," said the FBI man, "are reductions made from very large, soft-tissue X-ray pictures. They were taken with a concealed macro lens powered with extremely high-energy radiation. The location was the cargo area of U.S. Customs at San Francisco International Airport, the time was shortly after five this morning. The photos were shot through the sides of a fiberglass packing case. The seated person is Imry Kraskov. Do you recognize him?"

Jason felt a deadly chill, starting somewhere in his navel, thrust downward into other vital parts. But yet—the shots were so blurred, so obscure . . .

"I'm not sure."

"We're convinced that it is indeed Mr. Kraskov. The Soviets planned the operation carefully. First they disposed of Ellard. They had good input there. They also knew that Mrs. Gosch got off work at a certain time each night, so they set up the snatch practically on her doorstep. They didn't want a general alarm; they wanted one witness who would corroborate their charade, make it look real. Mrs. Gosch was the kind of lady who would notify authorities—nurses are trained that way. What they didn't count on was the speed of bureau reaction. The San Jose PD liaised with us not more than maybe fifteen, twenty minutes after the incident. And we took the appropriate steps."

For a few seconds there was total silence. Then Jason said, "What do you mean, charade? Imry was kidnapped, Miglio."

"No, he wasn't, Mr. Streck. There were guns and masks, all right. Real James Bond stuff, but it was all playacting. Kraskov must have notified them when he was ready to go. He probably sent his luggage on ahead. Obviously he'd been working for them for a long time."

Jason leaned across the desk.

"I'll never believe that."

Miglio's expression didn't alter. Neither did his polite, dead-level tone.

"With all respect, sir—may we review some facts?"

Jason seemed temporarily incapable of speech. Not so Kohn.

"Go ahead, sir."

"When Kraskov went to work for ADECT, his clearance was 'confidential.' Wasn't that later changed?"

"Yes."

"Once quite a while ago the DIS received a request to reclassify him. J. C. Streck, as CEO, signed the application personally. It was rejected."

"That is correct."

"But recently he was given work to do that called for a security upgrade. In this instance no application was submitted."

"I was not aware of that," said Kohn stoutly. Perhaps too stoutly. Miglio looked at him as if he knew that his answer was less than truthful.

"We reclassified him here at the plant," said Jason.

Miglio nodded. He had won that round.

Upgrading Kraskov or anyone else without DIS action was a breach of protocol. It was also unlawful.

"And after that he was given new work to do—work connected with the SEDAV program?"

"With a small part of it, yes. But that's all over. The SEDAV program has been canceled, as you may have heard."

"I'm speaking of the period before cancellation. In this period he had a job in the top secret category."

"Everything connected with SEDAV was top secret. His job, however, did not involve production. It was research, lab work, the kind of thing he was good at."

"Could he have completed this top secret work—had the data with him when he, er, walked away?"

"No."

"Can we really establish that? It would not have been possible?"

"Mr. Miglio," said Jason, "your bureau has its policies and at ADECT we have ours. Information about operations here is processed on a need-to-know basis. I would question your need to know."

"We have such a need, but at the moment I will waive the question."

"Do you mind if I ask one? If the Soviets wanted him back in Russia, why the cargo container? They could have just given him a passport and let him walk on to a plane."

"Yes, they could—but only at the risk of disclosing that he'd been their agent; the kidnapping facade would have had no value. He might have been recognized. Sure, he could have been disguised but disguises take time to perfect. The container was simpler and, as they thought, detectionproof. Up to date they haven't penetrated our X-ray techniques."

"Isn't there risk in nailing up a person in a box?"

"Not at all. It's been going on at least since the sixties, when the Egyptians caught the KGB freighting out a prisoner that way. In that case, the man was drugged and manacled. He had a doctor in there with him to supply life-support measures. Kraskov would have had every convenience—a comfortable seat, refrigerated food, lights and air conditioning from a microgenerator, a chemical toilet. Not a bad way to travel at all. Probably as agreeable as tourist class on most airlines."

Jason did not respond to the small joke. He sat doodling on a legal pad, his face drawn and pale: he was trying desperately to keep his control.

"Mr. Miglio, do you really believe in this fantasy? You've shown us what you call proof. I don't accept it. The seated person in those X-rays could be Kraskov or it could be someone else of his general body and feature structure. There's also another reason that convinces me that this isn't Imry. He got married last year. I know how deeply he was devoted to his wife, and she to him. He would never have gone off and left her behind."

Miglio glanced at the operations officer as if requesting his comment, then apparently changed his mind and made the reply himself.

"Mrs. Kraskov may not have known that her husband was a spy. We shall, of course, interview Mrs. Kraskov. I doubt if she'll have much to tell us."

"She might have a lot—such as the signs of stress he had developed, his insomnia, tending to indicate his knowledge that he was in danger."

"Had she ever talked this way before?"

"Never. So I took action."

"You ordered an escort for Kraskov."

". . . anytime he left here late at night or early in the morning."

"There was a guard last night?"

"There was supposed to be but a mistake occurred—what looked like a snafu by our security but turns out to have been a strategy planned by the kidnappers. Which again refutes your theory that he walked away, as you call it."

Miglio sat back in his chair. He looked at Jason with wonder.

"So you still have faith in him? No doubts at all?"

"Mr. Miglio," said Jason, "if I had any—and my knowledge of this man's character hadn't been enough to squelch them—let me give you one more fact that blesses him for me. While this plant was adjusting after the cancellation of the robot tank Imry invented and supplied us with a device for the private sector around which we're building a large program. A bonanza—and we got it free. Would he have done this if he had been about to make off with our battle secrets? Or had already furnished them to the Soviets? It doesn't make sense."

"I'm afraid it does. It was the next-to-last card in the game, the fake kidnapping being the final one. Without a perfect score—your trust unbroken—there would be no chance to collect the ransom. You talk about a bonanza—how about keeping a spy in place for years and then being paid millions for doing it? That's the ploy we're looking at now, wild as it may seem."

Jason had had enough of this. His legs were numb from tension and his maimed feet hurt. It was time to get rid of Miglio. He rose, balancing on his blackthorn . . . but he found he still had one more thing to say, if only to keep the FBI man from getting in the last word.

"You've told me, sir, that a man was shipped to the Soviet Union in a box this morning, but if so it wasn't Imry Kraskov. He's probably right here in California, in all likelihood not far away. The greatest service that the bureau could do right now would be to locate him and try to get him back before he comes to harm."

The first ransom call came in late that afternoon, a few minutes before the ADECT switchboard closed down for the night. The woman on the line identified herself as "a friend of Mr. Kraskov's, calling with a message for Mr. Streck."

The voice was mid-American, pleasant, business-trained. It conveyed Mr. Kraskov's regards and his hope that, in a matter vital to them both, Mr. Streck would be near the pay telephones in the lobby of the Los Gatos Motor Inn next day between one and two and that he would be kind enough to answer any one of the telephones that rang. He should come alone and bring with him a million dollars in used currency of the United States. It was important that the bills should have been in circulation and that they should not be marked.

THIRTY-TWO

The lady with blue hair in the Peruvian print dress had done her business at the desk and now sat decoratively, a suede pump dangling from one toe, facing the bank of pay phones which Jason was monitoring. Other folk kept passing through the lobby—late A.M. check-outs, early P.M. check-ins; a service club lunch group wearing Velcro identification stick-ons in the event that, lunching together only once a week, they forgot or confused Tex, Monk, Wooz, or Stew. Also some members of the Giacometti-Luro wedding (bulletined for 2:30), the young men in gray rented cutaways, the bridesmaids in deep-decolletage dresses of steamboat blue with blue-black bows shaped like hornets' wings behind.

It was five minutes of two. Jason wondered if he'd come on a fool's errand.

The million dollars in used bills filled three Samsonite attaché cases, these locked in the trunk of the Mercedes 500 SEL. The instructions had stipulated that he come alone and that was how he had come, despite the protests of Abe Kohn.

Three minutes of two . . . and now only one pay phone was in use. The salesman type who had been using it hung up and left; his phone immediately rung and kept on ringing. Then another phone at the far end of the console rang.

Jason picked up the salesman's phone.

"... hold for overtime charges on your Syracuse, New York, call ..."

He slammed down the receiver, ran to the other phone.

"Mr. Streck," said the woman's voice he had heard before, "I have Mr. Kraskov for you."

And then Imry was on the line.

"Jason, is that you?"

There was a kind of buzzing.

"Imry . . . speak louder."

Suddenly the voice came through as if from nearby, strong and urgent.

"*Jason, listen. I'm all right. Don't pay the sons of bitches anything. No matter what they tell you don't pay any—*"

There was a rasp as if the instrument had been snatched away.

"Excuse the delay," said the first voice. "Stay with us . . ."

Silence for a beat of four . . . five . . . six . . .

Jason's hands were shaking. He could feel sweat running down his armpits. Then a man's voice replaced the woman's, like hers agreeable and unaccented.

"Mr. Kraskov is understandably upset, but quite all right. You have the money?"

"Yes."

"Thank you very much. Your cooperation will make all this much easier. We should appreciate your proceeding at once to the San Jose International Airport where you should rent a suitcase locker; in the locker place what you have brought with you. Arrangements will be communicated later for payment of the balance and a drop-off location for the locker key. Is all this quite clear?"

"Yes," said Jason.

"Thank you indeed, sir," said the voice. "We shall be in touch."

"The real break is that he's still in the United States . . ."

"Oh, I hope. I hope you're right. But I don't know."

"You mean—a cassette?"

"That could be possible, couldn't it?"

"It could, but that message—that would have been too ingenious, even for *them*. I think it was Imry. And I think in a few days this will all seem like some weird nightmare. We'll get him back. I'm sure of it."

He had driven straight from the airport to the Kraskovs' house where Isabella had made him tea. This she served with homemade preserves and dark Polish bread; Jason, who'd skipped lunch, ate hungrily and talked optimistically.

". . . a terrorist power play. Hell, as you know, it happened to me . . ."

He mentioned other instances of bodily seizure, for politics and for illegal gain—she must have faith, she must hold on a little longer . . . and she smiled, she responded, but at length she said:

"Jason, I want to ask you something. Was Imry allowed to bring work home with him?"

"Well, no. But there are times . . . I mean, lately he'd been working on a new kind of office device that we think . . ."

"I don't mean his new work, his old work—with the robot electronics."

Jason shook his head. It seemed stupid to make excuses for Imry to Imry's wife for the breach of one of the company's most basic rules.

"That was top secret."

She rose from the table.

"Let me show you something."

In the family room she knelt on the floor, opening a cabinet in which there was a row of empty shelves.

"These were full of software. He took it with him."

"Aren't you jumping to conclusions? He knew he was in danger—you were so sure of that you came to tell me about it. Instead of taking it, he might have done the opposite—destroyed it."

"All right. But traveling in a cargo crate, that would have been a convenient way to . . . well, transport it, I would think. He might even have traveled that way so he *could* transport it."

"Isabella—you're too clever for your own good. You must stop these fantasies. I tell you, he'll be all right. We'll just pay what's asked and that will be the end of it."

Jason's optimism—almost if not quite sincere—weakened when, after days of confusing instructions from the "kidnappers," including a drop location for the key, the locker (staked out by company detectives around the clock) was opened with a passkey and the Samsonite cases discovered missing. The pleasant lady telephoned once more, this time accusing ADECT in general and Jason in particular of bad faith in setting up the stakeout.

"With regret," she said, "we must terminate these negotiations."

"KGB games," said Miglio.

"How did they get that million out of the locker?"

"I'm afraid I wouldn't know, sir," said Miglio.

Jason felt like busting the FBI man on his smartass, Ivy League jaw. Imry Kraskov was gone, that was for sure, but that he was gone of his own accord, by prearrangement, in an act of total betrayal after years of comradely trust and friendship Jason was still not ready to accept nor did he until the letters came.

There were two of them—one for him and one for Isabella. His came first. It was written on a manual typewriter with a queer old-fashioned type font, undated, and computer-coded instead of stamped:

Dear Jason:

Keep in mind that what I did, however abominable in your eyes, I would have done to my own son had he been in your place and I in mine. Also allow me to tell you with utter truthfulness that the feelings I hold for you are no different from those I would hold for such a son had fate allowed me one. Remember that no matter what may now befall as a result of my actions I shall always remain your friend and admirer,

Imry Kraskov

Postscriptum

I admired your father also particularly for the brilliance with which he came to detect what I had done to his pet TY6o. I regret that the discovery resulted so badly for him. Unfortunately there was no alternative.

Jason read the queer, horrible little missive first with disgust, then with irrepressible anger. The effrontery with which his correspondent nonchalantly confessed to J. C. Streck's murder was cynical and cruel beyond belief. One could conceive of it only as part of the spy's incredible capacity for deceit—equatable with his babbling about "an aura" as a key to the robot's outrages.

Possibly, he realized, his duty now was to pass the letter along to

Miglio or some other member of the intelligence establishment but this he found himself quite unable to do: after keeping it in his desk for a few hours, he burned it and flushed the pieces down the toilet.

For more than a week he didn't know that Isabella too had heard from her husband. Then she called and he went around to see her that last time.

He was struck at once by the extraordinary change in her. She'd suddenly come to look like an older, plainer sister of the ravishing bride he'd danced with on her wedding day or the lovely laughing wife who'd presided over his visits to her house. She'd taken few pains with her appearance, almost to the point of being slovenly in the sad way that women get when some vital pulse, some core of their being, has been snatched away from them; she'd also lost weight, so much and in so short a time that the bright clothes she'd once worn with such flair now hung on her like charity handouts.

"I could have taken the spying. I would have hated it but I could have held on . . . if only he'd *said something . . .*"

"He probably had orders against that."

"A spy's orders. How loathsome! We were together all those years. He must have sold himself *before we even met,* before he ever came to Poland and we . . . escaped, as I was supposed to think. Even that was a fake—the boat, the storm . . ."

"The storm wasn't a fake, for God's sake. The KGB doesn't control the weather."

"Perhaps not, though I'm sure someday they'll find a way. For him it was a wonderful convenience. It helped make him more believable, a *spy's storm,* though it almost drowned us. But even then, after we'd been saved, like a new life beginning, he never said a word. If only he'd *trusted* me, then I wouldn't feel . . . I wouldn't have lost my identity, don't you see?"

"Yes, I see, Isabella," Jason said wearily.

(When someone is dying or the body giving up, those are the words we say. Or "It will get better" or "I see . . . I see . . ." And eventually of course we walk away.)

It was a raw day in November. She'd lit a fire in the small living room but the air was musty; she sensed his awareness of this, saying, "I don't use this room much." He wondered, since the house was so small—with a cheery kind of mouse-house lived-inness he'd always liked—what room she did use, where did she curl up to think her thoughts and keep on getting thinner?

She had the letter in her apron pocket, it had come the day before.
She never took her eyes off him as he read it.

It was in English. The text set forth the reason for this.

My dearest wife:

I am well! I love you and miss you. I am sorry for the pain I have
caused you. I hope you can forgive me.

Those are the chief things I want to say and since this letter will
be short I must say them without shame and without preamble,
straight from the heart. I am assuming, of course, that by now you
know everything; I haven't seen the U.S. newspapers but I can
imagine the stink they will raise. Never mind. After a few hundred
or a thousand more such stinks it will all be forgotten, I can
promise you that. And I'll promise something else much more
important—someday we will be together again! I swear this on my
soul. I have asked my control about it, and they have agreed. After
all, it is no more than my due. I want no other reward!

I must mention also that honors have been given me or are at
least pending. Quite formidable honors . . . About these I shall keep
some degree of silence. Far more to the point (if you can forgive,
which in your openhearted way you will do, I know, even though
now, at this very minute, you may think and angrily declare—I can
just hear you!—that you cannot and will not!) the point is, *when,*
dearest? When can arrangements be made for you to come?

All right! They will be made. That is the main thing . . .

The date itself must be left open, at least for now. For you
see—though this too may be hard to understand—I have one last
test before me. I must renew my *bona fides* with the departmental
people here. Does this seem strange? Actually, it is routine. My
debriefing resembles what I underwent from the CIA—such a bad
time for both of us—when I ostensibly "defected." The process of
reestablishment is inevitable in the case of a person who has been
in deep cover a long time. Do you realize that party leadership has
changed four times since I first went on my mission? Let me tell
you something crazy. I had almost forgotten Russian! It came very
slowly to my tongue. It's what happens to languages if you don't
use them. You must keep in mind also that my original tongue was
not Russian but Ukrainian. Anyway, English seemed the best solution; it seems easier now to write in English.

Never mind! My work for the Soviet Union is impeccable and
will stand all tests—a notable breakthrough and an invaluable feat.
I have mentioned honors. One—the first—will be given to me any

day now—the Order of Soviet Scientist, First Class. So you see, I am on firm ground.

I have everything I need. I live not far from Moscow and the surroundings are very nice, even luxurious. We live and work in a scientific commune, a prestigeful group. The food is first-rate, there are exercise facilities and a bus to take us into town for shopping, movies, etc., whenever we wish to go. I have my own laboratory and an assistant, also a spirit stove to cook snacks. Really you must think of me as being quite pampered, surrounded by interesting and worthwhile people, achievers all. Some have wives or husbands also in residence or living in close proximity, as you soon will be, my dear one.

The interim period must be endured. It will pass. For the present I cannot give you a return address, but I am hoping this restriction will soon be lifted, so that you may reply. Meanwhile I send my steadfast devotion, my humble petition for your forgiveness and all, all my love—forever. I shall write again soon.

Your devoted husband,
Imry

"Do you understand what he's saying?"

"Obviously that he loves you very much and he . . ."

". . . tells me that in effect he is a prisoner and that he will never see me again! . . ."

"I don't read that into it at all."

"Don't lie. Of course you do, it's written in letters ten feet high."

She was right, of course; Jason sat silent.

"What's absurd is that he gave up science, which was his life—gave me up, who was at least part of his life, I can say without flattering myself. And what did he get in trade? A spy's life—a nonlife! Honors, he says. What kind of honors? Some miserable medal because he found a way to steal your robot tank. Also he seems to be in a sort of luxury jail, an elite Gulag. *They still don't trust him.*"

"They don't trust anyone. But he truly wants you to forgive him."

He spoke very gently—and caught himself up for it. The bitterness—the detestation!—generated within him by Kraskov's betrayal could have so easily lapped over, however unreasonably, to include the woman he had left behind. And yet . . . and yet in this strange miserable dialogue he could feel only compassion; her loss was so much worse than his.

She pushed back the great weight of black hair which kept pulling loose. In the firelight, with that fall of hair and the new thinness which accented the bony structure of her face she looked again, at moments, like the strong, striking woman she had once been.

"For what he did to me," she went on, "I can forgive him. What does it matter? It's all over now anyway . . . but for what he did to himself I can't and won't forgive him, I won't even try. He was such a man and he turned himself into . . . nothing!"

"Not quite nothing," said Jason.

"Nothing," she said, "nothing nothing nothing. A spy! A miserable worthless dirty little spy!"

Jason found that he was still holding the letter. He handed it back to her, and took his leave, never expecting to return again to that once-cheerful mouse-house on the hill. He was, however, back in it less than a week later. The Santa Clara police passed the news through Abe Kohn: Isabella Kraskov had rigged a piece of garden hose to the exhaust of the Honda Civic. Then she had sat quietly in the garaged car, breathing the fumes until she was dead.

THIRTY THREE

his time the Right Reverend Emmet Dalton Phelan did not deliver the eulogy at St. Athanasias. There was in fact no eulogy, no attendance by important people, no words of condolence from the great of the world, no choir, no incense, no hymns, although a neighbor who had met Isabella Kraskov in the Safeway and sometimes shopped with her could play the organ, offered to do so, and Jason, who had paid for the flowers and everything else, accepted her kindness.

Isabella had not fallen into the class of people who may not receive Catholic burial, a grace denied only those who have given no signs of repentance—and who was to say that no such signs had been given, for the sin of dying by her own hand, by Isabella Kraskov as she sat growing cold and sleepy in the Honda?

So under this dispensation the curate of St. Athanasias, Reverend Emilio Carriles Masvidas, conducted the mass and the Poles came, two of the men who had been at the wedding, with their wives, and several wives without their husbands, and Jason came and one very tall thin man, properly dressed, whom no one knew and might quite likely be the sort of man who goes to any funeral publicly scheduled, nobody knows why.

In slightly more than half an hour it was all over and Jason was back in the tower office surrounded by the historic battle souvenirs which he was now planning to donate, tax deductibly, to museums. The pace of production picked up at ADECT. Already, among other offerings, the fast little printer Imry Kraskov had designed was being rushed to market—an odd memorial to his scientific competence and his abysmal treachery.

As to the latter, far from all the questions had been answered:

Had he finished his work on SEDAV's self-destruct component?

If so, then he had surely taken his data with him and the entire U.S. battle robot program—once more up for bids—was compromised.

The Soviets could build the tank themselves. They might already be doing it.

Such reflections were bothersome but Jason had means of escape. They were no longer his concern. He was through with weapons making—home free!

He had the plant, he sat at the big desk vacated by the father who had rejected him. He had survived every threat including the Russian who for a little while had masqueraded in the attire of a substitute father and who had betrayed him even more despicably.

". . . feelings for you no different from those I would have had for such a son had fate allowed me one . . ."

The spy who loved me, Jason thought bitterly.

But the real hell of it was, a thing which he'd have admitted to no one, even if he was beaten on the feet again, he missed Imry's companionship. He'd catch himself wondering—what was the son of a bitch up to now in that Gulag of his?

The computer flea market was on again, the flags flying at the Santa Clara County Fairgrounds. Maybe he could get Ken Garay to go with him.

Christmas came and went—a forlorn time for many Valley companies that year but not for ADECT, where the spin-off of its fiber-optic division plus a new bank loan had restored fluidity. *The Wall Street Journal* carried the story on the first page of its second section, giving it two columns and on the day it appeared Odille Streck, long unheard from, rang up asking for an appointment.

Jason invited her to lunch.

She's coming for a handout, he thought.

It was like her to waste no time.

He had no doubt that she'd been hard hit by losses in the failed takeover bid. If so, she had quite enough brass in her to bid for his sympathy, play Mrs. Poormouse . . . but when he caught sight of her it struck him that she was overdoing the role. She had outfitted herself in a plain black suit—possibly a designer original, although to the male eye it could have come off the rack at Loehmann's—no jewels, little makeup, flat-heeled shoes, and a tender, worn expression. It was unreal—yet an inspired conception: had she sat on the sidewalk with a cigar box in her lap people would have filled it with money. She had even taken off her rings. Their absence left white circles on her fingers.

"Yes," she said, holding up a hand, "I left them all at home. I'm glad you noticed."

"Were you afraid we'd mug you here?"

"Not at all. I just thought modesty would be appropriate—in view of the surroundings."

He'd warned her that they would be lunching in the ADECT cafeteria.

"God, what a snob you are, Odille."

"Anything but that, darling. Or I wouldn't be here . . . or perhaps I would. I have something of importance to ask you."

Ah, here it comes, he thought—*the pitch.* But what he said was, "Well, in that case, we'd better get to it, don't you think?"

"I am getting to it. I must build up my strength."

He watched in awe as she attacked the second of two large breaded veal chops. Not the least of her many gifts was the ability to eat like a python without putting on an ounce of weight.

"First, about the takeover. If you think I went into it to make those two rascals rich you underestimate me."

"Who are you talking about?"

"Eric von Leventaller, of course. And that despicable Charlie Gitlin. But Eric started the whole thing."

"I had an idea it was Charlie."

"So did most people, I suppose, but it was Eric. I brought in Charlie myself. It was not the smartest thing I ever did. But there was that story going around—"

". . . about you and Charlie shacking up . . ."

Odille put down her fork in dismay.

"I'd rather have gone to bed with a toad. I mean the idea that you wanted to move the company out of procurement entirely. That was what terrified a lot of us. Charlie swore you'd said it to him face to face. He passed it on to Eric and Eric became terribly upset."

"It can't take much to upset a Swiss capitalist."

"It doesn't. But Leventaller Electronik was an original ADECT shareholder—two percent. Eric felt they either had to get out or get control and they decided on control so they bought more. I bought some myself. I make no secret of it. Charlie was going to replace you as CEO. He bought stock too . . ."

". . . with his golden parachute funds . . ."

". . . whatever. By this time the arbitrageurs were getting in. Shares were soaring. Takeover was in the wind and I was having second thoughts. I'd had a good ride. Did I really care who ran ADECT, with J.C. gone? And so I sold, right at the top. I did it as discreetly as I could but with these laws about insider trading it was all reported. I suppose when you read about it you thought I was starting something. Actually I was just getting out. Eric and Charlie were fit to be tied."

"You're unbeatable, Odille."

"No, just a woman who has learned to take care of herself. It was amusing to see Eric take a bath. The worrier! He can afford it. Of course it's different for Charlie, that toad. If he's broke it serves him right for spreading scandals. But now I have something to ask you . . . unless you're still angry with me."

"I have nothing but the highest esteem for you, stepmother."

"Well, I hope so, because this is a matter that concerns us both."

She finished her iced tea and began mopping up the veal chop gravy with a piece of bread.

"Would you mind dreadfully if I sold the place on Sand Hill Road? I've thought about it a lot lately."

"Meaning you're bored."

"A little. Your father was my link with the life here, and I enjoyed it. It's a perfectly acceptable life, if that's your style, but it's not mine. The Valley people and the Pebble Beach people. That's about what it amounts to, plus my guests, the ones that come and go. I've never fitted in. I don't want to sound self-pitying, but sometimes, darling, I've been homesick, stashed away among those trees up on the hill. What am I doing here, I've asked myself, so far from Europe where my real friends are? My house at Aix-en-Provence, for instance. And it makes no sense to keep two places going at the same time, thousands of miles apart . . . Don't even think you're facing a *fait accompli.* I was just wondering how you'd feel about it."

"What does it matter how I feel? It's your place, Odille. You can do anything you like."

"I know. But I have a responsibility to you. It's your home, where you grew up."

"Not really. We didn't move to Sand Hill Road until I was in Stanford."

"But you have memories . . ."

Her tilted eyes swerved away, she knew she'd made a gaffe. The memories that occurred to both now were far from good ones.

"In any event you have first call. If you should decide to buy it yourself I'll make you a special price."

He hadn't the slightest intention of buying it himself. But with Sand Hill Road on the block an era had ended, the wheel had come full circle.

A few days after the cafeteria lunch she called again, this time to tell him that some realtors were making an appraisal of the property. Would he, as a favor, meet with them and check their figures . . . or suggest another agent who might serve her better?

He had no suggestions. He met, as requested, with the designated people, two real estate ladies and their partner, a balding man with six pens in the breast pocket of his jacket; their business completed, he put off reporting to the main house, where Odille had invited him for cocktails. He wanted to walk down to the cottage, the one spot which today he had deliberately avoided.

The chain link fence was gone now as were the security dogs' kennels and the target range. Leaves had blown into the pool and a service man was vacuuming them out; the little patch of lawn once stained with blood and ripped by bullets was sere with winter brown but well trimmed and the paths raked. The doors were locked, as he'd expected, but in the old days, on the kitchen side, there'd been a key under the doormat; he looked and there was one there now.

He used it and went in.

There was no kitchen anymore. That room had been turned into an art gallery for Odille's photograph collection; the business machines were gone from the small rooms beyond but the living room with its big sofa and pale puffy chairs little altered (the chair in which J. C. Streck had bled to death covered now in some darker stuff but still in its former position).

Jason stood looking sadly and quietly at the well-remembered scene, realizing at once that it was no good place to be.

He wanted to leave. He had stepped through some kind of time warp, still with one foot in the present—a dangerous trap: the two zones in confrontation held him rooted and preempted his will and the function of his legs. Thus there was nothing left to do except to sit down as he had sat that night waiting for Kohn and Garay to come to his aid, on the floor, still as a rock, his back against the wall, the presence of his father heavy upon him. And gradually, an interior monologue with this presence took shape effortlessly and irresistibly.

You were certainly pretty stupid about my situation in Morocco. I don't know what in hell got into you. You were acting some kind of role, probably a temporary one without the slightest love or compassion, but I guess you just didn't understand, nobody could perhaps unless he'd been there, which you weren't. I don't hold it against you. I was on my way over here tonight to tell you that when I found you shot up and all. Anyway, I always loved you a lot, you son of a gun. You were a good daddy, so thanks, and thanks for everything, and most of all for that trip to Vegas when we saw the bomb go off. I learned a lot then. I made up my mind then, it was a killing thing and I want no part of those things. I've quit making them, as I suppose you know. No more robots. Let someone else make them if that's the drill—but you and I are home free now. And I've still got the plant.

The long speech, of which not a word was uttered, released him from the time warp. He got up and left the cottage, careful to lock the door behind him. Dark was coming on, lights were up in the big house where drinks were being served, and a wood fire burning but he was not in the mood for that or for the company of his vivacious stepmother; he rang her on the cottage line to tell her he was leaving. He'd told the real estate people to bring the appraisal along in the morning, it was all right, he thought.

In the end, of course, she'd negotiate the price herself. There was no one alive better qualified to negotiate a price than Odille Streck and he felt sure that she was doing right by selling, she would be infinitely better off in her rightful domain at Aix-en-Provence, her loneliness at an end; from all the more fashionable corners of the world the kind of people who get into planes and fly to parties would come flocking to her door.

. . .

The Department of Defense had by no means given up on fielding a proper and controllable battle robot. Once more bidding was solicited and this time around FMC got the contract, including all ADECT's patents—the rule being that when you worked for the government, the government owns everything pertaining to that work, even the ideas still yeasting in your brain should you leave the slightest residue of these behind when you clean out your desk.

Robotics still held high priority but lately interest had focused and funds clotted around a tempting new area—the combat applications of very high power microwaves (VHPM).

Would the next war be a sparring match of gigawatts?

It seemed possible. Wizard researchers in U.S. labs and think tanks had proved that a $30GH_3$ beam could detonate bombs and artillery shells at considerable ranges and dismantle the electronic systems of missiles, armor, satellites, aircraft, radar, and communications.

Intriguing horizons loomed but also, inescapably, certain ethical issues.

Would the employment of heat fluences as weapons violate agreements relating to the current nuclear phaseout?

Here one moved from the negotiable into the logistical. What would be the effect on troops? VHPM that merely stunned a soldier temporarily like the tranquilizers long employed to knock out cattle and subdue zoo animals were certainly more humane than lethal force but beams that blinded, boiled, flayed, deafened, maddened, eviscerated, or burned people to death fell into a different and of course abhorrent category.

The debates sure to follow in the international forums set up to rule on such matters seemed destined to be long, complicated, and acrimonious.

ABOUT THE AUTHOR

A product of Princeton, *Time,* and *The New Yorker,* NIVEN BUSCH has been a dynamic presence on the literary scene for a considerable segment of this century. He has written fourteen novels and more than twenty movies, some memorable successes in both forms. He and his wife, Sue, live in San Francisco, an area around which have clustered eight of their combined ten children.